D1489009

MINUS
TIME

NEW YORK

MINUS TIME

BY

CATHERINE BUSH

An excerpt from this novel has previously appeared in *Descant 8*.

The quotation from "The Idea of North: An Introduction" is used by permission. Copyright © 1984 by the Estate of Glenn Gould and Glenn Gould Limited.

Library of Congress Cataloging-in-Publication Data

Bush, Catherine.
Minus time : a novel / by Catherine Bush.
p. cm.
ISBN 1-56282-881-9
I. Title.
PS3552.U81625M56 1993
813'.54—dc20 92-32822 CIP

Designed by Holly McNeely

First Edition

10   9   8   7   6   5   4   3   2   1

For my mother,
who keeps both feet here on Earth

In memory of my father

And for Maija Beeton,
source of science stories and mucho inspiration

PART ONE

POINTS OF VIEW

"THAT CONDITION OF SOLITUDE
. . . WHICH [APPEARS] . . . TO THOSE WHO
HAVE MADE, IF ONLY IN THEIR
IMAGINATION, THE JOURNEY NORTH."
—GLENN GOULD

1

Tele-vision = Vision at a distance

This was the beginning, or one of the beginnings. This was minus time, which could either be the beginning or the end.

In darkness, hours before, we had parked on the gravel shoulder of a Florida highway, one among a row of other cars. When I turned off the ignition and the car radio went dead, the portable radio that we'd wedged between our seats continued the announcer's commentary, the slow countdown. Paul grabbed the radio as we stepped out of the car, into the cool blue, fervent air, into the suspension and anticipation of minus time, when at any instant, right until lift-off, the launch could still be shut down.

On the hood of the car, beside the radio, I set the thermos full of coffee. Binoculars were slung around our necks. No one stared at us. We were innocuous, invisible, just like everybody else.

Through binoculars—but my hands kept shaking—the whole launch tower seemed to shake, poised, there, at the edge of the world, on the pale green horizon. The astronauts, too, were invisible, shrunken, locked away in their sealed chamber miles from anybody else. Red liquid fuel tank, white solid fuel tanks loomed in the predawn light, searchlights veering across them as if they, after all, were the star attraction. The shuttle seemed so tiny, pressed against them.

On the radio a man said, *Time is holding.*

But the light kept growing, the sky paling tenderly in the east. Mist rose seamlessly above the flattened marshes.

When Paul touched my hand, his fingers were freezing. Both of us were shivering, not from the cold because it wasn't cold, but as if the ground beneath us were already shaking.

The man said, *The countdown has resumed.*

Huge jets of water spewed from the base of the launchpad, condensation billowing like smoke into steep clouds. A heron labored into the air and headed north. A salt breeze sang in our ears.

The man said, *Looking good.*

But my stomach kept coiling. Two red spots flared on Paul's cheeks. There was no way to prepare for this. A sick taste rose in my throat.

The man said, *Ten.*

Anything could happen.

In the clear, spectacular air, it seemed that nothing lay between us and the launchpad.

The metal arm at the top of the launch tower slowly pulled away.

Nine.

After all these years, after all these months and months.

And then the flames, just a small burst at first, like sparks flying, orange gusts from the engine nozzles. The whole launch tower seemed to jerk. Flames erupted from the liquid fuel tank, brilliant heat, molten, transforming, a huge, ripped-open sea of light. Golden, terrible smoke swelled, endlessly mushrooming. Enough heat to vaporize all of us, everyone watching, to power every city up and down the coast—and yet there was no sound. Blue, nearly translucent flames leaped from the liquid

4

fuel tank, yellow from the solid fuel tanks that once ignited could not be turned off, seven million pounds of thrust and all I could hear was the single cry of a marsh bird, the echo of a tiny human voice. The rockets rose straight upward.

I must have cried out—something. Tears were streaming down my cheeks.

My mother is in the air.

The air itself cracked open. A roar rose out of the ground until the ground was shuddering and they were shuddering with it, buffeted like pellets or seeds. Flames burned in a blinding particle dance, pure movement. Everything shifted. Helen was lifted off the ground, divided, pulled outside her body.

The spaceship rolled.

Roll maneuver completed.

The roar lessened. Tears were streaming down her cheeks. Through binoculars, she and Paul followed the thick trail of smoke that rose over the Atlantic Ocean, and *then*. She sucked in her breath. Far, far in the distance, flames flickered and surged—but this was normal, just the rocket boosters falling away while the shuttle went on climbing and their mother clinked with it.

Even through binoculars, the shuttle had diminished to a blip, a smudge, a lip of flame, a chimera, a tiny ghost.

On the road ahead of them, a small girl tugged at her father's trouser leg, crying for his binoculars because she could not see.

Their mother was gone.

All around them people were laughing, whooping, slapping each other's hands, dancing up and down.

There was almost no sign of what had happened, no trace except for the evaporating smoke and vapor trails—nothing except this whole new angle of vision.

Their mother had left the planet. Their mother, the Canadian astronaut whom the Americans kept referring to as "one of our international astronauts," was trying along with an American astronaut to set a record for human space habitation. She had left the planet and they had no idea when she was coming back again.

Even if one of them had had the crazy urge to follow her, it was impossible: She was encapsuled by all that blue. She would be in orbit, circling in the space station that floated invisibly in the sky above them. The time and space that lay between was not traversable. She was speeding into the future.

On the radio a voice called out velocity in thousands of miles per second, distance in nautical miles. They had spent months, no, years, of their lives in preparation for the launch and now it was over in seconds, like something only imagined, a trick of the eye. It had taken them days to drive two thousand miles south to see it—*and now?*

The speed was brutal, exquisite. It left Helen reeling, hollowed out completely, feverish for something more. She felt exalted and horrified; delayed shock shot through her, wild elation laced with panic. She had concentrated so hard on the launch and now she'd surged beyond it. In that instant, everything had changed. Her life, too, split into before the launch and after. She wanted to reach for the sky and howl out loud like a wolf—*what now?*

Paul dropped his binoculars, and when he put his arms around her she could feel how his whole body still shook slightly. "She's done it," he whispered. "Can you believe it?"

"We have to," Helen said. She squeezed his arms.

The people around them were already packing up their thermoses and binoculars and folding lawn chairs. Helen wiped her mouth with a Kleenex. By now the sun had risen, a bright, galvanizing light already warm against her sweatshirt. This was Florida in January. In eight minutes, maybe seven by now, the space shuttle carrying their mother, Barbara Urie, would stop climbing and enter orbit.

They should not, of course, have been where they were at all—not standing anonymously beside their mother's old green Volvo on the shoulder of an oceanside highway. They should have been in the official viewing stands along with the other astronauts' families. There were six astronauts altogether, Peter Carter and their mother, the two long-term astronauts, and four short-term ones who would only be staying up a week. Hours earlier Helen had heard herself and Paul described on the radio: *Urie, forty-five, is the mother of twenty-year-old twins, both college students.*

It wasn't true that they were twins. Even though they were born in the same year, she was eleven months older than Paul. In another two weeks she would be twenty-one.

Married to David Urie, a seismologist. Not seismologist but earthquake relief worker—Helen made the correction mentally.

They had not shown up at the official launch site, and so far nothing terrible had happened. The sky was nearly cloudless, luminous blue. There had been no search parties that she knew of. No one on the radio had mentioned that they hadn't shown up.

She crouched down at the edge of the marsh grass beside Paul. The smallest of smells, a dried stem of grass, heat on grains of sand, reached her vividly. They had seen the launch the way they'd wanted to, without interference, absolute and wonderous. She still felt a little knocked off balance. Even her skin felt different. "Paul," she said, "is this crazy? What if we go and get some breakfast?"

They took a booth right at the back of a place called the Ocean View Diner. Christmas tinsel still trembled over the doorway, and all the windows were dusted ridiculously with fake snow. A stuffed shark hung behind the counter. The wall behind their table was covered in a painted diorama of a rocket launch, but it looked old and faded—a black-and-white Saturn rocket with an Apollo capsule attached to it, from the years of the moon landings, just after they were born. On a TV set suspended from the ceiling, the morning's launch replayed, only on the greenish screen the whole thing looked as if it had taken place in the middle of the night, hours, not half an hour before.

A waitress, who could have been about their mother's age, came striding toward them with a steaming pot of coffee. She wore a red cardigan over her white uniform and smiled in such an emphatic way that Helen contracted, instantly terrified of recognition—as she had been every time someone unknown had approached her in public during the last few months.

"Hi there," the waitress said. Her voice was rich and kind and forthright, and it was clear as soon as she spoke that she had no idea who they were. She leaned over them in a way that was both sassy and maternal, pouring them coffee before they'd even asked for it.

"We probably need another minute," Paul said cautiously. He looked flushed and exhausted. A spaceship soared across the middle of their paper placemats, through a map of the solar system.

"Hey," the waitress said, "I bet I know where you were. I bet you were out watching the launch. There's a look people get, kind of a blown away look. I see it every time there's a launch but it's not so easy to describe it."

"Yes, we were," Helen said.

"Well, it's like nothing else, is it? I've seen one or two myself. When you live down here you kind of take it for granted. But take your time. After a launch people always are slow deciding what they want but they have great appetites." She set a handful of creamers on the table. "Here's what I like to do. This is a little game I play. I like to guess where people come from. You guys are tougher than some but I'd say somewhere in the Midwest."

"Minnesota," Helen said blindly. Anywhere. She barely knew where Minnesota was. She didn't want to say Canada because that might give them away.

"That's an awful long way," the woman said. "Did you drive it, too—all that way? But it's worth it, isn't it, to see one for real. I bet you two must be college kids. You're probably still on vacation."

"Yes," Paul said.

"You take your time," she said again and hurried away.

On the TV screen, the launch reappeared, flames surging as the rockets pulled the shuttle slowly into the greenish sky. It surged behind Helen's retinas; she felt branded with it. *Everything's going to be all right,* she told herself sternly. *Everything's going to be fine.* She breathed in the ordinary, greasy air. In the kitchen, the radio was playing country music, the twang of guitars seeping through the swinging doors each time an old stooped man in a baseball cap carried plates back and forth. Other people came in who must have been watching the launch, an older couple still clutching their binoculars, a family with two children who zoomed around making explosive noises, plastic rockets hanging from their necks. The whole world still felt gelatinous and shaky, charmed and changed. *My mother is in space.* Helen tested the notion delicately. Paul stared fixedly out the window, one hand clamped over his mouth.

It wasn't until we'd crossed the border south of Montreal and were driving through New York State that I finally said to Paul,

"We're not going to the launch site, are we?" And he shook his head.

We'd been working up to it, though, step by step. From Toronto, I'd called Paul in Montreal, where he was studying architecture, and told him I wanted to drive, not fly, since after all we had a car, our mother's car, which was parked in downtown Toronto in a long-term university lot. So I drove to Montreal and there, from Paul's apartment, we canceled the plane tickets the Canadian space agency had booked for us. It was that simple.

We knew, without speaking, what our reasons were.

We'd been through the crushes of journalists before, and each time they only seemed to get worse. Both our telephones had been ringing incessantly. There would be cameras everywhere, huge video screens jammed in front of the viewing stands and filled with blown-up images of the launch—and anyway, we weren't going to be able to see her. If we didn't show up, she probably wouldn't find out, or at least not right away.

Our father wouldn't be there. At first he'd said he would come up from earthquake-devastated Mexico City, which in itself would have been something since none of us—neither Paul, nor I, nor our mother—had actually seen him for five years. But there'd been an aftershock—and then an even bigger one. The airport runways in Mexico City had cracked open. *Like a war zone,* he'd said over the phone when the power came back. However much he wanted to, he couldn't get away.

Besides, doing it this way, on our own, gave everything a new cast of excitement. It distracted me from the fear I felt about the launch itself—in case anything went wrong. And after the launch, well, we'd worry about that then.

On the road we would be invisible, even with Ontario license plates, even though we were driving through a country where we were regarded as aliens. Americans never noticed us. And we weren't doing anything wrong—after all, we came from a family that specialized in disappearing tricks—and it wasn't as if we were planning to disappear for good.

We called her that night from a motel room in Pennsylvania. When Paul picked up the telephone, I could hear the low dial tone spilling into the room. We waited for the space agency operator to connect us to her. Her voice, when he handed the receiver to me, was lightly excited.

"Maybe this sounds funny to you," she said, "but we've passed through what I think of as the final stage. We've had to give up our wallets. They lock them away for us until we get back, all our credit cards, our ID. I waved goodbye to my old brown pocketbook, and now I'm trying as hard as I can to relax." Her passion, a hint of stubbornness, an undercurrent of longing traveled through the air between us: the shimmer of distance.

She didn't ask me where we were, but then she must have assumed we were in Montreal, getting ready to fly out the next day. And what else was there to say really besides good luck? We had prepared ourselves for so long for this moment, and yet we would still be able to talk to her over the phone and even see her on TV, on the private space station channel set up for the long-term astronauts' families, so in the end what difference was there really between this conversation and the next? We would simply be in different places.

"Take care of yourself," I whispered.

"I'll do my best," she whispered back. "You take care, too, all right?"

Everything else remained unsaid. I hung up the phone. When I raised my head, Paul was standing by the window, staring through the chiffon curtains. He turned toward me, his eyes solemn, shiny, as gray as hers. "I know she wants this. I know that, but sometimes it's hard, you know, that she wants this so much."

Halfway through her plate of French toast, Helen put down her fork, unable to summon the energy to pick it up again. With food inside him, Paul seemed less withdrawn, more himself, conversational and excited about the launch in retrospect.

They picked up the bill and headed through the restaurant toward the cash register. No one looked at them. The old man in the baseball cap glanced only at the green bills that Helen handed him, not at her. As long as they didn't call attention to themselves, they should be fine.

On the TV suspended above their heads, the astronauts and technicians walked along the catwalk high up on level 195 of the launchpad. They waved like cutouts in the floodlights. At this distance, Barbara was a tiny figure in the official blue worksuit that all the astronauts wore, nearly anonymous and yet utterly familiar, identifiable by her short, red hair, like a silhouette recognizable across a dark room.

Slipping away her change, Helen stared at her own wallet, checked to make sure the bright Canadian bills were still buried at the bottom. Paul grabbed her arm. Zooming toward the viewing stands, the TV camera began to pan: There was Nora Carter, Peter Carter's tanned and cheerful wife, and then—the ID flashed in yellow across the bottom of the screen: *Barbara Urie's family*.

For an instant, Helen could not quite believe what she was seeing: three people who—

Was that man, by some crazy chance, her father? After all, it had been so long since she had seen him. No. And yet this man looked so much like her father—at least her father as she remembered him—that it would be easy to mistake him for

David. A tall man with a high forehead, sandy hair receding at the temples, aviator glasses, a loose and long-legged body. Beside him stood a young man and a young woman, who resembled him, just as she and Paul resembled David: Both had thick, sand brown hair and dark eyebrows. The young woman's hair was tied back with an elastic. All three of them stared upward, mouths partly open, heads craned back toward the sky.

Barbara Urie has been affectionately known as the first Canadian mother in space, said the commentator, *and while there have been a few other mothers in space, she is the first to attempt a long-term mission.* With the roar still swelling the air around them, the other Paul and other Helen leaned toward the camera, looked straight into the eye of the camera, and shouted into the microphones thrust in front of them, "We're so proud of her. It was amazing. We're incredibly proud."

Then they were gone.

Alongside Helen, a woman in a striped T-shirt leaned forward, holding out her check as the old man's thickened hand reached out to grab it. Paul let go of Helen's arm. She felt stunned and determined to be practical. She smelled frying eggs, bacon fat, toast, the acid tang of orange juice, coffee on the point of burning, smells that descended to the pit of her stomach and began to churn. No one else seemed to have noticed anything. At least no one seemed to have made any connection between the two of them and the people on the screen. The two tiny figures turned toward the camera, shouting above the roar how proud they were. She saw them again and again, and yet there was no way, standing here in this Florida diner, to bring them back. The shuttle with its jittery trail of flame sped through the sky and disappeared. Perhaps it was only on this particular TV that the other family had appeared, some kind of wild hallucination surfacing out of the depths of their exhaustion. They had caused it; or only they had seen it. Perhaps it was some kind of private signal, a message for the two of them. But that was even more ridiculous.

"You saw that, didn't you?" Paul whispered as they hurried across the parking lot. "They're supposed to look like us. They're supposed to *be* us. How can they do that?"

Helen unlocked the door on the driver's side, stepped into the nest of warm, stale air, reached across to unlock the passenger side, and locked her door again as quickly as Paul locked his. The morning sun streamed through the windshield, nearly blinding them. She sat back against her seat. "It's a TV re-creation," she said. Her heart kept speeding. "The only difference is that they didn't re-create everything, they just re-created us. I mean, that other family was actually there, watching the launch. They didn't fake that. It would be terrible if only one of us had seen it. At least this way we know we're not completely crazy." *Anything can happen,* she thought dizzily. Then she thought: *It's not that unusual. It's absolutely to be expected. What else did we think they were going to do?*

"What if Dad had shown up?" Paul asked, turning toward her, in the funny, even tone that his voice sometimes kept even when he was upset.

"They must have known he wasn't going to."

"But what if we'd suddenly shown up?"

"Well, maybe they had to act fast, but at a certain point they realized we weren't going to. Maybe they always keep a family in reserve. A backup family, you know, like backup astronauts."

"They," he said. "They."

"Networks," Helen said, "the American space agency, the Canadian space agency, maybe all of them, who knows?"

She flipped the key in the ignition and glanced at Paul, who

14

sat with his feet resting on the glove compartment, arms clasped around his knees, hair standing in tufts, a deliberate expression on his face, as if he were simply trying to solve a problem. It felt suddenly as if they were in the midst of a real escape. "Do we want to do anything else while we're here?" she asked. "Now that we've driven all the way to Florida."

"What? Like Disney World? Space World? Like go to the beach? What if we just turn around and head back?"

"OK." And she wheeled the car fast and wild out of the parking lot. "That's what I was hoping you would say, let's just head back." Perhaps she really had divided in two. *We're proud,* the other Helen had said into the camera, as if what she felt were that simple and uncomplicated. *It was amazing.*

"What happens if people realize it's not us?"

"You saw them," she said. "They look enough like us to pass. If someone just assumes it's us, that's who they'll see. Because who's going to believe we weren't there? You see how they have us. Who are we going to tell that we decided not to show up? If we tell people that, they'll think we're nuts."

"She'll be furious," Paul said.

"They won't tell her. She won't likely see the shots."

"What if we lodge a complaint? What if we say they had no right?"

"If we talk, there'll be just as big a ruckus because we didn't show up. It'll turn back on us. And if we complain to the space agencies, it won't matter. They're not going to issue a retraction, say, whoops, sorry, that was the wrong family." They were tearing up the highway now. Outside, flat coastal grassland, marshes, a few desolate motorboats and lumbering recreation vehicles sped past. Time itself seemed to be speeding away from the launch, carrying them with it. There was no way back.

"What are we going to say to her?"

"Tell her we saw it, that's all, and we honestly saw it. We saw it better than we would have done if we'd been there. Paul, it's true. You know it's true."

Paul leaned forward and switched on the radio, shuffling through static up and down the dial. He cleared his throat nervously. "Maybe that family will be on the radio, too. She should have docked by now, you know. She should already be inside."

Three weeks before the launch, we had flown down to Houston for Christmas and to say goodbye to her; after that, all the astronauts went into quarantine, to protect them—especially Peter and my mother—from contracting stray germs or viruses.

The day before we were to leave Houston, she told us she had a surprise for us and drove us out to an airfield, toward a small space agency plane. I told her it had been years since I had flown in a plane with her rather than flying to visit her. She sat beside me, wearing a flowered shirt of soft old cotton, canvas pants, a light jacket, her clothes and skin scented with the sandalwood perfume she always wore. She had smooth, pale Scottish skin, which surprisingly didn't burn, just freckled a little and turned pale gold in the sun. Our skin was like my father's, sallower, slightly darker. We climbed out of the plane into the different air of Florida.

A van dropped us off at the launchpad, where the rockets and their shuttle attachment were already in place, all straining upward. "There," she said emphatically. How, I wondered, did you begin to describe something that huge? Everything around us stretched toward the sky, shrinking us, reducing us to ants, something crawling, microscopic. The huge tanks bulged with fuel. My mother pointed out the catwalk on level 195, her arm gesturing up the massive steel structure to the tiny, white preboarding room. Security personnel hovered around us. Years ago, she had shown us around her Toronto lab like this, taking us into each room, explaining how she studied the relationship between the body's balancing system and the nervous system, so that we would know intimately what she was up to.

Later, the three of us walked by ourselves along the edge of a Florida beach, among the broken seashells and tiny pebbles. In the distance I could still see the unmistakable silhouette of the launchpad, all the vertical towers of the launch complex, impossible to hide when the land was so flat.

"Look," Paul said, crouching down and picking up a small, frail scallop shell, each fluted line in place, a little pinker than skin. He dropped it into the palm of her hand. "I wish I could really give it to you for good luck."

"I wish I could take it," she said with a smile, and went on cupping it gently. "I do have some things, you know. A few photographs, things like that, but I'll still see you, I'll see you on TV, when we do what they're calling the live sessions, when you go into a studio and I'll be able to see *you,* too."

"Are you frightened?" I asked.

"A little," she said. "I guess that's just one among many things I feel. Listen, I know there are people who say why try to send people into space at all when we have such high-tech computer systems now. I don't believe in all-machine systems. You know that. I really think that's more dangerous, a more dangerous way to think about ourselves. And when it comes to long-term missions, and we have to begin to think in terms of long-term missions, there's only one way to find out what will happen. It's a frontier." She looked down at the tiny shell. "I really do think of us as all being in this together," she said softly, "all of us being on some kind of frontier."

The sky over the ocean was turning deep mauve-gray, a haze

across it, clouds gathering in streaks near the horizon. She stood up and started walking again, and every now and again I caught her glancing at the two of us in fascination: Perhaps she was trying to imagine what we would look like whenever she next saw us. How could she say we were all in this together and not see some kind of contradiction? But then she had also refused to acknowledge the fact that she and my father hadn't seen each other for years. If people asked, she said without elaboration that she was married, they just worked in different places, separate fields. That was that.

I had no idea when I was going to see her again or what she would look like when I did. That was a frontier. Anything familiar, the tiny lines at the corners of her eyes, the act of walking beside her along a stretch of water, became instantly irretrievable. The air around us flew into the invisible future, and not one of us could predict what was going to happen then.

I threw my arms around her in the Houston airport, late because my plane for Toronto left before Paul's to Montreal and we had not timed it right, all of us racing from the parking lot, my flight bag banging from my shoulder, through the check-in, damp with sweat. "Goodbye," I said breathlessly. She kissed me on the lips and then let go, and I wanted to squeeze her, bruise her, leave some indelible trace of myself before it was too late. "Goodbye," she said. "You'll have to run, sweetheart. I love you." She kissed me again.

Big transport trucks streamed long shadows in the pale winter sunlight, sweeping over their car, light, then dark, then light. At moments it seemed almost ludicrous to Helen that her mother only had to travel some three hundred miles to reach the space station and settle into orbit, while they had nearly two thousand miles to go before they would be home.

18

She accelerated, passing a metal tanker carrying something flammable, her windshield billowing suddenly in a sea of white, of feathers, chicken feathers from a poultry truck that had come barreling up beside them, until it felt like they were driving through a gale of furious snow.

She accelerated again, feathers dwindling behind them, glad to be speeding out of Florida. She wanted to make sure no one was trailing them, that no stray reporters had stumbled across them. At the same time, she was ready to believe that everyone, including reporters, had been taken in by that other family. She was learning to put faith in people's ability to see what they wanted to see.

A giant billboard rose in front of them advertising a roadside restaurant with a coin-operated mini TV at every table, ten miles farther on. "We have to stop," Paul said, pointing adamantly. "Helen, this is historical, this is our mother, and, no, the radio isn't good enough. Look, it'll be OK. I'll drive afterward, but I don't want to miss *seeing* anything."

A small TV set was fastened to each table, clamped down with bolts, a slot machine at the base. Fifty cents for fifteen minutes; it wasn't cheap, and Helen hated the idea of paying at all. "I'll pay," Paul said calmly, and pulled a handful of change out of his pocket. A flicker of screens, the low buzz of sound.

They found a special report on the docking with the space station, *which has taken place without a hitch*. They leaned forward. Grainy color, but there wasn't much color anyway, just the white space shuttle pulling up with an invisible computer whir, sliding slowly in front of the white deck of the space station, looking for all the world like a streamlined airplane taxiing at night into some clean, distant city. They peered closer as the astronauts in their blue suits floated forward into the entrance lobby (it was actually called the entrance lobby), steadying themselves with their fingers when they touched the walls. And there was Barbara's face, suddenly large and miraculous, mere inches from theirs. In the window behind her rose the curved transparent shell of the Earth.

Paul was driving. Wrapping an elastic around her hair, Helen leaned back and closed her eyes. "I wonder if she's had a chance to look down yet."

"Down?"

"Down at the Earth." Or back, because now there really was no down. This was the moment that Barbara had said she was more excited about than any other, more than the violent acceleration of the launch or her first real translation into weightlessness, because it was the moment that seemed most impossible to imagine in advance. *I can't wait to see what it actually looks like. It's the absolute shift in perspective, and I know we've all seen pictures, but everyone who's been up says there's this crucial moment that brings everything home to you. Where you are, where you've come from. I can't wait to describe what that's like to you.*

By now, whatever this moment was like, she must have been through it. After the shock and violence of the launch, did she feel wonder, pure joy, an ecstasy of exhilaration, a terrible ache, while her body floated effortlessly through the air and the Earth drifted calmly down below? Did she feel suddenly free, as if she had jettisoned a life behind her?

Where, Helen wondered, had her father, the itinerant earthquake relief worker, been at exactly that moment? Down a rubble-strewn Mexico City street he walked, lanky, distracted, past buildings that looked as if they had been blown open by a bomb, through air stewed and thickened with smog, past cars veering around ripped-open walls, piles of plaster, piles of stone. He headed away from the tiny old hotel without a telephone where he was living, he'd said, because it seemed solid enough not to fall down.

Perhaps that morning, filled with strange trepidation, he had walked into a darkened, twenty-four-hour bar where the television had only recently been repositioned among the remaining bottles behind the counter. Most of the high windows had been boarded with wood. Dark, small men waved their arms like antennae, gesticulating, glancing around warily every now and again in case the earth started moving. Leaning his long body against the bar, David argued with the bartender in Spanish, trying to convince him to switch to a channel with international news. *OK,* the bartender said at last and turned the knob, and at the end of a report about the Mexican president's request for international aid came a clip of the shuttle, in livid color, soaring upward, shooting flame. What expression passed across her father's face? Did he gasp quietly, wipe one hand across his eyes?

When Helen opened her eyes, Paul was singing along with the radio, with Patsy Cline it sounded like, holding on to the steering wheel with one hand. The sky above them was criss-crossed with a web of thick, dense vapor trails, ones that had spread out so much they could almost be clouds, newer, thinner ones slowly unraveling, trailing the distant needlelike glints of several airplanes. "Where are we?" she asked.

"Maybe South Carolina." He smiled. "Did you sleep all right? You're allowed to sleep. Our mother the international astronaut is keeping watch over us."

"Oh, look," Helen said, rubbing her eyes, "will you look at that?" There was a hand approaching them, a large wooden hand mounted on a pole by the side of the road, its fingers closed in a fist except for one finger pointing upward to the sky, a hand painted deep blue with silver stars all over it. On it were written the words: THE HAND OF GOD.

"Wow," Paul said, as Helen turned and followed the hand, watching it shrink away behind them.

No matter how much they had prepared, there was no way to be ready for any of this, the newness, the unpredictability. Their mother had achieved the thing she'd dreamed of, the plunge into space. Now, at the thought, Helen was filled with odd, enormous relief. Of course there was more to it than that. Something had been set in motion. Everything needed to be redefined.

In that night's motel room, she sat on the edge of the bed, a towel around her shoulders, tugging a comb through her wet hair. Newspaper pictures of rockets leaped at her from the other bed and the shaggy blue carpet, pictures of the other family waving and looking happy to be famous. Paul had insisted on going out to a phone booth to call the family liaison officer at the space agency, to let him know that they were safe, so word did not get back to Barbara that they'd disappeared. Helen had tried to argue with him, didn't know how to explain how much she wanted to prolong the sense of having stepped out of her own life, the extraordinary sensation that no one knew where they were.

Paul slipped back through the screen door. "I didn't even get to speak to the guy. All I did was leave a message, and I didn't even have to say where we were."

"No one asked?" He shook his head. And there was no point in being angry with him. It was always so hard to argue with Paul anyway; he didn't rouse to it. "What about dinner?"

"There's a restaurant."

They could go to the bar for a drink, and if they were lucky, no one would think they looked underage and ask them for ID. There would be a jukebox at the back, the name of each song glowing like a small white window of light in the smoky darkness, a thin melody weaving through the staccato blinking of a video game, a slow surge of longing. A cool breeze blew into the room through the webbed screen and with it the distant jigging of a radio.

"I wish I was home," Paul said suddenly.

"Where do you mean by home?" Helen asked.

"Montreal." It had been just over a year since they had packed up all their belongings in the Toronto house where they had both grown up, and Barbara had rented it out. Where Helen lived now, in an apartment with roommates down near the university, was fine, of course, but she didn't think of it as a home. A home, she realized, would be somewhere she could live by herself.

"Almost ready," she said.

"I still have to wash up. I want to throw some cold water over my face."

Already the launch seemed distant, as if it had taken place somewhere that no longer really existed. As Paul closed the door to the bathroom, Helen dressed and slipped outside. For all she knew, the people around them, eating in the restaurant, pulling off their clothes and sliding into motel beds, never even thought about expanding the possibilities of human existence in space or pushing at the boundaries of human adaptability in the name of survival. This was not what they saw when they thought about the future.

Out at the perimeters of the parking lot, the winter constellations hung amazingly above her, bright and dense, the familiar spread of Orion like a huge silhouette on a shore that led her home and away, a tiny yellow satellite roving like an extra belt across him; Mars, a minute globe, the roundness of reflected light. On top of the main motel building, above the neon sign and the windows of the restaurant, stood a satellite dish, glinting silver, a mouth open to the darkness.

The smell of exhaust rose up from the highway, gassy and strong. The stillness of this place somewhere in North Carolina shocked her, the way traffic, except for long-haul trucks, had fallen away as the light fell. All at once, walking back across the parking lot, she remembered an article she'd read in some science magazine about a group of animals the Soviets had once sent into space as an experiment in animal physiology: cats, rats, a whole miniature ark. All the animals had been kept in cages, including a monkey that had managed to free its left paw while in space. With its paw free, no one knew what the monkey would do, whether it could reach the spaceship's computer controls, and, if it started to play with them, whether it would be able to sabotage the whole mission. But the Soviet space experts did not panic: They had another monkey back at Soviet space headquarters in an exact simulation of the spacecraft, so they freed the second monkey's paw and waited to see what it would do.

Of course, they had no way to guarantee that the first monkey, whose name in Russian meant Trouble, would do the same thing.

As she drove through darkness across northern New York State, the other family floated across Helen's vision like ghosts. She imagined them as a family, even if they weren't really a family, saw them sitting down for lunch together in some diner. She saw her mother, setting off by herself in a rowboat, rowing across a lake brilliant and furious with stars, willing herself to push, needing to push beyond all limits.

Another Helen, not her, hailed a taxi at the Toronto airport, was whisked downtown, and walked in the door of her apartment, a Helen who believed that life could go on the way it had before the launch, who would pick up her own life exactly where it had left off. Now, right now, a young woman who looked just like her could be hurrying out of an anthropology class, down streets as familiar to Helen as the back of her hand. Perhaps the other Helen *was* a sign that said, *You don't have to go back to all that.*

Beside her, Paul stirred in his seat, stretching his arms, the bones in his neck cracking as he tilted his head from side to side. A few stars were visible as Helen rolled down the window on the driver's side and headed toward the green beacon that signaled Quebec. She pulled up at the Canadian border official's booth and longed for a whole new country to stretch ahead of them, a brand-new map. The round, moon-faced man peered down at them from his lit window, the entire contents of their car visible to him: their overnight bags, their gloves and scarves, the scrunched-up paper bags filled with apple cores and takeout coffee cups, the piles of newspapers with articles and pictures of the launch and the other family (which they had been unable to throw out), the transistor radio, the thermos, the twin sets of binoculars.

He asked them what their names were, where they came from, where they had been, what they had been doing, and Helen said they'd been to Florida, just on vacation, pleasure not business, no, no gifts, unable to resist the temptation to lie or at least to create some simpler truth than what they had really been up to. She needed to hold onto the sense of other lives, multiple possibilities, new beginnings. The border official looked at them hard, then waved them on.

The road signs swelling in the headlights changed. Distances elongated, kilometers now, not miles. The names changed. St.-Jean-sur-Richelieu. La Prairie. In just a week everything Helen could think of had changed. She breathed out giddily. Paul leaned forward, swiveling the radio dial, searching, she guessed, for a Montreal station, something he recognized. Satellite dishes rose from rooftops in the towns they passed. *Ici Radio Canada.* In a hotel room in Mexico City, David turned off a shaky, flickering light, rolled over, tried to sleep. Barbara circled through the night above them like an eye.

2

"Who am I?" Mrs. Hall, my new teacher, turned to face us. Sunlight poured across her blond, layered hair, across the newly sharpened pencil lying on my desk beside a shiny box of crayons. A blank, skinlike sheet of paper spread in front of me.

She turned and wrote this sentence on the blackboard; then she underlined it.

On the map in front of me, hanging above the blackboard, the provinces were cut as thick as pie slices, pink, orange, yellow, green, the colors so bright I wanted to eat them.

What is my name? Mrs. Hall wrote. "This will be your way of introducing yourselves," she said. "And you have a choice. You can either write your answers or you can draw them." The tassels on her boots swayed as she moved along the blackboard. *Do I have any brothers and sisters?*

I had said goodbye to Paul in the school yard, before he was engulfed in a crowd of other children and swept into another classroom somewhere. We were in the same grade, but we weren't allowed to be in the same class.

Are you twins? a girl had asked me, wedging her hands on her hips.

No, I said. *I'm six and he's still five. I'm born in January and he's born in December.*

No way. She gave me a withering look. *You can't do that.*

27

Yes, you can. Although there were times when I wanted more than anything to lie and say we were twins because it seemed so much easier.

Sometimes my father joked about it; he'd wink and call us twins just as he sometimes joked about our *astronaut food,* or our *space food*—in a hushed voice, cupping his hands around his mouth while my mother's back was turned. On the stove steamed the huge vat of chili that they were cooking together, enough to freeze so we'd have meals for weeks.

What do my parents do?

I wrote, *My parents are scientists,* because I knew how to spell scientist, even though what my father usually did was write articles about science. By training, he was a continental drift specialist. *This is nothing to be alarmed about,* he'd told us, *but the continents are always moving, very, very slowly creaking and shifting under our feet.*

When I told people at school that the ground, even the black pavement in the playground, was always moving, although we couldn't see it, they just looked at me blankly, as if I was trying to trip them up.

One afternoon, as an experiment, I'd walked to the back corner of our garden and stood behind the oak tree, my legs spread slightly apart for balance and my eyes closed, trying to feel the Earth spinning the way both my parents said it did. When I opened my eyes, my father was standing in front of me. When I told him what I was doing, he scooped me against him, against the smell of him that made me think of coffee and autumn leaves, a deep, rich smell. We both stood there dizzyingly, quietly listening.

What is my favorite TV show? Mrs. Hall spoke each word out loud as she wrote. We watched the news and science shows— all of them.

What do I want to be when I grow up?

I stared at the blackboard and instead of Mrs. Hall I saw my mother leaning over me in the darkness of my bedroom. It was still summertime. My hair, like my mother's hair, smelled of chlorine because she had been giving me a swimming lesson in our pool, holding my head and turning it gently, teaching me how to breathe. I lifted her hand and laid it on my forehead, feeling her warmth against my skin. In the distance, cars roared by on the 401, the highway that cut east-west across the city; and closer, the dense sizzling of crickets. She was telling me about the motion-sickness machine that she was building down at her lab, how she was trying to test the relationship between the nervous system and the vestibular system that made people balance; pilots and astronauts needed to know these things.

She riffled her fingers through my bangs and peered at me. "Helen," she whispered, "what do you want to be when you grow up?"

On the far side of the room glowed the star-shaped night-light that she had bought me. There was one in the shape of a crescent moon in Paul's room.

"I don't know."

"I'm just curious. Please tell me." She seemed very young, like an older girl, the way she leaned eagerly toward me.

"I don't know," I said.

Even in the dark, she looked mildly exasperated, then intent all over again. "Anything," she said. "Listen, it's all right. You have to tell yourself that nobody can stop you from being anything you want. Helen—anything."

"I don't want to be anything," I whispered.

I looked up at the dark edges around the loose ceiling tiles above me in the classroom, to check that none of them was about to fall. Everyone around me was either writing or drawing.

I knew, when my mother said *anything,* she really meant not anything but *something,* something nearly beyond reach.

Mrs. Hall walked softly up and down the rows. I couldn't leave the question blank. I gripped my pencil, breathed in deeply, and wrote down *astronaut.*

Sometimes, before we went to bed at night, my mother told us stories about astronauts, about an astronaut who dreamed, the night before he landed on the moon, that when he descended to the surface he found his own double, a man who said he'd lived on the moon for 500 years. She said this was a true story. In my memory, astronauts had been there since the very beginning of time. The first thing I could remember was my mother in a red sweater leaning forward, breathing out softly, the long, dark curve of my father's legs, a man in a spacesuit climbing slowly down a ladder. And even though people always said I was too young to remember the first moon-landing, just one and a half, I knew I remembered it: a man frail as a ghost, his huge blank head, the moon rushing through him, the living room we were sitting in growing grainy, late-night, far away.

We had watched all the launches, of course, from Seventeen counting backward to Eleven. The man in the spacesuit stepped down the ladder again and again, until I could see him with my eyes closed, floating inside me, couldn't help seeing him, and even though I knew he was American, I barely thought about this. He was so familiar, mine in some indefinable way, turning his TV head intimately toward me, a lunar landing module reflected across the dark TV screen of his visor minutely, precisely.

Mrs. Hall came up behind me, bending over until I could feel the warm drift of her breath on the back of my neck. "Helen, that's wonderful. How brave and adventurous of you." The eyes of everyone in the room turned searchingly toward me. "Helen wants to be an astronaut." There was pink lipstick spread across Mrs. Hall's wide lips, thick flecks of mascara around her brown eyes. My face flushed with embarrassment.

"Would you like to tell us why?" The excitement in her voice appalled me.

I knew it wasn't possible to say no. I did not want anyone to know that I had written astronaut out of desperation, because it was the only thing I could think of, because I was sure no one would *see*. "I want to go to Mars."

"Mars?" Mrs. Hall said brightly. "That's very far away."

"I know." Sometimes my mother would come up to me and say lightly, as if it was a joke, *Wouldn't I make a good astronaut?* She'd say it with her arms full of grocery bags or while tucking us into bed. Of course I knew it wasn't a joke—unlike my father's jokes—no matter what she was doing when she asked us. I never said anything but yes.

"The thing is," Mrs. Hall said, "if you really want to be an astronaut, then maybe one day you actually will be." I could hear the terrible eagerness in her voice. Couldn't she see? Did they really all believe me? Could I make them believe me? I tried to imagine what my mother would do if she found out, and my stomach began aching violently. Would she be proud of me or furious at me? Maybe all mothers secretly wanted to be astronauts. In fact, I couldn't really imagine a mother who did not want to be an astronaut.

The boy in the seat behind mine poked me in the back with his finger and whispered, "I want to be one, too, but I just didn't put it down." I grinned at him fiercely, trying to decide if he was jealous or simply being friendly. I sat absolutely still and watched Mrs. Hall as she headed down each row, gathering up our pieces of paper. I could not refuse to give her mine. There was no time to rip it up and start again. It was the first day of school and already I felt branded: This was the one thing everyone would know about me. Clasping the pile of papers to her chest, Mrs. Hall smiled.

Paul and I sat in the backseat while my mother drove down Avenue Road, downtown to the planetarium where we were going to meet my father and see a star show called *Red Giants and White Dwarfs.*

"You know how the telephone was invented by Alexander Graham Bell?" my mother said. Her voice had an intensity that made even impersonal things seem urgent and important. "He was originally from Scotland, except now the Canadians and Americans keep fighting over him. Well, the television was also invented by a Scotsman, did you know that? It's true, even though the Americans say they invented it. They didn't. I think there must be something about small northern countries, that's what I think."

"Why?" Paul asked.

"People need to invent ways to communicate," she said. We were just below St. Clair, slowing at a traffic light, when she turned and pointed across the street at an old, low apartment building. "That's where Nana and Grandad were living the year I was born." I craned backward to see. The building had a glass front door, a tiny lawn in front of it. She'd never told us this before. Sometimes I forgot my grandparents had ever lived in Canada, because as long as I had known them they had been living in a tiny town in Scotland, thousands of miles away. And then the light changed, and as we sprang forward, I swiveled around again because I didn't want to miss the huge hill that I loved. The road dropped away in front of us, the whole city spread below us, the gray concrete stump that was the beginning of the CN Tower visible in the farthest distance. The Tower was going to be the tallest freestanding structure

32

in the world, with a huge communications antenna at the top.

"OK," my mother said, "it's just after the last Ice Age and we're on the shore of Lake Ontario, because all the run-off water from the glacier has swollen the water level in the lakes until they're huge and high and this is where the lake begins. Look out now, we're going over the edge, we're diving into the lake, we're heading into the underwater city, and it's a good thing we brought our flippers and oxygen masks, because we're almost on the lake bottom." She grinned at us and we shrieked the way we always did as the car sped down the steep hill of the old lake, hurling us forward like a roller coaster.

"It's the Ice Age," I shouted. "We're on top of the ice. And there are mastodons." We had seen a movie like this in school, about a man who travels through time as he canoes across the lake.

"That's right," my mother said gleefully. "There are mastodons grazing at Yonge and Bloor." Between the tops of the bank towers and the Bay department store tower they grazed, hundreds of feet tall, bigger than any other animal that ever existed, swaying their huge, shaggy heads and enormous tusks from side to side.

She often told us stories like this, stories about the layers of things, how an ordinary rock from Minnow Lake, where we went for two weeks every summer, contained particles that had been in existence since the beginning of time, just as the jittery static on our own TV set could be traces of energy traveling across space from the earliest days of the universe. What you saw was not always what it seemed.

As we reached Bloor Street, a few stray flakes of snow began to fall, glancing across buildings, over cars, over the black snow encrusted at the curb. The museum with its huge stone arches rose on the far side of the street and spread south toward the white bulb of the planetarium. "Look," my mother said, "there he is, do you see?" A tall man in a dark suede jacket stood on the sidewalk, holding a soft-sided briefcase, sandy hair straying over his forehead, in aviator glasses, gazing distractedly in front of him, looking, not looking, as we came speeding toward him.

"Wave, Helen. Roll down your window and yell." My mother leaned forward eagerly. The planetarium gleamed like a half-moon, half-globe, and my father's eyes changed suddenly as I opened my window and my mother veered toward the curb. He hurried toward us, circles of snow dissolving on his dark jacket, his arms opening wide to gather us in.

I lay back in my chair, tilted toward the thick sky filled with stars, thinking about how my mother had said that looking at the sky was really looking back in time. We sat in a row, my father, Paul on one side of me, my mother on the other: It had been weeks since we had gone out anywhere as a family because my mother had been busy setting up the motion-sickness machine.

Once my mother had shown me the things that she put up on the walls of her bedrooms when she was a child. Even though she had been born in Toronto, her parents had kept moving, to Boston and Montreal and then to Edinburgh, and she'd told me how she put the same things up on the walls each time she moved: a mountain scene painted by her father the electrical engineer, a map of the stars, magazine photos of Marie Curie and Albert Einstein and Katharine Hepburn. When she told me that Katharine Hepburn would have made a great astronaut, of course I believed her.

It seemed odd that the apartment where my grandparents had lived still existed, while the house where my parents were living when Paul and I were born did not. It had been torn down to make room for a skating rink. Sometimes I even insisted that my father drive us down Robert Street, past the big Dominion store on the corner of Bloor, just so I could see where the house used to be, past the pale green boards and high fences around the rink, the light, swift skimming of the skaters' heads, no sign of any houses at all.

In the days when we had lived on Robert Street, my mother had been in medical school, and we had two regular babysitters: Magda and Diane, who always brought along record albums, Simon and Garfunkel, Neil Young, for us to dance to in the living room. Sometimes one of the babysitters would be there at the same time as one of my parents, except that my mother or father would be in the front room, which they used as a study, with the door closed.

I leaned back in my chair, tilting toward the ceiling as the stars above me slowly began to move. "Are you ready?" my mother whispered, and I nodded. We had watched the first moon-landing in the apartment on Robert Street. I remembered astronauts, but I remembered the door to the study just as clearly: white wood with thin lines of molding, faint cracks in the paint, a metal doorknob with the sheen rubbed off it, the low sound of a radio seeping through it. We had raced our orange plastic tricycles with the thick black plastic wheels up and down the hall, yelling and yelling.

If my mother was inside, we made up tests: We stood outside the door and told her things. *We're out of peanut butter. Helen hit me. A bird flew down the chimney in the living room.* It became a game, making things up. I egged Paul on. *A man in a black suit is coming down the hall and he is going to take us away.* We laughed and laughed. *Helen, Paul,* my father or Magda or Diane called softly.

It seemed as if everything around me was moving, the dark ceiling, the walls, the plush chairs.

On days when my father was between assignments, he met

us at our nursery school down the street and took us for walks in the afternoon, past the painted brick houses with their tall, sloped roofs, looking for wildlife, cats sleeping in windows, a squirrel quivering against a tree, a dog looping itself around a stake. He walked slowly, his jacket open, waiting for us, watching us carefully, meditatively. He took us up to Bloor Street and then west, past the Hungarian bakery where we sometimes stopped for pastries, sometimes as far as Honest Ed's Discount Warehouse, the largest store I knew of, with the world's largest sign, my father said, covered in lightbulbs that made the walls bulge into the street. From blocks away I could see the lightbulbs, the whole building, flashing.

I remembered what the inside of the study looked like: The same big wooden desk had stood in it that was in my mother's study upstairs in our house, the same office lamp pooling over books and graphs and papers, spilling heat, a small transistor radio set on the windowsill, antenna pointed to the glass, books growing in piles on the floor. A map of Mars glowed orange on the wall.

My mother sat at the desk, her dark red hair pulled back in an elastic, hunched over a pad of yellow paper, clasping a mug of coffee. She'd told us once that she worked so hard because it made her happy. Now she said she was studying for an exam. When she looked up at us, her eyes were heavy-lidded, gray circles underneath them. She pushed back her chair and crouched in front of us. "I want to ask you guys a favor." She spoke earnestly, her attention fixed on us. "If David were here, I'd ask him, but he isn't, so I want you to do something for me. This may sound strange but I'd like you to walk over my back."

"Why?" Paul asked.

"Because my back hurts," she said. "I've been sitting down too much. You're not going to hurt me. You're going to help me." She pushed aside some of the toy cars and lay down on the braided rug in front of us. Her body suddenly seemed very long. "Helen, why don't you go first. Start low down. Step onto my lower back, go slowly, just walk up and down." She lowered her head to the ground and closed her eyes. When I stepped onto her back, the weight of her body shifted underneath me, which made me feel curious and nervous, but she did not flinch as I walked up and down. I watched Paul take one step at a time, concentrating hard, hands out, wobbling for balance.

"OK." She sat up. "I'm not sure this is working." She rubbed her hands over her face, then peeled off her red sweater and lay down again in her T-shirt, her head resting on her bare, folded arms. "This time I want you to make your hands into fists, and then I want you to pound them up and down on my back. Pretend it's sand, OK? Pretend you're trying to make a flat, smooth place in the sand. Or you can knead me with your fingers the way you do with Plasticine, but don't worry about hurting me, because your father does it much harder, believe me, and if you do hurt me, I'll tell you."

She didn't close her eyes this time. I made my hands into fists, thought of drums and sand, and hit her. When I pounded her, it did not feel like sand. She had asked us to do this. I could not see Paul's face, just his hands and my hands, and I concentrated on my hands pummeling her back, feeling the quick, warm give of her body through her T-shirt. It was nothing like sand. I kept hitting her harder and harder, until I could feel my heart grow breathless and horrified, until my eyes were filled with tears. With a small sigh, she rolled over, laid both hands across her forehead, and smiled at us. "Thanks," she whispered. "That felt great." She stood up, tugging her sweater back over her head, and made her way into the kitchen where I heard the fridge swing open, the clatter of the freezer door, the scratch of tin foil on ice as she took out something that would be our dinner. We waited for her in the hallway, but she walked past us, lost in thought, and drew the study door nearly all the way closed behind her.

In the kitchen, low shafts of light fell across the red, tiled floor. We opened the wooden door of the tall, standing cupboard and took out boxes of cereal, Shreddies, Bran Flakes, and began eating cereal right from the box, scooping it out in handfuls and stuffing it in our mouths, stray bits of cereal skittering across the tiles. I pulled a chair up to the counter and climbed on it, prodded the long package in the silver sink, rimmed with snow but growing soft under the tin foil, a little pink juice on my finger. I poked Paul in the shoulder. "Blood," I said.

"Don't."

I poked him again.

And then he hit me, harder than I expected, knocked me off the chair and onto the floor, and I hit back until we were fighting the way we always fought, roaming through the apartment from room to room as if looking for someone to pry us apart. I kicked the wall outside my mother's door, shouting for her, while Paul shouted, too, trying to drown me out, and I pushed him aside, kicking and kicking the wooden frame of the door, but I did not touch the door.

She had to open the door. We had to make her open the door. Dusk was falling, but there were no lights on except the thin yellow line that shone through the space between her door and the door frame. We sat side by side on the floor in the hall, pounding our fists against the wooden floor until the bottoms of my hands were aching, until our shouting became a chant. *Come out. Come out. Come out.*

A chair lurched. She pulled open the door. "Will you stop it?" she yelled. "I can't stand it. I had two of you so you would keep each other company."

She pressed her hand over her mouth. The lamp shone on the desk behind her. The room was filled with the low chatter of the radio, a thick, human smell. She slid down the door frame until she was crouched in front of us again. There were white finger-shaped indentations in her cheeks.

"I'm sorry," she whispered. "Helen, Paul." None of us moved. She looked as if she wanted to touch us but was frightened to. There were tears in her eyes. She gave a small, strange laugh. "There's too much to do."

I stood very still as she reached out and stroked my hair, as she pulled Paul's head against her chest. Her hands moved gently over my skin, a doctor's, a scientist's hands. The hall grew dark around us as her hands smoothed over us, as we sat there listening in amazement to the quick luff-luff of her heart.

3

When Helen woke up, she had to remind herself where she was and what had happened to her. She was in Paul's apartment in Montreal, lying on the rolled-out sofa bed in his bare front room. Pale gray light needled through the bamboo curtains, which meant, presumably, that it was morning. She remembered waking once before in the middle of the night and she'd been starving. Paul had already been awake; he'd been sitting at the kitchen table drawing, and he'd ordered food for them both from his favorite twenty-four-hour Vietnamese restaurant just down Duluth Street. Hunched over the table, they'd eaten voraciously, right out of the carton, using the plastic utensils that came with the food.

Before that they'd slept through a whole day. And before they slept, they'd been driving. In darkness, they'd driven over the border. In the stretched, beyond-midnight hours they had driven north through the Eastern Townships, toward the island of Montreal, over a hovering, mist-covered suspension bridge and into the city. They'd unwedged their bodies from the car (now parked out of sight around the corner) and hurried to Paul's apartment, burdened with bags and newspapers—although there had been no one to see them.

Within her, Helen could still feel faint vestiges of motion, as

40

if her body refused to believe it was no longer hurtling relentlessly up the continent. She counted back carefully. Her mother had been up in the space station for four days.

She almost never allowed herself to lie like this, luxuriating in the quiet, although she was willing to bet that by now there'd be at least a reporter or two sitting in a car or café on the street below, scouting out the door of the building, trying to determine if she and Paul were back. She'd learned by now what to expect and to expect the worst.

From the hallway came the sound of a door opening—and if she reached with her fingertips she could, without rising from the bed, push her own door open a little further and see Paul in the kitchen, at the end of the hall. His hair stood up in tufts. He wore an old cotton Japanese-print dressing gown, cinched at the waist.

And as she watched, he began to touch things, touched them with small, precise gestures—the old refrigerator, a black vinyl kitchen chair, the gray Arborite counter—as if to reclaim them, reassure himself that they were really there, pure substance, and he was really home again.

She must have fallen back to sleep. When she opened her eyes, Paul was crouched in the hallway, talking on the telephone. "There's so much light," he said, "unbelievable amounts of light. The whole sky changes color, and the sound—well, the strange thing is you don't hear anything at first. It takes a couple of seconds for the sound to reach you."

What was he doing? Helen slipped out of bed.

"Even in the stands," he said, "you're a couple of miles away but it feels much closer. You've got these video screens all around you and the launchpad almost looks like it's balanced right on top of the digital clock on the ground in front of you, the clock that shows the countdown. It *is* scary, in a way. I mean I don't know if I'd compare it to a religious experience or anything but, sure, it's changed my life." There was a pause. "No," he said. "I wouldn't have missed it for the world."

He looked up suddenly, saw her in the doorway, put his finger to his lips. "I don't really know what it's like to have my mother living in space. She's only been gone four days." Then he nodded, said thanks, and hung up the phone.

"Paul." Helen crouched beside him, pulling the large T-shirt she was wearing down over her knees. Under the kitchen window, the radiators began hissing.

"There was a guy on the line," Paul said. "No, wait—listen, the machine was on but it hadn't clicked, nothing, and I just picked up the receiver to make a call and there was this guy already on the line. I said hello. And he said, hey, Paul Urie, you're back, great to get through to you. You're on the air. Helen, it was live radio—this morning show. I guess I could have—but I decided I'd just pretend I was there, at the official launch. *He* thought I was there. All I had to do was go along with it. And I guess I just want to do what's easiest, what will cause the least amount of attention, so that everything, my life, gets back to normal."

"Normal," she said and ran her hands through her hair.

"I made some coffee."

"Just a sec. I have to pee." In the bathroom mirror her outline trembled, restless at the edges. There were still dark circles under her eyes. She searched for exterior signs of change.

At the kitchen table, Paul was drinking coffee from a large mug.

"How can things return to normal?" she asked.

"They can," he said insistently. "They have to."

She walked past him, back down the hall to the bare front room that had belonged to Paul's roommate Marc, until Marc had moved in with his girlfriend two months ago. Despite the money, Paul didn't seem in a hurry to get someone to take Marc's place, which she understood completely. Through the bamboo blinds, she peered into the street. There were, as she'd suspected, a couple of people who were bound to be reporters: a woman in a CBC car talking into a cellular phone; a man with a videocam camped in the *bar laiterie* across the street, lurking under the illuminated plastic pictures of pizza and ice cream sundaes. Each lurid picture had its own name: *la suprême, la fiesta*.

An old man, clutching a jug of milk and a fistful of lottery tickets, tottered out of the *dépanneur,* which was what all corner stores in Montreal were called no matter who ran them; in this one, Helen knew, an ancient Portuguese woman ruled behind the counter.

If she made a dash for the car, to finish the drive to Toronto, it was easy to predict what would happen. And with Paul's voice issuing over the radio, everyone would know they were here.

She pressed her hands against her eyes. In another week she would be twenty-one, and she had no idea how to celebrate.

The answering machine, set along with the telephone on an orange crate in the hallway, clicked and whirred, Paul's voice automatically saying hello. In the kitchen, Paul was drawing, just as he'd often done in the past during moments of stress, as if the act of concentration became a kind of solace. Helen remembered him sitting at the kitchen table in the old Glenforest Street house where they'd grown up, folding scraps of newspaper into tiny origami cranes on the day their father had left for L.A.—only they hadn't known then that David wasn't going to come back.

Years before that, she had walked into the kitchen and found Paul and David sitting with drawing pads at the blue wooden table, shoulders knitted together like conspirators. She'd heard David say intently, as he flipped through a glossy photo book of the Galapagos Islands, *What do you want to draw? A tortoise or, no, look here, look at these ones. An iguana is almost as good as a dinosaur.*

"Do you want me to leave?" she asked Paul. "There *are* people out there, you know. I checked."

"No," Paul said and looked up. "No, I didn't mean that. I didn't mean to end up on the radio. I was trying to call someone to find out what I'd missed. And maybe that sounds obsessive, but in architecture they don't make it easy for you to miss anything—even though I know and they know this is an exceptional situation. Anyway, I *want* to get back to work."

On the fridge beside her was taped a schedule of his classes with their peculiar architectural names: statics, which, Paul had explained to her, was the science of how buildings stand up and why; infrastructure; applied engineering; pure design.

"What are you drawing?"

"Nothing." But that wasn't true. The page in front of him was filled with houses, strange, fantastic houses, each one different, houses sculpted in wild, geometric shapes: a house spanned by circular windows, a house that opened, atriumlike, toward the sky.

"I'll show you something," Paul said, pushing back his chair. He headed into his bedroom, which, from what Helen could see, looked nearly as bare as the rest of the apartment.

Leaning over her shoulder, he laid a sheet of paper on the table—a map of the space station that he'd obviously drawn himself, marking out the living quarters, the exercise area, the biological and physical science labs, the observation dome, the great winglike solar panels extending into the air at either end. "It's beautiful," she said softly.

"I wanted it to seem real to me," Paul said. "I want to

44

memorize it in a way so when she says, I'm here, doing this, I'll know what she means. I want it to seem like a real place."

The night before, after they'd eaten all the Vietnamese food, Helen had turned to Paul and asked, "Are you ready?" He'd nodded.

When they'd first driven into Montreal, he had been the one who wanted to turn on the television as soon as they reached his apartment, to try out the special channel that Barbara called the space station feed, set up for the long-term astronauts' families. The week before Helen had left Toronto, a space agency technician had come to her apartment to install a small and fairly unobtrusive satellite dish on the roof. But by the time they'd actually stumbled through Paul's door, they'd both been too exhausted to think of anything but instant sleep.

The television was the only object, except for the sofa bed, in the bare front room. Sheathed in black metal, large and bulbous, it sat on the floor beside a row of empty bookshelves. They pulled the blankets back over the bed and sprawled in front of it.

They had seen Barbara on TV before, of course. They had grown up seeing her on TV, in interviews and newsclips, and for a brief while they had curled up regularly on the sofa after dinner to watch her host a children's show called *Search for Science*. A TV camera, and the crew attached to it, were hardly unfamiliar. They knew (like it or not) how to gauge what the camera eye would see. They had seen shots of the space station before Barbara had even gone into space, and they'd caught TV glimpses of her at each stop as they'd traveled up the continent. So why, Helen wondered, did this feel different? Maybe because, since the appearance of that other family, there was a new element of surprise. Or because she knew this vision was private—only they, Peter Carter's wife Nora, the

Canadian and American space agencies, and mission control could see it. The space station appeared, beamed directly into their lives, their living rooms, like their own new continent.

"Here we go," Paul said, and he, too, was grinning nervously, pointing the channel control and zooming, station by station, into static until—that had to be it.

Down through the atmosphere the image came tumbling: a white room. It was clear but shimmery, its particles of composition visible, photons in action. A white hallway appeared, with a sealed door at the end.

"OK," Paul said. "OK, I think I know where we are. I think that's one of the transit nodes that link up to the labs."

They had been warned how it worked, how the picture would keep switching from camera to camera, room to room, although if you were in phone contact with one of the astronauts, the astronaut could choose to still it. There were also angles of vision they'd never see: the health-monitoring area, the astronauts' sleeping quarters.

In a lab whose four walls were covered top to bottom with drawers floated three astronauts, two men, one woman—Helen's heart beat faster—but they were two of the short-term astronauts and Peter Carter, black-haired, straight-jawed, who moved with the deftness and precision of a space mission veteran, using just the slightest nudge of his fingers.

Only three weeks ago, on Boxing Day, they and Barbara had sat down to dinner in a Houston restaurant with Peter and Nora Carter, almost, but not quite, as if they were some new extended family. In his terse but considerate voice, Peter had asked them both questions about college (*college,* Americans always said, not *university*) while Barbara threw in her own asides and Nora Carter, her white sweater slung over her tanned shoulders, watched them all a little anxiously.

What had Nora Carter thought at the launch? She must have

noticed they'd been replaced, but perhaps was prepared to keep quiet, to make sure no aura of the abnormal tainted the mission.

And then—"There she is!" Helen shouted. A woman's veined hand, a silver wedding ring, a blue sleeve. Her face.

"Oh, wow," Paul said, "you can see the difference now." In the couple of days since they'd last seen her, Barbara's face had grown rounder, or perhaps without distraction they were simply more aware of the change. They'd been warned about this, too. *It's only because in microgravity the fluids in the body rise and readjust themselves,* Barbara had said. *I know it may look funny but it's really nothing much.*

The skin around her eyes was puffier, the maze of tiny blood vessels in her cheeks had flushed. Her short hair floated away from her head as if it had a life of its own. Upside down (to them) she peered into a glowing computer monitor and the expression on her face became instantly recognizable, her work expression, as if she were solving several equations, balancing several worlds inside her head at once.

"The thing is," Paul said, "we'll get used to her looking like this. We'll reach the point where we won't imagine her looking any other way, and we'll have to look at photos to remember what she used to look like. And in a way I want to get used to it." The camera switched. He breathed out quickly. The room around them remained dark and midnight still. "So I guess that's it."

"Turn up the sound," Helen said, and when he did, they could hear a low babble of voices, their mother's among them, all talking in acronyms that could just as well have been another language.

"We could try calling that nine hundred number," Paul said, "the public access one where you can listen to clips from the astronauts and mission control."

"We don't need to," Helen said.

OK, turn around, someone said. The switch into English was so sudden, it was like being handed a clear glass of water.

"Hello," said a voice in the answering machine, as they leaned over Paul's map on the kitchen table. A small, tinny voice. "Paul, are you there?" A voice they both knew.

"Oh Jesus." Paul leaped down the hall toward it and grabbed the phone. "I'm here," he yelled. "We're here."

It was their father's voice.

"We got back yesterday," Paul said. Helen followed him down the hall. "Helen's still here. Well, the thing is, we didn't actually fly, we ended up driving instead—we decided it gave us a little more privacy. We did it each way in three days."

She could only imagine the questions her father was asking. "Oh, it was fabulous," Paul said, "totally." He looked at her pointedly, raising his eyebrows. "Where were you?" he asked into the phone. "What did you see?"

There was no extension line, no extra phone. It was driving her crazy not to hear what her father was saying.

"Here's Helen," Paul said, handing over the receiver.

"Hi," she shouted, just as a television or radio in the antique store beneath Paul's apartment began talking volubly in French. She tamped her finger over her ear.

"Hi," her father said, crackly, cheerful, like a tiny man standing on top of a mountain. Another conversation in Spanish, low and frantic, continued in the distance, beyond his voice.

"Tell me what you saw," she said.

"Well that's what I was telling Paul," David said, "how hard it was to see much of anything. There wasn't a lot on the news. I hate to put it like this—but somehow when you've just been devastated by an earthquake, an American rocket launch doesn't seem quite so important. I saw the launch itself, saw her go sailing into the blue. It looked like spectacular weather—was it?"

"They said it was almost perfect."

"But that was about all I saw. It's so strange to think she's—well, you know how strange it is. Thank God it went so well. And partly because I didn't see that much, I called her—"

"You spoke to her already?"

"Yes," he said, "after a couple of tries, which seems pretty amazing to me, too. The first time I tried the space station number they gave us I just got through to mission control and they asked me to try again later. Then—you won't believe this—I got their space station answering machine. They're so busy, of course, working out all the kinks with the short-term crew. And then, finally, I got through to her. She's fine, feeling a little under the weather but that's just the physical adjustment. She's frantic, barely had time to look at the view. She said she'd call you as soon as she can."

They were both shouting now. The babble of voices was getting louder.

"Where are you?"

"In a rather makeshift office, the relief team headquarters. I'm all right, just a little tired. They've opened up the markets again, even the flower markets, which is a testament to everyone's resourcefulness—just to walk into a square and see, despite the rubble everywhere, all these masses of flowers, roses, pink, red, yellow. Sweetheart, Happy Birthday. I haven't been able to send a card but I'll call again soon. Let me say goodbye to Paul."

His voice was the same as ever, wry, deliberate, slightly self-deprecating, there and then three thousand miles away. All she had was that voice. For years they'd talked to him but hadn't seen him, although in the beginning, for over a year, he and Barbara hadn't talked directly at all.

She pictured him in a room with a wooden desk and chair, a black old-fashioned telephone, fissures running through the painted walls—but that could be all wrong. Once or twice he'd sent photographs along with letters, grainy, bleached snapshots of a tall man in sunglasses, always in a hat, standing beside chasms or toppled houses in sultry open air. They were never close-ups. The point of them never seemed to be the man himself.

When he'd left to work on the Los Angeles quake, he'd talked about coming back, then about coming back for a visit; after a while they'd given up asking him when. Once Helen had asked if she could come and visit him, but he'd said it was too dangerous.

He was always so careful to explain to them in letters, over crackling phone lines, what he was doing, exactly what the work involved, how someone had to do it, how a city struck by an earthquake looked as if a bomb had hit it, how every earthquake seemed to breed its own nightmare that the people who survived it dreamed over and over again.

He'd never explained why he hadn't once come back.

"Helen," Paul said. He'd hung up the phone. "Why didn't we tell him?"

"About the other family? About where we really were at the launch?" She leaned back against the wall. "He didn't see. We don't need to tell him. He isn't here. He hasn't *been* here. It isn't really anyone else's business where we were. It's our secret. Paul, don't you want that? It's our own private version of what really happened."

She imagined an airplane landing in Iowa City or anywhere with wheatfields that was thousands of miles away. The young woman who had played Helen Urie stepped out, with her own secret like an extra pocket in her coat. Perhaps she'd been paid to keep what she'd been up to a secret, told to say she'd won a trip to Florida, and she'd agreed because after all she needed the money for tuition, because she, too, liked the idea of keeping a secret, and in the end all she really wanted was her own life back.

"There's this word," Paul whispered, sitting down opposite her with his knees tucked up, "this word that keeps appearing in all the newspaper headlines, and now I can't get it out of my head. ASTROKIDS. You know, like, ASTROKIDS WAVE BYE. I can't help it. It's stuck. I feel like an ASTROKID."

"You do?" Helen said. Did she?

They were children again, lying hidden under the sofa in the living room, reading comic books and the TV guide with flashlights. From the kitchen came the low voices of their parents, who did not know they were there.

She says we have such serious children: This was their mother's voice. Her firm, swift footsteps crossed the kitchen floor. *She called them old children, said they're cynical in the sense that you can't fool them.* Who had said these things? A friend of hers, someone at the lab?

The fridge door opened; the low gasp of their father opening a bottle of beer. *People sometimes say the strangest things if your children aren't like their children, but of course you're under no obligation to believe them.*

Under the sofa, Helen put her finger to her lips and looked at Paul, and in that instant the words *old children,* with their faintly illicit thrill, became a bond between them. They'd never needed to say them out loud. They were always there.

"I think I'm going to make a run for it," she whispered now. "Late tonight. I'll dash to the car and hope nobody sees."

"It's OK," Paul said softly. "About the launch. I'm not going to tell anyone."

Through the window of Helen's room, the lights of the CN Tower kept blinking. All over the floor lay boxes, newspaper, more boxes. Her two roommates were out. When the phone rang, on impulse she picked it up, ready to shock someone with the sound of a live human voice.

"Happy Birthday," said Barbara, close and crystal clear, nearly static-free, no echo. "You're there!"

"It's you," Helen said. "Oh my God. How are you?"

"I'm fine," said her mother's voice from space. "Now that the short-term crew has left we're finally getting used to the idea that we're actually staying here. We live here. Suddenly with just the two of us there's all this space—and all this room to think."

Helen looked around her—at the boxes, the heaps of clothes, spilled tights and T-shirts, piles of cassettes. She was packing.

Everything had happened with such incredible luck and speed. A week ago, just back, she'd been skulking down the hall of the anthropology department, when she'd overheard two men talking as they leaned against the department bulletin board. One in a knitted wool cap and black leather jacket said something like *The aboriginal is waiting for me at the gas station.*

"A gas station?" said the second man, who had his back to her. She loitered.

"Yes, I know," said the first man, whose face looked young although his ginger beard was streaked with silver. "He walked farther than he ever had before and he ends up at a gas station in the middle of the Australian outback. And no one knows what he's doing there or what he wants because they can't understand him. When they figure out he's never seen a gas station before, that he's never been in contact with the outside world, then things start moving very fast because this isn't supposed to happen any more. And of course people want to talk to him then, but there's almost no one who can. So when they figure out what language he speaks, I get a call because I'm the only anthropologist they can find who speaks it fluently. It's utterly amazing for me, too. I have to meet him there in four days. Everything's going crazy and on top of it all I want to find someone to sublet my apartment."

Helen took off the sunglasses she'd been wearing and stepped up beside them. "I'd be interested," she said. She had to pause and take another breath before introducing herself because she'd been so wary about doing this lately. "I'm Helen Urie."

"You're Barbara Urie's daughter?" Beneath the ginger beard he had a lopsided smile, a mouth that curved higher on one side than the other.

"Yes," she said quickly. "I mean it about the apartment. If you need someone now, I'm looking for a place and I'm available right away."

"You're a student in the department, aren't you?"

"Yes," she said, even though she hadn't actually been to any classes since before the Christmas break, and the dean of the department had begun calling sympathetically to see if everything was all right. Now that this apartment was materializing in front of her, she wanted it badly. There were for-rent ads in the paper but never for places she could afford by herself. She had to convince this man, with his dry stare and lopsided smile, to sublet it to her—in the interests of anthropology or *whatever*. She'd been feeling a lot like living anthropology recently; this was part of the problem.

"It's in the west end," he said. "Near High Park. Not too far?" She shook her head. The workboots on her feet were stained with winter salt and above them she wore tight green cotton pants, which some people might think was an odd combination. Her hair was tucked inside the collar of her overcoat. She didn't wear makeup. She was not always good at being charming. It wasn't simply that her life felt changed but that she wanted to change things herself. "It'd be for about six months, maybe longer, it's hard to say." He ripped an out-of-date memo off the bulletin board, wrote down his name, Sam Miller, and his phone number. "Helen Urie," he said again. "Tell you what, can you come out tonight and take a look at it?"

She had gone out there that night and agreed to sublet an apartment that by now she could only remember as full of books and furry circles of incandescent light and Sam's surprisingly garrulous presence telling her about the aborigine.

Now all she needed was a job, part-time anything, to pay her roommates the rent she still owed them.

"Have you got the TV on?" Barbara was asking her. "The space station feed. Tell me how that works."

"Just a sec," Helen said, and switched it on. There was her mother's new, round face, her buoyant hair; she was smiling delightedly, eyes bright, as if she could see through space. "What do you want to know? I mean, it's great. It works. You're right here. No problem with reception."

"You know what's strange," Barbara said, "being up here, it's that the layout, the whole station is exactly like the simulator we've been working in for months. I'm always doing these double takes—except, this time, we're weightless." She was holding a hand grip, wearing what looked like an ordinary navy blue T-shirt. "And by now I've had a chance to look at the view."

"Where are you now?"

Barbara leaned away from the screen, out of sight, then back again. "Over Europe. Everything's in darkness but I can see lights, all these glimmering lights of cities, even highways. That's the thing—the clue you'd have if you were traveling here from outer space and wondering if the planet was inhabited—the thing that gives away our presence as a life form are all the lights on the dark side at night."

"I didn't know that," Helen said, but she knew this pitch of her mother's excitement; it hadn't changed. And she knew how much Barbara wanted it to be contagious, to spin between them.

"Ninety minutes," Barbara said, "that's how long it takes us to complete an orbit. That means sixteen sunrises and sunsets a day if we're lucky. It's like having a new lens on your eye, that's how clear everything is. And it's not as though the Earth is some globe in the distance, we're 500 Ks away and what we see is the curve of the surface and then beyond it, darkness. Nothing. That's what makes it seem so contained; it's there and there's nothing around it. And when I look down I'm so aware of the details, the surface itself seems so vast because there's so much to look at."

"Like what?"

"It's like seeing two ways at once. Sometimes it's so clear I can see airport runways at night or tides of algae or lightning, tiny flashes from a tropical storm or smoke from those huge cut-and-burn fires."

"What about the cameras? You don't mind the cameras?"

"We get used to them. We learn to ignore them except that we know they're also there so you can see us, and sometimes that's good to think about. How has everything been? What have you done today to celebrate being twenty-one?"

"I'm going out later with some friends." Which was true. Helen licked her lips. "Actually, I'm moving."

"You are? Isn't that sudden?"

"It came up suddenly. It's a sublet. I can live there by myself."

"And that's all right, that's not something you've been forced to—because of any pressure, all the media attention? You know I'm sorry how much you two have had to put up with."

"It wasn't like that. I wanted it. It's in an old building, just off Roncesvalles, and it's quiet. It's for a few months anyway. But there's a story about it. I'll tell you if you want." In a way she wanted to prove that she, too, could tell stories, pass on odd collections of information, as Barbara always had.

"Helen, why wouldn't I want to hear it?"

"All right. First of all, an aboriginal man walks out of the bush in Australia—I'm not joking. Wait. This is a true story."

What she couldn't explain to Barbara was how she really felt about the aborigine, who would have had no idea what he was in for when he walked out of the bush toward the gas station, who did not know about the string of causality that spun out around the globe and linked them. She wished that by some chance the anthropologist named Sam Miller would tell the man, in his own language, that in Sam's Toronto apartment lived a young woman whose mother was orbiting the planet in a space station. She wondered what the man would think. At the same time she wanted to streak across the planet and whisper in his ear: *Slip out the door while no one's looking, don't tell them anything, stick to yourself, keep walking.*

She didn't know how to explain to Barbara her own restlessness, the low trembling inside her that had only grown stronger since the launch.

"At night," Barbara said, with a gleam of excitement still in her eye, "I sometimes think I can see nomads' fires in the desert, tiny, fuzzy orange lights that seem even more incredible than all the electricity, because people have actually lit those fires in some dark, bare place. That *is* a fantastic story."

"We're out of the news, you know, for the first time in weeks." Luckily, the other family seemed to have vanished without a trace.

"You must be glad."

Above the CN Tower rose the moon, clear-edged, still waxing, mottled with seas. They could both see the moon.

"There's been this other big news story. I don't know if you heard. About this big toxic disaster with seafood on the East Coast. Hundreds of people were poisoned. And they don't know—it may be caused by a natural mutant, but they think it may be linked to offshore dumping."

"People have died?" Her mother's forehead creased.

"Ten people so far."

"How terrible," Barbara said softly, "that it had to be something like that."

4

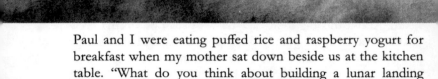

Paul and I were eating puffed rice and raspberry yogurt for breakfast when my mother sat down beside us at the kitchen table. "What do you think about building a lunar landing module in the backyard?"

Paul put down his spoon. "Like the Apollo one?"

"That's right." She leaned over to pat down his hair. "I thought it would be fun. You could play in it. Like a tree fort, only we don't really have a tree big enough for a tree fort, so I thought we could do something like this instead. I bet no one else has done it, at least around here." It was early July, just after the beginning of the summer holidays, time stretching ahead of us, each breeze filled with promise, like pollen or a scent.

"Instead of a pet," I said. I had wanted a pet, a dog or a cat, or even a rabbit or a gerbil, although neither of my parents was keen on the idea. They said we were on the go too much.

"All right," my mother said cheerfully, "instead of a pet."

"Is there room?" Paul asked with a small frown.

"There'll be room," she said, "beside the pool." Her arms, stretching beyond her sleeveless cotton shirt, seemed long and muscular, dusted with pale freckles. Three days a week, while my parents worked, we went to a YMCA day camp in the city, and on the other days we had babysitters or my mother kept

58

an eye on us in the mornings while my father was at the paper; then in the afternoon she went down to the lab and stayed into the evening. When she came home, she went swimming, even if it was after dark. At night, the inside of the pool was lit by floodlights, and sometimes I stood by the edge and watched her, watched the neat turns she made at either end, tucking her legs and then pushing off suddenly, exploding away from each cement side, her large, marvelous shadow soaring across the light blue bottom. Once, late in the evening, I came downstairs from my bedroom and looked out through the darkened kitchen window and saw my father in his bathing suit, his skin lit up strangely, slipping into the pool beside her.

She took a pad and pencil out of the drawer underneath the telephone. "We can make a frame out of wood," she said, looking at Paul, then at me. "How does that sound? It won't look exactly like the real one, but it'll be the same general idea, and we can probably use heavy-duty aluminum foil on the exterior. I'll get a picture of the real one and then we can look at it together. And we could always go over to the Science Centre to check out the space capsules there."

This was half her professional voice, quick and authorita-tive, the voice I'd heard her use when she took me with her down to the lab, and half another, softer, lilting voice. She laid down the pencil. "I know they've stopped going to the moon, but so what? It makes more sense to build a landing module than a command module if it's going to be sitting on the ground, don't you think? We can always just call it a landing module." She picked up the pencil again. "The legs of the actual lunar module were designed by Canadians, did you know that? Not the pads, just the legs. By a company in Quebec." She was always telling us about famous things that Canadians had done, things that no one else seemed to know about. She sketched a few lines on a piece of paper. "I'm not an engineer," she said, "but I bet I can work something out."

I knew that a lunar landing module had a bulging insect body and sticklike legs with round pads on its feet, that it shone a deep bronze in the wan light on the moon. "Call Dad and tell him," I said.

"I will." She smiled slowly.

"I know where there's a picture," Paul said, and he ducked purposefully under the table, ran through the kitchen, through the whole house and up the stairs, toward her study.

"Paul," she called and ran after him. "Paul, wait a sec."

We crouched inside our module. My father had cut a hole in the top and covered it with a plastic lid that you could tip back to look at the open sky. It was tipped back now to make room for my mother's telescope. She knelt on one knee in front of it while Paul and I huddled on either side of her, the flashlight standing on end beside the star map, shining at the wooden floor so that only a ring of yellow light filtered out around the edges.

It was a summer night, but we were wearing sweatshirts. A cool, clear sky seeped in through the hole at the top and through the window on the far side. Under the window my father had nailed a wooden shelf that was supposed to be the control panel; Paul's tiny transistor radio sat on top of it. Our unrolled sleeping bags lay pressed against the tin-foil-covered inside walls.

"Who wants to see the moon?" my mother asked.

"I do," I said.

"Just be careful not to knock the telescope." With her hands, she maneuvered me into place, and her excitement was like the light touch of hundreds of tiny fingers. There was just enough room inside the module for the telescope and the three of us.

The moon was huge. I could barely believe it was the same moon, the real moon, nearly full. Along the edge where it faded into darkness, the silhouettes of craters jutted out visibly from the surface. Lines ran down its sides like the seams of a beach ball, lines erupting from craters. It looked like the moon and some fantastic image of the moon.

"The first words spoken on the moon weren't really *a small step for man,* you know," my mother said softly. "Or even *a small step for a man,* which is what it was supposed to be. They were *contact light.* That's what one of the astronauts said the instant they touched the surface. You can hear it on the transcripts." The module bumped down, its feet lightly touching the ground, first contact ever, the words speeding back through the darkness toward Earth. "It was actually a light," she said. "A little red light that came on suddenly. Not a lot of people know about this, though."

"Now we do," I said. We were the lucky ones.

"It's my turn," Paul said, crouched and ready. "Mum, it's my turn."

"All right," I said.

I sat down in the doorway of the lunar landing module, at the top of its tin-foil-covered steps, and stared across the grass up to the second floor of our house, at the round glow of our plastic moon globe in Paul's bedroom window. My mother had brought it back from England, after a conference. She always brought us gifts after conferences, or at least gave us binders and pads of paper with strange scientific logos on them. The moon globe was inflatable, and there was a place to put a lightbulb so that it was lit up from within, an inflatable beach ball that looked like the moon, that shone like the moon. *Our moon.* Even from where I was sitting, I could see its craters and mountains and seas. When I was very young, I had stared at the moon when there were men on it and convinced myself that, even though I couldn't see them, I was looking at men on the moon.

Pool water gurgled in the filters like a voice. With the floodlights on, the pool was a blue rectangle, lighting up the whole garden, turning the metallic legs of the module blue.

"We can try looking for planets," my mother said from behind me. "It's hard to see much besides fairly large, bright objects from here, because even at night there's so much light, but we should be able to see Mars, and I think we may even be able to find Jupiter." She'd told us once that the Greeks had called the planets wanderers because from Earth they seemed to wander through the sky, through all the constellations.

"Why can't you become an astronaut?" I asked.

"Well, for a start," she said, turning aside from the telescope, "only Americans can become astronauts."

"There are Soviet astronauts."

"You're right," she said emphatically. "You are absolutely right. Except that I would probably have an even harder time getting into the Soviet space program than I would into the American one."

"Why don't you become an American?" Paul asked.

"Well, no," she said, "it's not as simple as that, and the other thing is, the Americans haven't flown any women yet."

"So you can't be," Paul said.

"Never say *can't* like that to anyone, all right? All right?"

"All right," he said quietly.

"There aren't any Canadian astronauts at all?" I asked.

"Not yet," she said, "that's all, just not yet."

I had never thought of it this way: However much she wanted to be an astronaut, maybe she could not be one. There were things that could actually stop her. And this was altogether different from the times when I hated the strength of her longing and wanted it to stop, and hoped that if I willed hard enough, it would stop.

"We should go to Sudbury," she said, "if you really want to see what the moon looks like. I think they took their moon vehicles up there to practice driving around."

"Where's Sudbury?" Paul asked.

"It's up north. It's where the nickel mines are and the land all around them has been so devastated that nothing grows there and now it looks like the moon."

"Do you really want to go to Sudbury?" I asked.

"No." She leaned back against a shiny wall, shook her head, and gave a quiet laugh. "Don't worry. I don't really mean it. We don't need to go to Sudbury." A car roared down the street. At night I sometimes dreamed about my mother hidden behind a white suit and huge visor so that I couldn't see her face but had to trust that it was really her. With a life-support system on her back, she climbed out the door of a real lunar landing module, one slow step at a time, utterly intent on what she was doing, descending toward the bare, Sudbury-like surface of the moon.

At night, when my mother wasn't around, the module became all ours. We were the wanderers. As it grew dark, we crept outside and up the tin-foil-covered stairs. I gripped the steering wheel and Paul pulled out the ignition, *throttle up,* and slowly, silently we rose above the garden, above the yellow windows of our house within its fringe of trees, above the glow of television sets spreading like a new constellation, like a row of blue runway lights along Glenforest Street. The rustling, unlit expanse of a ravine fell away behind us while the bright eyes of cars slid along Mount Pleasant. The lights of taller buildings loomed ahead of us. The murmur of Paul's transistor radio, crackling, then clear, became the chatter of mission control.

"Where are we going?" Paul whispered.

"Downtown," I whispered back.

We flew over the university, over the vast cement library hunkered down like a huge bird, over the Hungarian deli where my mother always bought us lunch when we came to visit her at the lab, whipped cream cheese on a bagel and a can of apple juice. Softly, we circled above the science buildings, over my mother's office, its walls as luminous as x-rays, so that I could see through them, see my mother's white lab coat hanging on a peg behind her door and, down the hall a little way, the motion-sickness machine in its own room. It looked so deceptively simple, not like something the American space program was interested in, although they were. Just a padded chair made of shiny metal and fastened to a horizontal pole that circled around a central unit. In the darkness, it gleamed with the strange frailness of a stilled amusement park ride. I had ridden it once, and I knew that my mother tried out experiments on herself sometimes, and that even though the experiments were about balance, you had to strap yourself into the machine's padded chair and ride and ride until you felt sick.

"Keep going," Paul whispered. "Where are we now?"

"We're banking a little," I said, "over the newspaper building." Over my father's desk surrounded by office dividers, its rack of manila folders and yellow legal pads lined in rows beside the silent hump of his typewriter.

We flew out across the harbor, rising higher, over the docked ferry boats and Centre Island where the leaves of willow trees hung like snakes' tongues into the water.

"Circle back, OK?" Paul whispered. "We have to check out the CN Tower."

And there it was, right in front of us, brand-new, solid

concrete, the tallest freestanding structure in the world, soaring above us, massive even in the darkness. The tiny lights on its great trunk blinked on and off. People waved from the slowly rotating windows of the restaurant, cameras flashed from the observation deck as we banked and circled giddily, swooping around and around. We had watched the tower being built: Each time we drove over the steep hill on Avenue Road it had grown a little bigger, one huge cement block set on top of another, until sections of its enormous radio antenna were being lifted into place by helicopter. *A new age in communications is born,* a voice on the radio had told us.

"Left," I said breathlessly. "West." Over the exhibition grounds and along the shore of the lake, over a stretch of pebbly beach and grass where my mother had taken me once for a walk. A dog bounded through the frothy waves. We walked under a gray sky, into a wind that batted our ears. *What a great day for a kite,* my mother exclaimed. *We could make one,* I suggested. *I have some string in my pocket. We could use a paper bag and see.* Grinning, she leaned over a garbage can, drew out a bag that looked perfectly clean. *You're so clever.* She flourished the bag and handed it to me. *What a fabulous idea.*

The four of us sat in a row close together, near the edge of a granite cliff. The air all around us was filled with the tangy, bitter scent of mosquito repellent. There was no moon. Down below, out of sight among the darkened trees, lay the cottage that we rented for two weeks every summer on the shore of Minnow Lake.

We had climbed up one of the narrow paths, following my mother's flashlight over the soft crunch of pine needles and the give of moss, while my father followed behind us carrying a second flashlight. In the round, bright beams, the trunks of trees lit up like eyes.

We were going to see the space lab. The linked Soviet and American orbiters were circling above us, both sets of astronauts floating inside. On this particular moonless night, everyone in the northeast part of the continent would have an especially good chance of spotting it. Even in Canada, spaceships became visible. If we faced north it would beam across our vision. *How often,* my mother had said in her urgent, splendid voice, *do you get an opportunity like this?*

Providing the weather holds, my father had said quietly, *because the one thing none of us can control is the weather.*

Pine needles crackled underneath us, as if we were owls or some animal family, while the air between us grew eager and staticky. The sky above was clear except for a few blue ragged clouds and the dense, close stars. Beyond the tops of the trees spread the bowl of the lake, a bowl of stars filled with shivering points and tiny waves of light that took my breath away.

One night my mother had taken Paul and me out in our rowboat, rowing to the middle of the lake, which was too small for motorboats. In the silence, she'd let the oars slip on their hinges deep into the water, the boat drifting gently as we stared up at the flooded sky. *This is what I dream of,* she whispered. Stars everywhere. Stars all around us. Everything slipped away from me. I held onto the side of the boat and looked around dizzily, searching for our cottage, some horizon, but all the yellow lights along the shore, even the line between the sky and earth, had disappeared.

When she dreamed of going into space, did she see us floating together in a gleaming silver spacecraft, waving to the people who watched us down below? Or did she see herself, floating alone, like a constellation, waving joyfully down at us?

"What if we miss it?" Paul asked. He tucked his hands inside the sleeves of his sweatshirt. My hands were cold.

"We won't miss it," my mother said.

My father lifted her hand to his lips and kissed it. Then he switched on his flashlight and glanced at his watch. "Still another minute." His voice had a scientist's calm, without my mother's fierce and electric edge. Both their faces were blue in the darkness. My mother pulled a roll of Life Savers out of her pocket without looking down, took one little white ring, and passed them to Paul. A bat flew through the blank space, the hushed air in front of us.

"There," she said suddenly, her voice low, "I think I've got it. OK, that must be it. There. Up to the right."

"Right," my father said with matter-of-fact assurance, as if they were just confirming an observation. "I've got it."

"Where?" Paul yelled, and his voice echoed out across the stilled lake, *where, where, where.* My mother cupped the side of his head in one hand and pointed her other arm up and out for him to follow along the trajectory.

"It's traveling across the sky from right to left," she said.

I could see a small, moving yellow light, but that was all.

"Can you see it, Helen?" my father asked.

"I can't see a spaceship," I said.

"It looks like a satellite," she said, "a little bigger than a satellite."

"I can see it," Paul shouted triumphantly. *See, see, see,* whispered the lake.

"Helen, can you see it?" my mother asked.

"I can't see a spaceship."

"It doesn't really look like a spaceship."

"So how do you know that's it?"

"It's over two hundred miles away. It *is* a spaceship but it's not like watching a launch on television."

"How do you know it's a spaceship?" It was just a tiny yellow light, it could have been anything, any kind of satellite, a chunk of metal, chunk of rock, there was no way to know there were people in it, nothing spectacular about it. How could this possibly be what she longed for? How would she ever see us from there or we see her?

"It's in the right place," she said gently, "and it's traveling in the right direction, so, of course, that's it. Don't you think it's incredible that we can see it at all?"

"No," I whispered.

"Oh my darling." She rocked her body against mine. "It's just the beginning. In ten years who knows where they'll be flying, but surely beyond the moon. Maybe people will really be living in space by then. Maybe they'll even be on their way to Mars."

5

DOMINION

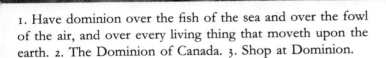

1. Have dominion over the fish of the sea and over the fowl of the air, and over every living thing that moveth upon the earth. 2. The Dominion of Canada. 3. Shop at Dominion.

Helen headed toward the back of the supermarket, looking for toilet paper, down the aisle filled with bright boxes of detergent, Zap, Ace, New Era. She thought about picking up some cans of soup as well, just so she had something to eat at home when she had run out of everything else. Soft, jangly music played over the PA system, pause, more music. There was almost no one around her. It was late afternoon, before the rush of people came in on their way home from work.

Maybe she should have been shopping in a health food store—after all, she *had* begun working in a natural foods café a few blocks west down Bloor Street—but the supermarket was cheaper. She'd just finished her daytime shift, leaving behind the converted diner with its bruised red booths and Formica tables. A handpainted sign over the door read THE MILLION. OPEN LATE.

There was no one in the back aisle of the supermarket except for a young man slapping stickers on packages of meat in the long refrigerator cases and on the metal frame underneath, moving very fast, with a cool, efficient, animal alertness.

69

He wasn't a store worker. No red jacket, no white jacket, whatever store workers wore. Dark hair, dark wool jacket, red hightop sneakers. He had his back to·her. He stopped like lightning, slipped his hands into his pockets, disappeared around the far aisle. A woman wheeling a shopping cart with a small child packed in it turned the corner and slowed in front of a display of potato chips.

Up close, under the bright glow of fluorescent tubing, the meat case gleamed with plastic, plastic packages covered in a mad, frenetic mess of stickers. EAT THIS AND YOU'RE DEAD MEAT. And beneath that: FACTORY FARMING. TORTURE FOR ANIMALS, TOXIC FOR YOU. Black stickers with white letters. Stickers on packages of chicken thighs, chicken breasts, pork chops, prime rib, rump roast, beef tongue. Everything shone, limp and moist. Helen tore a sticker off a package of drumsticks, ripped the plastic, too, but there was no point in worrying about that, tucked the sticker in her pocket and hurried *(walk, don't run)* up the far aisle, through one of the empty checkout lanes, past the old woman who always sat inside the door, her head covered in a blue kerchief, her belongings stuffed into the plastic shopping bags that sat beside her and filled the errant shopping car parked outside the door.

Out in the street, the young man headed determinedly east along Bloor Street without running. Helen hurried after him. The dense sky made the traffic lights ahead of them glow somberly, the air full of possible rain or snow. He crossed Bloor at the lights, turning north, and she followed him, dodging around people, guessed he was going to the subway but if he went in the tokens-only entrance then she would lose him. He didn't. He crossed the street again. High school students streamed around the corner in loud, smart packs. She could see the back of his navy jacket, red sneakers, fragments of him, one side of his face, stern chin, hollow around his eye. She just wanted to see him. Paper subway transfers swirled around the bottom of the turnstiles and in the eddies of air at the tops of the stairs leading down to the lower levels and the trains. Down the eastbound side.

And then she had to slow breathlessly because he was there, on the subway platform, among a scattering of people, standing by the stairs that disappeared up toward the other subway line, his hands still in his pockets. And finally she saw his face, deep-set eyes, everything about him lightly tense, poised. He glanced around sharply. If he'd seen her in the supermarket, surely he would show some sign of recognizing her now. She leaned back against the wall beside a man in a turban. Her bike was locked outside the supermarket. The voices of the high school students bounced off the walls. There was a faint breeze, a smell of grit as acrid as sweat, like the change in the air just before rain, and then a train rushed in.

Once in the train, she could have gone right up to him, pulled out the sticker, and asked him what he was doing, but she was more interested in following him. It thrilled her to be invisible, do just what he had done. There he was at the back of the supermarket, moving along the refrigerator case. It had been such a neat, swift act; he knew how to move fast, depended on staying out of sight. Now he sat on one of the seats that ran parallel to the side of the subway car, under an advertisement for new Canada Goose brand yogurt. Helen stood in the doorway. And even though part of her wanted more than anything to jump in a shower, wash away the restaurant smells of wet sponge and coffee and curried soup, she was alert, just as alert as he was. Their gazes met once, passed, nothing. She watched herself standing there, faking innocuousness, and wondered how long she could keep this up.

The train rushed into St. George, the green-tiled station, doors rattled open, a whistle blew, and then they closed again.

On to the white-tiled Bay Street station. She didn't worry much any more about people recognizing her on the street. Occasionally they did but not often, and for every person who stared at her, there could be someone on the other side of the city staring at a young woman who simply looked like her.

Half the people in the subway car stood up and clustered around the door, ready to switch to the north-south line at Yonge and Bloor. The young man stood up. Helen slipped through the crush of people on the narrow platform, briefcases hitting her knees, keeping her eyes on his dark blue shoulders, up the southbound stairs, and dashed behind him into the waiting train.

There weren't crowds yet on the southbound train, so it was easy to keep him in sight. She wondered what was happening back by the supermarket meat cases. Would a customer complain or a supermarket worker discover the stickers, which would not come off easily, either off the packages of meat or the metal refrigerator case? What would they do with all the meat? It had been over three years since she had eaten any meat at all. Cells of intense, hunched-shouldered activists gathered in small basement rooms, drinking Evian water and eating tofu burgers, planning this kind of speedy, anonymous action. The underground.

Loud voices, no, a man's voice, from a seat somewhere behind her, a father telling a story to a child maybe, to while away the subway journey. The train had slowed in the tunnel between Bloor and Wellesley, and now it stopped altogether, all its mechanical sounds dropping away to a low hum.

"Good evening," said the man's voice. "This is Peter Jennings, the voice of Canada coming to you from the newsrooms of America. Good evening, this is Barbara Frum. Hello, hello, hello." One voice doing other voices, talking to itself, a voice that probably everyone in the subway car could hear by now. "Good morning, Vietnam. Good morning, Basra. Good morning, Moscow. This is Channel 5, Toronto." Uncanny imitations of voices most people would know, a lifetime of TV voices. "Hello, hello, I'm here today to talk about safe sex safe sex, sex in a safe. Barbara Urie, thirty-five days in orbit. Now you know and I know that I have television sickness, that I am exhibiting all the symptoms of television sickness so what are you going to do about it? I am here today to talk about the problem of human waste. Now you know and I know there are too many people, there's no room for all these people. Dump them, dump them, dump the trash. He-ee-ere's Johnny."

The train rolled forward slowly, slowly, a little more speed. No one did anything. The man, wearing a gray suit, sitting by himself on an orange banquette, sounded as if he had been infiltrated by some satellite transmission. A human deathstar. "All used up and nowhere to go," he said in a deep voice. "Clean me up baby or spew me out." Probably everyone in the subway car was too busy concentrating to do anything, willing the train to move. "What are you going to do about it?" the man asked. "What are you going to do about it?"

Two young women in checked coats and bright, diligent makeup grinned at each other. The young man glanced warily past Helen down the car. She stared hard at the leached reflections in the window, suddenly terrified that the man doing the TV voices, of all people, would walk toward her, point, and say in his loud, clear voice, *I know who you are.* The advertisements above her head glistened, the floors shone, swept clean. And then, as the train pulled into Wellesley station, the man stood up, still talking, and exited, a sea of people parting around him as he disappeared down the platform.

A woman in a muskrat coat sat down on the banquette

where the man had been, and when people glanced at her, she glowered belligerently back at them. College station. The young man moved toward the door. Dundas, the mustard yellow station, Eaton Centre station, and all at once it seemed crazy to be doing this, almost rush hour, people jammed along the platform, clustering around the outside of the doors, waiting to push inside the moment everyone had streamed out past them.

The young man walked a little way down the platform, then glanced up at the electronic clock and backed against the tiled wall. Helen walked right past him. If she stopped, wouldn't it be obvious? There was nothing she could use as an excuse, no bench to sit down on. They were still some distance from the exit. The crowd around her began thinning out. And yet there was no reason to keep going, because if she simply gave up the chase and stopped following him, then all she really wanted was to get on the next train, ride around the loop, pick up her bike. So what if he noticed her now?

She stopped and turned just as he straightened up, as a woman in a dark coat came up beside him and touched him lightly on the arm. They kissed on both cheeks, European-style. He leaned down gently as the woman said something, then he nodded, pushing his dark hair back from his high forehead. They could have been any couple, any two people greeting each other before heading off to a movie. Helen felt a surge of disappointment, longing for some thin, gangly activist man or woman, small packages passed from hand to hand. Black hair fell sharply almost to the woman's shoulders; black tights, low black boots. She exuded a careful, streamlined sense of style. A narrow, pale brown flash of her face as the two of them moved to the edge of the platform. Lights in the tunnel. A bell pinged. The next train was coming in.

There were no windows in the studio. It was really a small, black booth with a TV monitor and a video camera built into a stand underneath it, set up in front of a metal stool that swiveled to different heights. Will, the space agency's studio engineer, crouched on the broadloom, untangling wires, and said, as he had done the first time, "Remember to look at the camera, not just the monitor, because that's when you look like you're looking at her."

"OK." Helen hooked her boots around the rungs of the stool. She had biked over to the studio even though it was raining, even though she had heard on a weather update that *Today's rain has the acidity of vinegar.*

On the black felt wall across from her someone had pinned a cartoon clipped from a newspaper. An astronaut joke: She'd read it the last time. Tiny caricatures of her mother and Peter floating in the space station. *How many astronauts does it take to screw in a lightbulb? One to take orders from mission control. The other to perform the experiment.* It still amazed her that no one associated with the space agency had ever said anything to her about the launch. Either they'd been told to pretend that nothing unusual had happened, or, like everyone else, hadn't noticed any discrepancy.

"Okeydoke, sweetheart," Will said. He stood up and rubbed his hands down his jeans. "Ready to go? Live session number two. Act natural." He headed into the control booth.

Even now she was being reduced to particles, she was speeding up through the ionosphere, the atmosphere, via satellite.

"There you are," Barbara said, and she smiled. "It makes such a difference to be able to see you. I think sometimes how crazy it is that I can see algae but I can't see you."

"I saw you," Helen said. "This was kind of scary. I turned on the space station feed and there you were, floating in space, nothing around you. You were checking the solar heat shields, I think. But it was a shock, seeing you out there like that, no warning."

"I'm sorry," Barbara said. "Will you forgive me? For a start, I can't see myself, and I'm concentrating so hard—but everything is very closely monitored. Peter is at the controls the whole time, moving the robot arm. It's actually exhilarating. There isn't really time to be frightened—mostly you're just concentrating on keeping yourself oriented, because if you look up from what you're doing there aren't any external visual clues. But you have to look, and then there's nothing between you and—not sky, just darkness. Nothing between you and the Earth. That's all there is. The stars are so bright they hurt. It's a moment of pure reckoning. I can't explain it. I wish I could whisk you up here and slip you outside so you know what it feels like." On the video screen her mother's eyes were luminous.

How, Helen wondered, could she not feel at least some terror? "You said you missed the weather, so I'll tell you about the weather. It's raining and it feels like we haven't seen the sun in weeks."

"How's everything? How's Paul? Have you talked to him?"

"He said he was staying up till two every night in the studio."

"How's school?"

"School's OK. Actually, I'm taking a new class. It's called garbology."

"Garbology?" Barbara sounded shocked.

"It's a way to study contemporary societies through an examination of their garbage."

"Is this an extension of anthropology?"

"Kind of. It's a new field. We take a lot of research trips, and it's not really as disgusting as you might think."

"And this interests you."

"Yes," Helen said. Working in the restaurant was grungy and often exhausting, but it was better than being in class. There actually *was* a course in garbology, although she wasn't taking it; she'd finally written a letter to the dean to say she'd quit. "Do you ever dream about being here?"

"I've dreamed about walking." Barbara gave a quick grin. "Just that. It was utterly simple. I was walking down a street. I'll imagine streets sometimes when I'm on the treadmill—or that park down by the lake. Once I had a dream about oranges, not even the shape, but more ephemerally, the smell, the taste."

Of course she would tell her mother what she was doing— just not yet. She'd already told Paul. All she wanted was a little autonomy, a little time, a sense of private space in a world where every ninety minutes her mother circled through the sky above her head.

Helen squeezed into a corner seat on the subway train and didn't look around again for the couple or even let herself wonder where they were getting off, just rode around the loop and walked back toward the supermarket. Her bike and helmet were where she'd left them, locked outside, under the red plastic letters, glowing now, that spelled Dominion. The sticker was still in her pocket, she touched it to make sure, but didn't go back inside to see if there was any sign of the stickers left or any meat on display, or no sign that anything had happened at all.

The sky was growing darker, nearly dark. The air seemed close and saturated, forming blurred rings around the streetlights. Damp air slipped past her face as she biked the wrong way down the one-way street, keeping close to the curb, south past the playing field and the skating rink that stood where the house they had once lived in used to stand.

Ahead of her, above the houses, rose the CN Tower, its thick gray stalk jutting into the close sky until it met the doughnut bulge of the observation deck, narrowing further toward the white rocketlike spear of the communications antenna. Red and white beacon lights blinked in slow, staccato unison.

For whole days at a time, when she'd first got back, she had gone biking, despite the slush and cold. In her helmet and sunglasses and gloves, no one had recognized her or stopped her. Biking comforted her. The risks were familiar risks: anonymous insults, skidding on streetcar tracks, car doors opening, an onion lying in the middle of the road. She'd tried to explain to Paul how much she loved the thrill of self-propulsion, feeling stripped down, sucked clean, swift and autonomous, warm in the raw air, the gas-sweet smell of car exhaust.

On King Street, she'd biked past construction sites, past the domed, retractable-roofed stadium swelling at the foot of the Tower like a huge egg or heavy-lidded eye. Past vandalized billboards, signs down by the toxic lake that read DANGER, KEEP OUT, new signs that had replaced the old SWIM AT YOUR OWN RISK signs. Outside corner stores, newspapers wrestled with the wind, held down by bricks.

At night she biked under stars that, for her mother as a child, a child moving between cities, had been the only stable thing. When she was a child, of course, the sky had looked different. The stars were just as luminous and beautiful, but infinitely changeable. *The stars we see are really old, traveling light,* Barbara had told her once, and she had hugged this secret to herself: *The stars are always moving. They are not what they seem.* And Paul? What did Paul see? The neat, mysterious map of constellations that spread hugely across the sky but still seemed human-scale—just as he'd once described to her how their family made him think of a sequence of points lighting up on one of those electronic maps. And her father? The hardest person to imagine a view for was her father.

And everywhere she biked, she ran into movie sets. A man threw a female dummy off a bridge. Floodlights bathed the yellow walls of an apartment building. A propswoman set up a blue mailbox on a corner. American movies mostly, the kind that transformed Toronto streets into New York or Boston or Baltimore. Ever since the big Los Angeles earthquake, there'd been a new stream of American movies shot in Toronto, turning it into Hollywood North again. The on-location shots touched her like a small bruise: They made her think of her father.

She took the EAT THIS AND YOU'RE DEAD MEAT sticker out of her pocket, laid it on the kitchen table, and stared at it. She knew about the huge poultry farms and pork farms where animals never saw the light of day and were stuffed with chemicals and antibiotics and killed in weeks. At the sink, she poured herself a glass of water and held it for a moment, water from the lake you couldn't swim in, water that tasted like chlorine, nearly like swimming pool water, as if it should have been some fake pale blue color, not unobtrusively clear.

She was still thrilled by her luck at finding this apartment, although she was at a loss to figure out what Sam Miller had taken with him to Australia, other than his computer. There seemed to be almost no dent in his belongings, even his clothes. It was as if one day he'd simply disappeared in some mad bolt across the globe. She kept meaning to pack some of his things away but hadn't so far, partly out of amazement, partly for company.

A bottle of shampoo and a couple of disposable razors lay on a shelf in the bathroom, beside the shower. A red terry cloth bathrobe hung on the back of the bathroom door. Her possessions lay like a grafted layer on top of his: her clothes, her books, her TV set, David's old computer, which she'd set up on the desk in the bedroom. In the kitchen, Sam had left all these matter-of-fact domestic touches, half-used candles, a lacquer bowl filled with matchbooks from restaurants all over the city, a shelf of cookbooks: Thai, Indian, Mexican, Indonesian.

The windows of the apartment faced the backs of houses on the next street—not much of a view but private. The day after she'd moved in, she had bought an aquarium and two goldfish whom she had named Clark and Lois. *I'm home,* she would shout to them every time she came in. Sometimes, perhaps in response, they swam around in circles. On the kitchen table, beside the aquarium, she set a hyacinth in a foil-wrapped pot, bright pink and luridly sweet-smelling, a bottled-up whiff of spring. She stepped back and stared at it in satisfaction.

Sometimes she combed Sam's bookshelves, moving aside the small wooden animals and clay heads. One day she pulled out *Madame Bovary,* which she read in hours, haunted afterward not by Emma but Emma's daughter, left behind at the end, ignored and half-wild, who had no clothes that fit her and had never been taught how to read. What, she asked the dead and faraway M. Flaubert, was going to happen to her?

After a shower, after scrubbing off the layer of restaurant smells, she carried the sticker into the living room, settling onto the blue sofa with a towel around her shoulders to watch the news. Dolphins were dying mysteriously up and down the east coast as they had been the night before, maybe from the same toxin that had been infecting seafood, no one seemed to be sure. *Dolphins are the smartest mammals on Earth,* she thought she heard the newscaster say, which made her laugh because it served the humans right.

A small boy, who had fallen from a balcony and lived, waved from his mother's arms while his mother sobbed uncontrollably. Helen leaned forward. Sometimes she watched for news of earthquakes. She'd sent David her new phone number but hadn't heard from him at all in a couple of weeks.

There was nothing, even on the local news, about people plastering the meat departments of supermarkets with stickers.

"Barbara Urie," the newscaster said, looking right at her, "forty days in space." She was getting used to this: Every evening, all over the country, news anchors announced how many days her mother had been in space, while a simulated shot of the space station circled through a black sky in the background. Just so no one forgot.

What are you going to do about it? When she shut her eyes, she could still see the man on the subway, sitting in his suit alone on the orange banquette, talking in all his revolving voices. *What are you going to do about it?* Sometimes she wondered why she didn't just run away, get out of Toronto, the way everyone else in her family had done. Partly it was stubbornness, partly a sense of responsibility that kept her, a feeling that someone should stick around in case anything (what kind of anything?) happened. And, anyway, you didn't necessarily have to go running off around the globe, like David, to *do something*.

Maybe the young man and the woman at Dundas station looked familiar because she had seen them at The Million. Maybe they just looked like other people she'd seen. They could have come into The Million. It served the kind of food that animal rights activists would eat, and it was often crowded in the evenings, a slightly spicy smell in the air. She was good at waitressing even when she hated it, good at the speed of it, operating in motion, the tricks it took to remember orders, people's faces, the illusion of everything going smoothly. A couple of people at the restaurant knew who she was and others didn't. She didn't talk about it. She'd been using her middle name, Stockton, her mother's name, instead of Urie.

When people asked why the café was called The Million, *the million what?,* and they asked all the time, she told them, *a million anything you want.* A million dollars. A million people. A million years. In the beginning, The Million had been a diner run by a Greek immigrant who had made his own hamburgers and moussaka in the kitchen at the back. People had laughed at the idea of a man hoping to make a million dollars from a diner and retire to a large house with a swimming pool, although it wasn't the diner that was worth so much now, but the land it stood on. What Helen liked more than anything was the man's exuberant optimism, and who was to say he had only been dreaming about money?

She pulled her feet up underneath her on the sofa, wished some kind of dinner, any kind of food really, would materialize in front of her, something that would fill her up, satisfy her, something substantial. She was savoring the sensation of being on her own, thick with latent energy and longing, and yet it was so difficult sometimes to figure out how to feed herself. Dinner like some kind of easy TV commercial, shiny and steaming. No, she told herself sternly, not food like that. The smell of someone else's dinner drifted in from the hallway, garlicky, slightly burnt. Reaching for the remote control, she switched over to the space station feed. She'd asked a space agency technician to reconnect the tiny satellite dish outside her window, close to the roof.

Peter Carter was working in one of the labs. Her mother floated in the observation area, under the clear dome, looking out at points in the black sky. Blue light filled the room. It was so easy just to go on looking, swallowing light, to fall out into that jittery, millions-of-years-old photon vacuum. It took all the will in the world to look away.

The line up to the cash register had stalled. Through the large, plate-glass windows, a streetcar blurred past on King Street. A young woman in a blue rain jacket with a hood pulled loosely over her head made her way through the entrance doors; black ski pants, low black boots. She didn't take a cart or a basket but kept glancing around carefully as she headed behind the twin lines of people, toward the back of the store. Helen stepped out of line, wedged her basket under an unused check-out counter in case she decided to come back for it (there wasn't much inside, bargain-sized white vinegar, oatmeal on sale, ginger preserves), and followed the young woman toward the far aisle. Midafternoon again. She'd been out walking. The meat cases were in the far aisle.

Somehow she must have missed the moment when the young woman picked up a basket, but she was carrying one now, lifting up cans of vegetables, checking the sales displays that faced the long, two-tiered meat refrigerator, looking around her, moving slowly toward the meat. Her face was the face of the woman on the Dundas subway platform. She put down the basket, slid one hand into her pocket, while Helen waited at the end of the next aisle, just around the corner, staring at cans of tuna. There was almost no one in sight. The young woman pulled her hand out of her pocket, moving discreetly, peeling stickers one by one off a roll, keeping her hand cupped so that it was difficult to tell what she was doing. One sticker, then another appeared on the refrigerator case, on the long mirror that ran along the top of the case, on the packages of meat and the reflections of the meat.

Quietly, Helen walked through the empty checkout line and

out the exit, leaned against the glass wall beside the doors, taut with excitement, the element of risk. High gray clouds scudded through the sky. Across the tiny plaza stood a bank and the Char-broiled Hamburger Restaurant. The dark, greasy smell of hamburgers char-broiling drifted toward her. On the inside of the glass beside her rose a stack of blue plastic bottles full of spring water, and above them big paper advertisements for President's Choice and bonuses from Mr. Grocer.

A siren wailed in the distance; lights flashed, approaching, and Helen froze, but it was just an ambulance and it turned a corner, streaming away in another direction. The young woman sped out the exit, blue jacket close enough to touch, grab, before she dashed across the plaza, Helen behind her. A rhythm in her feet, she was like Alice toppling down her hole: She wanted to go underground. Down an alley that led out onto a side street. The young woman was pulling her arms out of the blue jacket, bundling it into a paper bag, wearing another jacket underneath, a black fifties jacket tucked at the waist.

"I saw you," Helen said, coming alongside her, nearly running. The young woman didn't say anything. She turned the corner and headed back toward King Street, walking very fast, her black hair tangled, electric, full of static. She drove toward a break in the traffic, the two of them loping nearly side by side across the split seams in the road around the streetcar tracks. "I saw you," Helen said again. "I've seen you before."

"What do you want?" the young woman asked, and didn't stop. "Hmm? What did you see? Something you like? Something you didn't like?" Up the next side street, toward Queen Street where there would be plenty of small dark stores and restaurants for her to slip into.

"I saw you in the supermarket," Helen said. "I saw what you were doing. And I saw a guy in a Dominion last week. I have one of the stickers."

"So what are you going to do?"

"I want to know who you are. I want to talk to you about what you're doing."

"This isn't some kind of game."

"I know that," Helen said quietly.

The young woman stopped but did not come closer, pulled a strand of black hair out of her mouth, gave Helen an abrupt stare. A car swept past. Her pale brown skin was very fine, the bones of her face curved underneath it. She wore tiny gold rings in her ears, breathed quickly but silently. "I don't have any idea who you are."

"I work at The Million," Helen said. "My name's Helen."

"Oh, The Million." Her feet were moving again, edging lightly down the sidewalk, but she nodded. "Now isn't a very good time to talk. I could come by the restaurant. I know where it is."

"I work Wednesday afternoon," Helen called. "Or Thursday evening." At the same moment that she was certain the young woman would not come, she realized how much she wanted her to, for no other reason than that she'd said she would. A streetcar rattled across the end of the block. The young woman wedged the bag with the jacket in it back under her arm, and ran.

6

I was thirteen. I was walking along the dirt road from town back toward Minnow Lake, past the turnoffs for newer cottages, which were not like the cottage we rented, with its old white enamel stove and china teacups and an upright organ with embroidered foot pedals that you had to pump hard in order to get any sound at all. The roar of a motorcycle grew behind me. A boy zoomed past, spraying gravel and dust, spraying the scent of the creosote that the road crews used to cut the dust, and stopped a few yards up the road.

He turned around and looked at me. "Do you want a ride?" he yelled. I had seen him before, working in the supermarket and in line at the ice cream store and on a boat down near the docks. It was nearly dusk.

"Sure," I said. There was an extra helmet on the back of the motorbike.

"My name's Paul."

"That's my brother's name," I said. Then I was embarrassed. "I'm Helen." I could not really see the boy's hair inside the helmet, only his face, which was round and quiet-looking with thick, high cheekbones. He had tanned, bony hands and wore an "I Love Jamaica" T-shirt. Maybe he recognized me, just from being around town, but he would not know who I was, would not know my father's name from articles in newspapers and science magazines, or that my mother was an award-winning scientist who had briefly hosted a TV science show for kids and dreamed more than anything of becoming an astronaut. He didn't know that I was an expert on thawing times, that I could tell how long it took to thaw a package of ground chuck or chicken legs just by looking at it, and could identify the food my family ate even when it was covered in tinfoil in the freezer, or that I found it impossible to think about the future—what the world would be like or what I would be doing years from now. I was a girl in shorts and a blue T-shirt walking along a dirt road in Muskoka.

"How far are you going?" I asked.

"All the way round," he said, "back out to the highway." The road went in a circle, around the lake. Crickets were singing in the grass and in the gravel at the side of the road, still audible in the air around his engine as it idled. The clouds were white on one side, turning blue on the other as the sun fell and a breeze picked up. He handed me the extra helmet, and when I pulled it on, a strange kind of anonymity linked us, like two aliens. I climbed up behind him and slipped my arms around him, because it seemed like the safest place to put them.

"You can let me off right where the road starts to bend."

"Tell me when we get there." And then he did not look at me again, just turned and we were off, plunging into the smell of creosote with a noise that banged off the trees. Going fast, going faster. Anything I knew about elementary physics and velocity made it seem crazy and dangerous to be going this fast on a hilly dirt road at dusk, creating an inhuman amount of noise, and yet I felt curiously happy. I held on tightly. My eyes were watering. I did not want the boy named Paul to turn around and think I was crying. The lights of cottages shimmered, and even though the cottagers would be cursing us, I was determined not to care. We were coming up to the bend in the road.

"Keep going," I shouted, and he slowed for an instant so that there was a sudden shaft of quiet air between us.

"Do you want to see how fast we can go?" Did he see a girl or just another body on the back of his motorbike? Was he trying to scare me or prove something to me?

"All right," I said.

"You're sure?"

"I'm sure." I told myself that I was not afraid. He accelerated again, past the bend and the path that led down to our cottage and my parents' car, which gleamed in the fading light, and faster, faster than before, until there was nothing but the smell of creosote and a terrible roar and no longer trees, only sharp green air, then speed, just speed, hurling everything out of reach, as if time itself was spinning away from me. And yet I already recognized this sensation, of everything spinning beyond reach; I had just never thought of it as speed before. And then we were going so fast that I couldn't think of anything except that I had to hold on somehow to this boy's jeans. Nearing the highway we slowed while cars sped past us in their turn, cars that we could always hear, echoing over the water, from our cottage across the lake.

"Do you want to keep going around in a circle or go back the way we came?"

"Keep going," I said. We were breathless and covered in dust. He drove in a concentrated not a reckless way, as if he had an almost objective interest in seeing how fast we could go. It was an experiment, just as my parents sometimes joked that everything they did was some kind of scientific experiment. The wind we stirred up in the evening air was so strong that my arms and legs were growing cold, my ears burned with the roar around us, and then we passed the point where I had been walking along the dirt road back from town.

"OK," I yelled. "Right here." And suddenly, sliding back onto the ground at the edge of the road and pulling off the white helmet, I could hear everything from the outside again, how even the slowing of the motorbike was such an obvious sound that there would be no way I could sneak into the cottage as though that sound had nothing to do with me. "Thanks." I could not think what else to say. I slapped the dust out of my clothes.

"I'll see you," he said, but he said it casually. It did not necessarily mean anything. The engine revved and revved as I ran down the path toward the lake, where a pale sunset hung beyond the dock, long light falling among the birch trees. My parents sat on the small, dark green wooden porch, holding steamy mugs of coffee.

"Don't tell me you were on that motorbike," my mother said. Both of them held their bodies firm, in solidarity, my mother in a thick plaid shirt, my father with his straw hat on. They barely moved but kept their eyes on me.

"I was," I said cautiously.

"Who do you know who has a motorcycle?" my father asked.

"Someone named Paul."

"Someone you know?"

"I've met him in town," I said.

"Met him?"

"He works in the supermarket. You've probably seen him."

"I thought you went for a walk," my mother said, "and then you come back tearing around these crazy roads at some kind of crazy speed as if you want to break your neck."

"I don't want to break my neck."

"Then why go that fast? Why were you tearing around on a motorbike with someone you barely know?"

"You sound like an ordinary mother," I shouted.

"An ordinary mother," she said in amazement. "Helen, what's that supposed to mean?"

"Don't you like to do things that are dangerous?"

She was quiet for a moment. "I guess this seems reckless, not just dangerous." Her gaze met my father's, then turned back to me.

"I was having fun," I shouted. I could hear my voice soaring away from me. "I was just trying to have some fun."

"Helen."

"All right, I don't mean it." I kicked the edge of the porch. "I don't mean any of it." I sat down between them on the green wooden steps with my arms folded across my knees, the world still streaming around me. The lake washed and sang behind us. Mosquitoes began zizzing in my ears. I wondered where Paul was, if he was lying out on some patch of granite or in the kitchen, if he had heard everything we'd said.

"Maybe it's a matter of qualitative risk," my father said suddenly from under his straw hat. "The thing we'd like to teach you is how to avoid unnecessary risk." He leaned toward me, clasping his hands.

When I slammed in the back door, breathless from biking all the way home, I found my mother sitting at the kitchen table, which surprised me, because she was almost never there when we got back from school. Mrs. Agnelli, our housekeeper, had already left for the day. "Here," my mother said, "look at this." She held out the folded newspaper. Her face was flushed, and although she was still in work clothes, she had kicked off her shoes.

CANADIAN SPACE PROGRAM LAUNCHED, I read. *Applications for astronaut positions are now being accepted.* That was what it actually said, as if anyone who wanted to could apply. *Canadian astronauts will fly as part of the American space program on the returnable shuttle. The Americans have begun flying their small shuttle fleet as they proceed with plans to build a continually in-use space station.*

What caught me off-guard was how quiet the kitchen was, and how this was happening in such an ordinary, anonymous way.

"Did you try calling the number?" I asked.

"I did," she said calmly, "but it was busy." I wondered how many other people also wanted to be astronauts. Not just her. How could I ever think it was just her?

"Did you know this was going to happen?"

"I wasn't completely taken by surprise," she said. "I've known for a while this was coming, although I wasn't sure exactly when the ad would appear." I didn't know how I expected her to respond. Suddenly it was possible to be an astronaut, but what did that mean? Only that it was possible, not just some mad dream. The fact that she'd wanted to be an astronaut all my life didn't necessarily mean she was going to *be* an astronaut.

"You'll apply?" I asked, because the room was so quiet, because just for an instant I wasn't sure, because how could you anticipate that leap from the impossible to the possible?

"I'll apply," she said.

"So what will happen then?"

"Well, probably there'll be a couple of different steps. First they'll narrow down the applicants to those who are qualified to be serious candidates. And then they'll have interviews. And then they'll probably put the most successful candidates through a series of psychological and physiological tests, hook you up to electrodes and have you do all kinds of peculiar things." I had a horrifying vision of my mother with electrodes sticking out all over her shaved head. Who knew what was going to happen? I wanted her to apply, and I did not want her to. I was terrified as much by the possibility that it could still come to nothing, things could still go wrong: What if she applied and was not chosen?

When the science show that she had hosted for a season had been pulled from the air, she'd refused to talk about it. She had gone back to the lab full-time, working on a project with Tom Huang, co-authoring a paper that won some award. The American space program was still interested in her research. What if she had wanted to be something else, do something political, for instance, would it feel any different? Was that any reassurance? What was I supposed to do now?

I went to the sink and ran myself a glass of water. "Have you talked to Dad?"

"Not yet." She smiled at me complicitly. She wedged the newspaper under the telephone, turned, and held out her hand. "Helen, I really believe this is important work. And the thing is, I think it's important that people like me attempt to do this kind of work."

I set down my glass on the table. We had already drained the pool for the year; it was covered in black plastic with sandbags around the edges, leaves falling from the oak tree onto the plastic, brown as leather. How could you anticipate any of this, the sameness and the chasm from the moment before? Even if we had been shouting, there would still have been this quiet underneath everything, these gaps, the moments that in the end counted most of all.

I sat down beside her. "Maybe the possibility of something

is the scariest part," she went on in the same soft voice. "It's like when you've been in love with someone for a long while and suddenly it seems that they are interested in you. For a moment you don't know anything. You have to reconstruct the whole way you see things. You may not even know for an instant what you really want."

7

GRAND UNIFIED THEORIES = GUTS

The subway train sped out of the tunnel, over the great Roman arches of the Bloor Street viaduct and the Don Valley Parkway, which streamed like a river up the middle of the wide ravine. The train sped through the arms of a deep, red sunset, and into the tunnel again. In her pocket, Helen had the address of the woman named Elena, a map that Elena had drawn on a napkin from The Million, the pen lines bleeding a little at the edges. She had decided not to ride her bike, hadn't felt like concentrating on traffic while she cycled the long way east. This way she could think, wonder what was in store for her, try to keep calm.

Elena had invited her for dinner. That was all she'd said, but maybe it wouldn't simply be dinner. A slide show afterward, shots of caged animals, cats with shaved skulls hooked up to electrodes, rabbits with their eyes mutilated in cosmetics product tests—or slaughtered seals, beluga whales dying in the St. Lawrence, so toxic that they had to be buried as contaminated waste. Maybe dinner itself would be a kind of test: three plates of unidentified food set down in front of her. She'd have to choose one. Elena would stop her and ask fiercely, *Do you know what you're eating?* Would she have to make a big deal out of the fact that she didn't eat meat? That she'd bought two goldfish to keep her company? Would they make her fill in a questionnaire? Sign petitions? Give them money? How many people would be there? As Helen walked south from Pape station, starlings massed on all the telephone wires, chattering loudly. In her knapsack she carried a bottle of soda water and a baguette.

Go to the side door, Elena had said. It was an older house, its brick walls painted pale green. Elena lived in the basement. Her grandmother lived on the first floor, and a tenant lived upstairs. One evening the week before, Elena had come into The Million, slipped into a booth in Helen's section and ordered a cup of coffee. She was reading a magazine called *The New Ark* when Helen sat down across from her. There was no sign that Elena had recognized her as anyone other than a waitress at The Million, but then someone like Elena probably didn't waste her time reading magazine articles about astronauts' families.

Bangles jingled on Elena's arm as she lifted her coffee cup. Her black hair was pulled back in a silver clip. She didn't seem either as severe or wary as she had on the street, although Helen had been prepared for both. The stickers, Elena explained in a low, clear voice, were just a small part of what she and the people she worked with were trying to do. During the day, she worked for a company that developed alternatives to animal-testing techniques: cell cultures, for instance, or computer programs. Before that she had worked as a lab technician. They talked about the food at The Million, about downtown rents. Then Elena mentioned dinner, took a fountain pen out of her canvas bag and wrote down her address.

Now, when Elena came to the door, she was wearing black tights, a black miniskirt. Helen wasn't sure why she found it odd that Elena seemed so fashionable; on the other hand, it added to her fascination. "Hi," Elena said warmly, "come in."

Face to face like this, Elena was shorter than Helen. She

moved with economical, decisive grace. The steps down to the basement were lined with wood paneling and smelled of food, something spicy, although there was no sound of anyone else, no voices.

In the basement itself, the walls shone plaster white, like the walls of some small Mediterranean cottage, windows set high in the thick stone. The concrete floors were painted a shiny, startling turquoise. Everything seemed very neat, spare, even elegant, a storybook place, like a floating island. There was no sign of banners, no radical posters, no EAT THIS AND YOU'RE DEAD MEAT stickers lying around, no blue raincoat on the coat rack like the one that Elena had worn the day Helen had accosted her on King Street. There had been fifteen other supermarket attacks in the city that day; three people had been arrested. Helen had heard about it on the news when she'd arrived home.

"You don't mind living in a basement?" she asked.

"Given the choice, I'd prefer not to, but it's all right," Elena said.

On the fridge were two postcards that Helen hadn't noticed at first: One read, "Biotic equality not biomachines." On the other, which read, "One man's meat is another nine men's bread," a red slash had been drawn through the words *man's* and *men's*.

"Foster just called," Elena said. "He'll be here in a minute." She took off her bangles and laid them on the counter, unfastened the watch on her other wrist, a man's watch with a thick metal band, laid it beside the bangles, and tucked her black hair behind her ears.

"Does Foster live here?"

"No," Elena smiled. "Foster's my partner. Foster and I work together. He's the one you saw in the Dominion. We're part of this group, as I guess you've gathered. Basically we started it together."

Helen nodded, took the bottle of soda water out of her knapsack, and laid the baguette on the counter. She still felt nervous. Even though she wanted to take Elena's friendliness at face value, she was finding it hard to do. It wasn't that she distrusted Elena exactly, but she was conscious of ulterior motives. For all she knew, Elena had people over to dinner like this regularly, went through all the same sleek and cheerful motions. Dinner was a lure, a seduction, a professional technique.

There was no table in the kitchen, just two stools lined up at a section of counter that jutted out from the wall. A small white cat roamed into the room, then out again. And yet, in spite of her nervousness, Helen felt curiously safe. She was free to say whatever she wanted among these people, be whoever she wanted.

A pair of red hightop sneakers strode past, framed in the window above the counter. The screen door slammed. Footsteps hurried down the stairs. When the door behind them opened, Foster looked almost exactly as when Helen had followed him through the subway, the same blue jacket, hair pushed back from his high forehead, deep-set eyes, only this time he carried a bottle of wine in a paper liquor store bag in one hand.

She guessed that the two of them were in their mid-twenties, maybe Elena was a little older. Seen at a distance, down the subway platform, Foster had struck her as feral; up close, he seemed quick but touched with jumpiness. The skin under his eyes was darkened. His lips were chapped. "How was your day?" he asked, as Elena kissed him on both cheeks. Then he turned to Helen. "I'm full of admiration for Elena because she has a full-time job, a very serious day job, on top of everything else she does. Did she tell you?"

"Helen works at The Million," Elena said.

"That's right," he said. "I live on Shaw, north of Bloor, not that far from The Million. I go there sometimes. Maybe I've seen you." He leaned against the counter and took the bottle of wine out of the paper bag. "It's rat for dinner," he said quietly, his eyes stilled, looking right at Helen. "Organic rat, actually. You're lucky. Did Elena tell you?"

"It's ratatouille," Elena said evenly. "Foster always calls it rat. Some people we know think it's in very poor taste."

"I don't care," Helen said. She looked from one to the other, aware of their faint air of mutual protectiveness.

"OK." Foster grinned. "Do you want some wine?" Elena handed him three glasses and he set them on the counter, poured some wine in each of them. "We're going to have a little toast to the future," he said graciously. "We always try to, if that's all right with you."

"Fine by me," Helen said. She didn't really see how it was possible to say no to a request like that. They each took a glass of wine and clinked them.

Foster had long hands, deft hands, hands that kept moving around the edge of his glass, pulling back the metal collar around the neck of the wine bottle. He sat down on one of the stools, resting his feet on the rungs of the other. "So Elena says you saw me in the Dominion."

"Yes, I did."

"She said you even followed me out the door." He stopped and coughed quietly. "It's kind of unnerving to know that, actually. Because I didn't see you. And I guess in a way I have to admire you for being able to do that. Usually I'm very good at telling if someone has noticed me, because you have to be able to tell."

"Why do it like that? With the stickers, I mean. Isn't it kind of risky?"

"Well, it's just one of the things we do."

"You have to start somewhere," Elena said and leaned across the counter. "It's nonviolent and on our end pretty inexpensive, and people can go in and do it on a small scale if that's what they feel comfortable with, or you can do something larger-scale. You can't tackle everything, can you—and this is what we've chosen to do."

What am I supposed to say? Do I just have to agree with her?

"So," Foster said abruptly, "what's in it for you?" Elena was lifting the lid off a pot, a cloud of steam rising around her, looking nothing like a wild fanatic.

"For me?"

"You wanted to meet us. Well, what do you see yourself doing? Can you see yourself in a supermarket, slipping down an aisle with a roll of stickers in your hand? Another thing you can do, if you're not up to that, is just puncture the plastic over the meat and leave the package behind a row of tins. After a while it starts to smell. Of course it's not just stuff like this. This is the frontline work but how you live counts, what you eat—you know. You've probably thought about it if you work somewhere like The Million."

"Sure I have," Helen said. She looked right back at him.

Foster stood up and began taking plates out of a cupboard while Helen found herself wondering ridiculously *where* they were going to eat, since there were three of them and only two stools, barely enough room in the tiny kitchen. Then he turned around again. "How did you get here?"

"By subway."

"Is that how you usually get around?"

"Usually? Usually I bike."

"You don't find it too dangerous these days?"

"No," Helen said warily, "not really. And even if it is some-times, it's faster than any other way."

"My bike got stolen," Foster said, "and I didn't have insur-ance, so right now I walk."

"Do you ever drive?" Elena asked. *Drive?* Why drive? Per-haps this was some kind of trick question.

"I can drive," Helen said, "but I almost never do."

"Here," Elena said to her, perfectly pleasantly. "Can you carry these things through? We're eating in the other room."

In the back room, a futon folded on a wooden frame seemed to be in use as a couch. There were bookshelves, a low wooden coffee table, another chair, a trace of classical music, soft footsteps padding past overhead that probably belonged to Elena's grandmother. Did conversations drift up through the floor? Maybe she was some kind of radical herself. There were no voices from the kitchen. On the other side of the wall, the furnace clicked and churned on softly.

When Helen returned, Foster was back on the stool, slicing a carrot into a salad bowl, Elena at the sink. "I don't suppose you have a car," he asked.

"No," she said, "although I can get access to a car."

"Oh." His gaze fixed on her newly, very clearly. "Access. Does that mean it's a family car?"

"No," she said instantly, "not really." Elena, too, had stopped at the sink, her shoulders under her sweater held acutely still.

"Can you get access to it whenever you want to?"

"Why?" she asked. She was too shocked to backtrack, to try claiming that for environmental reasons she stayed as far away from cars as possible.

Foster rested his elbows on the counter. "I know you'll think it's contradictory." His voice had gone quiet and serious. "And as a rule we don't have much to do with cars, but the problem is there are places it's impossible to get to without a car. And there are things—things it's very important that we do—that we can't do unless we have access to a car."

Helen was lucky to see him, because it was dark and Foster was crossing Bloor Street on Shaw Street, his street, walking south, head tucked, hands in his pockets. She braked, hauled her bike onto the curb, locked it outside a Korean video store, then jogged back to Shaw, keeping to the far side, still in her helmet, black biker's tights, quiet rubber soles on her boots. She was far enough behind him that there was no particular reason why he should turn around, and anyway it was dark; as long as she kept the curve of his shoulders in sight, the gleam of the top of his head. Past Harbord, past the black box of a high school just below it, flat asphalt with a tall fence around it, past College, a stooped man and a dog tinted dusky orange, the parking lot and loading dock of another supermarket. Even then he didn't stop. Bulbs shone on the front porches of the old, brick houses. At Dundas he turned east. A streetcar was coming, and at its serene, electric approach, she lost her nerve and climbed in, grabbed the last seat by the window that looked out over the sidewalk. She could see the flecks in Foster's jacket now, an old suit jacket, the red stain of his running shoes, the streetcar whirring, speeding up to a thin, high-pitched whine as it clattered along its tracks, headlights of cars stealing past. A band of wan, fluorescent light ran under the row of advertisements. Long reflections in the window made everyone look malnourished, takeout restaurants, Portuguese bakeries shining behind their eyes.

She lost him. One moment he was standing at an intersection, the next he wasn't. What did she want from him anyway? Simply the thrill of following him and finding out where he was going? Across the aisle, a man in workboots sat hunched over dreamlessly, hands heavy and dusted in gray, holding a paper bag between his knees. Two young couples sitting in front of her chattered in voluble Cantonese. Both of the girls wore white blouses under their coats and spiked heels, and spoke in high, breathless voices. The streetcar headed toward Chinatown, through Chinatown, toward the glassed-in bulk of the Eaton Centre where the teenaged runaways in ripped denim jackets with their tufted hair stood staked out inside the glass doors. Helen stared hard at all of them, all these private journeys, everyone wandering like planets. Everything had the shaky clarity of travel by night.

"Imagine the Earth as a basketball," Barbara said, "and then imagine sticking a piece of Scotch tape on it." The picture that was Barbara's face dissolved into the image that she was looking at on a screen in the space station, a luminous, computer-generated shot of a basketball with a hand coming toward it, flattening a piece of tape along it, a basketball that floated in deep space. Of course, these were things that her mother could only imagine: *basketball, Scotch tape.*

Other words that were now beyond her mother's reach floated through Helen's head: *Mona Lisa, McDonald's, canoe.*

"The thickness of the tape represents the layer of the atmosphere that sustains us and life as we know it on the planet." The TV guide from the Saturday paper, which lay beside Helen on the sofa, had another picture of her mother on it, smiling above the blue collar of her astronaut worksuit. Barbara was advertising the premiere of *Frontiers,* the science show from space. "Without that thin and fragile layer of atmosphere, our skins would burst, unable to contain bodily fluids. Without oxygen to breathe, our lungs would cease to function."

Her mother's voice was assured in a way that at moments made her sound almost cheerful, which was alarming, but at other moments her seriousness was alarming, too. Her bright gray eyes fixed right on the camera, barely blinking, staring confidently out at everyone watching in Canada, the United States, and around the world. Was Paul watching? "Now imagine the planet as a spacecraft."

Helen stretched out on the couch and pulled a cushion over her head, thought about trees burning, animals burning, insects burning. *The Earth is not a spacecraft.* She turned on the TV set floating across the silver sky inside her head and focused on her mother's face. *There are all kinds of frontiers,* she said. She heard the phone ring suddenly on the floor right beside her and sat up, thinking for some reason that it might be David calling her out of the blue, although probably it was someone from the restaurant.

"Hi," said a voice she did not recognize. "Is that Helen?"

Someone from the space agency, a reporter, a TV producer, someone who automatically assumed a kind of familiarity with her. "Yes," she said tersely.

"I got your number from Elena," said the voice. "It's Foster."

"Oh, right." She turned down the sound, but Barbara's lips kept moving. He could not see what she was watching. He was not going to ask her what she was watching, although she would lie if she had to. There were any number of American sitcoms that she could have tuned in.

"I met you at Elena's."

"Yes, I know." She switched the picture off as well, instantly gray, except for a thin bright line in the middle, like a mouth closing, still glowing.

"I was calling about the car."

"Yes," she said. She propped herself against the arm of the sofa, his voice coming back to her now, easy on the surface, then suddenly purposeful. *The car?* "What about it?"

"I was wondering if I could see it."

"See it?"

"Take a look at it. I was wondering if we could meet and you could show it to me." Was there a moment she had missed or conveniently covered up that other night at dinner, some point when she had agreed to let them use her car? "Do you have any time tonight?" he asked.

"Not tonight." She was amazed that he would even suggest it, that he'd think she was ready to get up and leap out the door. "Maybe tomorrow."

"All right," he said easily, "tomorrow night."

"It's in an indoor lot on McCaul Street." The tips of her fingers grew cool, but that was all. She couldn't believe she was doing this. "Below College."

"I'll find it," he said. "I'll meet you outside, but later, like nine, say, or ten, because I have to work. Is that all right?"

"Nine-thirty," Helen said, "all right."

"I have to go," she said softly, and there was just a touch of vindication in saying it, because of all the times that David had cut short phone conversations, because of all the bad, static-filled lines that often made it impossible to talk for long, because of all his endless talk about earthquakes, because of all the weeks he did not even call. She switched off the kitchen light, unlocked the front door, and leaned against it. In her free hand she held her bundle of keys, the keys to the Glenforest Street house, her old apartment, her new apartment, her bike lock, the station wagon, journeys radiating out of each of them. She held them so tightly that the edges bit into her skin.

"Can you give me a minute?" David asked, and on this night, of all nights, the line was not wavering but fairly clear. "I'll be quick, as quick as I can. I just wanted to hear how Barbara's show went."

She wondered sometimes if he still pictured her as she had been at sixteen, with short, spiky blond hair, or if he tried to re-create her, tried out different pictures, makeup, no makeup, imagining the tilt of her body, the kind of clothes he thought someone her age would wear. "Really well," she said. In the dark, she slipped her wallet into her pocket, pulled on her orange safety vest with its reflecting lime-green X across the back, so lurid that drivers were guaranteed to take note of it.

"Is it at all like the other show, the one she used to do?"

"Well, it's not just for children, and, of course, it's from space. They're using a lot of space station footage, interior and exterior shots, and that's getting a lot of attention. It's quite high-tech and glamorous, lots of computer graphics. They didn't have all that stuff when she was doing *Search for Science*. And she's good at it, you know that. She loves explaining things, she's better than ever."

"I was just wondering," he said, and he sounded almost wistful, "because probably I won't get to see it, at least not right now."

"You could see tapes."

"At some point I'm sure I will see tapes."

"You could call her up and ask her how it went."

"Oh, I will, Helen, I will, but I was just curious to hear what you thought."

"I have to go in a sec," she said. Her heart was beating fiercely. "What have you been up to?" Imagine Foster. Imagine the car, an utterly ordinary, dark green Volvo, slowly rusting in a parking lot, and why should it make a difference that she had driven the car to Florida for her mother's launch and had not gone near it since? No reason to be nervous, because how could a car give her away? There was nothing for him to see.

"I was working out in the mountains this week," David said, "in what remains of this village, only there's not much left.

Everyone's still sleeping out in the open or if they're lucky in tents. Just getting there and back was terrible, because of the roads. Are you on your way out, is that it?"

"I'm going to a movie." It made her sound so petty.

"All right then," he said quietly, "I'll let you go."

Helen slowed as she biked up McCaul Street, narrow and quiet at night, past a corner barbershop, a dim sum bakery with empty trays lying behind its darkened window, a garage full of trucks from one of the huge bread chains, an outdoor parking lot where an attendant sat in a lit-up white booth, eating from a box of doughnuts, in what she had always thought of when she was younger as a little house. The indoor lot was almost at the top of the street, near the southern reaches of the university, and when she pulled up across from it, a figure detached itself from the wall, turned toward her, then jogged across the street, dodging a car, to meet her.

In the dark, Foster smelled faintly of soap and seemed more sinewy than ever. He greeted her with what was either coolness or instant familiarity, and although she had thought he might bring Elena with him, obviously he hadn't. He held onto her bike, eyeing the street around them while she searched for her keys. She wondered if someone like Foster would get a kinky thrill out of driving around in Barbara Urie's car. It was hard to tell. She could still turn around, leap back on her bike and ride away.

"I never asked you what kind of car it is," he said.

"A Volvo. It's a station wagon."

"Oh great." He seemed genuinely pleased. They crossed the street. When she held open the door of the pedestrian entrance for him, Foster grinned, hands in his pockets, while Helen eyed the hunch of his shoulders, watched his eyes glide over the man in the booth by the exit ramp, who seemed to be reading a book. The inside of the lot was quiet, no sound of cars at all.

"You haven't told me what you want to use it for," she said.

"Nothing violent." He grinned again. "We don't do violent things."

They headed through another door, up the concrete stairway to the second level.

"You must have had access to other cars before this."

"Oh yes," he said. "And, I mean, we still do, through other people we work with. But it seemed worth looking into something new."

She thought about telling him that she hadn't just followed him out of the Dominion that day but had trailed him by subway all the way to Dundas station, off the train and onto the platform, too. She could tell him about the night she had followed him down Shaw Street, except that she wanted to hold on to this private way of seeing him, this break in his alertness, a point of vulnerability.

The station wagon was parked against a side wall, just where she had left it, between two concrete pillars painted an unappealing brown. It seemed like such a peculiar way to phrase the question, to ask if he could *see her car*. What was he looking for? What did he expect to see? Foster leaned against the next car, a blue sedan, looking expectant, the edges of his face whittled to fine lines, down to curves and hollows. His presence filled her with a low excitement. All she had to do was open the door. She opened it. On the floor, on the passenger side, lay a sunbleached Burger King bag, which was hilarious really, and when she opened the other door, she saw Foster glance at it immediately, although he didn't say anything. She reached over and tossed the bag into the backseat.

Barbara's university parking sticker was still on the windshield. Sprigs of heather, picked from a field outside the town where her grandparents lived in Scotland, were tucked against the sun visors. Sand on the floor. The air inside the car was dense and sweet, contained air, like the air in a capsule. She couldn't quite believe that he sat there without picking up some distant smell of Florida, some trace of that journey, of all the other places trapped inside the car, everything leading back to that arc into flame and booming, endlessly reverberating sound. He didn't seem to notice anything. This was in its own way reassuring. And anyway, even if he had seen newspaper or magazine photos of the launch—she wasn't in them.

"Aren't you going to start the car?" he asked. Helen had thought he would look at the car, check to see if the seat folded down, size it up somehow, not bend forward, waiting for the ignition to catch, and then switch on the radio.

"Well it works," she said, "is that what you wanted to know?"

"Are you busy?" He smiled and ran one finger along the dashboard, picking up grit.

"Why?"

"There's something I wanted to show you. We'll have to drive to get there, but the problem is I can't show it to you until later, quite late actually."

"Are you going to tell me what it is?"

"No," he said gently. His eyes were very dark, very lucid, very round, and it struck her that this was what he'd been leading up to all along. "It's a surprise."

She pulled into a parking space down the block from a twenty-four-hour Galaxy Donuts. She'd been searching for a Dunkin' Donuts, a Tim Horton's Donuts, anything other than Galaxy Donuts in a city filled with doughnut shops, but they hadn't passed anywhere else that was open. Foster sat quietly beside her, his eyes wide open, staring impassively straight in front of him. The sky was calm and clear, an ordinary night blue, brown just at the edges. A streetcar clattered past.

Inside, they ordered coffee, which Foster drank black with a lot of sugar, leaning toward her across the tiny Formica table, both of them sitting on plastic chairs attached to the table by metal rods. He told her that he worked as a freelance proofreader for a group of law firms and often worked night shifts, so he was used to staying up late. At times he didn't even know how long he would end up working. Once or twice he had worked twenty-three hours straight in a small, wood-paneled room without windows, reading legal briefs until he couldn't see clearly and his hands shook. On the other hand, he said, it was useful for him to be familiar with legal language, and he loved getting off work when other people were just waking up, being sent home by taxi at dawn.

"How did you first meet Elena?" Helen asked.

"At university."

"Here?"

"No, at Western." Western was in London, Ontario. "Elena was studying biology, and I was studying history. One year we lived in the same house." He folded the paper sugar packet between his fingers with a taut energy that made her think of people who smoked, of people who smoked to distract themselves from all their energy.

"Where does her family come from?"

"From? Her father lives here, but she doesn't ever see him. It's kind of awful, actually. I know what you're asking. Her grandmother's Czech. And her mother's from India, but now she lives in New Jersey." He shoved his coffee cup out in front of him. "Look, I don't want you to think that we do any of this for sentimental reasons, just because we love animals or think animals are better than people. We think they have rights as species, like all other species; they should be treated not just as something that's around for us to use however we want. But it's not the same as being sentimental about them."

"What made you say that?"

"I just wanted to be clear."

"Do you have to hide what you do from people?"

"Sometimes." He shrugged. "Not that often."

"What about your family?"

"They know basically how I feel. My parents live in a condominium up in North York. They're older than a lot of people's parents. They know I won't eat steak if I go home for dinner, so we always have takeout Chinese and I order vegetarian, and they know I write articles but they don't know what about. They're not the kind of people who read a lot. I don't get on with my brother at all, and that upsets them more than anything, because they think it must be partly something they've done. But I don't live at home and I support myself, so I must be doing all right."

"I used to think the most horrible question you could ask someone was what they wanted to be," Helen said. "Because I didn't see how you could answer it without knowing—well, everything. And what I wanted was to open my arms and feel the world, feel things press against me, just swallow all this stuff somehow. I don't really know how to explain it. But it's not the kind of thing you can say when people ask you what you want to be."

"People been bugging you?" His voice astonished her, the way it veered from being imperious to instantly kind.

"Well, I was in university, and now I'm not. That's OK. It's not really a big issue. Maybe I'll go back and maybe not."

"University here?" She nodded. "Then you found out about us."

"I needed some time to myself," she said. "I needed to sort some things out."

"What do your parents do?"

"My mother's a doctor. She works for the World Health Organization in Australia." It was out, it was easy. She could reinvent herself endlessly. "They're divorced. My father's a CBC radio producer and he's in Yellowknife. The car's his, but he lends it to me. He's not really living here right now."

"I've always wanted to go to Yellowknife."

She asked him quickly if he had ever been arrested, and he told her about one time, early on, when people had gathered and spread out on the ground outside a Yonge Street fur salon, and he had been hauled to his feet and taken away in the back of a police car, along with several others. Then he said he had to make a phone call.

The only other people in the all-night doughnut shop were an older couple, sitting a few tables away, clasping hands and looking slightly embarrassed, as if unaccustomed to being on a tryst. The woman wore a green silk scarf tied over her hair. The man's brown hands were long and elegant. The boy who had served them was sitting on the counter, the headphones of his Walkman hanging around his neck. Helen glanced at her watch. Her hands were cool and nervous. It was already after midnight. She glanced at Foster, leaning against the wall, the phone pulled close to his face, at the blue jacket hanging over the back of his chair, and wondered whom he could be calling, what exactly Elena had meant by saying, *We're partners, we work together.* They had the ease, the apparent closeness of two people who could be involved or perhaps had once been involved with each other.

If they'd both been at Western, perhaps they had taken part in the lab raids there a few years before, raids that were famous because not only had animals been released but a lot of documents stolen. She wouldn't put it past them. And what about in Toronto? She'd seen drugstore windows plastered with lists of companies using animals to test products, items on drugstore shelves slashed with a red Magic Marker X. Maybe they'd had something to do with the sabotaged billboards that she had biked past, or at least knew who was responsible for them. An air of illicitness trembled over everything around her.

Maybe Foster was going to show her a billboard, a drugstore, another supermarket. *It's a surprise.* Maybe she was crazy to go with him. Maybe he was going to truss her with ropes and dump her in a ravine. Should she be worried, call someone, explain where she was and what she was up to, just to be safe?

They were somewhere in the west end, far west, in an industrial area not far from a railway line because they had crossed over the tracks once, red signal lights distantly glowing. Helen had let Foster drive because he knew where they were going, and it seemed easier than trying to follow his directions. She watched the thick, long warehouse buildings with their corrugated garage doors slip past. Poised on the edge of her seat, she listened to his low voice read out street signs.

He pulled into a small alleyway and parked, handed the keys politely back to her. Outside, everything was desolate and still, one solitary truck parked by the side of the road. *And now,* she wondered, *what now?* "We still have to walk a little," he told her. Her eyes felt tired and metallic, as if they had wires coiled inside them. It was after four in the morning. The sky hung like a skin of deep, swollen blue above them.

At the end of a darkened driveway Foster stopped abruptly. There were two loading docks at the other end, lit up, garage doors already raised. A man strode up and down behind the doors in heavy rubber boots, hosing down the concrete floor and smoking a cigarette, exhaling little tufts of gray. Behind the man, a single chicken wandered across the empty floor, taking aimless, staccato steps, looking completely out of place, as if it were on the moon. From down the street behind them came the sound of trucks, brakes heaving, exhaling pressure. "No one's going to see us," Foster said. And even though his whole body rippled, tensing again, he seemed, like the first time she had seen him, completely unafraid. They stood at the top of the lane, in the lee of a garbage dumpster, beyond the reach of the floodlights above the doors, as a truck began backing past them, the driver just a shadow in the cab, head twisted behind him, dark tarpaulin pulled down over the back of the truck.

Feathers blew past. And even over the throbbing of the engine and the brakes, Helen could hear the chickens, a high-pitched rasping, the sound of their bodies rubbing, crushed together, because that was also a sound. She felt her heart slide, speed up. Smell of gasoline, a mouthful of exhaust, a moist, dense reek.

The men unloaded cages stuffed so full of chickens that it was almost impossible to tell that there were individual birds inside, bits of chicken stuck out at broken angles through the wire, bent feathers, flattened beaks, feet smashed up against the wires and curled around them, tiny chicken eyes. The cages fell onto the loading docks, chunk, chunk, chunk. She was going to throw up. The air filled with incessant shrieking. "You can see the racks on the assembly lines," Foster said in a crazily matter-of-fact voice, talking very close to her ear but shouting just to be heard. "That's where they get strung up feet first, and then they ride along until their throats get slit." Helen stared at the still brick walls, at the bent-over men, at the cages. Sweat was gathering around the edges of her lips. Was it better to look or not to look? "I know it's horrible," Foster shouted. "I know that, but the thing is people never have to think about this part. This is what they're eating. This is what chicken means, and it isn't just chicken either." Why had he brought her here? Did it excite him to show her this? Did he assume that she wanted to see this, that she ought to see this? The bodies disappeared and were chopped into pieces. Did he want her to prove she was tough enough to stand her ground and confront the sight, or run outraged down the alley in some mad effort to stop the men, or keel over and vomit in horror? Did he want her to feel branded forever? She was on the verge of wheeling around and trying to shake that fierce, insistent voice right out of him.

They sat in the station wagon with the engine running and the heater on, Helen behind the wheel, the car filled with the scent of dying chickens, the smell in her clothes and Foster's clothes. She swallowed with great care. "You know what they're called when they come out the other end?" Foster whispered. "They're called Chicken of Tomorrow."

"I've seen them," Helen said.

"Not many people ever get near slaughterhouses, you know, it's not that easy to do, especially now that a lot of them are moving out of the city. I thought at least once you would want to see what really happens." From the corner of her eye, she saw him looking at her thoughtfully.

"I'm fine," she said, before he could say anything else. The smell was in her hair and in her skin. In front of her, the sky was already lifting, a deep, high blue, the one or two stars slowly draining of light. She wondered if Barbara was awake or asleep. She had seen mice killed by the dozens in the labs of her mother's colleagues when she was a child—you had to be tough then, too, and it was the same toughness as now, only it wasn't.

Another night, years ago, came back to her: She'd gone down to the basement to get some ice cream from the freezer and hadn't bothered to turn on the light. When she pushed up the freezer lid, the interior light didn't go on. No hum. She looked down: A pool of water was spreading at her feet. And when she peered closer, she could see—even in the dark—how all the tin foil packages had grown soft, months of dinners dribbling at the edges, ice cream oozing out of the sides of the cardboard container. The creeping decay had terrified her—the waste. She screamed because everything seemed alive.

"The thing is," Foster said softly, "there's still time for us to change things. You have to believe that." He seemed so clear, so electrically sure.

"I know," Helen said. "I really do."

"So, listen." He brushed one finger over her hand, pulled back instantly, a nearly invisible gesture. "There's one more thing I want to show you, and then I'll treat you to breakfast, somewhere good I like to go."

"No." Helen set the key in the ignition and turned it. "I mean, it's good of you to do all this, but I think I've had enough. I have to work later. I need to get some sleep."

"I can't just take you out and show you a slaughterhouse. Don't you think that's incredibly rude? It'll give you completely the wrong impression. Listen, we'll go get Elena, if that will make you feel better. We'll drive across and pick her up, it's not really out of the way." His voice was growing insistent, although there was another undercurrent to it, as if she could actually disappoint him. When she said in amazement that Elena would probably be asleep, he told her emphatically that it was all right, Elena wouldn't mind if he woke her up; she got up very early anyway.

I'm going to be so exhausted at work I'm going to drop things. But it was true that she was almost never up at this time of day, to see the stilled intersections, lights changing luxuriantly, wastefully from red to green, a man placing a ladder gently against

115

the side of a house. The few cars eyed one another as if each one were driven by some private, unspeakable mission, and Helen realized all at once how utterly strange and wonderful it was to be moving through a world with so few cars in it. A woman and a small child walked down the sidewalk, hand in hand, and maybe the child had been shaken out of sleep, noticing at once how tense and pale its mother looked, and then how unusually quiet and clear the world looked, or maybe they got up this early every day. Still restless, still apparently wide awake, Foster stirred beside her. She had walked down this street once before at dusk, listening to starlings, turned in at this pale-green house.

"I'll just be a minute," Foster said. He opened the car door and ran up the side path to Elena's door.

They had already climbed up six flights of stairs, surrounded by walls of painted concrete and fire exit signs, in a deserted office building where Foster said a friend of his worked. He had keys to the back door. Elena was laughing. Her face had the slight puffiness of someone who had just been woken up, paler patches of skin under her eyes. She wore socks, long underwear, a skirt, an oversized green sweater. Helen kept trying to imagine her in a white lab coat, hands flattened on a metal lab counter, that veneer of scientific authority. She didn't seem irritable at being woken up, just slightly giddy, and she grinned at Helen behind Foster's back. She didn't ask where they had been either, which made it seem as if she already knew.

"We're almost there," Foster said. The stairs narrowed a little on the last flight, and at the top he held open the door. Helen stepped out onto a flat tar rooftop. The sky was pale green in the east. Behind them, to the west, rose the conglomeration of Bay Street bank towers, an edge of the CN Tower beyond that. Little gray waves rustled out on the lake. They walked separately around the edges of the rooftop. The view glimmered and teetered around her. She wondered if Paul, walking home at dawn from the architecture school studio in Montreal, noticed only the buildings, the way the frail light traveled along the edges of the buildings. She imagined him hurrying along determinedly with a black drawing case in one hand, and then stopping, caught all at once by the sky. "It's my favorite place to watch the sun rise," Foster said from behind her. How often did he come here and watch the sun rise? No eyes, she told herself: It was just a sunrise. She loved the wash of light over his face and Elena's: a shot of the three of them, held forever, sitting on the raised roof of the ventilation system. The horizon turned a slow, effortless, demented pink. "Was it worth it?" Foster whispered in her ear. "Isn't it worth it?" It was going to be a beautiful day.

8

When my mother stepped through the back door from the garden, I could tell how nervous she was. Her fingers were breathtakingly cold when she touched my hand. My father lined up four glasses on the table and said we would drink the bottle of Dom Perignon he'd bought, no matter what happened. She tried to smile. On the floor, Paul was tying multiple knots in his shoelaces, sitting under the sign my mother had taped to the refrigerator: CLEAN OUT THE POOL!

The smell of lilacs drifted through the open window. We all tried to stay calm. Outside, black winter plastic still covered the pool, heavy sandbags holding the plastic in place around the edges. Paul's ten-speed stood upended on the tiles. It was a late-spring Sunday afternoon. "You know what's going to happen," my father said quietly. "The phone is going to ring and it will be some press person calling to find out whether you know if you're an astronaut yet."

And then the phone rang. No one moved.

"Barbara, do you want me to answer it?" He picked up the receiver and said hello brusquely, as if trying to scare away an obscene caller. "I'll get her." His voice grew quiet. He handed over the receiver.

She said hello and nodded, and then she kept saying yes, but there was a moment when you could tell by her eyes, by some

118

instant expansion in her gaze, by the way her free hand balled into a fist and released, and my father popped open the champagne as if he couldn't wait, the cork thrusting against his palm in a cloud of vapor. Paul gave a whoop. I stared at her. My stomach began fizzing. She held one hand over her ear, was smiling, taking notes on a scrap of paper, saying matter-of-factly, "Yes, tomorrow, yes, we'll be there." The champagne spilled a little between glasses because my father's hand was shaking as he poured. My mother put down the receiver and didn't say anything.

"Please," I said fiercely. "You have to tell us."

Resting her elbows on the blue table, she pressed her head between her hands, shaking it gently. "First he asked me if I was having a good weekend, and if you were all here, and then he just said, well maybe you've guessed already, but we've decided to accept you into the astronaut program, so are you sure you want to do this?" Her mouth kept slipping into an uncontrollable smile. "It means I go into training with the other Canadian astronauts, that's all it means. It doesn't mean I'm going anywhere yet."

Paul passed her a glass of champagne. "Wait," my father said and, like a ballroom dancing partner, pulled her to her feet, wrapped his shaky hands around the sides of her face, and kissed her. I watched their mouths, his hands, the way her hands gripped his back, the sleeves of her striped cotton shirt rolled up above her long, muscular arms. An old shirt, a favorite shirt that she had been wearing while she weeded the garden maniacally for hours. The strange fact that she was now an astronaut slipped seamlessly over her, easy to accept because it didn't make sense, she was still here, right in front of us, exactly as she had been a moment before. Nothing had changed yet.

My father gave us each a glass, and we stood, raised our

glasses in the air, and clinked them together, shouting out toasts. *To Mum. To Barbara. To us.*

The doorbell rang. "Oh no," she whispered, pressing one hand over her mouth. My father hurried to answer it. There were tears in her eyes. When he came back, he said with a grin that it was only the paper carrier collecting.

"No one is supposed to know," she said. "We can't tell anyone yet, not until after the press conference tomorrow when they make the public announcement. They're doing it here, not at the space agency headquarters in Montreal so that we can all be there—it would give everything away if we all got up and flew to Montreal. And there'll probably be a little more fuss than usual, because of you, because after all I'll be the first Canadian astronaut who is also a mother. And people leap on these things. The word is out that there will be some kind of announcement, but we can't give anything away, we have to act as if everything is absolutely normal. You guys even have to go to school in the morning and you cannot, *cannot* say anything. A taxi will come an hour later to pick you up, and we'll meet you downtown. But until then we can't do anything to celebrate, nothing public, we can't even go out to dinner in case anyone suspects, and we can't yell too loudly in case the neighbors hear and some journalist calls to ask them if they've heard anything unusual. I know it's crazy but that's what the man actually said. And if anyone calls for me, tell them we've gone to a movie. I can't even call my parents."

"We have to do something," Paul said softly and stood up, wrapping one arm around her shoulder. "We can't just ignore it."

"We could order in something for dinner," my father said.

"Indian food," I said.

"Pizza," Paul said. "You can order whatever toppings you want."

"Sure." My mother rested one hand against her forehead. "Whatever."

"I think we'll be glad to have a quiet evening at home," my father said, "before all the craziness begins."

She sat down again suddenly. Pulling Paul into the chair beside her, she touched the edge of her glass to his and then to mine. "I'm doing this for you." Her voice cracked to a whisper. "I am. For you."

I sat in bed with my head against the wall, closed my eyes, then opened them. I could not fall asleep. My parents' voices murmured in the distance. *I am sixteen years old and my mother is now an astronaut.* For years, it seemed, she had been going through tests, with weeks and sometimes months between them. After she had passed through the first round, she had started flying back and forth between the Montreal space agency headquarters and Toronto; she'd walk around the house attached to her Walkman, saying she didn't care if she looked ridiculous, whispering in French, because one of the psychological requirements was that Canadian astronauts had to be functionally bilingual.

We have to give these talks, she'd told us one night, *on preassigned topics like "Technological and Communication Frontiers of Space" and "Heroes of the Future." So I've decided I'm going to do mine on "Heroes of the Future," and this is how I'm going to begin.* She stood up and stuffed her hands into her pockets of her jeans. *Hero?* She dropped into a fake, deep voice. *Do you think I want to be a hero?* Then she stopped, waving her arms, and said, no, she was just kidding; she couldn't do it like that.

She told us she was going to renew her small craft pilot's license, promised she would take us both up with her sometime, although when I pictured her flying, I imagined her private glee at being alone in the air. A week later, I biked home and found a microwave sitting on the kitchen counter with a sign taped to it in her handwriting: THAWS FOOD IN MINUTES. WOW! I OWE THIS TO YOU.

I had grown so used to the test days that I had even stopped thinking about what the end point *meant,* just as I had grown accustomed to the American space station slowly being built in the sky above our heads. Photographs appeared in the paper every few months, and each time it had grown a little bigger. In the last photos, there had been huge advertising billboards for high-tech communications companies on its sides. BIG BUCKS EVEN IN A VACUUM, one caption read.

We were, in our own way, going to become famous. I stared into the darkness. My life was going to change. But it was not as if we'd had a choice in this. It was not because of anything we'd done. It didn't matter what we wanted. My arms felt like a puppet's arms, waving up and down.

"You ran out of that school like escapees," the taxi driver said, then turned around, set the meter, pulled away. He did not know who we were, but maybe he would turn on the evening news and start forward in surprise: *It's them.*

Paul had worn his new pair of running shoes, his red nylon knapsack squeezed between his feet. I was trying to gauge his mood beneath his usual deliberateness. A month ago, I had cut my hair very short and bleached blond streaks into it, which my friends liked and my parents had barely commented on. When I'd cut my hair, Paul had walked in a thoughtful circle around me. "We're going to be on TV," he said now in a low, astonished voice, looking at me as he scraped his fingers down through the hair above his eyes.

We had seen her on TV before. We had heard her easy, authoritative voice on the radio. We'd even had our own photos in the paper, but we had never been on TV.

"People we know are going to go home and turn on the news and see us," I whispered.

"We'll see ourselves on TV," Paul said softly.

The room was warm and filled with journalists, a ring of television floodlights, a stale, slightly hysterical eagerness, as if everyone in the room were flapping their arms. There were no windows. In the midst of the flurry, she was a still point, poised, expectant, unusually still. In the suit he almost never wore, my father sat with his hands clasped in his lap, staring out across the room. Paul and I perched on slippery chairs on either side of him.

"I'd like to introduce you to Barbara Stockton Urie," said the tall man at the podium. "She's forty years old and a distinguished scientist who has won a number of awards for her research into the relationship between the vestibular system and nervous system. She's no stranger to the idea of space flight or the goals of the space agency, since her research has had direct applications to both the Canadian and American astronaut programs. Originally Dr. Urie trained in physics; she went on to receive a degree in medicine. Among her many other talents, she's a former competitive swimmer, has her small craft pilot's license, and once hosted a children's TV show about science—and on top of this, she's the mother of two children."

Lights flashed. Everyone rose to their feet and clapped. My mother made her way to the podium, sudden propulsion, vivid in her bright green suit. "I can't tell you how glad I am to be here." She leaned toward the fistful of microphones, a low, vibrant, not-quite-her-usual voice. "This has always been my dream. My family can vouch for that. They've put up with me talking about wanting to be an astronaut for years and they've been very patient, and now—I can't think of anything more exciting than participating directly in the astronaut program and the space station project, and finding out firsthand about the human capacity to adapt to microgravity and life in space." She paused calmly.

"Now I know people have asked me, and maybe some of you even wonder, why bother to send people into space at all? Because machines can never be programmed to do everything that humans can, for a start. It seems to me, though, that the line between life on Earth and life in space is growing increasingly thin. There are practical applications to be gained on Earth from space research and exploration, but in a fundamental sense, if we are to survive as a species, we *must* be able to move beyond our own planet, and I believe the need to do so, like the need to survive itself, is built into our genes."

She sounded passionate and determined and touched by wildness. Were those real tears in her eyes? Did she feel as if she could do anything? Did she believe everything she was saying? Was there any room in her right now for uncertainty, for doubt? She was smiling into the cameras, the tips of her fingers pressed lightly against the podium, the only sign, if it was a sign, of nervousness. I could not quite believe this was my mother. Did she truly think that the need to move beyond the planet was built into her genes, my genes?

"I understand," she said, and smiled, glanced very quickly at the three of us, "that you'd like to ask me some questions." A couple of journalists had already raised their hands. The tall man came to the podium and stood beside her, whispered something in her ear, then pointed at one of the hands.

"Dr. Urie," said a young man, "we all know that you are the first Canadian astronaut who is also a mother. Are you proud to be setting this precedent?"

"Well, I don't think it's all that extraordinary," she said dryly. "Quite a number of the astronauts who have gone up have been parents. I'm not sure what the distinction between mothers and fathers proves in this context. Of course I wouldn't do something like this without the support of my family, and I'm lucky that my children are old enough by now to be fairly independent human beings, and I'm happy to be married to someone who has always been very supportive and very involved with our children. I wouldn't want to stop him doing something like this any more than he has stopped me."

"Dr. Urie, now that you actually have an opportunity to go into space, do you think more about the Victory disaster? One of the American astronauts killed in that shuttle explosion was also a mother."

"Of course I think about it," she said levelly. "I don't think it's only astronauts-to-be who think about it. There are dangers, the explosion highlighted the dangers, but whatever kind of life you lead, you end up taking risks. You have to satisfy yourself that the risks are under control and that what you are trying to do justifies them."

"Dr. Urie, I've read that world-class women athletes have been encouraged to have children because it seems to increase their endurance and strength. As a former competitive athlete, do you believe this?" A woman in a red suit asked that.

"What are you asking me? Are you asking if I believe people are being encouraged to do this or if I believe it really makes a difference? I think anyone who has children will argue that it increases endurance and strength." This made them laugh.

The only break that I could see in her self-control, the only hint of impatience, passed in a thin line along her lips.

At the reception they lined us up in a row and took pictures of us. She rested her hands on my shoulder and squeezed.

I watched my father lean against a wall with a drink in his hand, chatting with a couple of journalists who, it struck me suddenly, were probably colleagues of his, other science journalists. He worked with people here, had one foot in each camp. "She looks so young to have children that age," said a woman's voice behind me. "Think how young she must have been." I found out soon enough that all the reporters who asked me questions simply wanted me to agree with them, to repeat back to them what they had said: *Isn't this wonderful, yes, it's wonderful, are you proud, yes, I'm proud.* If I tried to say anything else, their eyes just turned to sieves.

We were out on the street, running through the dull afternoon drizzle toward the lot where my father had parked the car. Paul and I sat in the backseat while my father drove east toward Jarvis and then north, until Jarvis turned into Mount Pleasant. He seemed to be driving home. Were we going to act as if nothing had happened, as if we'd all met downtown by accident? No one said anything.

What was the point where the excitement had dissolved, or shifted, where I'd begun to feel as if we were sitting in that room like some kind of zoo exhibit? My mother rose and walked to the podium, without looking back. From across the reception room, my father winked at me, turned, went on talking to the other journalists. Once you started, anything could turn into a question. I felt as if someone had pulled up my shirt and then didn't even want to look at my body but instead pushed a hand through my skin, worked it around inside, fingering the articulation of my joints, the squish of my organs. What held them, held any of us together—glue or centripetal force?

We passed the Chinese food place north of Davisville where my father always went to get takeout, a movie theater, a store that sold only dollhouses. Everything seemed unstable, very frail, as if we were driving along the edge of a cliff. I wanted Paul to look at me in his even way and moor me. I tried to stare out the window through my mother's eyes: Did houses suddenly look different if you were planning to go into space? Did people? Did they look less substantial, did they start to disappear? What did your own family look like?

"Barbara," my father said softly, "just be glad you weren't the first person with green hair to go into space, because if you were, people would concentrate on that."

"I know," she said.

"Are we going straight home?" I leaned forward between their seats. "Is that all we're going to do?" All at once I didn't want to go back and watch myself on TV.

When she swiveled toward me, her skin seemed very pale and fine, her lipstick almost faded away. "I want to call Scotland before it gets too late," she said, "before someone calls them first."

"It's up to you," my father said.

"I'd like to go home."

"The phone will be ringing."

"David, I know."

"Fine," I said, and sat back in my seat.

"Helen, for heaven's sake, don't be angry."

"When do you have to start giving your talks on what it's like to be an astronaut trainee?" my father asked, cutting in smoothly.

"In a month or so," she said.

We made piles of newspapers on the floor of my mother's study, as we clipped the articles about her out of the papers and discarded those with the articles already cut out. Her voice rose above the sound of the radio, talking on the telephone in the hall, the cord pulled through the room and under the door. There were newspapers strewn all over the house, in the front hall and the living room as well as the usual pile rising beside the kitchen table. My father had come home the night before with an answering machine under his arm and plugged it in next to the kitchen phone, just down the counter from the microwave. *More new technology,* he'd said.

Sometimes people even came to the door, not just journalists but neighbors, people we didn't know, sometimes with children, people who just wanted to introduce themselves and meet my mother. Every night I sat up in bed in the dark, listening to the hushed voices of my parents talking.

After a while it made me dizzy to read the articles, because there were so many of them and the facts were so often wrong: Sometimes Paul and I were sixteen, or fifteen, sometimes twins and sometimes not, sometimes my mother was described as a doctor, sometimes a physicist. Our lives became infinitely malleable, as elastic as the limbs of a contortionist, stretching and bending in all directions. Paul held up one clipping with a picture of the four of us and the headline ASTRO FAMILY LOOKS TO FUTURE.

I needed time to assimilate things. It was all I could do to cope with the present. I was already tired of explaining to people at school that we wouldn't be moving to some kind of astronaut compound and we had no idea when my mother would be going up in space.

The door opened and my mother set the phone back on the desk, her eyes heavy-lidded, exhaustedly bright. The day after the press conference she had flown to Montreal. Her rolled-up swimsuit and towel lay against the wall in a plastic bag, reeking of chlorine. What did she see when she thought about the future?

Silently, my father appeared in the doorway, his glasses tilted on top of his sandy hair. I hadn't heard him come upstairs. "How's everything?" he asked cordially.

"Fine, my love," my mother said and reached for his hand.

"I'm wrapping up this piece on fault pressure." Although he gave one of his loose and easy smiles, I had the sudden sensation that he was lying. When I'd walked into his study the day before to use his computer, the top page of his yellow legal pad had been covered in drawings—no notes at all, just doodles of forests and volcanoes, strange elaborate landscapes.

I clambered over the fence to the golf course after my boyfriend Trig. In the night sky the stars were blurred by a slight, invisible haze. I'd told Trig how, when Paul and I were younger, my mother had been the one to climb first over the gate, ignoring the PRIVATE, NO TRESPASSING sign, before turning to help the two of us over the fence and into the deserted driving range. It was the only real expanse of darkness that we had, a wide stretch of sky, far better than any view we could get from our garden. In her knapsack, she'd carried her portable telescope wrapped in a towel while we took turns carrying the telescope stand. Once we'd even watched a lunar eclipse.

Crouching in the middle of a sandpit, Trig pulled two small paper bags out of his knapsack—one which I knew contained brown sugar and the other saltpeter; we'd done this before. He dug a small hole and emptied the bags into it, then lit a match, tossed it in and covered the hole again quickly with sand. We both bent over it, hugging our knees.

"This is for you," Trig said, and when he smiled, his full, mobile lips gleamed in the dark. Someone had given him the name Trig early in high school, before I met him, because he was good at math but in an easy way so that he never really had to work at it. We were both good at science; we liked experiments. Trig ran cross-country, and this was perhaps the thing that I loved best about him: his steady, muscular, containable speed.

A trail of smoke filtered out of the sand and crept into the air, as I slid my arm around Trig's back and tucked my hand in the edge of his jeans until I touched skin. It was hilarious to imagine the daytime golfers roving around in their electric-powered carts, swatting at tiny balls, having no idea that at night we tramped across their lawns and dew-lit putting greens and dug holes in their sandpits to make smoke bombs.

"I saw you on TV," Trig whispered in my ear. "What was it like to be on TV?"

"It wasn't like anything," I said. It had made me uncomfortable, actually; it made me feel we looked ridiculous. My hair looked strange.

Smoke rose out of the sandpit until a gray, burnt-smelling cloud filled the air, a cloud that seemed to have no source but to be materializing out of nowhere.

"How can it not be like anything?" Once he'd told me, with a note of amazement in his voice, how he used to watch my mother's old TV show, before he'd ever met me. I'd showed him the dents in the grass where our lunar landing module had once stood, although he said he barely remembered the lunar landings.

The smell of smoke breathed from our clothes. The edges of our mouths were wet and slick. Trig looped his finger through my belt buckle, and we walked back through the wet grass toward one of the hills that led up into people's lilac-scented gardens, into the thicker darkness under the trees. The air under the trees was cool but not too cool, quiet enough for us to keep our voices down even though there was no one to hear us. Trig lay down on the ground and I rolled beside him, burying my face against his neck. Then he pulled me on top of him, my legs spread around his legs. I worked his arms out of his jacket and flattened it underneath him, although he stopped my hand for an instant, pulled out a condom packet, laid it gently on the ground. I pulled his T-shirt over his arms and head, felt the streak of muscles over his stomach suddenly tightening. He smiled at me and slid his fingers inside my pants and then inside me as far as he could reach.

I tried not to think about astronauts, to concentrate on our own immediate aura of risk. I took off my shirt and bra but not my jeans, not all the way, and then he rolled us over and I reached for the buckle of his jeans, pulled them, pulled his underwear down over the smooth bones of his hips. The heat of his skin against mine was a relief.

I kept trying to tell if Trig was looking at me differently, if he really saw me or some picture of me on TV or in the paper, if he saw my mother in her green suit talking intensely about the exploration of space being in our genes. I could hear cars on the 401 traveling with a low roar across the city. Thin spring leaves and distant stars flickered above us in the dark. When I closed my eyes, Trig's body was reduced to fragments, only the parts I could feel, his vertebrae, small nipples, skin like pieces of broken glass, his hands on my skin. I held on to his shoulders edgily and pushed against him until he came, everything tense, and I could still feel pain, the same pain I always felt deep inside me. I pushed to keep myself from floating in terror off the ground.

After a moment he ran his tongue over my collarbone. "Helen, what is it?"

I did not know how to explain what was wrong. The ground was cold underneath us. Trig peeled off the condom, wrapped it in a pile of Kleenex, put the whole pile back in his knapsack, leaning across me, dirt on the pale undersides of his arms. My mother, in a white spacesuit, bent slowly over me. I closed my eyes until they bulged. *I'm pinned in a spaceship, hurled forward like a fireball.*

When I opened my eyes, Trig was standing in front of me, yanking his jeans all the way off. "What are you doing?"

"Helen," he whispered. "I'm putting on my running shorts. I'm going to run home and then I'm not going to take a shower, because I love you, because I want to lie in bed covered in sweat with your smell all over me."

When I opened the door to the house, Paul raced into the front hall. "They've been wondering where you were." His voice rose distraughtly. "Helen, there's been an earthquake." There was something in his bewildered, frantic tone that made me think he meant disaster, any disaster, the only one I could think of: Our mother was not an astronaut. There'd been some mistake. The new world we'd constructed had collapsed. We'd have to go back to the beginning and start again.

"Where?" I said. "Here? What kind?"

"What kind? Helen, a big one—*the* Big One. In L.A. there's just been a huge earthquake, and they think it's the one everyone's been waiting for."

The TV was talking urgently in the living room. "It's that terrible?"

"Horrible." Trig knew nothing, racing furiously home through the dark. A small pile of newspapers with articles about my mother in them lay at the foot of the stairs: out of date. We were old news already; gone. I told Paul I had to go to the bathroom.

When I entered the living room, my mother and father were sitting side by side on the sofa, my father leaning forward with his elbows on his knees, rubbing one hand over his mouth in distraction, my mother in jeans and a sweatshirt, legs curled up, lips parted.

"Where were you?" she asked.

"You saw me go out," I said. "I was out with Trig." Trig's pale body under trees in the darkness.

"Oh no," she said softly, staring at the TV screen.

132

"Eight point one," my father said. "Jesus, eight point one, and they don't even know that for sure because the L.A. seismic equipment was knocked out." There was an almost wondering note to his voice.

A view from above, from what seemed to be a helicopter: It was dusk in Los Angeles, and up through the blue light rose billows of smoke and flickering orange that had to be flames, street after street, some houses still standing, some with visible roofs and windows but structurally collapsed, stretches where you could see streetlights and darker stretches without, and then the hills.

A massive temblor, said the newscaster's voice. A word that always sounded to me like *tremblor,* shuddering down through hills and mountains, capable of pushing millions of people into the ocean. The words REAL FOOTAGE appeared in white in the corner of the screen. The helicopter flew in a little lower, faster, trying to make the most of the light while it lasted, over a street with cracks erupting in it, leading into a freeway littered with abandoned cars, people who stared upward violently, shaking their fists, the road rising like lips around a deep gash. Then the freeway crumpled and twisted, leaving a hole in the air, because the bridge underneath had collapsed. The earth had done all that, I thought. How little time it took: I'd been lying on the ground with Trig. You could count in seconds while the walls fell down.

"Where was the epicenter?" I sat down on the floor next to Paul, pulling my knees against my chest.

"Near Palmerston," my father said, clearing his throat and recovering his scientist's voice. "To the northeast. The helicopter's flying along the fault line. My God, how can these things happen? Look, there, that's right near where I used to live." He leaned forward again, but all I could see was the edge of another fissured highway, more disappearing houses. When

133

my father was ten, his family had gone out there from England for three years, because my grandfather, a screenwriter, had been asked to work on the screenplay for a TV series that never came to exist. After that they'd packed up and gone back to London. No one ever guessed that my father had grown up in England, because he did not have an English accent. By the time he met my mother in Toronto, both his parents had died of emphysema. He almost never talked about them.

"Have you ever been in an earthquake?" I asked quietly.

"Yes," he said, "but not like this."

"What an awful time for it to happen," my mother said, rubbing the side of her hand against my father's leg. "Just before dark. The looting must be terrible. Think of being there in the dark unable to see anything. That has to be the worst kind of darkness, being in a city when the power goes out."

"Remember the thunderstorm when all the lights went out," Paul said, "even all the streetlights and you couldn't see anything." Darkness when you didn't expect it, which was not like the darkness out on the golf course, or darkness in the woods around Minnow Lake, or even the darkness of deep space, which my mother had told us wasn't really darkness at all, but filled with light traveling from stars so distant that the rays simply hadn't reached us yet.

There is no word yet as to the full extent of the damage, but numerous movie and TV lots have been destroyed. Universal Studios is in ruins. The Hollywood movie industry will take decades to recover. The new fall TV season may have to be canceled. There is no word as yet from Silicon Valley. The governor of California has declared a state of emergency. In the twilight, behind the man's shiny silhouette, stood the remains of the fake Matterhorn at Disneyland, flattened and crumbling like an atoll or a volcano, and then a billboard for Coppertone appeared, folded like an accordion.

The phone wasn't ringing. For the first time in three days

our phone had stopped ringing. We were sitting quietly in our living room, watching TV, like any ordinary family, bound together by long-distance disaster, America invading our lives again. Paul stood up, reached over and turned off the lamp in the corner so that we were enclosed in semidarkness.

"At least it was after rush hour," my father said. "At least people weren't in their offices."

"If there's no electricity, how can the TV crews be filming anything?" I asked.

"There must be some electricity," Paul said. "Maybe they have their own emergency supply."

I have a shoe store in the mall, a man said, gesturing behind him to where there was no mall. His heavy face was glazed by floodlights. Tears were streaming down his cheeks. *I was closing up and then I was going across the street to get some takeout, but I fell down into the curb because the street was shaking so hard. It went on and on, and I knew it was the Big One. I knew.*

Everyone has been expecting the Big One for years, a woman reporter said resolutely, while behind her a roar of sirens and muffled voices rose out of the darkness. *While seismologists had said that some quake activity was likely, no one seemed to know that this was going to be it. It was dinnertime. Restaurants were full of people. I'm standing on Wilshire Boulevard.* Then her face just went blank and she stopped, the picture dissolving.

My father got up and walked out of the room.

"But they knew," I said. "They knew one day it was going to happen."

"There are a lot of things that people know are pretty likely and that doesn't stop them, they just keep on doing whatever they're doing," he said loudly from the doorway.

My mother turned and stared at him. L.A. in darkness was dotted with wavering flames. He came over and crouched down beside me, pulled me against his shirt, toward his scent that still made me think of autumn leaves and coffee, kissed my cheek. "Helen, I'm sorry." He touched the tufts of my blond hair wonderingly, and I shrugged, because it wasn't like him to be so edgy or volatile, but maybe it was just one thing after the other the last few days.

"I'm going to bed," Paul said. He stood up and kissed them both, but I stayed where I was, watching my father sit down again so that my parents were on the couch side by side the way they had been when I came in. My mother pressed her head against a pillow, her eyes shadowed and tired, frowning at the TV like a sober, willful child.

"Mum, you should go to bed," I said.

"I will." But she said it distractedly, barely listening, as the buildings on the screen began crumbling again.

I knew by heart the contours of my room in the darkness, the way the leaves on the tree outside moved like mouths on the ceiling. The numbers on my traveler's alarm clock read three o'clock. My hands were growing shaky from lack of sleep. For a while I had listened to the low buzz of Paul's radio through the wall, wondered if he was listening to music or the news turned up loud, until at last he switched it off. I thought about knocking on his door and asking him if I could come in, waking him up so that at least someone else in the house would be awake with me, the way we used to wake each other in thunderstorms and lie in one bed or the other, curled up side by side, warm, not sleeping, listening to the thunder roll into the distance.

I told myself there was no reason to be frightened. I was here in our own house, safe. My mother was simply going to begin traveling, between her lab in Toronto and the space agency in Montreal, and eventually to training sites in the States. There was no need to think beyond that.

At dawn the air was more still than before. I pulled on some clothes and crept downstairs, half expecting to see the TV quivering silently, but the screen was blank, just the house ticking, full of rooms, hushed, no rattling. I went outside and unlocked my bicycle and biked up Glenforest Street, past the solid, two-story houses, under the gently flowering trees that shed their tiny green flowers all over the flat, continuous sidewalks. Venus hung in the sky between the roofs. The paper girl reached the end of the block, then turned the corner. And even though everything seemed stable and in place, the world still felt thin and porous, as if there were another layer moving through this one, reducing everything to ever-increasing speed. Time itself seemed suddenly compressed and uncontrollable. Faster, faster. Didn't everyone feel it? Was I the only one whose stomach was being turned inside out? I biked south down Mount Pleasant, west toward our school, past a square in the sidewalk whose location I remembered exactly because of the grafitti on it, RON + JESSICA = MC^2. Ron and Jessica soared together into the air, exploding convulsively into flame, which seemed horrible and absolutely perfect.

When lights came on in the first floors of houses and people began heading to the subway, I parked my bike at the side of Trig's house and knocked on the back door. His mother answered it. I asked if Trig was there, but of course he would be. I had no school books. I was in track pants, an old T-shirt, shaking slightly, covered in sweat.

I made my way into the kitchen and sat down in a chair, wished that Trig's mother would ask me in an ordinary voice if I wanted something to eat: *Would you like some toast, Helen, some scrambled eggs?* She leaned against the counter, her business jacket slung over her shoulders, alert but bemused, as if still in the middle of her first cup of coffee. Antique china plates hung on the wall behind her. "What a crazy week," she said. "First your mother, then this in L.A."

"It's what she's always wanted."

"Will you congratulate her—" Before she could stop me, I dashed through the hall, up the stairs, toward Trig's room at the back of the second floor, beyond the squeak of his father's shoes in the master bedroom. In the tiny bathroom just off his room, Trig was brushing his teeth. He spat toothpaste in surprise into the sink.

"I can't sleep," I said softly.

"Not at all?"

"Not for days."

"You heard about the earthquake?"

"It's everything," I said. "I don't know—the speed." He wavered a little, receding into the distance. Puzzled, newly reconstituted, he looked the way people do first thing in the morning, a way I almost never saw him. He wore an old gray sweatshirt with a small hole in the collar. His mother called his real name, *Rick, Rick,* from the bottom of the stairs.

"I'll be right back," he said.

I lay down on Trig's bed. All I wanted was to close my eyes and fall asleep. I pulled Trig's pillow against my face, breathing the slightly oily smell of his hair, my heart pounding wildly like a child's heart woken suddenly, craving everything around me: Trig's toothbrush, his calm toast, the still gray walls of his room, the Indian cotton bedspread. I longed for everything to stay just as it was, for someone to look after me. Trig came back and lay down gently beside me.

"My mother knows people who live in L.A.," he whispered. He slid one cool hand under my shirt and then his head, running his tongue over one breast and then the other, sucking them gently. I tried to relax. The front door slammed, and two pairs of footsteps hurried down the front path to the sidewalk.

138

I unzipped his cotton slacks and licked the palm of my hand until the saliva glistened and then ran my hand over his penis until it was straight and hard, licked both hands again and kept on until I made him come with a low groan. Then I let go. "Do you want to stay here?" he whispered. "Do you want to sleep? Helen, just tell me what you want, I want to do things for you. Do you want me to make you a sandwich?"

The bed was soaking wet, the sheets, the mattress. I wanted both our bodies to grow thick with liquid inside and out, get away from the bones, the questions, all that anatomy. Everything ached. The sky outside Trig's window turned white, clouds scudding past. I thought if I lay still for a while maybe I would fall asleep, but when nothing happened, I got up and took a shower and wiped myself off with Trig's towel, got dressed. It was early afternoon. I went downstairs, made us each a cup of coffee, and brought the cups upstairs to the bedroom where Trig still lay on his back, eyes open. Too late for either of us to go to school. Trig's smell and my smell were still mixed together all over my hands.

"You don't have to go," he said with a slow, uneven smile.

"Maybe I'll just go home," I said.

I didn't expect anyone to be there, but when I came in the front door, I heard loud voices upstairs, my parents' voices. In the living room the television was on, but the sound was turned down. On the steps inside the front door, beside my mother's briefcase and her handbag, lay the day's newspapers with their three-inch headlines: L.A. DESTRUCTION, EARTHQUAKE TERROR. I wondered if in the morning they simply thought that I had gone in early to school. "How long?" I heard my mother say.

"I don't know how long," my father said. They must have been in their bedroom with the door open, because their voices carried easily, so I sat down by the bottom step with my back against the wall. "I know they need people to help. They're still digging people out of the ground. Whole neighborhoods have been destroyed. And, sure, it helps that I know something about plate tectonics and seismology, because I can gather data, take part in the research end, but maybe knowing about earthquakes seems like all the more reason why I should simply go out and help."

"Are you planning to write about it?"

"No," he said loudly. "I am not doing this so I can write about it. That's not the point at all. We're talking about a terrible disaster, a situation where a tremendous amount of work needs to be done, and I feel some kind of responsibility to do it. I need to. I don't know how else to put it. I've never stopped you doing what you wanted to do."

"But now," she said, "right now?"

"Look," he said, "if you go to give a talk and someone asks you where your husband is, if the people in Montreal ask you where I am, you can tell them I have gone out to join an earthquake relief team in Los Angeles and how can anyone, anyone, possibly object to that? And if anyone, any reporter, wants to check up on me, fine, I'll be doing exactly what I've said I'll be doing."

"Can you just give me some idea?" she said. "This is so sudden. What about Helen and Paul? Are you talking about a week, three weeks?"

"I'm not sure. At least a few weeks."

"You know I have to start traveling back and forth a lot," she said. "You know I'm practically going to be living in Montreal part-time. We've been talking about all this."

"I know that," he said, quietly but vehemently. "I have to do this, Barbara. If you love me, please accept that."

"So how long?"

"Barbara, we're dealing with the massive destruction of a city, and the massive rehabilitation of a city, as well as gathering scientific data to find out exactly what happened and also research data about the effects on people who have to live through something like this. So I'm really not sure how long."

"What about your job at the paper?"

"They've given me a leave of absence to do this," he said. "All right, it's true, I may write once in a while but not regularly."

"David, what are you trying to tell me?"

"I'm going to L.A. Nothing more, nothing less. I've weighed the risk, and it still comes down to the fact that I need to do this. It's one of those situations where you have to make up your mind in a hurry, where, in a sense, your humanity is being tested. If Paul and Helen were younger maybe it would be different, but, as it is, I can't stay here and not do anything."

There was silence. "This isn't going to work," she said at last, her voice gone low and raw. "How can we do this? How can you just spring this on me like this? What am I supposed to think when you won't even tell me if you mean a few weeks or a few months? We've always talked about things being dynamic, but we can't—David, please, I need you to be here. Why does being here have to mean not doing anything? I want you to be part of this, even in the simplest way, I want to tell you things, not close you out or be closed out. Are you listening to me? What *about* Helen and Paul?"

"I've talked to Tom."

"Tom?" she said. "Tom?"

"Tom, your lab associate. He would be willing to live here with Helen and Paul if that's all right with you. I'm not trying to go behind your back, Barbara, but I called him to see if he could suggest any graduate students who might want to, so that I would have some ideas to present to you, and he said he would be happy to. He doesn't really care for where he's living. He said he'd been thinking about moving."

"When did you talk to Tom?"

"I called him at home this morning before he went in. I told him I wanted to have a chance to talk to you. Barbara, I'm trying to behave as responsibly as I can. And all I can hope is that our children are smart enough and independent enough and enough like us in the end to have some sense why we choose to do these things."

How dare he, I thought. All I had to do was walk upstairs, break in on them, and say, *Why are you treating us as if all you want to do is get away from us? What do you think we are, aliens?*

My mother walked out of the bedroom, and at first I thought in horror that she was going to come downstairs, but instead she headed down the hall to her study and closed the door. I didn't care if they heard me make my way through the house to the kitchen. I sat down at the table and tried to peel an orange without crying, tried to concentrate on Tom, who had started working in her lab as a grad student, who used to babysit for us, who had once given me a peach pit carved in the shape of a monkey. I liked Tom a lot, his attentiveness, how generous he had always been to us; I tried to concentrate on all the independence we would have living with Tom, and how enviable that would seem to all our friends. *How could they?* The earthquake was supposed to stay screen-sized, chopped up, far away, not reach out a temblor hand and grab me.

But my mother was only going into astronaut training, and my father hadn't said he was leaving forever, which was a possibility that my friends and I learned to live with when it came to our parents: Marriages could always split up.

The front door slammed. Footsteps came toward me through the house.

"You're here," my mother said from the doorway. She did not ask me what I was doing there. "Did you hear all that?"

"Yes," I said.

"He's going to catch a plane." She put her hands on my shoulders and squeezed so hard it frightened me, as if she were trying not only to hold onto me but to herself, as if she had forgotten her own strength. Then she let go. "I'm sorry," she whispered. "Helen, I'm sorry. I'm sorry you had to hear it like that."

I pushed the chair back and stood up and put my arms around her. We were nearly the same height. I could feel the muscles in her back, and for a moment, hugging her, I felt stronger than her. "We didn't know you were here," she said. In my mind's eye, I followed my father up the street: He was walking resolutely, a small flight bag in one hand. The scent of orange filled the room.

"Is it because he's angry?" I asked.

"I don't know if that's being fair to him." As she talked her fingers wandered slowly across my back. "I don't think of him as someone motivated primarily by anger, but I don't know. This is so unexpected. There's no reason for him to be angry. Helen, he loves you both so much. He said he would call when he got there. He said he would talk to the two of you then."

She dropped her hands and sat down, tilting her chair back against the wall, the way she always told us not to because we would break the chairs, her head turned upward as if otherwise, looking anywhere other than above her, she would fall. Her eyes were thick with tears and the corners of her mouth trembled, but she did not cry. When the phone rang, she jumped but made no move to answer it, let the answering machine pick up. For one wild moment I thought it might be my father calling from the corner, saying sorry, saying he had just wanted to make a point, but it wasn't, it was someone calling for her. With his flight bag in his hand he kept walking toward Yonge Street, the subway, a taxi, the airport bus. My heart kept splitting. Part of me hurried desperately up the street behind him. I wondered what it would feel like to be hurtling on a roller coaster, to be standing on the staircase in Sleeping Beauty's palace at Disneyland as the earth began to heave beneath me.

"We almost went to L.A. once," my mother said, "after we were married. There was some conference but in the end we didn't go, and I've been there since but we've never been there at the same time. It's horrible. It's an earthquake, and it could have been anywhere. It's important work—I know that. You know how some people crave a cigarette in moments like this? Well, all I wish is that a pool would open up in front of me and I could dive in and swim, because it's the only thing that calms me, that ever lets me clear my head." The front legs of her chair came crashing to the ground. "Helen, I'm sorry."

"Don't keep saying that."

"It's just I'm frightened," she said in a low voice. "I'm frightened that you'll blame me." She stood up abruptly and left the room.

Paul and I were eating dinner when my mother entered the kitchen. We had fixed tomato soup and cheese sandwiches for ourselves, rudimentary comfort food, both of us standing by the stove waiting for the soup to warm, watching the cheese grill under the broiler. I kept wondering where my father was and if he was thinking about us, and why he hadn't at least given us some kind of warning. My mother had talked to Paul when he came home from school so that he didn't have a chance to ask me where I'd been all day. I didn't really want to talk to Trig.

On the surface Paul didn't look upset, but then he always took things in slowly, as if trying to solve a problem, trying to be as evenhanded as possible. Why shouldn't we take Dad at his word? So he wanted to do some emergency earthquake relief work. He would go away for a few weeks, a month maybe. Why couldn't it be as straightforward as that?

He didn't finish his sandwich but began folding the corner of a newspaper into accordion strips as he talked. Ripping off a square piece, he began to fashion it into an origami crane. He was bending intently over the folded paper when my mother came in and sat down at the end of the table, her hair newly combed and glossy, her arms slipping out of the sleeves of her cotton Chinese dressing gown. She must have taken a shower. Her eyes were still red. Paul started up, fingers stopped in mid-fold, in surprise.

"There's no way I can put this so it seems like a fair question." She looked from Paul to me. "But if either of you feels really strongly that I shouldn't be entering the astronaut program, I want you to tell me right now before anything goes any further. I need to know. I don't know exactly what David is planning to do. I can't ask him not to do this work. How could I? But I've committed myself to something that's going to be tremendously time-consuming and that will take me away from here a lot and maybe at some point involve risks to my life. Now Tom has offered to live here, but if this situation, if what I'm doing, is intolerable to you, then tell me now, because it will be so much easier to know now than it ever will be later."

Everything in my head was turning into a question, as if my brain itself had become a jumble of reporters. Questions grew and pushed against the inside of my skull: *What does it feel like to have the thing you have always dreamed of come true? What if one of us or both of us said that we didn't want you to be an astronaut, would you tell the selection committee that you had changed your mind, or that*

145

we had changed your mind? Would that make the news? Would people admire you or think you were crazy to give up the opportunity you had been working toward your whole life? What would people think of us? Which of us would be accused of being completely selfish? If we said we didn't want you to do it, would you go back to the lab or do something completely different? Would you never in the slightest way hold this decision against us? Would Dad feel guilty? Would he come back? Wasn't he needed in L.A.? Wouldn't we feel guilty if he came back? If we asked you to say no, could we live for the rest of our lives with that?

Her eyes looked across at us, very clear and gray.

"I think you should do it," Paul said slowly, holding the frail paper crane in his fingers, and then he dropped his shoulders, as if saying this were a kind of release.

"Do it," I said, because when I looked at her across the table, I did not see what else I could say, how there could be any solution more elegant than this one.

"You're sure," she said.

"Yes," I said. And so we implicated ourselves. We chose this.

9

Q: Why do Canadians talk on the phone so much?
A: Because there's so much space between them.

Helen was holding on to a ladder that climbed up the side of an enormous Kentucky Fried Chicken bucket, a bucket that she had seen who knew how many times from the expressway below, without ever imagining herself clinging to the side of it, glancing over her shoulder into the darkness, toward the dark lake. Her heart beat furiously. And yet there was a kind of exultation in being up so high, nothing between her and the air. She had offered to climb the bucket in Elena's place. It rose on the metal stilts of an old water tower, inside the fenced compound of a darkened warehouse, surrounded by other warehouses, dead-end streets. It looked just like an ordinary chicken bucket, only blown up, mutant, out of scale. She was waiting for Foster, climbing ahead of her, to stop and wedge himself against the top of the ladder so that she could open the knapsack slung over his shoulders and pull out a square of folded, thick black plastic, a roll of weatherproof duct tape. And all the while she had to be careful not to look straight down at the large, vertiginous outline of the colonel's face, the ground, her invisible parked car on the far side of the fence, invisible Elena pacing beside it.

A breeze blew up at them, north off the water. They barely spoke. A forest of billboards stretched along the expressway, down the lakeshore, thicker than trees. The lifesize fiberglass front of a car stuck out of one billboard; a giant bankcard flashed, dissolved, and flashed again. Pixelboard time was 3:08. Foster took one corner of the plastic sheet and Helen grabbed another, shaking the taped-together garbage bags out into the air until they fell, huge, down over the side of the bucket. Then he set off, sliding carefully along the bucket's edge. She swore under her breath just watching him, at the slightest sign of imbalance, at his apparent lack of fear. It wasn't a sheer drop on the inside of the bucket, only a few feet down, but what if he fell, what if either of them fell and went floating down over Elena like angels?

Beyond the billboards, the old glass domes of the halls on the Canadian National Exhibition grounds shone like blue-green cupolas, just across the highway. Invisible satellites scored the brown sky above them, manned, unmanned, weather satellites, communications satellites, spy satellites. The line between the visible and invisible seemed particularly thin. *Hi, I'm Barbara Urie,* a voice said, *and this is Frontiers, the science show from space.* Another mother, a doctor for the World Health Organization, crouched behind a small, dusty office in southern Australia and rubbed a piece of grass pensively between her fingers, while inside a house in Yellowknife, a man paced back and forth, listening to voices on the radio, the rush of water and ice. *The Soviet Union was the first nation in space with Sputnik, and then the United States, but it's a lesser-known fact that with the launch of Alouette in 1962, a satellite designed to study the ionosphere, Canada became the world's third nation in space.*

Cars sped along the expressway, but how many people at this time of night were likely to look up and see what they were doing, even though, high on the floodlit chicken bucket, they

148

were certainly visible? And how many people, glimpsing something as they shot past, the road a clear streak ahead of them, were likely to do anything about it? Foster had stopped, was taping down the far end of the garbage bag sheet, ripping the tape off sharply with his teeth. She still had to wait for him to make his slow, precise way back, watching his hands in cotton work gloves grip the edge, the roll of duct tape slipped over one wrist, feet in their perpetual hightop sneakers clamped against the side of the bucket.

They had spent the night before at Elena's cutting open the bags and taping them together to form what they had taken to calling the garbage bag shroud. Other people were there: a lean, practical woman named Julie who worked for the Humane Society, who was part of a larger environmental action group and had organized a lot of the billboard attacks (she called them *billboard projects*). She and Elena seemed to be good friends. A tall, dark-skinned young man named Raj leaned against the wall, eyeing Elena, speaking very quietly every now and again. A boy who had dyed his hair green said that being green was like being part of a new race; at least these days everything was so mixed up that you might as well think of yourself as green, or anyway that was how he thought about it. He had bright, wicked eyes and played in a band called The Mutants and was the only one who looked at Helen curiously. With white paint they had written across the garbage bags in letters huge enough to be read from a car below: FINGER LICKIN' DEAD.

Helen moved a few rungs down the ladder so that Foster could lower himself carefully onto it; he leaned suddenly toward her, grinning, breathless, the tendons in his bare arms visible. "If people think it's funny, that's OK, as long as they notice it." His voice caught in the air so that Helen could barely hear him. He seemed garrulously happy. She could smell

149

the peppery scent of his sweat. The biggest Kentucky Fried Chicken bucket in North America, he'd told her, and she was prepared to believe him, guessed there'd be someone in the city that was home to the world's largest freestanding structure crazy enough to build the continent's largest chicken bucket.

Lights bounced off the bodies of the tiny, fleeting cars. A brown glare on the horizon across the lake might be Rochester.

"Helen, go," Foster shouted, and she started down, reaching one foot toward the next invisible rung and then the other, moving across the main white body of the bucket, past the colonel's square black glasses, neat goatee, trying desperately not to look at the ground.

"I'm eating a sandwich," Helen said. "I'm sorry, I was starving. I couldn't wait. That's why my voice sounds funny."

"Is that your dinner?" Barbara asked.

"It's my dinner. You don't need to say anything."

"I didn't think I had said anything."

She was sitting at the kitchen table in a way she presumed her mother, like most parents, would prefer not to see: boots up on the table, a plate balanced against her legs, the phone held to her shoulder. Her bike helmet lay on the other chair like an extra head. She had not turned on the TV to the space station feed. Then again, she didn't see why she had to turn it on every time she talked to her mother. Seeing her mother's face did not necessarily make her feel closer to her. Why pretend she wasn't in a room by herself hearing a voice from faraway? "Are you adjusting now all the short-term astronauts are gone again?" She took another bite.

"Actually, it feels as if things are getting back to normal," Barbara said. "We get used to having a certain amount of room to move around in and we get ridiculously possessive about it."

"You don't get lonely?"

"Well, Peter's here. And David calls pretty regularly."

"He does?"

"Yes, he does."

"How regularly?" She had assumed their contact was still fairly sporadic, related to exterior events like the launch, another aftershock, Barbara's new TV show. More informative than chatty. She hadn't even heard from David herself in close to two weeks.

"Well, it depends what he's up to," Barbara said, "but usually about once a week."

That often. Perhaps more often than David talked to her or Paul, which made Helen feel odder than she expected. "Sometimes people make comments, you know," she said softly. "I mean, I've seen a couple of comments in the paper, kind of jokes, about you and Peter." There had been an editorial cartoon she'd stumbled across in a magazine not that long ago, which had left her both numb and irritated, because even though she wondered about them (wouldn't anyone wonder?), she tried not to be too suspicious.

"They were doing that before," Barbara said, "don't you remember? After we were chosen. Before we left. We were told to expect it. Put a man and a woman anywhere together and everyone thinks something's going to happen, but especially here. You learn to live with it. I know some people think we have a scientific obligation to have sex in space, but, Helen, we were chosen because we work well together, and the fact is we work very well together." She sounded defiantly matter-of-fact.

"Do you still look down as much?"

"Of course I look down."

"Does everything look pretty much the same?"

"Things change. You notice new details constantly. We can

see smoke from that oil fire in the Middle East, we've been monitoring atmospheric conditions this week—a little grim at times, I'm afraid to say."

"I didn't know you were doing that."

"Helen? Listen, I called because I wanted to ask you a favor."

"What?" She put down the last bit of sandwich cautiously.

"The people running the event down at the Tower, the celebration on the day we've been up for six months, would like one of you to be there. I said I thought you could."

"Just be there, or actually do something?"

"I think they want you to talk to me. There'll be some video screen set-up. There'll be other people, too, so I don't even think they'll need you for that long."

Helen tipped her chair back slowly, resting it against the wall. Tilting her head back, she could balance there, as if in a seat at the planetarium. Need, she thought, although it didn't really feel like need but the same assurance on her mother's part as always that what she wanted would somehow be communicable.

"Helen?" Barbara said. "Did you hear me?" She sounded as if she were frowning. "What is it? Surely it's not too much to ask? All I'd like you to do is talk to me."

Elena took one hand from the wheel and handed Helen the screwdriver, which she pried around the lid of the paint can wedged between her feet, working in the traveling glare of streetlights, until the lid came loose. She handed the screwdriver to Foster in the backseat. They all wore knitted hats and gloves, which looked ridiculous, and she wanted to laugh out loud just for the release, even though her stomach kept turning over and over. She had to trust the two of them.

"If this was all we were doing," Elena said—she sounded as if she were arguing with herself—"then it would be a stunt. But it's not all we're doing. And you can do all you like on your own, but you still have to try to change the way people see things, and the only way seems to be to do things that will get attention. Which may be sick but it's true." She smiled and stopped when Foster touched his gloved fingers to the back of her neck.

As they crossed the west-end railway tracks, the inexplicable scent of lilacs drifted in, mixed intoxicatingly with the heady waft of paint. Newspapers lay in layers over the floor of the car, the only stipulation Helen had made: They could use the car as long as they didn't get any paint on it. And if they ever got caught in Barbara Urie's car—if it happened, she'd deal with it. They had offered to let her drive, but she said it made more sense for one of them to drive, since they knew the way.

The station wagon was slowing. Elena switched the headlights off, strained forward but composed, the green glow of the dashboard disappearing. A small click as Foster's door unlatched. Helen grabbed the handle of the paint can, opened her door, and held it closed until Elena pulled up alongside a stretch of low, dark buildings and the lane between them. Then Helen pitched herself out the door, freefall, was running up the drive with the can of paint, lifting the can as high as she could, hurling paint forward in a red arc, over the driveway. The paint from Foster's can went higher, over the slaughterhouse walls, windows, over a sign. A light blinked on and off, then on.

"OK." Elena accelerated, both of them in, as Helen grabbed her door, pulled it shut with a bang, almost a cry. She peeled off her gloves, fast, wrapped them in a piece of newspaper, tore off another piece and wiped ferociously at the paint she had smeared on the door handle with her gloves.

"As long as some of it dries," Foster said.

"If the trucks go over it while it's sticky," Elena said, "it'll still get on the wheels, leave traces."

"As long as they don't get a chance to hose it away."

They drove down one wide, barren street and turned down another before Elena switched on the headlights again. "If everything else goes well," she said, and her voice had relaxed a little, "then we're doing OK." Out there, somewhere, sliding down other streets, were other cars with empty paint cans dripping in them, dark figures moving swiftly outside supermarket windows, flattening paper posters against them with long-handled sponges dipped in buckets of glue.

"Time to stop for coffee," Foster said cheerfully.

"Foster," Elena said, "don't be crazy."

They told bad jokes and jibed each other with the endurance of people who had spent a lot of time together, and Helen knew now that they had once been involved for a period of months, although it had been years before, when they were both still at Western. Elena had been the one to get out of it, *because we fought,* she'd said, *because we argued all the time.* Foster's version was different: *It ended,* he'd told Helen, *when Elena fell in love with a woman named Simone.*

"So what's it going to be?" he called out, leaning forward between them. "The front page, the local news, the *Globe,* the *Star,* CITY-TV? Helen, what do you think?"

"You're sure there'll be something," she said.

"There should be," he said emphatically. "There'd better be."

"The *Star,*" Elena said.

It wasn't the same to be making the news in this anonymous way, when it was just the act, the signs you left behind that counted. It wasn't like being part of the spectacle surrounding her mother.

They were canny, even cynical, and yet their eagerness struck Helen as terribly naive; she squirmed to hear them sound so hopeful. Couldn't they see that trying to get into the news was like striking a bargain, and it wasn't necessarily going to be on your terms?

"Are you all right?" Elena asked solicitously, glancing across at her. "Not everyone feels comfortable doing this kind of thing, and we don't want to push you into something you don't feel comfortable doing."

"No, I'm fine," Helen said, "I really am." Sometimes, one on one, Elena seemed difficult and private; around Foster, she usually eased up. She talked about her grandmother, about what she called the Czech Ladies Radio Brigade that met and listened to the shortwave news in her grandmother's kitchen. Without warning, she would reveal what seemed like quite personal, even painful things. When she was six, her mother, who hated living in Toronto, had tried to move back to India with her: They had stayed in Bombay for just two weeks. In the middle of a terrible fight she had refused to let her father in the door of her grandmother's house, where she had been living since she was sixteen.

They passed a place called Cosmo's Diner, or was it Cosmos Diner? The stars on its plastic sign were extinguished for the night, just little black shadows. Neither of the others seemed to notice. One hundred and sixty-five days in space. *Don't think.* There were new layers that Helen could press down over the others, over the launch and the layers before that: nights, and they were almost always nights, new coffee cups, maps that Elena had drawn, Foster's loose change. They drove down streets that she could swear she'd never driven down before, that stretched ahead of them like long, straight limbs, like something asleep, tenderly and violently exposed, like the intricate field of lies that she was drawing for herself. She lux-

155

uriated in the sense of a new skin forming around her, a new world taking on its own independent life, as if even the city around her, even streets and places she'd known since childhood, were growing a new skin. There were plenty of ways to travel right here. She would lie and go on lying, making up stories for them about her invented family and herself: As a child, she had moved from city to city, she had never lived in a house with a swimming pool.

She watched both Foster and Elena with a fierce, precise kind of passion, a mixture of love and hunger, watched each tiny move they made, Elena's eyes flicking up to the rearview mirror, Foster's fingers beating out rhythms on the edge of the seat, as if this were a way to claim them, come closer and closer. She'd forget, for full minutes at a time, about anything else.

Foster came in the front door of The Million carrying a newspaper, two newspapers, tucked under his arm. He stood by a table in her section, right at the back, and raised his eyebrows, and when Helen nodded, he sat down. He opened one of the papers, the *Sun*, the tabloid paper, with a photo of a young woman in a green bikini on the cover, not what she thought of as his usual reading material, and apparently began to read. She could see his red sneakers under the table, one leg crossed over the other.

"Here," he said, when she stopped beside him and folded the paper open for her. He seemed quietly jubilant. MEAT VIGILANTES, she read. Under the headline was an inky photo of a supermarket with its windows plastered in posters, and a report about the slaughterhouse attacks. "It's something," he said. "Something's better than nothing. OK, wait." He began leafing through the *Star* as well.

"I'll be back," Helen said. It was late in the evening; the last rush of people who had come in after the late show at the cinema down the street had begun to leave. She poured two glasses of iced tea, set them on the table, and sat down opposite Foster, keeping her eyes on the couples still huddled in the bruised red banquettes. He pushed the *Star* toward her, pointed a finger at the words, ACTIVIST ATTACKS. "Well?" He was still smiling.

"OK," she said, "so what now? So people see it, what then?"

"Well, it's not like we're out there bombing slaughterhouses," he said levelly. "But if people find these things harder to ignore, then of course it helps."

She took a sip of iced tea, crunched an ice cube between her teeth, thinking about how the names of the newspapers, *Sun, Star, Globe,* assumed galactic prominence, as if the news they spread were winging through the universe.

The fact that Foster didn't seem to mind coming into the restaurant and talking about what he was up to meant he must consider the place basically safe, which made her feel safer, too. He was less likely to discover anything about her that she didn't want him to. Anyway, as long as they kept their voices down, under the music, no one could really hear what they were saying.

He leaned forward, hunched over, twisting the napkin beside him into a thin column with his fingers. "Elena was in the paper last week as well. I don't know if you saw. There was an article about the alternative lab-testing program she's working on, and it's great, because she's kind of becoming the spokesperson for it, but it's a little difficult, because she can't let anyone there know she does underground work as well. If she gets too visible doing one thing or the other, it could be tricky, but she says she wants to keep on doing both."

"I don't know how you feel about this," Helen said slowly, "but I was thinking that it would be a good idea to have a name."

"A name?"

"So even if people don't know who you are, they have some idea that it's one group doing all these things, like the chicken bucket and the supermarkets. Something you use as a tag line on signs or posters."

"Well, we already work with groups," he said, "organizations, the Green Brigade, the New Ark people, you know that, but we like to keep our own small core. Sometimes it's safer."

"Why not come up with your own name?"

"Like what?" he asked. She took out a pen, wrote UNITED SPECIES on a napkin, and passed it to him as she got up. She'd been having trouble sleeping the past few nights. The night before she had given up and lain in the dark trying to think up names instead.

When she sat down again, wiping her hands on the cloth looped through her short, black apron, Foster seemed to be lost in the paper, elbows on the table, head pressed between his hands. "So?" she asked. He had folded the napkin into a neat, small square.

"It might work." He raised his head. "It's catchy. Like a real slogan."

"Doesn't it say exactly what you want it to?"

"Yes. Absolutely."

"Can you think of anything better?"

"Probably not." He grinned. "Talk to Elena, or do you want me to?" He shook the ice cubes in his glass and leaned toward her, close enough that Helen could feel his breath. "Have you heard about the lights going out?"

"The lights?" The couple in the nearest booth were counting out change.

"When all the lights go off for the Barbara Urie show, like a big flashlight, on, off, so that she can fly over in her space station and see us during that celebration for her while we sit in the dark. How long do they go out for? Five seconds? OK, but we don't get a choice about it, do we? No one asked me if I wanted my electricity turned off."

"Blink and it will be over," Helen said quietly.

"Oh great," he said, "great, is that your solution?"

"It's just a suggestion, not a solution. Why? What are you going to do?"

"Don't know yet." He shrugged. "They're leaving on street-lights and emergency services, but it's the principle of the whole thing, isn't it?" He folded his arms on the table and pressed forward. When a strand of dark hair fell across his cheek, he pushed it behind one ear. "I'll tell you something, though," he whispered. "This is my impossible, technological dream, so don't laugh. I would love to send up millions of people into orbit, not just a couple of astronauts. All we have to do is find a way to send them up without using so much fuel, use slingshots maybe, and then everyone can look down and see how small and fucked up the planet is and how everything connects."

Helen had a sudden vision of millions of tiny people soaring up through the atmosphere, wearing white protective suits and hats and goggles, gliding and wriggling like butterflies as they looked down in amazement. Her mother in the sky waved at them, urging them higher and higher. "How do you know what they'll see? How do you even know they'll want to come back?"

"You're making fun of me." Foster looked shocked. The skin stretched tight across his face.

"No," Helen said quickly. She pulled her own hair out of its elastic, tied it back again, and rose to her feet so that she was

159

standing right beside him, fingers prickling, desperately trying to stop herself from touching him. "Really, Foster, I'm not. I'm sorry. I'm just tired. And I have to go clean up."

He stood abruptly, kissed her on the lips, and headed out.

"It's not like the launch," Paul said. "In a way, she'll be there. You'll be talking to her."

"I know that." Helen tried to keep her voice as even and as reasonable as his was. "I'm not even thinking—all I'm asking is why don't you come for the weekend, then we could do it together."

He told her that he couldn't, he was too busy to get away, and in any case he'd said he would show up at the space agency headquarters in Montreal for some smaller affair. The Toronto celebration was going to be the big one, the real circus. They both knew that.

"It would be good to see you."

"Helen, I can't," he said. She had begun to notice how nervous he got these days at the whole idea of going away; all he seemed to want to do was stay in one place and bury himself by working as hard as possible. Even though he'd always been edgy about work, he seemed to be getting worse. She had asked him once before about coming for a weekend, but he'd said he needed the stability of staying put for a while; when she'd mentioned coming to Montreal instead, he didn't seem much in the mood for visitors, either. Maybe this was just how he coped. Did she have any right to complain about that? Even when Paul seemed calm or hard to ruffle, she knew this hid a kind of concentration, his way of willing things not to fall apart.

"I guess it's just there may be protesters."

"There've been protesters before," he said. "You'll have to ignore them."

She ran a finger over her lips, but of course he couldn't see. "I've been doing some work for this environmental group."

"You have? Oh, so you mean you may know some of the people protesting. Like what? Doing what?"

"Disseminating information."

"What?" he said. "Oh, OK. Do people give you a hard time about her, is that it?"

"No," she said, "not really."

"You haven't told her about this, have you?"

She could sense his slight impatience, even though she didn't think he had much right to be impatient. She looked at the wall across the room, lined with Sam's bookshelves, at the clay heads and wooden animals set in rows along the edges, ran a finger worriedly over her lips again. "Maybe it's because she wants all this contact. She goes away and expects us to be independent, for years now, and we are, and then she goes as far away as you can go and wants more contact than ever."

"Don't you think it's important?" She could hear him shifting—from the bed to a chair, from a kitchen chair to the floor?

"I don't know if it's fair."

"If it's fair?"

"In a way, it doesn't really matter where she is. I think I would feel the same wherever she was."

"Helen," he said in an odd, crunched voice, "of course it makes a difference where she is."

A man came into The Million, sat down at a table in her section, and when Helen brought him a menu, he pointed to the small, white sign in the front window that read A GARBAGE CONSCIOUS RESTAURANT, and asked her what it meant.

"It means we use as many recycling techniques as possible to cut down on trash," she said. "We're part of a whole group of restaurants that work together."

"Do you recycle food as well?" the man asked. "If I don't eat what you give me tonight, will you serve it to me tomorrow?" He was wearing a turtleneck (at the end of May, she thought, in the middle of a heatwave). A scarf and pair of gloves lay folded on the table. His eyes gleamed, anxious to please.

"I'll give you everyone's leftovers," she said. "How would you like that?" The ceiling fan above their heads whirred like a propeller. The square hole above the front door where the air conditioner used to be was covered on the inside with a piece of wood. She walked into the tiny bathroom, locked the door, leaned her head against the cool surface of the mirror.

If only everyone in the restaurant, the man sitting by himself, the loud group clumped in one booth, the couple doing a crossword together in another, would leave big tips and go home instantly. Home, crazy word, all she wanted was to go home. Her eyes felt grainy, possibly from exhaustion, possibly close to tears. It was a Wednesday night, and before they left, she and Robin, the other waiter, and Byron, the cook, had to make sure all the nonreturnable bottles and plastics and flattened tin cans and biodegradable waste were put out for collection. Garbage was no longer garbage. If they were lucky, Byron would tell them stories while they worked about his cousins in Jamaica or eating goat stew on a beach or being scared off by wild dogs' eyes that glared from the darkness when once he went in search of the house where he used to live.

When she came out again, Elena was standing by the cash register. The tops of her dark shoulders shone. A water bottle protruded from her shoulder bag. "Hi," she said, and kissed Helen lightly on both cheeks. "I can't stay. I was at a meeting down the street. We're organizing this demonstration down at the Tower on the day of the astronaut celebration. Did Foster tell you? It's not just us, there'll be other groups. Can you come?"

"I have to work that night." Helen was amazed how calm her own voice sounded.

Elena smiled and tucked her hair behind her ears, the bracelets on her wrist clattering gently. "You could get off, couldn't you? Couldn't you trade your shift?"

"It's kind of a bad time." She envied Elena's conviction, her compressed energy, her unusual beauty, whereas she felt as if she were walking around on a pair of stilts, the fragile balance of being held in the air by everything she kept hidden about herself.

"You look tired," Elena said quietly. "Get some sleep. Don't get sick."

"I won't get sick," Helen said.

She bagged a chunk of fake cheesecake, made from tofu, although it was almost impossible to tell, and set off quickly on her bike, west along Bloor Street, away from the darkened restaurant, longing for comfort, distraction, real contact. At Bathurst, the thousands of lightbulbs on the signs covering Honest Ed's Discount Warehouse turned themselves relentlessly on and off, a miasma of white light, the sound of a single lightbulb magnified so many times that it became audible, while inside fields of china ornaments and diapers and kitchen utensils and children's clothes spread in all directions, every discount good imaginable.

At Foster's street, she pulled her bike up onto the sidewalk and leaned it against the side of the phone booth on the corner. She waited for a moment before slipping her coins into the slot, although at least when she dialed his number, she wasn't afraid he would be asleep. They didn't have to talk

163

about the demonstration. She told him, a little nervously, that she'd brought him something to eat.

Trees stirred and settled above her, the air still humid, nearly summer air. A wedge of yellow light shone from Foster's doorway. He was waiting for her out on the front steps and stood as she approached, helped her hoist the bike onto the porch, whistling lightly as she locked it to the railings. He wore a black T-shirt with a white fish printed on it. In the glow of the porch light, the bones in his long face seemed particularly elegant. But then, as she headed up the inside stairs behind him, he started to come apart in small, physical pieces. His hair, which he appeared to be growing out, was pulled back from his face and tied with a rubber band. What was she doing here? When he turned at the top of the stairs, his deep-set eyes seemed rounder than ever. And then, just as elastically, all the pieces came back together and formed Foster. She longed for the small electric shock of touching him, just to prove that he was really there, to check that she still had a firm enough grip on what was real and what wasn't.

"I brought some cheesecake." She watched his face go blank. "It's all right, it's fake." She was never sure quite how far Foster's vigilance went, or whether he ate dairy products. Mostly he seemed to subsist on a lot of Indian and Chinese food, washing everything down with liters of water and black coffee.

Ostensibly, a roommate named Peter shared Foster's apartment. He was never around, and Helen didn't even know if he slept there, which was just as well since all the rooms in the apartment were like oversized cubicles, even the kitchen. Foster pulled two forks out of a drawer and set the fake cheesecake on a plate.

In his bedroom, the computer at his desk was on, the screen emitting a blue glow that bounced off the walls. In its circuitry

164

lay a million things she did not know about him, articles, letters, plans for other underground activities, raids, newsletters, mailing lists, a whole history of him. On the floor, beneath his bookshelf, sat a globe and a brown bag from a fax shop, more signs of all the matter-of-fact technology upon which even he and Elena depended. Helen stood in the doorway, her skin like a million probing filaments, fascinated by this whole world that he carried around inside him. She watched Foster work his way around the bed. Then he pushed open the window and leaned out.

"It's a nice night." He maneuvered himself over the windowsill, set the plate on the ledge, and jumped. Helen leaped across the room after him. The roof of the lower part of the house had to extend farther out than the third floor, not air, he hadn't just stepped into air. When she got close enough she could see that it did. Slinging one leg over the sill, she grabbed the plate, and climbed out onto the roof.

At first her eyes had to adjust to the darkness, before she could make out Foster crouching by a piece of foam mattress. He had turned to watch her. Beyond the roof rose the thin trunk of a sumac tree, spreading out at the top into long branches and rows of prehistoric-looking, toothlike leaves that seemed, drooped above them, amazingly lush. There was just enough room on the mattress for them to lie side by side, eating the cheesecake under a starless, dark brown sky.

"I always think of sumacs as trees that can grow anywhere, out of rocks or in back alleys," Helen said. "I think of them as being like cockroaches, these things that will be around long after we've gone."

"When I was thirteen," Foster said quietly, "I ran away from home and lived in the ravines by myself for over a week. I was thinking about it because of the leaves, because it was just this time of year. Actually I caused kind of stir. I was called the

Ravine Boy in the news, I had my picture in the paper, and afterward the police were kind of freaked out that they hadn't been able to find me. I started out in Wilket Creek Park and made my way down, south of the Science Centre. Down toward the Don Valley Parkway. I was really lucky that it didn't rain. I had a sleeping bag and I'd brought food and I was careful because I didn't want to be found."

"And then what?" She watched him poke the fork delicately against the plate as he talked. He'd never said anything about this before, that he, too, had had his brush with fame.

"Well, after a week I got bored and lonely, and I figured my parents had had a chance to really miss me and even think I was dead, so I made my way to a supermarket parking lot and convinced a woman to drive me home."

"You just slept on the ground in the woods and you weren't afraid."

"Well, I was, kind of. I didn't sleep very much, so I was also exhausted and filthy. But I was smart enough to bring a flashlight, only the last night the batteries ran out."

She stared up through the thick branches of the sumac tree and tried to imagine what Foster could have been like at thirteen. Could she remember ever hearing about the Ravine Boy? *The year I was thirteen was the year the astronaut program began.* "When I was thirteen," she said, "we drove cross-country to L.A., because my father decided he wanted to write screenplays. My mother couldn't stand L.A. She'd steal away with my brother and me and take us camping in the desert as a kind of protest." The lights of a plane floated past above them.

"That doesn't sound so bad."

"Well, it was and it wasn't. Sometimes it was fun and sometimes it was horrible, but it was so hard to judge because we didn't know anything else. And sometimes both my parents would be away, and they'd leave us with this babysitter who got us to watch him doing tai chi in the evenings instead of television. He was amazingly good."

"We ate TV dinners."

"We ate lots of frozen food but never TV dinners." She turned toward him. "Why did you decide to run away?"

"I was unhappy," Foster said. "My brother and I fought all the time. It seemed like we had been genetically programmed not to get along."

When she asked him what his mother was like, he shifted onto his side, pressing his fingers into the foam mattress. "Quiet, fastidious about certain things, like buying things on sale and always turning off lights when you leave a room. She used to work in a bank."

"What did she do when you came back?"

"She took me out to a movie and asked me to tell her why."

His teeth shone in the darkness. He told her about the woman he'd been involved with until a few months before, who was older and married, an ecologist. It had been painful and difficult and ended when she'd moved away. Helen reached out and ran a hand over his back, over the thin cotton of his T-shirt, the flat planes of his shoulder blades, the skin at the back of his neck, and felt herself shiver, felt the breath sighing out of him. Her hands, even her arms still smelled of food; sometimes she felt as if they always did. There were still parts of her that craved touch, the feel of someone's fingers moving inside her, as a way to stop thinking, a kind of oblivion. It wasn't that she thought this was a good thing. It had been months since she had slept with anyone at all.

A few faint lights and voices drifted out of other houses. Why did inviting someone to trust you necessarily mean you had to reveal everything, give up the power to re-create yourself? Why did people act as if revelation always equaled honesty, as if this were the only way to be true to yourself?

Foster sat up suddenly, undid the buckle of his belt, and pulled off his T-shirt, then leaned toward her, pushed the hair away from her ear and whispered, "I have a condom in my pocket, do you?" Helen nodded. "So we're even," he said. "I was just wondering. I just needed to know that." He drew a strand of hair, probably her hair, out of his mouth and lowered her head down onto the mattress. When she slid her tongue between his teeth, his saliva tasted clean and lightly metallic. She watched his face screw tight, struck by his air of utter concentration. She held onto his arms. The night was so still it amazed her. It was crazy to be the one feeling nervous, to feel jumpy just because they were outside, as if the air itself were too crowded, too much floating through it. She wanted to climb back through the window and pull down the covers of Foster's bed, lie with him on his clean white sheets. But it was a beautiful night; it was true that it was a beautiful night. He took off her boots and socks and ran his tongue gently over her insteps. "Don't worry," he whispered, "no one's going to see us."

She came out of the bathroom with a towel wrapped around her and found Foster in the kitchen in his jeans, cutting up fruit at the counter. "I feel happy, you know, I really do," he said. "I was scared I would wake up feeling very odd and tense because sometimes that happens, and I've always been very uneasy about getting involved with someone I'm also trying to work with, especially after Elena, even though we managed to get over that."

"Will she feel weird about it?"

"No. Maybe. I don't think so. I mean, really, what is there for her to feel weird about? Anyway, she says she's too busy to be in a relationship, *and* she's still kind of involved with this woman who lives in Vancouver." He handed her a cup of black coffee and carried two bowls of fruit salad to the table.

There was no milk. Her body hurt a little, all her muscles stretched taut: She wasn't sure what was going to happen next.

"So." Foster sat down, stretching out his arms and legs, smiling effervescently. "Here's what we need to do. What we really need to do is take a hostage."

"A what?"

"A hostage," he said, just as cheerfully. "It doesn't have to be anything violent. We just have to find the right person and abduct very carefully and then we can use them as bargaining power. Get some nightly news coverage. Make sure world destruction and speciesism are treated like a real crisis, daily front-page news coverage, worse than plane crashes. There are times, you know, when I get really sick of plane crashes."

Helen stared at his high forehead, his thin chest, the bones of his rib cage, impenetrable parts of him, felt as if she'd collided with him, gone reeling backward. "How can you do it nonviolently?" she asked. She pulled the towel more tightly around her. "Why a person? Why don't you take an animal hostage, some famous animal, an animal from the zoo?" And yet she could see with absolute clarity why, with a mother like hers, she would be the perfect person, an ideal way to get attention. If she said anything. *Perfect,* Foster would say gleefully, spinning them both around the room. *It's perfect.* Her shoulders were shaking, they would not stop shaking. Maybe she looked as if she were laughing. She spat a melon ball back into her bowl.

"Helen," Foster said nervously, pounding her on the back, "are you all right?"

The clock, which sat on a small table beside her bed, along with the telephone and a bottle of flat Coke, said just after

6 P.M. Helen kept thinking about hostages. *It was a joke.* She kept telling herself that Foster couldn't possibly be serious. Then again, how did she know? She hadn't seen him in a week because he had been doing a massive proofreading stint, and she had been sick. Did it make any difference whether she was really sick or had made herself sick? In two hours the celebration for her mother would begin. There had been a rehearsal two days before, and she'd asked to be excused from that. The man she'd spoken to had said all right but he'd fax her a script. *A script?* She told him she didn't have a fax machine. *As long as you think you can manage, we'll give it to you when you get here. Barbara's seen it, okayed it. You'll just ask the questions, she's the one who has to answer.* They were sending a limo for her in a little over an hour. A limo. Why hadn't her mother said anything about a script? *I'm going to be interviewing her.* In a peculiar way that she couldn't ignore, Barbara was depending on her.

When I said one hundred and eighty-two days in space, she told me I'd forgotten the half, David had joked over the phone from Mexico City. *She's very particular about the half. After all, that's what puts them over the so-called American record for space habitation.* It bothered Helen that he had begun taking these light, affectionate pokes at Barbara again, as if without warning he'd reclaimed some kind of intimacy. *I've been a little under the weather, nothing too serious, Helen, really, I'm fine. And you?* Yes, she'd told him, she was fine, too.

She had slept all morning, woken at lunchtime, and gone down to the corner to buy a paper, couldn't stop herself. ASTRO STAMINA HOLDS STRONG. URIE ON SPACE RECORD TARGET. A man had been arrested in Vancouver as an alleged terrorist. A violent typhoon was blowing toward Indonesia. The newspaper lay in a pile on the other side of the bed, headlines reaching toward her like hands. It was hard to believe that her mother had already been in orbit for six months. Six months. How much longer, a little voice asked. It got easier and it didn't. She was used to her mother's image on the TV screen. The impression of her mother's body, the scent of her perfume, the weight and presence of her skin were disappearing; she had to fight to hold onto them. *I miss you.* Helen sat up suddenly.

She left a message on Foster's machine saying she didn't feel well enough to make it down to the Tower, and if she didn't answer the phone it was because she was asleep. She had to believe that Foster and Elena would be too busy protesting to notice her. What would happen if they did notice her? Had she really thought she could divide herself and live two separate lives at once? Everything she had done seemed all at once like a collision, bodies spinning wildly out of control, not like stepping into a new skin at all. What if, no matter how hard she tried to block things out, they didn't stay blocked out, if one world refused to stay separate from another?

She scrambled out of bed. Opening the doors to the closet, pushing aside her own clothes, she eyed what Sam had left, clothes that Foster and Elena would never recognize. Right at the back, under plastic, hung Sam's black leather bomber jacket and a man's quilted kimono (what incarnation of Sam was this?). Helen pulled out the bomber jacket. It was hilarious really: like wearing a mustache, going in disguise, ridiculous to feel that for once she was going to be safest in leather. It was like being out in the woods, ducking between trees.

The limo came to a stop near the base of the Tower, beside the glass-walled conference center, tiered with lights inside, the tinted limo windows turning the sky artificially dark, like some kind of nighttime preview. A man waiting at the curb opened the back door, took Helen's arm, and helped her out. "You look so different from your pictures with your hair combed out like that." He smiled at her.

Part of the street had been blocked off with blue police barricades, and people were already gathering, spilling from the bottom of the steps that led to the entrance of the Tower and into the street. At the edge of the crowd, by one set of barricades, stood the protesters, although it was hard to see them because of the lights in her eyes, a tight crowd around her, the man's hand on her, maneuvering her toward the steps. Shouts. White placards. They were so intent on themselves that they would never see her. BILLIONS FOR SPACE IS A DISGRACE. WE WANT A PLANET NOT ASTRONAUTS. YOU DON'T NEED TO BE A ROCKET SCIENTIST TO KNOW WE NEED LIFE ON EARTH *NOT* LIFE IN SPACE. A glimpse of something that might have read UNITED SPECIES, she wasn't sure. No faces.

The man beside her whistled a little tune. "Six months, eh," he said, "and how could we possibly have asked for a better night?" There were microphones, another man pushing the microphones away. *Hey,* someone shouted, *what do you think of* . . . Helen was sweating a little in the leather jacket, although there were other people wearing leather, too, and it was true: no clouds at all, a calm, lavender, midsummer night. New buildings surrounded them: the hotel attached to the domed stadium, lights blinking in its windows, the plate sides of the broadcast center across the street, something that might be Venus, another light, rising in one of the gaps. The cement trunk of the Tower turned sand-colored as dusk fell. Everything seemed eerily, futuristically beautiful.

A stage area had been cleared at the top of the steps, in the plaza in front of the Tower entrance. At the back of the stage area rose a huge screen, like a screen in a stadium, square, but white as a moon. "That's where she'll be," the man said, nodding toward it. He was younger than Helen had first thought, in spite of the gray suit, good-looking in a slightly gawky way. He handed her a page with a short, typed list of questions. When she turned around again, the crowd had grown; the people right below her, at the bottom of the steps, must have been there for hours, sitting on jackets, blankets, newspapers. Families had brought picnics. A plastic lid skittered through the air like a tiny wheel. Any moment now.

"We're already planning what we'll do when she's been up there a year," said the woman dabbing makeup over Helen's face, "because I believe they're going to make it past a year, I really do. And you're an old pro. You'll be great tonight, we'll make you beautiful." Someone pointed out a chair, pinned a badge to Helen's jacket that would let her up to the observation level of the Tower afterward to see the lights go out, although there were cameras stationed up there that would project the whole view down onto the huge screen for everyone stranded on the ground.

The woman playing emcee, who had been an evening news anchor for a while, shook her hand, and then headed out smartly toward the microphone, wishing everyone good evening. Her name was Barbara, too.

Shots of the Earth appeared on the screen, a blown-up sequence taken from the space station cameras, the surface moving, shifting, dark brown, covered in clouds that looked like swirls of smoke with scattered fuzzy orange lights shining through. A man who had been one of the first Canadian astronauts stood at the microphone and identified what they were seeing. "That's Africa," he said. "OK, now we're moving toward the Atlantic." Helen could hear people breathing out softly, wonderingly, a sigh that moved her inexplicably.

A seagull blew past, lavender-colored, arcing on a breeze. The sky grew deep blue, rich blue. On the screen shone pictures of the simultaneous celebration going on in Houston. It was exactly in situations like this that her mother never lost her cool. All she had to prove was that she could do it, too.

"Congratulations," Helen said. She'd said it enough times that it was easy. Her voice rang out around her.

"Thanks," Barbara said delightedly. "I'm happy to be here with you—with all of you." The particles that composed her face and her skin trembled like huge pores, larger than ever, her large mouth widening at the edges into a smile visible on the far side of Front Street.

A CBC crew stood to one side of the stage, a CTV crew on the other, a CITY-TV crew right in front of Helen, Live Eye emblazoned all over their equipment. Helen stared down at herself, her long hair, her bright red mouth. At least she couldn't see the crowd of protestors. *Have you enjoyed the last six months?* the teleprompter asked.

"Have you enjoyed the last six months?"

"Enjoyed isn't the word," Barbara said. "I feel in a way as if I've been completely transformed. And even when I'm utterly exhausted, I never lose the pure emotional high of being up here."

"Do you have a clear view tonight?"

"Perfect," Barbara said. "Utterly clear. Just what I came up here for. Right now I feel more like a tourist than a scientist." Only at that moment she was not looking out a window, Helen knew, but into a video monitor or a computer screen, her other windows.

Are you all set for the next six months?

"Are you all set?" Her mouth was open but nothing came out. This was crazy. They were turning themselves into some kind of simulated family. How could they reduce their conversation to this? There were real questions she needed to ask, they were rising upward, pressing at the back of her mouth. *Are you set?* A roar rose up around her, a huge, exultant cheer. No one made any move to stop her, as Helen dashed off-stage, slipped through the people at the side of the stage, and disappeared.

The ride in the elevator up the side of the Tower was very quick, crush of bodies, scent of perfume, smell of sweat. Everyone squashed around her wore VIP badges, like the one pinned to her jacket, or clutched invitations in their hands. There were too many heads to see the view. When the elevator slowed into darkness and stopped and everyone hobbled out, one or two people stared at her but no one said anything. She knew that as soon as she'd left the stage, she would have been covered over seamlessly, as if that was exactly how things were supposed to happen.

Windows ran in a circle around the exterior of the observation level, floor to ceiling. Low pop music poured out of the bar, drinks clattering. The gift shop was closed. On the far side, people were beginning to press near the windows. Were they simply excited, like children? Did the idea of the lights going out unnerve any of them at all? A boy in a baseball cap, the only real child Helen had seen, licked his tongue around the edges of his lips. *The lights will go out,* said a voice over the PA system, *at exactly ten oh six.*

Outside, the sky was dark, except for a pale turquoise line in the west. Helen worked her way between people, didn't care if they stared at her now in annoyance, until she was standing where she wanted to be, facing north toward the bulk of the city and the blinking lights along King Street West, the steak restaurant and Chinese restaurant and theater all owned by

Honest Ed. Beyond this block of lightbulb-ringed billboards, like another star cluster in the distance, she could see the faint blinking at the heart of his empire: Honest Ed's itself.

The only other time she'd been up the Tower had been in daylight, with Paul and her mother, the city bleached by sunlight, spreading out undisguised in all directions, abrupt pockets of taller buildings. They had tried to find their house, or at least the place where their house ought to be.

The lights around the observation deck dimmed to a low glow. The voice of the woman named Barbara, piped up from below, began a countdown: *seven, six, five, four, three, two.* It was strange to realize that she was standing as close to the space station, as close to her mother, as she possibly could, short of climbing mountains. Like her mother, she was looking out a window, looking down. The lights touched her, like a child, in a way the daytime view never had, filling her with wonder, a lake of light.

Whole floors of Bay Street bank towers, the curved, scintillating walls of the Roy Thomson concert hall went dark as if at the flick of a switch. Billboards, pixelboards, the garish block of lightbulbs, dots that had to be houses disappeared, everything swallowed up, consumed, leaving just a brown glare, a trace among the wavering outlines of streets and hospitals lit by their own generators, all so that her mother could see it. It seemed like such an effortless, American kind of power. Everyone around Helen looked so still and tiny. Had cars stopped in the streets? Where was Foster? What was he thinking? Five seconds. It was only going to last five seconds. And yet while the darkness lasted it began to seem obscene. What if the city really disappeared? How could she ever think that hiding, disguising, trying to make herself invisible was going to be enough, that not talking about things would somehow make them go away?

I remember a room in darkness and your voice over the telephone. *This is what it was like.* In your study, with your books and papers and files of newspaper clippings stacked neatly on your desk, I turned off the lamp and waited, concentrating on the stilled, expectant hush of your voice. "Where's Paul?" you asked. "Is he there? Can you ask him to pick up the extension?" There was a click of the phone down below in the kitchen, before I had time to say anything, the gust of his breath. Snow ticked faintly against the window, against the brick wall of the next house. "I've been assigned to a mission."

Paul whooped and made fanfare noises into the phone.

"What kind?" I asked. The darkness bred an air of urgency. Already it was not like the first time, when the four of us had gathered in the kitchen, toasting each other over a bottle of Dom Perignon. You were in Montreal, we were in Toronto, and we knew by now that, whatever his plans had been in the beginning, David was not on his way home.

"I still don't believe it." The edge of hysterical laughter was not like you, the hint of being slightly out of control. "I would never, never have guessed that I would be selected for a mission like this, and I keep telling myself that it must be because my profile is so different from the other astronauts—I'm prime experimental material. No, I'm sorry. Don't listen to me. I don't mean that. You're both so strong and brave and adaptable, and I know we ask so much of you. I admire you. Listen." That hush again. "There's been a change of direction, a new kind of long-term mission—preparation for a possible Mars mission. There'll be two of us, an American astronaut and myself, and other astronauts who will come up and go back for shorter stays, but mostly it will be the two of us—and the idea is to try to set a record for space habitation, to see, in the end, how long we can stay."

"How long?" I asked. "A year? Two years?"

"Maybe a little over a year. It'll go so fast—it won't really seem like that long. And whatever happens there will always be contact, always, by television hookup, not just by phone."

"So this is a really huge deal," Paul said.

"Absolutely. Everyone here is nearly out of their minds."

And maybe, in a way, it was easier to hear the news by phone, without being face to face with your animation, the pull and tug in your features as you tried to hide—although I could hear your radiance translating itself unmistakably over the phone. If I took away your restlessness and love of distance, then I had nothing: no mother at all. Our father had vanished in an instant; you unpeeled yourself from us like skin, piece by piece. No. You hurled us with you into the dangerous future. We soared over other people's barbecues and skating expeditions and shopping trips, an atomic family, fracturing in all directions, spiraling through the air.

"Listen," Helen said. "Please, listen." No one turned to look at her. All around her lights burst on. "Where do we go from here?"

PART TWO

POSSIBLE WORLDS, POSSIBLE MOTION

"LET US BEGIN THE WORLD."
—CHARLES DICKENS, *BLEAK HOUSE*

10

There was a knock on Helen's apartment door, which meant that whoever was knocking either lived in the building or had somehow got in past the front door. It was ten-thirty on a Tuesday morning. Maybe it was Foster, although she tried as much as possible to keep him away from her apartment. When he did come by, she always hid the remote control device in a drawer in her bedroom and made sure they never watched TV. She clambered off the sofa, where she had been sitting in front of the rotating fan, eating a bowl of yogurt and reading the paper, feeling radiated by heat and information. Maybe it was Sam, come back without warning from Australia, wanting to reclaim his apartment. Most likely it was someone in the building with a small, ordinary request: *Can I borrow an egg? I've run out of coffee.* A man's voice tentatively called out her name. Someone who knew her, who at least knew who she was. Perplexed, she opened the door a little, holding on to the handle firmly.

A man stood in the dim, pink light of the hall, a tall thin man with a windbreaker folded over one arm, small round glasses on his tanned face.

"David," she said softly, and opened the door wide, and it wasn't until a moment later that she realized she had called him David, not Dad, as he pressed her against his chest, his arms pulled fiercely around her, her own hands flattened against the real skin and bones of his back.

"So you're here," he said. Suddenly he was standing in her kitchen. It terrified her that in the first second she hadn't recognized him, but he was stripped down, weathered, older, his tanned skin had the creased tightness of someone who spent a lot of time outdoors. His hair had receded noticeably, winnowed at the top to a few thin blond strips. This man. This man who was—

Helen locked the door behind him, watched in amazement as her father sat down at her kitchen table and stared at the goldfish in their aquarium, as he slid his windbreaker over another chair. "What are you doing here?" she demanded.

"I came to see you."

She saw the room all at once through his eyes, new eyes: the old cupboards, heavy with layers of paint, the plum-colored curtains, Sam's international collection of cookbooks, her paperback flattened on the table, the calendar on the fridge still flipped to July. She tried to imagine herself through his eyes: the surface things, black lycra biker's shorts, white T-shirt, her longer, five-years-later, natural-colored hair. She probably looked more muscular, maybe a little tougher.

"It belongs to an anthropologist." She hugged her arms around herself, didn't know where to begin, wasn't sure exactly what she had told him about her life or what details he would remember. "He's in Australia. Do you want something to eat? To drink?" All the questions. Begin with ordinary questions. The air in the kitchen was hot and still. Sweat shone on David's forehead. Had he brought a windbreaker because he thought it would be cool in Toronto, cooler after Mexico at least? Didn't he remember that it got hot here, too, or realize that even in Canada this was the hottest summer on record? What did it mean that he had just appeared like this? There was muscle but no excess weight on him. Once or twice over the last five years, David had sent her photos of himself, one taken in northern China against a panoramic shot of mountains (nearly a tourist shot, as long as you ignored the foreground rubble). In the other, he was standing beside a broken statue in Guatemala City. But these had been mere outlines, just suggestions of him, impossible to tell from them how much he had changed. He might be thin but he was still substantial enough that she could reach out and poke him in jubilation. "You look so different."

"Well, so do you," he said.

"Older?"

"I guess you do look older."

"Why didn't you tell me you were coming? What if I hadn't been here?"

"If you hadn't been here right now I would have left a note."

"How did you get into the building?"

"The superintendent let me in."

"Why didn't you at least call beforehand?"

"Nerves," he said quietly. "I'm sorry. I kept getting worried that for fairly good reasons you wouldn't want to see me, and somehow after all these years I couldn't see just calling up and saying, 'Hi, I'm in town.' I knew I risked barging in on whatever you were doing, but I decided it was better to do it this way and simply come."

She had a sudden, horrifying fear that this was not her father. Surely, even after all these years, she'd know if it was the wrong man, some bizarre impersonation. Perhaps this man *was* her father but had changed in profound and as yet unidentifiable ways. She sat down dizzily across the table from him. *Do you remember?* she could always ask him. (But what if they remembered different things?)

"Did you just come from Mexico City?"

"The night before last."

"You mean you were here yesterday?"

"I decided I needed a day to walk around and reorient myself."

"So what are you doing, are you visiting, are you coming back?"

"Just visiting for now," he said, "although I'm not going directly back to Mexico. I've been invited to speak next week at a conference in the States, about procedures for dealing with people who lose their homes in natural and manmade disasters."

"Speak about what?"

"Well, about that, as it relates to earthquakes, although of course the implications go beyond them."

"Is that why you came back?"

"No," he said. He smiled at her. "Perhaps it was an excuse, in a way. I've been invited to conferences before and said no, but this time I knew I wanted to come up and see you, so I said yes, so that I couldn't back out of coming. This way I had most of my airfare paid, too."

"Where are you staying?" Her mouth was full of questions, questions like jewels, like pebbles.

"At the Park Plaza for now."

"How long are you going to be here?"

"I'm not sure yet."

"Have you talked to Paul?"

David shook his head. "I'll go to Montreal after this for a couple of days. So I won't call him just yet. I'd like to make it another surprise." He reached out and touched his fingers lightly to the back of her hand. "Could I have a glass of water?"

"Sure." She stood up abruptly, took a glass out of the dish rack, and opened the fridge.

184

"Not the tap?"

Helen shrugged.

David stood up, too, rubbing the back of his neck, and began walking slowly back and forth as Helen poured filtered water out of a container. He drank the water in one gulp and leaned back against the counter. Even now he seemed tall to her: a long-legged man. "I had to use a map to get here," he said, "which felt strange, because even if I've been away, I've still lived in this city for the better part of my life. I never came out to the west end much, though. I took the subway and then walked."

"I like it out here," she said. Her father wore round, wire-rimmed glasses now, not aviator-framed ones. She remembered leaning over his desk as a child while he drew a map of North America for her on his yellow legal pad, showing her all the fault lines, describing why there were small earthquakes even in the middle part of the continent where they lived. Everywhere she had looked there were fault lines. She used to keep some of the sketches that David had made for her, his private explanations about the world; for all she knew they were still stored up at the Glenforest Street house. When she and Paul were young, he had taught them to pour beer from a bottle into a glass so that there was no foam, holding their hands beside his, just so, and then he'd let them sip the rich, malt fizz. He said it would teach them moderation. These moments came seeping up like bubbles, like a history she needed to reconstruct for herself. The scent of David's body was the same, the hint of leaves or coffee, drier now than she remembered, more piney.

When he moved toward the living room doorway, Helen froze. Everything was just as she'd left it the night before. On the sofa, only partly hidden by the newspaper, was a letter that she and Foster were drafting, using the name United Species, in support of the international Amazon or Hamburgers campaign, an article entitled, "Human Growth Gene in Cows: The New Cannibalism?", a newspaper ad for a new chicken product called Bigger is Better, *featuring 20% More Breast*. The chicken, with its huge bosom and wings folded like arms, looked disturbingly like a woman. On the floor in a plastic bag lay some more EAT THIS AND YOU'RE DEAD MEAT stickers.

David did not look down but simply walked across the room toward the television and turned it on. Then he stepped back, flipping between channels until he reached the space station feed, concentrating on the screen, his gaze fixed straight in front of him. She remembered now what his presence in a room felt like: his keenness, his deliberate energy, that small, nearly unconscious smile. There was no sign of the astronauts, just a bright, empty corner of their living quarters, while on the floor, the fan swiveled back and forth, rippling the newspaper and the rest of the papers on the sofa. It seemed too late or too obvious to try clearing things away.

"You know I've never seen this," David said. "I told them if they couldn't get me portable access to it, it wasn't going to do me much good and, do you know, they actually said they're working on it. I'm sorry." He turned around again. "This is rude. This isn't why I came."

"If she comes to the phone, then you'll see her."

"Do you think it's been useful?"

"I guess. I watch it sometimes but not all the time. Sometimes it just makes me feel like I'm spying. And I know she's in space, but I don't feel like I need to see her, just because she's not here. I'm old enough by now that I can cope with that."

"I see."

"Why, after all this time, did you decide to come now?"

"Don't you think it's about time?"

"Well, yes," she said, but that wasn't good enough.

David switched the television off and looked around quizzically, at the shelves lined with books and small artifacts, the clay heads and wooden animals with their beady eyes, the black lacquerware boxes, toward the bamboo blinds on the living room windows. "It's strange to be here," he said, flexing his tanned hands. "It's strange to see you here surrounded by someone else's things—although I guess I'm just as glad not to be going back to the Glenforest Street house."

"Do you want some coffee?" She simply wanted to get him out of the living room. In one quick dash, she picked up the rotating fan and her empty yogurt bowl, set the fan up in the kitchen doorway. She would have to call people from the restaurant, see if she could find a sub for that night and the next night, too, hoped that Foster wouldn't call, or Elena, wanting her to come out and meet them suddenly.

The sight of her father stepping back into her kitchen shocked Helen all over again, a new wave breaking joyfully over her. She had stopped expecting, even though he called, even though he wrote letters, that he was ever going to come back. *Cities take years to rebuild after earthquakes,* he'd written. *As soon as they're out of the news, everyone forgets.* It was like stepping without warning into some realm of imaginary time. The relations, the balances between different parts of her life suddenly changed. When she pushed aside the curtains and shoved up the window, a fly was hurling itself against the screen. Ordinary things. A trickle of breeze drifted in, while outside, somewhere in the dirt and grass below, crickets were strichilating—a word David had taught her. *Put on the kettle.*

"I had dysentery," he said suddenly from the table. "That's how I got so thin. This is only a recent development. I was working outside the city for a while, and I guess it was some water, although I'm usually very careful about things like that."

Helen turned and stared at him, thought about Mexico City smog, the thick, black layer of it probably still coating her father's lungs, big risks, little risks, how his own parents had died when he was only a few years older than she was.

"You're all right?" She sat down across from him.

"I'm all right now. I've been on antibiotics. I just lost a lot of stamina. Maybe you don't even want to hear this, but I've actually gained some weight."

"Were you in hospital?"

"Just for a day or so, mostly for tests."

"Why didn't you tell me?"

"I didn't want to worry you. Helen, there wasn't even an easy way for me to get hold of you. If it had really been serious, of course you would have heard."

"You're sure you're all right?"

"I'm all right," he said in his calm, steady voice. He reached across the table and gripped her hand.

She called David and waited until he was standing right behind her, in front of the bathroom mirror. This way she could see the two of them, have some renewed proof of the ways in which she actually looked like her father, the physical grounding, the reassurance of biological connection that she could not get with her mother. Her rounder cheekbones were like David's; they had the same dark eyebrows, a hint of wariness in their eyes. The invisible camera that pinned them together confirmed that he was really here: Now she would be able to see them standing like this again and again.

"I'll tell you what I've been longing to do when I got here," David said. "Eat a meal in Chinatown. I'd lie awake in Mexico City sometimes and think about Chinese meals I'd eaten here, restaurants that Barbara and I used to go to years ago, places we took the two of you, fantastic noodle dishes, marvelously spicy meals. And even if I can't eat anything really spicy at the moment, I thought maybe we could head out and have lunch together, if you're free." His voice became all at once very serious and courteous.

"Of course I'm free," Helen said.

They walked north on Roncesvalles toward the Dundas streetcar. Warm, wet air blew up from the lake, over the expressway, through the heavy trees, tinged with hints of sulphur. The Polish delicatessens were hung with sausages and stacked with loaves of bread. Greengrocers spilled piles of waxy, shiny fruit onto outdoor counters. The strains of a local FM station wafted out of the Polish Old Home restaurant. At one moment everything seemed familiar, places Helen walked or biked past nearly every day, and David, striding beside her, seemed someone wholly out of context; then she would look at him with a burst of warmth and wonder what either of them was doing here. Her feet stepped lightly along the ground.

"After I left," David said, turning to her intently, "when you were still in high school—I know this probably seems like eons ago now—but did it work out all right having Tom live with the two of you?"

"Tom was great," Helen said, "he really was. He was very kind. He had us do tai chi with him sometimes because he said it would help us deal with everything. I mean, mostly we looked after ourselves, and at least there were two of us, right? And Mum came home whenever she could on weekends."

"Do you see Tom at all?"

"Not now." She could have called him, kept in touch, since he still ran Barbara's lab, but she hadn't mostly because he was linked to a whole world, a part of her life she'd needed to leave behind. Although there were still memories of Tom that she carried with her. His meticulous, passionate presence in the kitchen: He'd bought them a wok, insisting there was more to cooking than making foods you could freeze for weeks. He'd introduced them to dim sum.

Summer nights, with a citronella candle at her feet, she had sat on the back porch and watched him, shirtless, amber-skinned, standing as still as a heron in the evening light beside the pool where her mother had once swum endless laps—no, not completely still, one arm imperceptibly moving. His concentration, his capacity for slow, utterly focused movement was so unlike her mother's or even her father's restlessness. And yet Tom worked with Barbara on the motion-sickness machine, inventing vestibular-system experiments for astronauts to perform in space. *Why,* he'd said, when she asked him, *does there have to be a contradiction?*

"You seemed to have managed with everything," David said. "I've always been very impressed with the way you handle things."

"Mum says that."

"And at the moment you're working in this restaurant?"

"It's a café, a natural foods café up on Bloor Street. I don't mind it."

"And then in the fall you go back to university."

"We'll see." She wished she had pockets that she could shove her hands into abruptly.

"Does that mean you might have other plans?"

"Maybe I'm not sure it's the right thing for me to be in university right now."

"Ah," David said carefully. And then, after a moment, "Have you decided not to go back?"

In the distance, a cat jumped in one lithe motion over a fence. It was crazy, after so many years, to want his eyes to fix on anything but her. "I haven't been at university." Helen tried to keep her own eyes on the horizon, feel lucid and sure about what she was doing. "Not since January. I've been working."

A streetcar passed, heading up toward Dundas, but they did not get on. David cleared his throat. "I know I've been here the least of anyone, and forgive me if I've got things mixed up, but am I wrong in thinking Barbara doesn't know this?"

"I'll tell her," Helen said. "I really will, but I wanted to wait until things settled down. Please don't tell her. It was my decision, and I didn't want her to think it was somehow her fault." She could tell David was frowning through the odd little clip-on sunglasses that he'd attached to the frames of his regular glasses, as if the light had changed or he were trying to see her more clearly. "I'm looking after myself, aren't I?"

"Yes," he said, "yes, I'm sure you are."

"Did you tell her you were coming up here?"

"All right." He gave her a small, sideways smile. "We talked about the idea, but I've been so—I haven't told her finally, decisively that I've gone through with it."

They sat at the back of a restaurant called The Shining Palace, in a cool, dim room that made it seem as if it could have been any time of day or night, a room that equalized them. Deep, red walls held them in place, away from the hot, quick rush of people and the tall, new buildings built with Hong Kong money, the flashing banks, the time blinking from the computerized sign at the top of the glassed-in Dragon City mall. They had made their way past crates of tubers and fish and watches lining the sidewalk until David gave up searching for a place he remembered and Helen suggested the Shining Palace. She wanted to tell him about the huge new dim sum restaurants opening in malls all around the city, about an ordinary suburban mall that was being redesigned with a traditional Chinese gate over the parking lot entrance, how much things had really changed. She tried to imagine him stepping off the plane in

Toronto, carrying the same flight bag as when he'd left, filled with taut expectation, rigid with anxiety.

"It's so good to see you, you know." He clinked his bottle of beer with hers. He had grinned as he'd asked if she wanted to order her own bottle of beer.

"You, too." A small spot burned at the back of her throat. The menu blurred, then coalesced. She thought suddenly of the father she'd made up for Foster, the one in Yellowknife. She could still see him pacing up and down in a small house, or in a felt-walled, soundproof booth, funneling voices out over the radio. "Just for your information," she said, "I don't eat meat."

"You don't." David looked up. "Since when?"

"The end of high school."

"For moral reasons or health ones?"

"For both," Helen said, "mostly moral ones. I guess it's not the kind of thing I talk about in letters or over the phone."

"Well, I would like some hot and sour soup, if you don't mind," David said politely. "I know there's meat in that. And then perhaps we can compromise on a few things."

She nodded, didn't care that much what she ate, actually. Her body felt sharpened with a different kind of voraciousness, hungry for words, some substance, *the real meat*. She took a sip of water. "So did you come back to give me an explanation?"

"An explanation?"

"For why you left. A real explanation, instead of just talking about earthquakes all the time, about why you need to work on earthquakes and all the terrible things that happen after earthquakes, because that's all you ever did in the letters you sent and it's not good enough."

"That's partly why I came back." David ran his fingers back and forth across his lips.

"Did Mum ask you to check up on me?"

"Helen!"

"When you left, were you trying to prove something to her?"

"More to myself, I think."

"But you knew—didn't you always know she wanted to be an astronaut?" No matter what she'd done in the last few months, no matter which of all possible Helens she had become, this remained a constant, a point of origin.

"I knew she'd always been interested in space," David said slowly. "That's what I knew when I met her. She was studying astrophysics, although she was already talking about doing something more hands on, more practical, like going to med school. But she didn't talk so much about astronauts. Maybe that's hard for you to believe. At least she didn't talk so much about it out loud, and when she did, she often joked about it, we both did, especially after the moon landings." He stopped, looked past her toward the front of the restaurant, then began again. "Maybe I underestimated how much it was something that she actually wanted to happen, that she would put everything on the line to do. It wasn't just the kind of desire that drives you without your needing to have that desire fulfilled."

"She's always been very determined."

"Oh, I know. I know that." The tiny lines at the edges of his eyes kept creasing as he talked, small slivers of pain, and yet he spoke in a low, steady voice, as if he'd been carrying this stream of words in his head for years, formulating and reformulating it, and now the words were bursting out of him. "Sometimes all this seems so long ago, and sometimes it doesn't, but I guess I wanted there to be room for compromise, even the possibility of compromise. Maybe that was where it started. Maybe I ignored—and yet I knew that if Barbara was actually accepted into the astronaut program, there was no way she was going to say no. And when I realized that, I started to question

things, everything really. I began to feel somehow as if everything we'd done together had been a mistake, as if we'd made
the wrong choices, or I'd made the wrong choices. It's complicated, and maybe the best way to think of what happened to
me is as a kind of disease. I lost some kind of ability to look
toward the future, and I started to feel guilty. I would look at
the two of you and feel guilty, even though I knew this wasn't
fair to you. And when Barbara was actually picked to be an
astronaut, everything suddenly got much, much worse."

"Did you try to tell her?"

"Then? I didn't really see how I could explain it then. I
didn't know how I could explain the guilt. She said that entering the astronaut program or wanting to go into space didn't
mean she loved me, loved any of us any less. It was only a
contradiction if I insisted on seeing it that way, and yet the
worse I felt the harder I found it to be around any of you.
Maybe this doesn't make sense to you, and maybe there are
ways in which what I did shouldn't make sense to you. And
then there was the earthquake, and I felt all of a sudden as if
I had to do something, as if this might be a way to combat
what I was feeling. In some peculiar way I felt responsible. The
Earth can still act in uncontrollable ways. I'm not sure that
realizing this is such a bad thing. It's still no reason to give up.
You find a way to rebuild a home. It gives you a reason not
to give up."

"You didn't have to stay away for years."

"No," David said, "I know." One small, blue vein pulsed at
his temple. He stared down into his miasma of soup and
stirred it carefully. "Maybe I was frightened of what you would
say. Maybe I wasn't sure what I would come back to, how I
would resolve things with Barbara or what I would do. I did
not want to go back to being a journalist, and everywhere I
looked there was always so much that needed to be done. And

then someone convinced me to go from L.A. to Guatemala City for the initial rescue operation, and when I got there, I didn't see how I could leave. All these wrecked lives, Helen. All these people living in houses that crumbled like cardboard boxes, or homes that *were* cardboard boxes. Maybe I let myself be enveloped by all this, but then again, what else could I have done? I don't want you to underestimate those reasons. They were real reasons."

"Didn't you wonder what was happening to us?"

"It's not as though we've been out of touch entirely. I haven't been completely cut off. I mean, reporters were even following me around L.A. the day that Barbara's mission was announced."

"That's not the same," Helen said, "that's really not the same." For a start, he had no idea what that particular day had been like. *It will probably be a little crazy,* Barbara had said, and it had been. "The three of us went to Montreal, you know, for the announcement, and when we came out of the space agency headquarters, all the reporters who hadn't been let inside suddenly charged us. And I know it's not like earthquakes, it's nothing like earthquakes, but I really thought I was going to be crushed. We were pressed up against a wall. I was smashed up against her. There was nowhere to go. People were shouting and throwing things from the street, bits of paper and rice." There was more but she'd managed not to remember it. There was a moment when the lights in her face grew so bright that she'd felt totally devoured, as if she had no body left at all. And afterward, when they'd come back to Toronto, there were one or two times when each of them had picked up the phone and it had been some crank caller telling them that Barbara had no right to be doing what she was doing. Helen remembered the first time this had happened, the way her mother had stood there silent and blanched.

"No," David said quietly, "it's true, I don't know what that was like."

"So how much do you talk to Mum?" Helen leaned forward across the plates between them.

"Now? It depends on when I can get a clear line through and how much time I have, but sometimes once a week, sometimes more, sometimes less."

"Do you call her?"

"Usually it's easier if I call her."

"What do you talk about?"

He gave her one of his loose, slow smiles. "We've talked a lot about these things. We talk about what it is we're trying to do."

Two fortune cookies and two curved slices of orange sat on a plate in the middle of the table. "So what else keeps you busy besides working in this restaurant?" David picked up a fortune cookie, set it down, but did not open it.

"Why does there have to be a what else?"

"There doesn't. All right, I was just wondering about something in particular." He slipped his hand into the pocket of his canvas slacks, pulled it out and, with an unobtrusive deftness that impressed her, showed her the sticker cupped in his palm. His eyes were filled with wry curiosity, carefully withholding judgment. "Maybe I shouldn't have taken this."

"No," Helen said, although her pulse had quickened, "people are supposed to see them." She reached for the other fortune cookie and cracked it open. Maybe it was time to stop hiding; invisibility was not good enough. If you don't tell your own story, you'll be discovered. What did she have to fear from telling him? "I'm doing some work for an environmental organization, kind of an animal rights group."

"Animal rights," David said.

"Well, a lot of what we're involved in has to do with animals, only it's not just animals."

"What kind of work exactly?"

"Organizing product boycotts, distributing information, protests. Nothing violent, don't worry."

"Is this something you're quite involved in?"

"I guess I'm pretty involved." She watched his face, which stayed very still, the ghost of a smile hovering over his lips, perhaps because he wasn't sure how to respond. "I know life isn't bad here compared to the places you've been, but there are other ways for things to collapse. And maybe you think it has nothing to do with animals, but it's about the same kind of attitude, it all connects."

"You think this is the best way to deal with things."

"I think just looking after humans isn't good enough anymore. It isn't just about houses—and I believe you have to do something."

"Well, I agree with that." David slipped the sticker away. And what more, really, could she expect him to say? Although part of her wanted him to argue with her so that she could defend herself.

THERE WILL BE GOLD BUCKETS AT THE END OF YOUR RAIN-BOW, her fortune read. Helen stared at it blankly. GOLD BUCK-ETS? What she hated most about fortune cookies was that however stupid their messages were, part of her always wanted to believe them. David handed his fortune across to her: WORK HARD AND LIVE LONG.

"You probably haven't told Barbara about this either," he said laconically as he dropped the slip of paper with his fortune on it into the ashtray.

"I will," Helen said. "I promise. Soon." With her teeth, she pulled her piece of orange away from its skin. The juice spread cool and tangy through her mouth, the taste her mother dreamed of.

There was a point sometime in the afternoon when she started to relax a little and it began to seem almost natural to be walking beside her father through the streets of Toronto, keeping pace with his long, easy stride, a point when she stopped worrying what would happen if they ran into Foster and Foster began asking David questions about Yellowknife. The man in Yellowknife seemed far away. In his level, urgent voice, David told her stories, about a woman in northern China whose body was found amid the bones of her house, clutching an unbroken egg in one hand. How researchers were no longer talking simply in terms of fault lines but fault segments, which responded differently to the buildup of stress: Some crept, some lurched, some waited years then ruptured. About a man in L.A. who had gone after him with a baseball bat because he wouldn't let the man back into his house. *It looks exactly the same,* the man kept shouting, except of course the foundations of the house were shattered, while everything the man possessed, his socks, his compact discs, his photographs of his dead daughter, remained inside. These were the layers her father carried around with him.

They sat in the late-afternoon shade of a plastic umbrella, outside an Italian café on College Street, drinking orzata and soda. "There's something I wanted to ask you," Helen said. David raised his eyebrows. "You and Mum used to fly together. I know that. But did you teach her?"

"To fly? Not exactly. Although you could say we met because of it. At a party. Barbara came up to me to ask about flying. She'd found out from someone that I flew during the summers, on geological survey teams in northern Ontario, and she wanted to know about it. So we started talking. And then of course I had to decide what to do, because I was supposed to be heading up north two weeks later. If I'd gone, maybe nothing would ever have happened. And I really didn't know what I was going to do, until Barbara told me she would learn to fly if I stayed. You have to take a proper training course, which she did, but we flew together. And it cost money, so we'd scrounge like crazy until we'd saved up enough and then we flew. And most people we knew thought we *were* crazy, that I was crazy to move into her tiny apartment only two months after I'd met her, which I did, and that we were crazy to live like dormice and spend all our money flying, but we didn't care. It was a badge of pride, I guess, because we already felt like these two weird hybrids, these unlikely scientists. I came from a family that had nothing to do with science and thought it was ludicrous when I went off to Toronto to study plate tectonics, and Barbara was in this program surrounded by men, completely used to ignoring what people thought about her."

"So why did you stop flying?"

"We decided to get married. Of course it wasn't that exactly, but Barbara wanted to go to Scotland so I could meet her parents, even though she hadn't seen them in a couple of years. Anyway, we saved up to do that. And then we had you."

"But didn't you miss it?"

"In a way," David said, "but in other ways, no. I always wanted to take Barbara flying up north, over that land, over lake after lake. But there were other things I wanted to do. I wanted to write. I wanted to be this amazing science populist.

And there was Paul. And we had kind of an agreement that if we had children, we couldn't both fly, or at least we wouldn't fly together. Maybe it seems foolish. Maybe it was unnecessary. Maybe it wasn't. It wasn't the main reason."

"You could have gone back to it."

"No," he said, "it really wasn't that important. And there were practical reasons. I'd have to renew my license." He smiled at her easily. She was still amazed at his new loquaciousness, his determination to explain—to justify—himself. "I started out as a geologist. Maybe it made more sense for me to try out my luck on the ground."

"Did you mean to have children so close together?"

He looked genuinely startled. "Yes," he said. "Yes, of course. I mean, I don't think we exactly planned to have both of you born in the same year, but Barbara was always adamant that she wanted two children and she wanted them close together. Why?"

"I was just wondering," Helen said.

"You're sure," David said urgently. "Listen, I don't want you to think that what either of us has done, we've done simply from ambition. Barbara's been terribly successful, but she's never just been motivated by ambition."

"No," Helen said, "I know that." She took a slow sip of her drink, breathing in the scent of almonds. "Do you miss her?"

"Yes," David said quietly, "I do."

The phone rang. And rang and rang. "Helen." She could hear her father's voice speaking into the hollow machine, urgent, puzzled, as she struggled back from miles away. "Helen, are you there?" She ran on slow, loose legs to reach the voice, through the blue and limpid darkness, from one room into the other, the sky through the window too blue for it to be the middle of the night. They had eaten dinner in an Indian restaurant on Bloor Street, and then walked west down Bloor, past The Million, which she had pointed out to him, and they had talked about taking the ferry out to the island in the morning or meeting at the museum the day after that, making oddly formal plans, as if, Helen had thought, to prove they could make plans. They had kissed goodnight outside the subway, and then David had headed down the renovated blocks, back toward his hotel.

"I'm here," she said, crouched on the floor. She thought instantly of her mother, the constant low-grade fear of catastrophe surging up, remembering the time one of the routine missions had been delayed for days because the onboard computer kept shutting down, and another time when there'd been problems docking; of course it made perfect sense that her father would be the bearer of terrible news.

"Listen," David said softly, "I hate to tell you this. I hate to wake you up like this, but I had no idea this was going to happen. I have to leave again."

"You what?" She rocked back on her heels in disbelief.

"There's a gas fire, not here, in Ohio. They've called me to help with the evacuation because it's grown a lot worse than they first thought, and they're evacuating a lot more people."

"Why you?"

"Because I know how to lead evacuation teams. I know how to deal with people who may lose their homes, and a lot of these people may lose their homes. It's horrible. It happened last night. There was some kind of explosion but it's still burning. I'll be protected if I have to go in close, don't worry."

"You don't have to go." A dog barked. The fan in her bedroom whirred and turned, stopped and turned. Her head was reeling. It had to be sometime in the very early morning.

"What do you mean I don't have to go?"

"You just got here."

"Helen, it's an emergency. I wouldn't go if it wasn't an emergency. A state official called me. They need me. They're trying to put some kind of international relief team together."

"You could have told them you just got here."

"How could I say that?"

"You could have told them you hadn't seen me in five years."

"Helen, it's not that—"

"I don't believe you. I don't believe they called you."

"Turn on your TV. All you have to do is turn to the news channel right now. Do you think I wanted something like this to happen? Why would I lie to you?"

"Because you want an excuse to get away."

"No," David said, "no, you mustn't think—this isn't like L.A. This really isn't like L.A. I'll come back."

"In five years," she shouted, "in five years you'll come back. How can you expect me to believe you? And maybe right now you even *think* you'll come back, but you'll get somewhere else, somewhere as close as Ohio, and there'll be so much to do that you won't come back."

"I'm not running away. I've told you. Helen, you have to believe me."

"But how do I know that? How do I know I don't frighten you? How do I know you're not more frightened by what I've turned into?"

"Don't say that."

"All you want to do is save people."

"That's not true. Helen, I haven't even seen Paul. I thought you of all people would understand why—after everything you said."

"Please go," she said. "Please." Her father had the power to invoke disaster, leave a trail of disasters behind him. The room, the blue sofa, the TV set didn't move.

202

"I'll call you," David said. "I'll try to call you tonight if I can. And I mean this absolutely. I'll see you soon."

"I'll see you." She kept fighting the urge to burst into tears, fighting a crazy urge to say, *I could help you.* No matter what happened, she still felt split in two. "I believe you." She held the telephone up in the air, dangling at the end of the receiver, and threw it across the room.

11

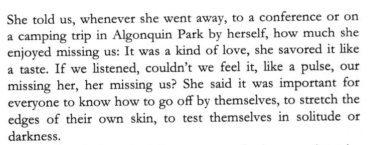

She told us, whenever she went away, to a conference or on a camping trip in Algonquin Park by herself, how much she enjoyed missing us: It was a kind of love, she savored it like a taste. If we listened, couldn't we feel it, like a pulse, our missing her, her missing us? She said it was important for everyone to know how to go off by themselves, to stretch the edges of their own skin, to test themselves in solitude or darkness.

The night before she left our cottage for her camping trip, she unpinned the star map from the wall and spread it over the floor in front of us. "When I'm out there and you're here," she said quietly, "we'll look up and see the same constellations. I'll put up my tent and then I'll walk down to the shore. That's why people imagined a sky full of men and women and animals—to make it seem safer. So wherever you are, you can look up and see a reflection of home."

Mosquitoes flared up as it grew dark. We'd driven her north to Algonquin Park, dropped her off, then driven back to the cottage. At the edge of the lake, Paul and I sat on a slab of granite, watching my father grill hamburgers on the tiny barbecue. He handed them to us without napkins or plates. We were

204

quiet, as if we could feel but not express the looseness in the place where my mother's energy usually settled between us.

The Big Dipper, when it appeared, would be right above us.

My father stretched out his long legs and crossed them at the ankles, as the charcoal toppled into embers. We leaned back against his warm T-shirt, listening to the wind rising, making different sounds in each different kind of tree: the poplar leaves clattering, the rush of air through the pines, the quiet whipping of the almond-shaped birch leaves, nearly invisible now. The stories he told us were like and unlike my mother's stories. He read to us from the *Field Guide to Rocks and Minerals,* the *Field Guide to the Weather,* and made up contests for us to guess at kinds of clouds: altostratus, stratus, cirrocumulus. Now he explained that he was in the middle of writing an article about a chimpanzee named Lucy, who lived in a suburban house like a human child, and a gorilla named Koko. Ruffling our hair, he asked us if we knew that humans and chimpanzees shared over ninety percent of their genetic material. "No," Paul said, "really?" It was true, my father said, and it's an amazing thing, look into their eyes sometime, and then he smiled.

I listened to my father's voice, the comfort and steadiness of his voice, the gentle scratch of his fingertips against the back of our necks, a father's voice, a mother's voice that carried us and held us. I wondered where my mother crouched in the rustling dark, under the August stars. Was she afraid? I wanted to believe she felt that pinch in her stomach, her throat seizing up.

In the kitchen window, set against the screen, the radio played a weather report for the whole province, the world streaming softly around us, other places pouring through the window like ghosts: Temiskaming, Kapuskasing, North Bay, Sudbury.

"Will you keep us safe?" I whispered to my father.

"Yes," he whispered back, "of course I'll keep you safe."

12

Helen moved quickly, stuffing clean clothes into her overnight bag. Outside, the sky was growing light. The phone lay where she had thrown it, like a body on the floor, the receiver flung out like an arm, a small black knick carved in the living room wall above it, no sound coming out of it now at all. At the foot of her bed, the fan turned jerkily back and forth. She had taken the goldfish to her neighbor's. In six hours, once she got herself to the car, she could be in Montreal. The most important thing was to keep moving. Everything would be all right as long as she kept moving.

In the bathroom, she soaked a washcloth in cold water and pressed it over her face. By now David should be in a plane on his way to Ohio, flying toward all those people who were going to lose their homes to toxic contamination. And if there was a fire, there would be fumes, tall pillars of toxic smoke, a cloud that for all she knew was blowing east across Lake Erie, over Lake Ontario, traveling with all the usual industrial emissions toward Toronto; Ohio wasn't that far away.

She kept thinking how much better it would have been if David had never come back; then she wouldn't be able to see him so clearly, an endless film loop, here in her own living room, the exact shade of his blue T-shirt, the way he tilted his head and looked around probingly. She would not miss him with this immediate intensity. If he hadn't come back, she wouldn't be tempted to blame herself, berate herself for telling him anything. A garbage truck heaved distantly down a street. Anything could happen. She'd told herself this before and it was just as true as ever. The ground kept shifting underneath her, knocking her off balance. Nothing felt safe. She zipped up her bag, lowered all the blinds, and let herself out.

The air in the street was already hazy, leaves on the trees rustled like boiling soup. At the convenience store on the corner, she stopped for a paper and bought the *Star* because of the headline about the Ohio fire across the front page. With the paper under her arm, she hurried toward the nearest coffee shop, bacon and fried eggs like flying saucers painted on the windows, lost objects floating in a vacuum. Water dripped into a bucket set just outside the door, and as soon as she stepped inside a blast of cooler air hit her: No way to avoid air-conditioning.

At the counter, with her bag on the seat beside her, she ordered Breakfast Special Number One, eggs and toast and coffee, and in her head heard Foster's tiny, worried voice: *Helen, you're not going to eat those eggs. Because if you're not going to think about what people do to battery hens to get those eggs, at least think about the risk of salmonella poisoning.*

Yes, I am, she said. *I'm hungry. I need some protein.* In one long gulp, she swallowed a glass of water that she had watched the waitress run straight from the tap; then she began to devour the paper. *Intensity of flame holds back containment crews at the toxic chemical fire in Lagoon, Ohio.* Another place that no one had heard of before, to add to the list of all those other terminally infected places. Lagoon, what a crazy name, Lagoon. *So far twenty thousand people have been evacuated.* And the thing was, it could have happened in Toronto. It was not like a massive earthquake. Nowhere was safe. How could you really believe there were things you could do to make yourself safe?

"The wind's coming from the wrong direction," she heard the man in the booth behind her say. "It's not going to blow on us. If we're lucky, eh?" But something would still be in the air, even if there was no cloud, there would be particles slowly, invisibly dissipating, nothing to smell, no sign at all but spreading every which way.

At the bottom of the page she found an article about Soviet plans to send a two-person crew up to their smaller, currently unoccupied space station, *another step in preparation for the international Mars project.* Her mother probably knew about that already. And even if a colonizing party did set off for Mars in the not-so-distant future, *there's no reason to think that someone like me would ever be picked. I'd be left down here with everyone else to be contaminated or radiated, pickled for the future.* She remembered that horrible moral-values game where everyone had to pretend they were adrift on a boat and argue about who should be saved. Or the ark. Not many people ended up on the ark. All those people in Ohio. How could she possibly feel safe? She drank her coffee so fast she burned her tongue, shoveled down her scrambled eggs.

There was a phone booth right at the back of the restaurant. Helen paid her bill, walked to the back, and pulled the paneled doors of the phone booth closed behind her. The air inside was warm and close: no air-conditioning. Settling onto the metal stool, she wedged her overnight bag on her lap and dialed, waited what felt like long moments for the connection to go through, until she heard a click, a distant ringing, and Peter Carter's voice said hello. "Hi, Peter."

"Helen." His voice altered, instantly kind. "How are you?"

"I'm fine," she said, "but I'm in a hurry. Can I talk to my mother, please?"

"Surely." It was the first time in all these months that she had tried calling the space station from a payphone, even though they had been told all along that it was possible: Any time, from any corner, contact was always possible.

"Helen," Barbara said. "It's morning for you, isn't it? I don't usually get morning calls from you."

"David came back."

"So he did it. Helen, I'm so happy. Tell me what happened." It was impossible to miss the surge of pleasure, her fierce curiosity.

"He appeared on my doorstep yesterday morning—he didn't even call, just knocked, I opened the door, there he was—we talked for a long time. We spent the day together."

"He seemed fine, changed?"

"I don't know." She heard his voice, calling her name in the darkness, into her answering machine. "He seemed glad to be here. He was trying to explain things. He looks different. I can't tell if he's changed."

"But he's there. At least one of us is able to visit you."

"He left this morning."

"He left? What happened? I thought he was staying—"

"There was a fire, a chemical fire in Ohio."

That fire. Oh God, I thought I could see flames from that fire."

"They called him up to help with the evacuation."

"Helen, it's not like L.A. I don't want you to think this is L.A. all over again. I don't think his reasons are the same. Even if he left, I'm sure he'll come back."

"That's what he kept saying. He kept repeating it's really not like L.A."

"Did he say how long he was going to be gone?"

"No," Helen said, "of course he didn't." The air inside the booth was growing warmer, stuffier, smelling of other people's cigarettes, old sweat, old breath, the forced intimacy of many people, even one at a time, occupying the same small space. Only a few feet away, the cook was having a loud conversation with a young man whose shoulders curved under his T-shirt, a cigarette pack tucked like a bicep up one sleeve.

"Helen, where are you?" Was Barbara staring in bewilderment at a blank screen, an ordinary computer monitor, a window? "Aren't you at home?"

"I'm at a payphone."

"Why a payphone?"

"My phone's broken."

"Are you getting it fixed?"

"As soon as I can."

"Will you call me as soon as it's working?"

"Of course I'll call you." She closed her eyes. When she opened them, the man with the cigarette pack was standing against the opposite wall, staring at her through the plastic doors, at her bare arms and legs, her breasts. It was only funny if she reminded herself that he had no idea who she was talking to. She turned and gave him the finger.

"You're sure you're all right," Barbara said.

"I'm all right." She felt all at once like bursting into tears. She was so out of practice when it came to imagining a private dialogue between her parents, their mutual explanations for their own behavior, their possible discussion of her behavior or Paul's. It was like plunging into a new wilderness.

There was nowhere to park so Helen drove the station wagon onto the sidewalk outside Foster's house, switched on the hazard lights, then dashed up the porch steps to Foster's front door. When she had tried calling from the parking lot, his line was busy, but that could simply mean someone else was trying to reach him. His running shoes appeared at the top of the inside stairs—he *was* there—his black jeans, the neat line where his T-shirt met his jeans, filling her with relief. He loped down the stairs, opened the door, and kissed her on the mouth. "Surprise," Helen said. "Were you on the phone?" She kissed him back.

Foster nodded and touched the tips of his fingers to her forehead. "You're really sweating. Are you coming in? Or are you off somewhere? What's with the car? Is this business or pleasure? I hate to put it like that, but I have to go proofreading soon."

"In a minute," Helen said. "I'll explain in a sec. Can I get a glass of water at least?" She remembered suddenly that she had forgotten to say anything to Barbara about going to Montreal.

"Sure." Foster bounded ahead of her up the stairs, his undone laces skittering.

On the kitchen table sat a large, empty bowl with a pair of chopsticks in it. "Oh good," Foster said gleefully, standing in the middle of the floor and stretching out his arms. "Now I can show you something." He pushed up the window beside the counter and pointed to a bucket rigged to a rope and a pulley, like an old laundry line, except that the rope descended vertically to a black plastic composting bin with a hole cut in the top. The bin sat on the ground, up against the wall of the house. "There's another string so I can tip the bucket and everything falls pretty much right in. Everyone's lazy, I'm lazy, and now I don't have to run downstairs every time I want to use it. Maybe I could market it, for people who live at the tops of houses, or in apartment buildings, who don't like composting with worms."

"Sure," Helen said, "why not?" She positioned her legs

around the nearly empty water container, pulled up hard on the pump, then pressed down until she had enough of a stream to pump herself a glass of water.

"Maybe I could *patent* it." Sometimes she felt bowled over by Foster's energy, as if the air around him were licked with tiny flames; she was reassured by it, infuriated by it. Sometimes she couldn't believe he had never suspected anything about her family. "More stories in the news this week." He was clearing the table, talking animatedly, self-absorbedly, pale skin over taut muscle jutting beyond the edges of his salmon-colored T-shirt. A fan whirred from the top of the refrigerator. "Finally, finally, it makes front-page news here that forty-eight species become extinct every day."

"Forty-eight?" Helen said softly. "I thought it was only twenty-four."

"No." He stopped with the dishrag in his hand. "That's an old number. I don't know how exactly they figure it out but there are ways. For all I know, it's even more by now." His hand touched her back, between the shoulders. "Hey," he whispered. "I didn't mean to make you so upset." He began to wipe down the counter. Nimble, moving beyond reach: From the start, she'd seen how good he was at dodging around corners and staying out of sight. She had admired his ability to disappear. The old song, the loss-tied-up-with-longing song was rising in her again even as she tried to push it down. Even if you trusted someone enough to reveal yourself to them, how did you know they weren't going to turn around and walk out the door a moment later?

"Foster, listen." Helen gulped down the water. Her mouth felt desperately dry. "I'm on my way to Montreal for a couple of days."

"You're what?"

"I'm going to visit my brother in Montreal."

"You're driving the car all the way to Montreal?" He pulled out a chair, sat down backward on it, and stared at her fiercely. "Why don't you take the train?"

"Because it's last minute. It's cheaper. All right, I know these don't sound like good enough reasons, I know it's not consistent, but I just want to get up and go. Because of the privacy." And the speed and the possibility of self-propulsion, and there were probably a million reasons why she shouldn't feel this way but she did. Surely Foster remembered learning to drive a car, the freedom and independence tied up with soaring down a road on your own?

"How you live counts."

"I know." She hugged her arms around herself. "I know it does, but don't tell me everything you do is always totally consistent, because it's not, and at least I'll admit to being inconsistent."

"It's not like it's somewhere you can't get to any other way."

"Foster, I know."

"We could have gone somewhere together. Did you think of that? Camping. We could have gone up to Algonquin. Maybe I'd like to get away, too." Suddenly his eyes seemed very dark, very deep in their sockets, his arms long and pale lying along the back of the chair.

"We still could," Helen said softly. She crouched down in front of him. "Even if we don't do it this weekend. It's just that I haven't seen my brother in months. I want to get out of here for a couple of days but I also really want to see him."

"OK, fine." Foster stood up.

The eggs and whatever else was in her stomach were starting to make Helen feel slightly ill. What had she told Foster about her brother? She couldn't remember. Before her eyes, Foster began to come apart in pieces that this time she could not put back together, his hollow cheeks, his wet hair combed back from his forehead, his long hands endlessly making small adjustments, tucking his T-shirt back in.

"Elena's thinking of starting a hunger strike," he said. "She did one before, I must have told you, when she was still mainly protesting animals in labs."

"I'm not Elena," Helen shouted. "And I can't do all the things that Elena can do."

"I'm not saying it to make you feel guilty," Foster said. "I was just telling you because I didn't think you knew. She's thinking about doing it outside the corporate headquarters of banks or investors in big development projects that destroy wild habitats and species—not just animals, all species. And I know it's a little different than what we've been doing but maybe it's time to expand our scope. That's what she's been saying. She was talking about building this huge clock or some kind of timer that would count out each time another species disappeared."

"Why does it have to be a hunger strike?"

"Well, that's how Elena is. It's a way of showing that she's serious. And it's a good way of focusing people's attention."

"You don't have to go on a hunger strike to be serious. It's like taking a hostage."

"Helen." He cupped her face between his hands. "I'm not about to take a hostage. Anyway, what's the point of arguing with me about it?"

"Have you heard about the chemical fire in Ohio?" She wanted to slip through his hands and out the door, stick to herself, burst into tears by herself, eliminate risk, escape the possibility of loss.

"I've heard," he said. "I bet there are all these people who keep sticking their heads out the window to check if the wind has changed." How could he possibly sound so nonchalant?

214

"I have to go," Helen whispered. "I don't want to get a ticket. I'm parked up on the sidewalk."

"Just a sec. I want to show you something." He headed down the hall and into his tiny living room. "Are you coming?" A tiny spinning fan was plugged into the light fixture on the ceiling. Another fan turned slowly on the windowsill. He knelt, slipped a tape into the tapedeck, then stretched out languidly on his back on the wooden floor, hands folded under his head. "It's cooler down here," he said gently and grinned. Helen lay down on the varnished floor beside him as a voice began pouring out of the speakers: a smoky, nightclub voice, a wry, sad voice that seemed so incongruous weaving through the dull, mid-morning light. She frowned in puzzlement.

"What is it?"

"You don't recognize it?" He turned toward her in surprise. "Helen, didn't you ever watch *Sesame Street*? It's the frog song, the Kermit the Frog song, it's Lena Horne singing 'It's Not Easy Being Green.' "

"No," she whispered, "I never did."

He looked solemn, wily, too quick to trust. Leaning over her, he traced his finger across the outline of her lips. "Just relax," he whispered. "You can't walk around thinking things are as terrible as all that."

Hot air rushed through the vents and open windows, and everywhere Helen looked she saw traces of Foster and Elena, making their own field of static: a pen, their maps, a note in Foster's writing that said *I'll meet you at 8,* an extra pair of sunglasses Elena had bought one day that Helen was wearing because she had forgotten her own. She drove through endless suburbs, past the industrial towers and the nuclear power plant towering along the gray shore of the lake before the trees began, hills rising and falling like dinosaur backs, the high, gray-white sky scattering oblique light across them. Maybe it was a good thing to get away from Foster for a little while, and from Elena, too. She was feeling too *entangled*. It would do her good to sit down and talk to Paul. And being in motion cheered her, with its sense of escape or arrival, the possibility of going in a straight line from one place and ending up somewhere else. It had been months since she had gone anywhere outside the city. She slipped off her running shoes and grinned. Wriggling her toes, she drove in her bare feet.

When she switched on the radio, a voice said, *In twenty years even the maple tree may be extinct.* She hurriedly turned the radio off again.

Our land, another voice whispered over the rushing of air through the vents, *is like an animal, and if you take away that piece, or even if you just chop all the trees down, it is as if you are cutting off the foot of the animal.*

A car sped past, easily at over 130 kilometers per hour, a blue Mazda with BLAST U on its license plates, and then, hours later, after she had stopped for coffee and a baked potato, as the clouds broke up, fissioning into blue, she passed another car with VIRUS 1 on its plates. Who were the people in these cars? Should she laugh at them, be terrified of them? Where was her constantly metamorphosing father—balanced on the edge of a metal chair, patiently explaining to a young girl why she could not go home again? Walking up an innocuous driveway lined with flowers, zipped into one of those white toxiczone suits that looked like the old balloon-sized astronaut moonsuits, trying to convince some last desperado, a young man, an older woman camped defiantly in an Ohio basement, to come out?

———

A light shone from the front window of Paul's apartment, through the matchstick blinds, although when Helen tried the bell, no one answered. He was probably working late at the architectural firm where he had a job for the summer. From what he'd said over the phone, architects habitually slaved like maniacs. It was only dinnertime. She tried to imagine his face when she told him about David. In the *bar laiterie* on the corner, with its glowing plastic pictures of ice cream sundaes on the wall above the counter, *la galactique, la supernova, la futuristique,* she tried to decipher, from the swirls of ice cream, what the difference was between them.

Outside again, a cool wind began to blow down Duluth Street, carrying the sharp scent of bleach from the laundromat next door to Paul's building, a raft of voices rising over the churning of the machines, something about *une catastrophe écologique.* Leaning against someone else's car, Helen watched the sky gain an aching evening clarity as the sun set behind the tree-covered mountain, blue folding into green, colors growing quietly prismatic. The black lines of the wrought-iron stairs climbing up to front doors slowly sharpened. There weren't stairs like that in Toronto.

She looked across the street: Paul was coming toward her, scooping his hair back from his forehead. But he wasn't looking at her. Beside him walked a young woman in low black heels, sunglasses hiding her eyes. Both of them wore what were probably their work clothes but even so they gave off an air of easy stylishness, the way people in Montreal often seemed to.

Helen had never thought of Paul as looking stylish. This was her brother who wore turtlenecks that bagged at the cuff, whose hair stood on end, her steady but workaholic brother. His body and the young woman's body bumped lightly, unselfconsciously together. For as long as she'd known him, he had never had a girlfriend, or at least she'd never seen him with anyone, never heard him mention anyone. He'd pined after girls in high school, but that was not the same.

Across the street, he took his keys out of his pocket. The young woman leaned toward him, talking vivaciously, the hair that fell forward from the shaved nape of her neck catching red in the light. Paul opened the door and closed it again behind them.

So what now? *I'm like David,* Helen thought. *If you surprise people, then it's easier to find out what they've been hiding.* She picked up her overnight bag and walked a few steps down Hôtel de Ville, shivering in the breeze. Upstairs, Paul's kitchen light flicked on, the shadow of heads, blue light. She headed purposefully back around the corner and rang his bell.

From the top of the hall, he stared at her, before racing down the wooden stairs toward the door. "What are you doing here?" His voice rose, nearly cracking. "I thought it was going to be someone trying to sell me Bibles." He was laughing, hugging her, practically shaking her while she gripped him back, until her bag slid off her shoulder and pulled both their arms down.

"I just decided to come. I know I should have called, but it came over me all of a sudden, I wanted to see you, so I got in the car and drove."

"Is something wrong?"

"Why does something have to be wrong?"

"What if I hadn't been here?"

"I didn't think that far. I guess I assumed you would be, and, you see, you are."

He picked up her bag, started up the stairs. "There's been this terrible chemical fire in Ohio," he said over his shoulder.

He didn't seem nervous. He didn't act as if he was concealing anything from her.

"I know." She wondered if, by the time she reached the top of the stairs, the young woman whom Paul still had not mentioned would have disappeared without a trace.

From the hallway Helen could see her: She was standing in the kitchen, in bare feet, as solid as ever. Her shoes lay on the floor under the table. Holding a glass of water in her hand, she looked inquiringly toward them, her gaze tinged with possessiveness. Another pair of women's shoes—red pumps— were stacked on a metal rack inside the apartment door.

"Helen just drove in from Toronto," Paul said. "This is Helen, my sister. Helen, this is Carla—Carla Blaise." In the background, a voice began the evening news.

Was Carla a new roommate? If she were a roommate surely Paul would have mentioned her.

"Hi," Carla said and held out her hand. Her bare arms were golden brown. Her hands were small and neat, precise in their grip. Her toenails, but not her fingernails, were painted: a row of tiny red half-moons. Around one ankle she wore a chain of minute silver links. "Are you totally exhausted?" she asked. "Do you want something to drink? There's juice or wine or iced coffee or water."

"Just water," Helen said. "Thanks."

"If we eat here," Paul said, "is that OK? I said I'd cook a stir fry and we already bought all the ingredients, but there'll be plenty of food for you, so don't worry."

"Sure," Helen said, "whatever. Maybe we could go out for coffee somewhere later."

If Carla *was* his girlfriend, did she have any idea that Paul had never mentioned her? Not one hint or murmur. Did Barbara or David know? She couldn't believe he'd tell them and not her. And yet Paul was acting now as if there was nothing odd about his behavior, as if he'd made all the explanations he needed to, whistling as he carried her overnight bag down the hall to the front room. His cheeks were a little flushed, but this was the only sign that she might have caught him off guard.

The kitchen itself looked different—still spare but not quite as stark as before. A small TV, emblazoned with the face of a male news anchor, was set on a shelf above the kitchen table. It hadn't been there in January. On the table, a spray of dried rosebuds arched from a glazed vase. And the black and white tiles on the floor—had they been there?

On the TV screen, a figure in a white moonsuit walked with lumpy grace toward them. Helen opened her mouth to speak. *Ici Radio Canada,* said a voice from the antique store under her feet.

"Sorry," Paul said. "I have to watch this." He turned up the sound.

A caravan of cars and trucks traveled slowly before them, from left to right, *stretching now for hundreds of miles.* And what would happen if their father's face suddenly appeared—David Urie, the international relief specialist—talking about evacuation procedures or the way people in manmade disasters suffered the same kinds of nightmares as people in natural disasters, and no, he didn't know when people would be going home again.

"When did you last see Paul?" Carla asked in her slightly raspy voice, a voice that probably a lot of people found appealing. Handing Helen a glass, she sat down on one of the black vinyl chairs, tucking her legs underneath her, glancing every now and again at the TV.

"Seven months ago," Helen said, "just after—"

There was a photograph of Carla taped to the fridge where

Paul's schedule of classes had once been—Carla in a black velvet hat and red lipstick, mugging for the camera—beside a second photo, a picture of Barbara, her hair blown aloft by what Helen knew to be a breeze racing down a Florida beach.

"The launch," Paul said. Why did it make her jump to hear him say it? Of course Carla knew who their mother was. She'd probably known who Paul's mother was when she met him. "Your hair's gotten so much longer." With his hands on the back of Helen's chair, he leaned over her, tilting her toward him. "Seven months longer. It's weird—this whole time—in some ways it's gone so fast."

Carla leaned toward the window and shoved it open, the new, cool breeze funneling in. "All I can say is, thank God we don't live in Ohio."

"And thank God to be released from all that heat." Paul took off his jacket, his skinny blue tie.

"It was like a furnace in Toronto," Helen said dizzily. "I really thought I was going to lose it. That's partly why I came here."

"News is over," Carla said, cupping her chin in her hands, and a hush fell through the air between them as the newscaster announced: *Barbara Urie, 212 days in space and going strong.*

"Chalk up another one," Paul whispered.

Une attaque, whispered the voice underneath them, *dans le Métro.*

"Should we switch to the feed?" Carla asked.

"Sure." Paul nodded. "See how they're doing."

They made it seem so ordinary. It shocked Helen how domestic, how unweighted they made all this seem. They made her feel as if she'd dropped in from another world, raw-edged and awkward, as if she didn't know the customs here or wasn't the right shape.

"What happened to the other television?" she asked. "The big one."

"Oh," Paul said. "It's in the bedroom. I spliced the cable, the cable that's connected to the satellite dish, so now we can get the feed in both rooms."

In front of them, Peter Carter whipped something into the space station's tiny microwave, floating lazily as it spun inside.

The bedroom door was closed.

When the telephone rang, Carla leaped down the hall, waited for the machine to pick up, then answered it after she'd heard the voice. *"Oui, allô?"* she said. "I'm here." With her back to them, she wrapped one leg around the other and began to speak quickly, inaudibly in French.

Now Helen could say something about David, *now,* ask Paul to come out with her *now* for coffee, leave Carla on her own for awhile. She would pull him into the car, drive off with him down some highway, and they would talk in a way they hadn't in months, except she had the peculiar feeling that if she tried anything like this, he would only get angry, as if her whole purpose were to disrupt this life he'd painstakingly created for himself.

"Do you remember the wok?" Paul asked as he set it down on the stove. "It's the wok Tom gave us." He'd insisted on taking it with him when he left for Montreal, determined to follow Tom's precepts about the abandonment of frozen food, although until now Helen had never seen him cook with it. Neither of them had ever shown much inclination to cook.

"Paul," she said. His back was to her. Carla hung up the phone.

"Oh, look." Carla padded back down the hall. "What's Peter eating? Is it a tortilla?" She spoke his name with the familiarity of someone who watched him regularly, even if she'd never met or talked to him.

"It probably *is* a tortilla," Paul said. "They're great in space, you know. They're easy to freeze dry, very easy to store."

What would they do if Foster suddenly materialized in the room or floated slowly past the kitchen window like some new kind of angel, laces dangling from his sneakers, holding a SPECIES SUPREMACY IS DEATH banner in his arms? Perhaps they would be shocked. Perhaps they wouldn't even notice. Helen's heart stretched out toward Foster, this figment of him.

An eggplant lay in front of her on the table, a zucchini, red and yellow peppers. Paul had poured her a glass of wine, and she was getting drunk faster than she wanted to, still dazzled by the receding heat and the shock of arrival. Outside it was growing dark. The room was settling like a nest around her and whatever she had meant to tell Paul was fading, fading, fading. "Do you study architecture, too?" she asked Carla.

"I finished in the spring," Carla said. "I was a year ahead of Paul, and now I'm working for a firm—Paul has a summer job working for a rival firm."

"Not rival," Paul said emphatically, "just different ones. And Carla's a vegetarian, like you."

Carla raised her head. "Paul says you work for an environmental organization."

"Kind of," Helen said, "when I'm not waitressing."

Although the feed was on, they were barely watching it; it hummed and flickered away like a layer in a cocoon. She was the only one who saw Barbara float past them. Maybe the point wasn't to watch it, but to contain the distance between here and the space station, make it feel safe. *What was the point of making it feel safe?*

"Can I do anything?" Helen asked.

"No," Paul said from the stove. "Don't be silly. You drove all that way and you're supposed to be on holiday."

She wanted to ask him if he remembered the time, years ago, when they'd set off after school to go shopping for peanut butter and toilet paper because they couldn't find any in the house, and she'd yelled his name in the middle of the supermarket because he'd disappeared down another aisle and she thought she'd lost him.

"Can we turn off the feed?"

"Why?" He was frowning as he turned around.

"Because I came here to see you. Paul, we can watch the feed anytime. Don't you think having it on all the time makes it seem—I don't know—more like some kind of entertainment?"

"No," he said. Across the table, Carla was staring in front of her, a small smile on her lips. "Helen, that's horrible. Don't you think we owe it to her to watch it?"

Her brain had a certain furious speed on the nights when she didn't sleep, nights when she knew from the start she wasn't going to sleep. Over the years, she had given up trying to fight it. She lay on the sofabed in the front room, where she had always slept in Paul's apartment, although she hadn't bothered to pull out the bed or turn off the light. She'd just taken off her boots and stuffed the pillow and sheets that Paul had given her under her head.

This room looked different, too: The walls had been repainted salmon pink. The sofabed had been draped in canvas. Two drafting tables had been set against opposite walls, black drawing cases leaning against them. The speakers from a miniature stereo system balanced on top of two tiny white columns. A row of videotapes lined the bottom of the bookshelves, each week's episode of Barbara's science show from space, *Frontiers,* scrupulously labeled by Paul. Everything looked so meticulously arranged, so perfectly designed. If she moved, she would probably break something.

At dinner, she had watched how attentive Paul's whole body

was to every move of Carla's, and how Carla folded herself neatly against furniture, her mixture of languor and stability. He did not seem so much flushed now as basking in an interior glow. In the candlelight, she'd asked them what kind of buildings, given the chance, they wanted to build.

"Well, we don't really build buildings," Carla said. "We design them."

"The thing is," Paul said intently, "often the most interesting designs aren't the ones that get built."

"So what's the point?"

"To have a vision."

"A vision?"

"Of a city, or how to use space in new ways, a vision that isn't like anybody else's."

Now their murmuring voices drifted down the hall toward her. Helen closed her eyes and tried counting constellations, then reciting the names of all her classmates in Grade Six. There was no reason why Paul's apartment should be exactly as she remembered it or why she should have any monopoly on change. Why should it shock her that he also seemed to have a secret life? In a way she deserved the surprise, like a pendulum she'd set in motion that, with exquisite neatness, came swinging back.

But all these months she'd imagined the two of them, alone in their separate apartments in different cities, turning the feed on now and again, going into studios for their live sessions, bound together by this experience, since it was what remained of their family life after all. He'd violated this privacy. She'd imagined it all wrong.

Was Paul drawn to Carla partly because she seemed so matter-of-fact about his family? Would Carla deny the allure, the small thrill that hovered like an electromagnetic field around Paul?

Was she jealous of them? Were they watching the space station feed in bed, even now, watching it like a late-night movie, astronauts flickering just beyond their feet as they rolled slowly toward each other, pushing back the covers, mouths on each other's bodies, forgetting to turn it off? Stop, that was enough. She really had to stop.

A door opened. Footsteps padded toward the bathroom, down the hall where, in the darkness, lay the telephone. She wanted to call Foster, just to hear his voice, ask him simple, urgent questions: *How are you? What are you doing right now? Is it still so hot?* Five hundred kilometers away and he came in strongly, a clear signal, his dry, persistent voice, his constantly moving hands, and now, of course when she was nowhere near him, she longed for him to walk into the room. She wanted to kiss him slowly and luxuriantly. The smell of his antiperspirant clung to her T-shirt. Desire, stretched over distance, seemed stronger than ever.

Maybe this was what her father had begun to feel, late at night in Guatemala City or in Mexico, after the bitterness and anger had cleared—because even if he denied it, she was sure there had been anger. Before that, he could have been involved with someone else, for a while or just a fling, both her parents could have been: another relief worker, astronaut, physicist, a Mexican actress with two children of her own. She had needed to imagine this, had created for herself other people for her parents to be involved with, just as she had sometimes wondered if, in his understated way, Tom Huang had been in love with her mother for years, and this was why he'd come to live with them. In all this time apart, surely there had been affairs, complicated or uncomplicated passions, distinct from or caught up in her parents' passion for their work. Even if both Barbara and David refused to talk about them, how could there not have been?

And yet at some point David must have begun thinking about Barbara again, imagining her, just a point in the sky at the beginning, slowly gaining shape, becoming a tiny human figure that hovered in the dark. Then, by himself in the dark at first, he must have started talking to her, trying to explain himself. Perhaps the sky had introduced a new element of desire between them, although Barbara had probably always felt this keenness, longing pulled tight between one place and another, like a humming string; this was why she argued that going away didn't mean she was abandoning any of them. The distance would hold them together. In orbit. It allowed them to dream. As long as they all felt the same pull and tug.

Helen stood up abruptly. Cool air was pouring in the window now, smelling of bagels, a smell that she knew blew down from the streets north of Paul's apartment, from the bagel stores where the back walls were filled with enormous ovens and men shunted rows of bagels on long paddles into the raw, transforming heat of the fire, then pulled them out again.

She waited a moment before slipping into the darkened hall. A blue stream of light issued from Paul's bedroom, through the door that had been left slightly ajar. No voices. She made it silently past the door, searching for the orange crate where the phone used to be, before she turned.

Blue light spread across their bodies on the futon. Carla lay curled in a neat fetal ball under the sheet, Paul like a spoon against her, one arm flung around her chest. And all around the bed were buildings, model buildings, architectural models, bathed in the light of the blank TV screen that glowed on the floor behind them. They weren't ordinary buildings: a spiral-shaped tower that curved upwards like shell; one that reached toward the ceiling like a tree or a candelabra; another that climbed like stairs; buildings that rose in multiple facets, sharp angles, not the usual four walls; buildings linked by archways, causeways, gyre wires; houses, more houses; a house shaped like a boat; a house like a snail shell; an oval shape that rose in Lucite tiers, like some kind of swimming pool.

Helen breathed out softly. The shadows of the buildings fell hugely across the bed and over the ceiling. They formed a circle around the wall, filled shelves and dressing tables. They were mad, beautiful, frightening. How long had he been working on them? When Paul looked to the future, he dreamed a city, a city full of houses, distorted houses, transformed houses, his designs like a new map for the world. How could she blame him for longing to build himself a home?

As if in a dream, she watched Paul's eyes open, watched the methodical way he slipped on his Japanese dressing gown before stepping out of bed and into the hall, pulling the door shut tightly behind him. "What are you doing? What do you think you're doing?" He was whispering, shaking her shoulders with a violence that shocked and did not shock her, because of course there was no way she could entirely justify what she'd been doing.

"Let me go. I'm sorry. I got up to make a phone call. I saw the buildings."

He dropped his hands. "Helen, you were spying on us." She could feel his anger, even though he refused to raise his voice, even though she could barely see his face.

"Why does everyone in this family keep hiding things?"

"You're one to talk," he said. "You can't accuse me of anything."

"Tell me about the model buildings." She was on the verge of tears. Her chin was shaking. "Paul, please—tell me. What are they for? Did you build them yourself? With Carla? We're so much like them, you know. We're all these big, crazy dreamers."

"It's none of your business."

"We don't talk about things. All of us. We keep refusing to talk about things."

"Helen, why should I—"

"What about Carla? You've never said a word about her, and all right I barged in on you but you still haven't told me a thing. Are you just waiting for me to leave so you won't *have* to tell me?"

She heard the faint quaver in his breath. "I just needed a little more time," he said.

"Can we go into the front room? Can we go somewhere we won't disturb her?"

For a moment she thought he wouldn't follow her, but he did. He looked at her still-folded sheet and pillow and sat down on the edge of the sofa with his hands clasped between his knees. "We just wanted a little privacy," he said softly. "I wanted to give things a chance to see what would happen without feeling any more pressure about anything."

"Didn't Carla mind?"

"We made a decision. We both knew it wasn't an entirely ordinary situation. We met in the winter. Not that long after the launch. We met in the architecture school studio. I mean, sometimes you just know right away, it's very clear. It's like you make a choice and you absolutely know it's right. Well, that's what it was like, but I wanted—I wanted to make sure. All right, I liked it that no one knew. And then Carla moved in maybe two months ago."

"Paul?" He looked up. "What did you say about the launch?"

"About the launch?"

"What did you say to Carla about where we were?"

"I told her what really happened. Helen, what else could I do? I needed to talk to someone, someone *not* my family—not confess but, I don't know, confide in someone."

How could she admit to him how much this hurt, perhaps more than anything else? She'd trusted him. She'd stuck to her word in this and it didn't seem to have gotten her anywhere.

"Dad came back."

"What?"

"David—Dad—came back."

"Came back where?"

"He came back to Toronto. He was there just for a day, and then he left again."

"When?"

"Two days ago." His whole face shone, creased, pale and covered in a sheen of sweat. The light flickered, but it was just the refrigerator motor surging quietly in the kitchen. "Paul, that's why I came," she whispered. "I came here to tell you."

"Where did he go?"

"He's in Ohio. Lagoon, Ohio. He was going to stay longer, he was going to come here and visit you, but then he got called away to help with all those people who've been evacuated, who are losing their homes after that toxic fire, because that's what he seems to be doing now—not just dealing with the earth moving but moving people. And when they called, of course he went. Because they needed him."

"Why didn't you call me when he was there?"

"He was going to surprise you. Paul, that's what he wanted. He just appeared on my doorstep. I opened my door and there he was—nothing, no warning."

"And then?"

"And then we spent the day together and then he called me in the middle of the night to tell me he was leaving again."

"How can he go on doing this?"

"He said he'll come back. He said he'll call from Ohio."

"It's like asymptotes."

"Like what?"

"Like asymptotes. It's like these waves on a graph and they keep getting closer and closer as they run toward infinity but they never touch. That's what it feels like."

"Paul," she said softly. "He'll come back." She'd always thought of Paul as the reasonable one, the less volatile one. He was able to perform some inner act of will, and this was the secret of his ability to reassure himself. She'd always trusted him to be like this: dependable, the one who believed in things being fair. In his eyes, the world was malleable but not about to disappear; people came back.

"Maybe I should fly to Ohio." He kept squeezing and squeezing his hands. "No, why should I? It's toxic in Ohio. Helen, what did he look like?"

"A lot thinner. His hair's nearly all gone on top, and it's grayer. He's so thin because he had amoebic dysentery, but he says he's fine now—although he *was* hospitalized. He's very tanned and weathered, kind of the same, more intense. There's less of him, but he's more concentrated." For an instant, she heard an echo of her mother in her own voice— saw some eerie ghost of Barbara in the fixity of Paul's expression.

"So maybe he'll come back," Paul said.

"It's nothing I did," she whispered. "Paul, you mustn't blame me. He said he didn't want to call us before he appeared because he didn't know how we'd react. And it was great to see him—but then he left. It felt like the first time all over again. So I just got in the car and drove here. All right, that's not all of it. I've been involved with someone, one of the people I work with, one of the activists—his name's Foster. And I don't think it's working out. I didn't tell him—he doesn't even know who my mother is."

"Helen!" She'd shocked him again; she'd probably go on shocking him.

"All right, it's a mess," she said. "Paul, what should I do? It's such a mess."

"I can't tell you what to do."

"Do you wonder—do you lie there sometimes and wonder how long she can possibly stay up there?"

"Until she breaks the record."

"Does that matter?"

"No," he shouted. "Yes. Because that's what she's worked so hard for. Helen, don't you care?" He stood up facing her.

"I thought you'd tell me to trust him—to believe he'll come back."

"How can I tell you that?" Now he was backing away from her. When he got to the door, he bolted through it, and she couldn't hear if he'd whispered anything else, like goodnight. She imagined him sprinting down the stretch of hallway to his bedroom, into that nest of blue light, into his hypnotic model city, plunging toward Carla, wrapping his arms and legs around her so that she would stay and stay and stay.

There was nothing to pack.

Go to sleep, he'd say to her. *Stop running and go to sleep.*

If he tried to stop her, she'd tell him to leave her alone, she could look after herself. She could not possibly stop now.

She switched off the desolate light. In the dark, she made it to the front door, turned the lock with one furry click, and opened the door.

13

These are the gaps, the moments I've tried not to remember.

In the living room, with the door shut, my mother was watching tapes of her science television show for children, on a monitor and machine that she'd brought home from work. The ratings were down. There was talk of pulling it off the air. Under the door came the sound of her televised voice, then music: an hour, two hours. I checked the kitchen clock. Something was thawing in the sink. Paul had stayed for dinner at a friend's house. Until I couldn't stand it anymore.

When I opened the door, she looked up with a start from a corner of the sofa, an old cardigan pulled around her hunched shoulders.

On the screen, in the white lab coat that she hated, smiling under her carefully hairsprayed hair, she opened the door at the back of her TV lab. Beyond it lay an animated vista of deep space: clouds of nebulae, the whirl of spiral galaxies. I'd always liked that effect. On a lab stool sat her scientist companion, played by a red-haired child actor whom I could not stand. He waved goodbye to her as she stepped briskly through the door.

"If I'm going to fail," she said from the sofa in a small, disconsolate voice, "I at least want to know why."

"Helen." I sat bolt upright in bed. Paul shone faintly in the darkened hallway. "Someone's in the garden."

"OK," I said, "I'm coming." I slipped past the chair where all my clothes lay haphazardly, too surprised and in a peculiar way excited to be frightened. On the walls, the photos I had cut out of *National Geographic* and other magazines formed rows of dark and shiny windows. We made our way quietly down the hall to Paul's bedroom at the back of the house. He was shivering a little, although it wasn't cold, a trace of summer warmth lingering even in the night air. His walls were covered with drawings. The moon globe no longer hung in his window but sat high on a shelf on top of his desk. Side by side in the dark, we peered into the garden, careful not to call attention to ourselves.

A man was standing down below, lit blue by the pool floodlights, holding a hammer. There was no lunar landing module—or at least its walls were no longer standing, only its tin-foil-covered legs and floor; the walls leaned against them. I had noticed, maybe a day, maybe two days before, that one of the walls had come loose and fallen, its tin foil tearing a little in the breeze, but I had glimpsed it casually, hadn't done anything or said anything about it. We hadn't actually played in the module all summer; we had ridden our bikes to the park and played baseball or hung out with the kids there instead. Sometimes my mother still drank her morning coffee on the module steps. For over three summers, the module had stood in our garden, like something that had grown there, like some kind of extra limb or wing of our house, covered in a tent of plastic in the winter, uncovered like the pool in the spring, something that by now it was possible both to ignore and take for granted. Even if we outgrew it, I had assumed, I realized suddenly, that it would always be there.

"Did you ask them?" my mother's voice said. She was

standing just below the back porch with her hands on her hips, right at the edge of my vision, half lost in shadow.

"Barbara, it's broken," my father said. The sleeves of his shirt were rolled up above his elbows. The hammer quivered in his hand. The dark air and choppy, mottled light from the pool made him look stretched, his gestures elongated and unfamiliar. Beyond him, beyond the trees at the edge of the garden, shone a few lights in other houses. "They don't even play in it anymore." Through the screen in Paul's window, their voices rose toward us.

"You don't need to do it now."

"Well, when? I've been working a crazy schedule the last few weeks, this is about the only free time I have, and I honestly didn't think you wanted to be the one to take it down."

"In the dark?"

"Better now, don't you think, than to have it fall down."

"I'll fix it."

"Barbara, don't be crazy, it's structurally unstable. Look at it." When he pushed the module with one hand, it swayed: an eerie rushing sound.

"Are you doing it like this to hurt me?" She was walking slowly toward him around the border of the pool. "Are you doing it because you're jealous, because somehow by getting into the communications business I've been encroaching on your territory, in spite of whatever we've said about not doing that to each other?"

"I'm taking it down because it's broken," he shouted, "because it seemed better to take it down than have it fall down. Why do you have to start imputing motives to me? It can't stand here forever. It isn't a real lunar landing module. Would it be better to wake up one day and find a pile of wood and tin foil lying on the lawn?" He wiped one hand over his mouth.

"Maybe you can't always have things your way. Maybe that's something you'll have to learn. So the TV show didn't work out, Barbara, so what? You're a successful research scientist. I'm sorry you're exhausted, but there are times when I need a little recognition that I'm working a crazy schedule, too. I have my own job. I worked on those scripts with you for months. And if you want to do something for our children, then for heaven's sake spend time with them. I am not trying to sabotage you."

He took a step onto the tiles just as she lunged at him—to embrace him, hit him, in the tangled darkness it was impossible to tell, only that she'd moved with swift, precise violence and that their bodies heaved together, tottering, arms around each other, knocked off balance. Still struggling, holding onto each other, the hammer still clutched in my father's hand, they toppled toward the pool. Their faces, lit from below, were pale blue with horror. Their bodies hung in silhouette, the whole world grown utterly silent around us, suspended in the instant before the water splashed and swallowed them. The impact pulled them apart. The hammer sank gently to the bottom. They gasped as they surfaced, a hollow, unknowable sound, and swam separately toward the edges of the pool. The tiny hairs all over my skin stood slowly on end. In the filters, water slopped and coughed. Grasping the side of the pool, my mother pulled herself out sleekly, in one long motion, her clothes streaming water; then she turned and held out her hand to my father. As he clambered onto the tiles, she knelt beside him, pushing the wet hair back from his face and carefully removing his glasses. His hands were on her shoulders. She gave another sound—a gasp, a cry. "We weren't going to compete with each other," she said.

"I know." He tilted his head up toward the sky, then lowered it. Was he crying? She pressed her lips to his as they rolled back suddenly, soundlessly against the tiles.

Beside me, Paul jerked away from the window, crawling maniacally across his sheets back into bed. He lay there, staring at the ceiling, his hands flattened at his sides, like an animal trying to stay out of sight by remaining as still as possible. "Please stay with me," he whispered in a small, desolate voice, as if he'd simply knocked on my door in the middle of a thunderstorm, lightning raging all around us.

14

1. See under *Florida.* 2. If Florida doesn't work, try Toronto.

The bedroom was filled with white, bright light. Helen had no idea how long she'd slept or when she'd fallen asleep or even when she'd climbed into bed. Sitting up, she felt sharp and clear, as if certain difficulties had clarified themselves, as if while she'd slept her edges had been newly defined. Perhaps the air just seemed so bright because she'd finally been able to sleep and wake up hours later, like any normal person.

She remembered arriving back from Montreal in the very early morning and watching the light rise through the back window, above the trees and houses, wondering how she was going to explain to Foster and her mother that there were things she hadn't told them, parts of the story they knew nothing about. It was fine to feel ready to do this, but how did you begin? She remembered lying down on the couch and closing her eyes; nothing happened. The light flattened and grew gray. Aching with exhaustion, she had reconnected the phone and retrieved the goldfish from down the hall, watched them swimming silkily. Later, she had sat on the couch with her knees hugging her chest, staring into the dark: She imagined a young girl walking hand in hand with her mother along a strip of sand beside a lake, some deep and simple pleasure. And after that, thank God, she must have slept.

The linoleum tiles in the kitchen were cool under her feet. She opened the blinds on all the windows. Her muscles felt loose and invigorated. Sipping from a glass of filtered water, she crouched down and rewound the messages on the machine, voices she must have slept through. In the bedroom doorway, the fan still turned, squeaking slightly. *Hi,* Paul's voice said softly. *I'm sorry everything was such a mess. I just wanted to make sure you got back all right. Call me.* David had called, which was some reassurance, a small sign that he hadn't disappeared again for good into the oblivion of rescue missions. Foster. Someone from the restaurant. Foster again: *Are you back? I can't remember when you're coming back. Call me as soon as you can. It's important.* Important how, Helen wondered, what was important? She ripped the bent corner off a paperback book in distraction. Should she call him now? The light shining through the window seemed fiercer, nearly electric. The phone rang and she stared at it, then grabbed it.

"Hi," Foster said, as insistently as ever. "You're there. You're back." He was nearly shouting.

"I was here," Helen said. "I've been asleep. No, wait. I went to Montreal but I got back early, and then I couldn't fall asleep. I'm kind of an insomniac sometimes, I've told you. I just woke up. What day is it?"

"What day? It's Saturday."

Which meant she must have slept pretty much all Friday, and all Friday night: She'd skipped a day. "I'm glad I went," she said. "I really am. It was a little weird, but OK, and now I'm glad to be back."

"Have you drunk anything yet?"

"Have I what?" She already felt like Sleeping Beauty, as if she'd slept far longer than she should have done, and now as

239

if she'd stumbled into some other fairy tale: Drunk what, some kind of potion? "I'm drinking a glass of water."

"What kind of water?"

What kind? Now that she'd actually plugged in the phone again, it seemed ridiculous to be playing what sounded like a game of broken telephone. "Filtered water," she said calmly. "You know I started to filter my water."

"But tap water," Foster said. "Helen, there's been a spill." She saw water pouring out of a row of overturned glasses on a table, a neat, domestic image, even though she knew at once that this was not what Foster meant, hearing the note of terrible consternation in his voice. "On Thursday, there was a spill from a tanker in the lake, a chemical spill, a lot of benzene, other stuff. There was a fire on board and the tanker started to sink. They managed to tow it to safety but not before the spill—right out in the middle, right near our water intake pipes. And not only that, but the wind's been perfect, the worst—from the south, blowing the stuff this way."

She set her glass of water gingerly on the floor, as if even through glass it could contaminate her—but this was old water, water she had poured through the filter before she'd gone to Montreal. Only now there was almost no more of this water left.

"You're saying no one's supposed to drink the water." She felt as if she were stretching and stretching, wider awake than ever.

"Well, no," Foster said. "I mean, that's what I might say, but the official word is that it's basically OK, they're checking the water stringently at the filtration plants, and it's maybe a little less safe, but it's still within acceptable limits. Of course you can always change the acceptable limits, can't you? You can't just suddenly say to a whole city, sorry, don't use the water. I mean, finding a new garbage dump is bad enough, but you can't just go and scout out a whole new body of water."

"So what does it mean?"

"Well, you can't buy any bottled water anywhere, for a start, or much else to drink, for that matter. I went down to the lake yesterday, out in the west end. You can't really see anything, just the usual, a few dead gulls. And you can't do much to contain it, because it's not just on the surface."

"But can you shower in it? Have you showered in it? Did you brush your teeth in it?" She knew this wasn't the whole issue, but these were the things she thought of first; the instinctive, self-preserving urge kicked in, even if it seemed hopelessly petty to be more desperate for a shower than anything else.

"I took a quick shower in it."

"I'm drinking water I poured through the filter last week, but that's it."

"We're having a rally at one at City Hall."

"Who's we?"

"United Species," he said. "And also the Green Brigade people, but mostly us. It's easy to think we're the only species affected by all this, but we're not. We had an organizational meeting on Thursday night. You missed all that. Anyway, it's two hours from now. Bring some rubber boots and a padlock."

"A padlock?"

"A lock. You know, a heavy-duty lock, or use your bike lock but then you'll have to throw away the key. I was getting worried about you. I figured you'd have heard about this on the news or something, only I had these horrible visions of you sprawled on the floor after drinking all this toxic water. I know. It sounds crazy, but there you are. It's probably easiest if you just meet me down there."

"If you hadn't called," Helen said softly, "I wouldn't have known a thing, do you realize that? I'll be there. I'll see you."

"Right," Foster said, "then I'll see you."

As soon as she got off the phone, she wondered why she hadn't asked him directly what they were going to do with the boots and locks. Maybe because on some level she didn't really want to know. Because the locks still made her think nervously of hostages. Maybe because she felt miffed and also guilty that she'd slept through all the preparation. She'd slept through a day, but just one day, and all this had happened.

It wasn't just speed but the speed of disasters that threw her, small ones, big ones, local, global; at a certain point what difference did the scale of disaster make? They kept accumulating, coming faster and closer together until one day they were all going to start erupting simultaneously, across all borders; even buried disasters, things hidden underground, would come leaking, spewing out of the past. A hair had already fallen into the glass of water sitting on the floor in front of her. Four days ago, when she'd left for Montreal, everyone had been worried about the air, about a cloud of detritus speeding across the lake from the fire in Ohio. And now the water, an indigenous disaster; of course disasters could happen here.

Would her father come racing back from Ohio, hearing word of trouble in Toronto, the one sure thing that would bring him back? But how, if the speed of disasters kept increasing, could he ever keep up? You could not keep bolting day after day from one place to another. Perhaps David would only come if people were forced to leave their homes, but in a situation like this there was no way to evacuate a city, no way to move millions of people to a brand new source of water. You could build your own home and even that would not protect you.

She was thirsty. Her mouth tasted horrible. She could drink

the rest of the water in the glass slowly, savoring it sip by sip, or swallow it all in one fast gulp—either way it wouldn't last long. Did Paul know? Did it make him glad to be living 500 kilometers away in Montreal? Pulling herself to her feet, she made her way into the kitchen and poured another glass of water straight from the tap, into a different kind of glass this time so that she wouldn't confuse the two. She set the glasses side by side on the table. Tiny air bubbles rose to the surface in the second glass, but other than that the water looked the same, crystalline, smelling faintly of chlorine.

But maybe right now it wasn't that serious; maybe dead gulls didn't make it that serious. There had been dead things and chemical spills before. In their aquarium at the back of the table, Clark Kent and Lois Lane swam obliviously back and forth. She had called them that as a joke, because of something Barbara had once said, that Clark Kent and Superman were invented by a Canadian, not an American. Sometimes she had been driven crazy by all the bits of reclaimed history that Barbara had insisted on passing on to them. *If I were Clark Kent, I'd strip off my clothes and find a second, impermeable skin underneath, I'd zap the tanker, tie it in a knot, tie up all the industrial drain pipes, the sewer overflow pipes, zap the intake pipes, the filtration plants, the lake, Pow, Zoom. It would be so easy.*

She felt as if she had entered the future without warning; she was saturated with it. Dipping her finger into the second glass of water, she licked it, tasting skin but no strange tang, then spat in sudden fear into the sink. Of course the water wouldn't have to taste any different. All David's long-ago jokes about science experiments in the home seemed eerily ironic, now that they had come to this. Her body, like everyone else's body, was going to be a test ground for the future whether she wanted it to be or not. For an instant, just an instant, Helen held a shiny picture in her head: She and Foster were driving as fast as they could in the station wagon toward Algonquin Park, toward lakes and trees (after all, he'd said he wanted to get away)—but this image had no substance either. He was not going to be interested in escape. And what about Elena's plan to start another hunger strike? It seemed crazy, because surely their bodies were being subject to enough already. Above all Helen hated the thought of someone starting another countdown, another feat that depended on *how long*.

The biggest experiment we're doing up here these days is on our own bodies, Barbara had said jokingly a few weeks before. She was exercising as she talked, walking the treadmill, sweat gathering in globules on her arms instead of running in rivulets. More and more, Helen would see the astronauts exercising as they worked, up to five or six hours a day, to counter calcium loss and muscle atrophy. The hydroponic vine in the corner of the space station exercise area had bloomed, as if, even in space, seasons were passing; now orange pumpkins floated from it, undulating among the leaves, weightless and perfectly round. The astronauts grew pumpkins because they produced oxygen. Of course she worried about her mother's body, her lean, athletic mother's body, about radiation exposure as well as deteriorating muscles and brittle bones, but these days she was growing just as worried about her own body. *What,* she wanted to shout, *is going to happen to all our bodies down here?*

She'd better hurry if she didn't want to be late. She fed the goldfish, looking thoughtfully at their water. At least there was an old, wizened orange in the fridge that she could eat. She closed her eyes and drained the first glass. There. Gone for good. In the bathroom, she stripped off her T-shirt and underwear and dove under the new water, as hot and steamy as the old water, dove out again as quickly as she could. As far as she knew she didn't have any rubber boots. Feverishly she toweled herself dry, muscles tingling, edgy with the sense of danger but welcoming the need to hurl herself into it, because there wasn't any other choice left. Gulping down the sections of orange, riffling through the mail stacked on the kitchen table, she found a new postcard from Sam, another photo of Ayres Rock in Australia, glowing red. *Don't worry,* he said, *will be here for months yet.* Perhaps the aboriginal man had a lot to explain about where he had walked from. Perhaps it was taking a long time to describe to the man what kind of world would come zooming toward him if he kept walking. Perhaps Sam had decided to set out on his own trek.

The first thing Helen noticed, biking east along Queen Street, were the posters. They were bright yellow. She was pedaling as fast as she could. She caught the words UNITED SPECIES in large letters. Tacked to hydro poles and telephone poles, they stretched like a trail ahead of her. There had to be a number of people involved if the postering had been this extensive on two days' notice. The sun slipped in and out of clouds. The street was crammed with Saturday shoppers, shopping carts, strollers, straining children, bulging plastic bags. LIMIT OF ONE 2L BOTTLE WATER PER CUSTOMER! proclaimed a sign in a supermarket window, the first real sign that everything was not as usual. The jostling people looked the same. Maybe they clustered together, shoulders hunched, talking more animatedly than they ordinarily did, but no one seemed hysterical. The spicy smell of roti fillings poured as always out of a roti shop. But when Helen searched for the outlines of bottles in people's shopping bags, she found them, definitely more than usual.

A man leaned precipitously against a streetlamp, clutching a bottle of undisclosed liquid in a paper bag. ONLY CHEMICALLY TESTED SPRING WATER read a sign in a restaurant window. GATORADE, THE ULTIMATE THIRSTQUENCHER, was on sale in a cornerstore. SPILL SPREADS BUT DILUTES bulged a newspaper headline. In the distance, like a blue moon, a tiny crescent at the end of one street, hung the lake. Even rain would be no consolation, because who in their right mind was going to tilt their head to the sky and drink those cool, acidic drops? Across the street, starlings quietly pecked at the grass around a sign that said KEEP OFF, PESTICIDE IN USE. Layers of pipes and cables streamed by underneath her, the whole precarious, invisible web that held each building, each house suspended in the air. All at once, with the wild, swift love reserved for things that could disappear, she wanted to embrace the whole messy vision in front of her, as if her own fierceness had the power to make this place as real as possible. She loved the long, low stretch of the street, the gray, wobbly haze over the peaks of office towers on the horizon, even the sewage, the TV programs, the toxic water rushing by under her feet.

In a hardware store, she grabbed a heavy combination lock, paid for it, and dropped it into her knapsack. Maybe they were going to parade into the lake, rescue dying gulls, storm a water-treatment plant. There was a piece of new graffiti scrawled over the railway bridge: DRINK CANADA DRY AND DIE, it said. She was thirsty again because of the heat and the exhaust from the cars still jamming the streets, partly because a glass of water now had the allure of something nearly unattainable. A lone bottle of Coke in a convenience store window shone like a beacon.

Glancing down between parked cars, Helen saw an arrow painted on the sidewalk, canary yellow like the posters. There was still a trail of posters. Another arrow. How had they managed to do this? How could she have missed all this? A man with a camcorder videoed his way down the street, past the arrows, filmed the handwritten sign in a coffee shop window that said, NO WATER IN OUR COFFEE. She was traveling as fast as she could, speeding into whatever future this was, craving wings. Her heart kept beating, harder and harder, as if trying to make itself visible.

More arrows, and not just arrows now: the painted outline of the lake, the skeleton of a fish, a bird, a human figure, a glass with what had to be a skull and crossbones inside it. Low over the handlebars, Helen sailed over sewage grates, all the way across wide University Avenue on a yellow light. She locked her bike and ran the last stretch, toward the huge square and the white lunar glow of the City Hall's tall, curving walls, past the outer ring of tourists clutching cameras as if the cameras were their only eyes. Then she stopped in astonishment, staring at all the people.

"Here," Foster said, "I brought you something to drink." He swung his arm around Helen's shoulder, and released it. She bent over double, hands on her knees, trying to catch her breath. Her face felt crimson. She took a sip of warm and fruity-tasting water from the bottle that Foster handed to her, grinned, and handed it back. Trust, she thought with a small shiver, total trust. She could be drinking anything.

"Who did all the arrows?" she gasped.

"We did," Foster said. "I organized it. We went out in groups last night."

"What kind of paint?"

"Totally safe." He smiled. "Safer than the stuff we used on the slaughterhouses. Water soluble, chalk-based." He swigged a little water, too, then slipped the bottle back into his knapsack and handed her a tube of sun screen. "Not to tan," he said dryly, when Helen looked surprised, "just to be safe." He smelled of coconut. Through her sunglasses, his dark hair, pulled back in a ponytail, was flecked with red. He wore the same red hightop sneakers as always, and a black-on-white

United Species T-shirt that she had never seen before, with a logo like a galactic spiral made up of different species, ending with a crawling human baby. One more thing that must have happened while she slept. He seemed excited, taut and ready for action, as if, for the moment anyway, the event counted for more than the disaster.

"I missed you," Helen said. But when she looked again, Foster was gone, like lightning, leaving just that coconut scent, the trace of his voice in the air, saying emphatically, *I'll be back.*

There was no stage. A huge white banner with UNITED SPECIES written across it stretched across the open area where a sound system had been set up, big speakers on each side. Foster was swiveling a microphone into position and testing it. Helen didn't know how many people she'd expected there to be—not this many. It was not a huge crowd, but large enough, not on the same scale as the crowd at her mother's six-month celebration, but still. There were thin people in stretchy black outfits, people in bright, kaleidoscopic clothes carrying their own cardboard banners with slogans like WE WANT OUR ECOSYSTEM BACK, a group of teenagers with brilliant dyed-green hair bouncing up and down like pogo sticks. Behind the crowd of people rose the tops of the three cement arches that looped over the long rectangular pool. In winter, the pool became a skating rink. Now a cascade of water soared upward from the fountain at one end.

"Here," Elena's voice said suddenly, "you need a T-shirt."

"Your hair," Helen exclaimed, because Elena had cut her hair, which made her, in the first split-second, unrecognizable.

"I needed a psychological change," was all Elena said. She gave a wry twist of her lips, then slipped into focus, a new Elena with short black hair that made the smooth line of her pale-brown cheekbones and her high forehead seem more spare and striking than before. She wore a T-shirt, too, but with a jacket and short black skirt that gave her a newly professional air. She looked like she meant business: tough and graceful; the dark curve of her lips. *Why shouldn't I wear lipstick?* she'd said once, almost belligerently, as if someone had been hassling her about it. *As long as it isn't tested on animals and doesn't contain any animal products.*

"Are you going to speak?" Helen asked. She pulled the T-shirt that Elena had handed her over her own sweat-covered T-shirt, which seemed the best she could do under the circumstances.

Elena nodded.

"Are you still planning to start a hunger strike?"

"Not today," Elena said. "Why?"

"Foster mentioned something about it. OK, it worried me. The whole idea of it worries me. I know you've done it before, but I just don't like to think of you doing that to yourself. It doesn't seem necessary. I mean, if you need attention, there are other ways to get people's attention."

"Of course there are." Elena sounded conspiratorial and serenely sure. "Helen, don't worry. Nothing like that's going to happen today." And yet, on second glance, Elena also looked tired. There were dark rings under her eyes, a stark edge of exhaustion, as if she had been working too hard, up for too many late nights.

Helen searched for Raj, the tall young man who had leaned quietly in the corner at meetings, but couldn't find him. There was Julie, though, the woman who had worked for the Humane Society and organized the billboard projects, talking to a man and a woman wearing Green Brigade T-shirts, looking casual and big-boned in contrast to Elena. Waving her arms directorially, Julie was in jeans, a shoestring holding back her hair. Behind her curved the low, mushroom-shaped pod at the center of the City Hall: It looked incongruously like a space capsule. There were people with armbands, carrying buckets, to gather money presumably; people selling buttons. Everything seemed so *organized*.

"Did you bring boots?" Elena asked.

"No," Helen said carefully. "I don't have any."

"You could probably do it without them."

"Do what exactly?"

"Foster didn't tell you? I was sure Foster had told you." She pressed her lips to Helen's ear. "We're going to stand in the pool and chain ourselves to the arches. We'll be totally visible and not in anyone's way. We're just going to let everyone know that every species that lives around here, including us, needs a lake not a glorified sewer system."

"That's where the locks come in."

"Yes," Elena whispered. "Isn't this exactly the kind of action you wanted?" Her eyes shone intimately, bright and close. "You look a little nervous. Helen, really, if you're nervous, don't do it. Don't do it just because Foster's doing it, or I'm doing it. I guess we assumed you would, so Raj is expecting you to be with the rest of us. He's over at the pool. He's in charge of that part. But if you don't feel comfortable about it, then don't. You've still got a few minutes to decide." Had they found her out at last? Were they proposing this to her as a test? They wanted to be as visible as possible. This was completely different from the slaughterhouse attacks. Taking a folded piece of paper out of her pocket, Elena scanned it, whispering under her breath, until Julie beckoned and Elena hurried away. Helen stayed where she was, eyeing the gathering people and the sun as it skimmed out of the clouds again, brightly, dangerously.

"Elena quit her job," Foster whispered. He had crouched down beside Helen for a moment. Elena stood at the microphone, pushing up her sleeves, speaking in a sure, clear voice. "She quit her other job. She figured if she was going to go public with this, then she couldn't also be a spokesperson for alternative lab procedures. Anyway, they wouldn't have let her. So she wants to find a way to make United Species a full-time thing, but that means we'll have to raise money. She's not just being an opportunist. You know she's not like that. She thinks we can really have an impact. It *is* a good name. I hope you like the T-shirts."

"I do," Helen said. Elena's transforming, she thought. Her enlarged, passionate voice poured out of the loudspeakers, a voice that held people's attention, that for an instant made Helen think of Barbara's voice. *We live in the middle of the most toxic ecosystem in North America.* Strands of black hair flickered across Elena's forehead.

People cheered—and probably some of them were discussing what they had eaten or were going to eat for lunch, but some of them were definitely cheering. The green-haired teenagers jumped up and down. Did people listen to her because she was beautiful? No, not just that. There was one TV camera, Helen could see it out of the corner of her eye, on the far side of the open area, a Live Eye crew. She felt dizzy. She was trying to think about consequences, about what was likely to happen if she went through with this—if, like Elena, she went public. *We're being held hostage,* Elena said. *That's what it feels like. We're being poisoned along with every other species around.*

"Foster, listen," Helen whispered, "if we're arrested—"

"We're charged with mischief. It's not a serious offense. It's happened to me before." He seemed foreign and far away, suddenly receding, wiry and feline and too absorbed in what he was doing to notice anything else. He had no idea what she was trying to say to him. He grinned and whispered in her ear, so loudly that he made Helen jump. "It's working."

We're fighting for change, Elena shouted, *change so fundamental that we're going to transform the face of the Earth.*

The last time Helen had been in a crowd this big, under the missilelike CN Tower, they had stared at video images of the Earth from space, luminous and finite. The world had seemed full of theme-park beauty. *When I looked down,* the astronaut had said, *I barely even felt human.*

"Are you ready?" Julie prodded Helen between the shoulder blades.

"Here," Foster said quietly. "One last sip. Then that's it." The water in the bottle was nearly hot by now. It was still her choice. Whatever she did, it would be her choice.

"OK, go," Julie said. "This is the tricky part. This is the point where you must absolutely not call attention to yourself."

Foster nodded and sinuously disappeared. People were whooping and clapping. Elena had finished speaking. There was a line of sweat on Helen's upper lip. She started to dodge slowly through the crowd, slipping her way toward the pool, toward the net screens set up in front of the cement arches to stop people from climbing them. She had skated here with her family, in winter, long ago: A blue winter sky slashed with vapor trails came surging without warning out of the past. She eased herself behind the screen. At least the water in the pool was shallow: It looked cool and utterly clear, like a dead lake, an acid lake, no goldfish, barely even any coins. A man's voice, presumably the man in the Green Brigade T-shirt, began talking. Foster was in the water. If she didn't do this, what else was she going to do? As long as she was prepared to face the consequences. A young woman in black with bleached blond hair pulled a long coil of chain out of a heavy knapsack. Tall and methodical, Raj stood behind her, his skin shining, glancing around as if he, for one, was slightly nervous. He grabbed

252

the chain and looped it around the closest arch, moving silently but very fast.

Elena appeared, breathless and pleased, still in her jacket, and bent down, wiping her face with a cotton handkerchief as she tugged on a pair of black rubber boots. Slipping her knapsack off one shoulder, Helen pulled the lock out of it. Foster stood against the arch while Raj wrapped the chain tightly several times around him. A lock clicked. Someone scooped away the lock that Helen was holding. She stepped into the water, which was warmer than she expected. A helicopter swam past overhead. There was a Live Eye van pulled up at the curb, a CBC truck: She could see them in the distance. In a heightened, fiercely tangible way, she was aware of the bodies pressed beside her, Julie on one side, Elena on the other, the drops of sweat at Elena's temples, the ridiculous coconut smell of Foster's sun screen, Raj's arm pulling the chain around her, the dark, curling hair under his arms, each pale line across his palms, vanilla perfume, thick breath. There was something heady and almost sexual in the air between them. "Here," Raj said. Helen snapped the lock shut herself. And now there really was no escape. Disappearing acts were no longer possible. Her running shoes were clogged with water. She felt anxious but also strangely solid, ridiculously happy. She was here. She wanted to be here. She needed to be here, needed to be doing this. Raj had locked himself in at the end of the row. They all wore United Species T-shirts. People cheered as the man from the Green Brigade stopped talking. Two young women with empty knapsacks slipped inconspicuously away. Silver flecks of light jumped over the water.

A policewoman had stopped at one end of the pool and stared at them. People in the crowd were turning. The tourists goggled through their camera eyes in dismay.

"Courage," Foster shouted.

"You're animals," a man yelled.

"That's right," Elena yelled back.

"Elena, don't," Foster said sharply.

Two more policemen made their way along the tiled edge of the pool, one of them talking into a cellular phone, but they hesitated when they reached the first arch, as if they did not want to get their feet wet. There was a sudden commotion on the far side of the pool. A cameraman peeled off his socks and shoes, hopping from one foot to the other, and then, hoisting his equipment umbilically onto his shoulder, he took a delicate step into the water. One of the policemen called out, but more people cheered, ringing the sides of the pool by now.

"No lake," Elena shouted, "no life," until the rest of them began shouting with her, until other people took it up. The man from the Green Brigade stood at the far end of the pool, shouting, one arm raised.

"I'm thirsty," Foster whispered hoarsely; then he grinned. They wrapped their arms around each other's shoulders. Hotels and office towers surrounded them. The CN Tower rose higher than ever, soaring above everything. The TV cameraman waded resolutely toward them, as if across a jungle.

"Look right into the camera," Helen said. Her heart beat faster and faster. Because there was no way to avoid the cameras, there were always going to be cameras.

"I know that," Elena said.

Up in the sky shone one vulnerable triangle of blue. The cameraman had stopped and was tilting his head, scrutinizing them carefully. Dark, soaked patches crept up the legs of his jeans. At the far end of the pool, water from the fountain kept falling. Helen's heart felt light and almost free. She could see everything unfolding. "Hey," the cameraman said, "you." Coming closer, his camera whirring.

"We don't have to say anything," Julie whispered.

"You," he said, "what's your name?"

"Don't tell them," Elena whispered.

A peculiar smile quivered across the cameraman's face. He opened his mouth again. The lens of his camera shone like a tiny globe, fixed right on Helen. She could see herself reflected in it: that doubleness, as if she were still floating just above the ground. *All I want is to be human.*

"I'm Helen Urie," she said.

15

VICTORY

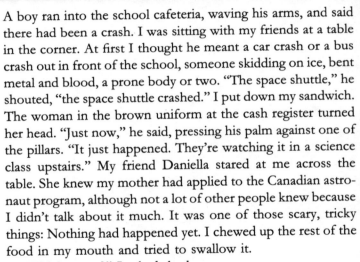

A boy ran into the school cafeteria, waving his arms, and said there had been a crash. I was sitting with my friends at a table in the corner. At first I thought he meant a car crash or a bus crash out in front of the school, someone skidding on ice, bent metal and blood, a prone body or two. "The space shuttle," he shouted, "the space shuttle crashed." I put down my sandwich. The woman in the brown uniform at the cash register turned her head. "Just now," he said, pressing his palm against one of the pillars. "It just happened. They're watching it in a science class upstairs." My friend Daniella stared at me across the table. She knew my mother had applied to the Canadian astronaut program, although not a lot of other people knew because I didn't talk about it much. It was one of those scary, tricky things: Nothing had happened yet. I chewed up the rest of the food in my mouth and tried to swallow it.

"Which room?" I asked the boy.

"They're setting up TVs in the auditorium," he said. His plaid shirt sleeves were bunched above his elbows.

I dumped the rest of my lunch in a garbage can, banged through the cafeteria doors, and ran down the basement hall. People were still opening their lockers, taking out books, and closing them again. No one else was screaming about a crash. I smelled sour food and sweat and the dry, acrid furnace odor but that was all. I took the center staircase, leaping two stairs at a time, and when I came out at the first floor and looked down the hall, another figure was hurtling down the stairs at the far end, like a mirror image, pulling open the glass door: It was Paul. We met breathlessly in the middle of the hall.

"How did you hear?" I asked. The hall was very quiet except for the muted voices of classes in session.

"I saw it," Paul said. "I got permission at the last minute to go into one of the science classes and watch it. It was horrible. Helen, it was really awful." His eyes stared past me down the hall. His hair splayed in all directions over his head. "It was just these streams of smoke spreading into the air. Right when it happened people thought maybe they had ejected away from it, but they didn't, they couldn't." He wiped the back of his hand across his nose. "They burned up," he whispered. "There isn't anything left."

"Where upstairs?" I asked. "Where is it?"

"They're moving the TVs into the auditorium. It's horrible up there. Everyone's trying to see it. Wait till they bring it down here. We should call her. Do you have a quarter?"

There was a payphone at the end of the hall by the auditorium. I still had my wallet on me from lunch, and I opened it as we walked back down the hall.

"She'll be all right." I put one hand awkwardly on Paul's shoulder and squeezed.

"All the families were there," he said in a fast, flat voice. "They kept showing all the families screaming."

A man in a suit, one of the science teachers, bumped a television on a tall metal stand along the hall from the other direction, from where the freight elevator was. *They burned up,* Paul had said. *They burned to a crisp.* Ahead of us, people were hurrying through the doors from the stairway and disappearing inside the auditorium, boys' voices yelling, while I leaned against the wall, away from everyone I might know, watching Paul's fingers dial my mother's number at the lab, as if that whole school world had momentarily shrunk away from us.

"Can I speak to Dr. Urie please," he said. "It's Paul." In my head I saw astronauts falling, I saw tiny pieces of astronauts falling, hands and feet and heads, bursting and shriveling and dropping toward the ocean. I tried to block them out. Paul was frowning at the numbers scribbled softly on the white paint of the wall. "Thanks." He hung the phone up abruptly. "She left," he said. "They think she went home."

"Probably she knows already. That's why she went home."

"So we should go home. No one will care if we leave now." He pressed his lips seriously, tightly together. Right now, I thought, at the other end of the continent, the astronaut families would still be sobbing, reeling in horror and disbelief.

"Let's get our things," I said. "No, wait. Paul, please wait." We both slipped inside the nearest set of auditorium doors, because even if it was terrible, I did not want to be the only person who had not seen what had happened. An announcer was talking. In the background spread a panorama of the official launch stands filled with twisting clumps of people. The shuttle soared into the sky, flames beating the air behind it, spewing a plume of smoke through the blue, and then there was a puff, that was all, a small gasp. Tails of smoke went whirling like pinwheels in all directions. Like a star, like a fireworks display, only everything was white, pure white. Sucked in by gravity, the white trails began falling gently down and down. *That was all.* I thought I could hear screaming. In the viewing stands, the astronaut families jerked their hands and mouths and eyes and fell against each other. One of the astronaut children stood absolutely still, staring straight ahead. We were almost there. We were traveling, tilting through the television, closer and closer toward them. The science teacher, standing by the TV, did not say anything.

"Let's go," I said to Paul and ran out the doors again. My eyes were burning. "Fuck," I whispered. I put my hand over my mouth and made it to the basement without looking at anyone, because the last thing I wanted was to cry in school. There was no one else in the basement now. My ski jacket, my knapsack, my boots. Our lockers were at different ends of the hallway, because even though we were in the same grade we were always put in different homerooms.

"We can take the bus," Paul said, leaning against the locker beside me.

"I want to walk," I said. "I'll go by myself, I'll just get there a little later."

"Why?"

"I just need to."

"OK." He nodded and wedged a blue student ticket between his teeth. "I'll take the bus." His eyes were steady but raw. Without running, we hurried up the side stairs and out the side doors of the school. No one stopped us. The air streamed with bright, January light, clear as knives, barely afternoon light, cold enough to pinch my nostrils. The sidewalks in front of us had all been salted, black and clean. Traffic rose up a small hill on the main road, billowing exhaust, betraying no sense of emergency, no screams, although inside each sealed car, the drivers could all be listening to the news about the shuttle crash. Nothing like this had ever happened in our lives. A bus with its headlights on appeared in the distance, and Paul began to run.

How had she found out, I wondered as I watched Paul climb onto the bus and be carried away. Had she been watching the launch at the lab? But that was unlikely: It was just another routine launch, and I didn't think there was a television at the lab. Listening to it on the radio was a possibility. Had someone called to tell her? The arms of the astronaut families jerked, their bodies toppled, my mother's face blazed and crumbled. I saw another phone booth on the corner two blocks ahead, and began to run.

There was a quarter in the front pocket of my knapsack. I had to take off my ski gloves to dial, each breath puffing like smoke into the air. I dialed my father's extension at the newspaper; a strange man's voice answered the phone and said David Urie was on another line.

"Can you tell him it's his daughter," I said. "Please. I need to speak to him." For an instant I was frightened that he had gone home, too, or that they would not put me through to him.

"Helen," he said.

"Did you see the crash?"

"The explosion. The Victory explosion. We're covering it right now. Where are you? Are you all right?"

"We saw it at school. Paul's on his way home. Mum already left the lab."

"Listen," he said, "it's a terrible thing. Sometimes you can take all the precautions in the world and a terrible thing like this can still happen. I think you should go home. I can't leave here, you know. That's the horrible, ironic part. It's a science story and I have to cover it."

"Did you talk to Mum?"

"Yes," he said, after a brief, odd pause. "I called her up right away to tell her. She hadn't heard until I told her."

"You think I should go home?" I whispered.

"Yes, I do."

I stood in the phone booth for a moment longer, staring out at the terrible, brilliant blue of the winter sky with the spreading vapor trails across it, imagining my father in his shirt-sleeves, jockeying between phone lines, forced to stay cool and respond as a professional. My stomach was growling ridiculously because I had barely started my lunch when the boy ran into the cafeteria waving his arms. It seemed obscene to feel so hungry, but I couldn't help it. The astronauts believed they were hurtling into space, they believed in everything they were doing, and a second later they were dead. And their families were *watching,* clapping, shouting because the astronauts were in the air, they had conquered space and gravity, they were already on their way. It was no comfort that they were all Americans. I started running, gasping for breath, trying with each step to stamp those faces out even though I didn't know how I was ever going to blank those faces out.

At Yonge Street, I stopped and looked south, at the traffic streaming downtown, toward the bank towers and the department stores and the CN Tower and the distant lake, away from our white brick house and the frightening, unimaginable presence of my mother's grief. Then I turned and headed north up Yonge Street. A woman in a gray trenchcoat was loading grocery bags into a station wagon. Children from the public school where Paul and I used to go were milling around outside the Happy Convenience Store talking about candy. The part of me that wanted to cry had curled up deep inside my stomach. Other parts, like seeds, were springing up elsewhere, not walking more and more slowly up Yonge Street, but running as fast as possible downtown, trapped inside a television set in Florida, inside the body of that frozen astronaut child.

When I stepped inside the Chinese grocery at the corner of Glenforest Street, the air was warm and comforting. Flattened cardboard boxes had been spread out over the floor to stop it getting covered in muck. In the corner, on a shelf behind the cash register, the shuttle exploded gently on a tiny black-and-white TV. *In hindsight it seems doubly ironic,* said the newscaster's voice, *that the shuttle's name was Victory.* Along one wall stood bunches of flowers propped in buckets, carnations and roses, freesias and irises even in the middle of winter, all wrapped in shiny plastic. I picked some freesias because I knew my mother liked their scent, and when I asked for a package of cigarettes, du Maurier only because I knew the name, the woman behind the counter gave them to me without asking if I was old enough. I looked tall enough to be sixteen.

I had never bought cigarettes before. In a crazy way I wanted to smoke one now as a distraction, do something simple that was not approved of, make a different kind of mark on the day. I had to take my gloves off again to light one, backed under an awning out of the wind, and still it took a couple of tries for it to stay alight. The back of my throat burned. My mouth filled with the taste of smoke. I tried to swallow some of it. My eyes stung. Millions and millions of people had watched the astronauts die on TV: One instant they were alive and the next, nothing. No warning. The plastic wrap over the flowers crinkled in my knapsack. I breathed out smoke in horrible fascination. No one could save them, do anything except watch them hungrily from all over the world. I turned onto Glenforest Street, stamped the cigarette into the snow, and began to run.

Our house looked just as it had when we'd left it that morning. A light shone in the living room. I crouched on the doorstep, took out the flowers and my key, and opened the door. Paul's boots, my mother's low leather boots were already on the plastic mat. Then I heard her swift, decisive footsteps coming toward me. "Helen?" she called out.

"Here," I said, holding out the flowers. "I'm sorry." Her face looked wan but calm, her hair standing on end in a wild, tired way as if she had been running her hands through it. She still wore the blue wool blazer that she'd worn to the lab that morning.

She opened her arms and hugged me. "My darling," she said. I felt one small shiver run through her. "I'm glad you're here." I held onto her lean body. She took the flowers, tore the plastic off and pressed them to her face.

"Are you all right?" I asked.

"I'm upset," she said quietly. "It's a terrible shock, but basically I'm all right. Are you?"

"I'm OK." I pulled off my jacket and boots as she rubbed my shoulders. "Did they really die right away?"

"It seems as though they did."

"Did you know any of them?"

"I didn't know them personally but I knew who they were." I remembered the time that one of her colleagues at the university had died in a car crash and she had bundled herself in a sweater and scarf and set off through the late-autumn dusk, striding down the street by herself.

In the living room, Paul was sitting on the sofa with his arms clasped around his knees, his face solemn, his hair as skewed and messy as my mother's, his navy turtleneck pulled up around his chin. "Do they know how it happened yet?" I asked him. My mother had carried the flowers into the kitchen.

"They think one of the fuel tanks exploded, but they don't know why." On the television, a woman was explaining the force it took to escape the Earth's gravity: An ordinary launch was like six people strapped to an explosion with a force of over two million pounds that used up several tons of liquid and solid fuel. My stomach turned over. I had never heard it put like that before. When Paul switched the channel, a voice described the backgrounds of the dead astronauts over flat, smiling photos of them. The sight of the television made me feel sick. "One of them was a mother," Paul whispered. "That one. She had two young children, a boy and a girl."

"I didn't know that." The woman had thick brown hair, narrow, far-apart eyes, a wide smile. She looked grainy and ordinary.

My mother came back into the living room carrying the flowers in a vase, which she set on the coffee table. I stared at her carefully. Her eyes seemed slightly bloodshot even though she wasn't looking at the TV. A Kleenex was tucked inside her jacket sleeve. She sat down on the sofa beside us, spreading her veined hands tightly over her knees, her silver wedding ring shining on one finger. She had to know that one of the astronauts had been a mother.

"Was there a TV at the lab?" I asked her.

"No." Her eyes were gleaming. "That's partly why I came home."

"Did you see the families?"

"They shouldn't have shown the families like that. They should have given them some privacy." On the screen, the shuttle named Victory was beginning to rise into the air, spewing huge bursts of flame, and yet everything seemed so quiet, almost motionless until that moment when the white puff appeared and the sky bloomed with all those petals of vapor trails.

"Will they stop?"

"Stop what?"

"Stop flying?"

"I don't think so," she said quietly. "There'll probably be a hiatus while they conduct an investigation, but they've already initiated plans for the space station and I don't see how they can just stop."

"But if it's too dangerous."

"Airplanes crash," she said. "You need to find out what

happened, if there's a problem that needs to be fixed, if it's a human error or computer error or structural flaw, but that doesn't mean people should stop flying altogether." These were not exactly the things I had expected her to say.

"But it's an explosion," I said. "The woman was just saying that a launch is an explosion."

"That's what rockets do. I know it seems scary but, Helen, you need that force. Even cars, even the internal combustion engine in a car runs on the principle of explosion." It wasn't just about going into space. So much of her research was tied up in the space program, too.

"But no one was talking about it like that," I said. "No one was talking about the risk. Just this morning they were saying how routine launches were."

"Even if they're routine, there's still a risk. There's always a risk."

"So why don't people talk about it? Why don't people talk about how dangerous it is to actually get into space and not just about what happens when they get there?"

"Well, they do," she said. "They acknowledge the risk but maybe they don't want to concentrate on the worst that can happen. And even now, when something like this happens, you have to believe in what you're doing and be prepared to go on." She stood up and began pacing back and forth across the living room, holding her arms tightly around herself.

"Maybe the families didn't know."

"They would know."

"But maybe they didn't know it was such a big risk. Maybe they didn't know it was reckless, not just dangerous."

"Helen, that's not all it is," she said firmly, although there was an undercurrent of sharpness in her voice.

"But you have to talk about it," I shouted. "If there's a risk, everyone has to know about it." I dove off the couch and through the kitchen doorway toward the box of Kleenex on the counter and pressed a Kleenex to my mouth in dismay. The last thing in the world I wanted was get into an argument with her now, especially now. My mother stood on the far side of the living room, as if rooted in place, bent slightly in the middle. Tears were streaming down my cheeks. I could see the pain creased through her face, in the stopped arc of her whole body, an arc that I had partly made. I wanted her to move, please move, at least to stop staring at me like that. Harder and harder I pressed my hand over my mouth and could not stop crying.

16

THIN AIR

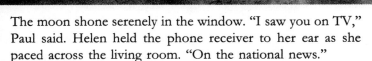

The moon shone serenely in the window. "I saw you on TV," Paul said. Helen held the phone receiver to her ear as she paced across the living room. "On the national news."

"Yes, I know." She'd seen herself, too: the shot of the five of them in their United Species T-shirts chained in the pool, the frame slowly zeroing in on her; quick cut to her mother, wearing her blue astronaut worksuit, but standing, earthbound, speaking at a press conference a month or so before the launch; then back to her. A shot of Foster looking lean and defiant. A shot of the police leading the five of them away. They'd kept her separate from the others; she wasn't sure why. Maybe because the crush of cameras around her had been much worse. There'd been time for more crews to arrive while a police-led team removed the locks and chains. She'd kept telling herself, *There's no going back.* And it was true. Foster and even Elena, beside her, would barely look at her, as if, in their eyes, part of her had disappeared. There'd been no chance to explain anything to them in front of all those people. *I'm doing this because I believe in it,* she'd said into some microphones as she was being led away. *This has nothing to do with my mother.* But then she'd clamped up, refusing to say anything else, wondering suddenly about her rights, frightened that she'd somehow incriminate herself, make everything worse. The possibilities for distortion were huge; she knew that. She might not have a chance to make herself clear.

"Helen, you've just been arrested," Paul said. He sounded terse and bewildered. Sitting down on the edge of the sofa, she pushed one hand into her hair, watching the moonlight stream through the window and onto the floor.

"When you do a protest like this, you usually do get arrested," she said, "and maybe you have to pay a fine, but there are people who do these things all the time, you know." The intercom buzzed, as it had once or twice in the past hour. Another reporter, Helen guessed, although she couldn't believe any of them actually expected her to let them in. She hated the fact that she couldn't see what was going on, how many people were actually milling about outside her building. She'd tried calling Foster: no answer. Would he have given away her address? If only her apartment had faced the front, then she could peer down and keep an eye on things. She tried to ignore the buzzing.

"Have you got a lawyer?"

"Mum's lawyer called me, if I need one."

"You knew they would pay attention to you. You must have realized there would be a fuss because of who you are."

"That's not why I did it," she said fiercely. "I didn't do it to get attention. I didn't even know for sure they'd recognize me."

"You didn't have to do something like this." She knew why his voice sounded so disapproving, as if in some way she had betrayed him personally, broken some unspoken pact about privacy, about keeping to themselves.

She wanted to explain to him that the worst thing about the police had been their condescension, only she didn't think he wanted to know the grimy details. When a male and a female officer had led her to the squad car, they had addressed her curtly but like an overgrown child, as if she had been coerced or led on and either way was not entirely responsible for what she was doing. They kept glancing down at her sodden running shoes, her leaky trail of footsteps. At the police station, some-one had even phoned for a cab to take her home, and a woman had escorted her out a back door, away from the press, before any of the others, so that she had no chance to wait for Foster or talk to any of them. The woman didn't even let her give her own address to the cab driver; before Helen could open her mouth, she was rocketing swiftly home.

"I know about the water," Paul said. "It's horrible—but it's just *how* you did this. *How* it happened."

"There didn't seem to be any other way."

"You can't expect to hide this from her."

"No, I know. I don't."

"She's going to be upset, not just angry."

"Paul, I know. I'm going to talk to her. I didn't do it to make her angry. That wasn't the reason. Look, aren't you frightened by the way things keep happening? Is it really just me?"

She thought of all his towers, his houses, all those fragile and fantastic buildings. "It's not just you," he said quietly. "Only I couldn't do what you're doing. Helen, what am I supposed to say when Mum calls me? What about when she asks me if I knew what you've been up to?" A worried crease had formed between his eyebrows: She could see it clearly.

"Say you knew I was working in a restaurant and that's all."

"Maybe."

"Paul, trust me. Please. Please, even if you don't agree with me?"

"Helen, I do trust you." Although she heard him pause fractionally.

Moonlight poured along her arm as she hung up the phone. Leaving the lights off, she made her way across the apartment, into the kitchen, as silently as a cat.

When she had arrived home in the taxi, a Live Eye van was already parked outside the building, a TV crew leaning against it. She had run past the two men as swiftly as she could, in through the double set of doors. Upstairs, she'd grabbed a black marker and written on a piece of cardboard, PLEASE DO NOT LET ANYONE IN WHO DOESN'T LIVE HERE, hurried back downstairs, and taped the cardboard to the inside glass doors, the scrutinizing eye coming closer and closer. Mustering up her courage, she had headed back upstairs, along the pink-lit hallway, and knocked on her neighbors' door. Only Sando, the man, was at home; if he had seen her on TV, he didn't say so, although he stared at her in careful, puzzled amazement. She asked if she could borrow a couple of eggs and possibly a little milk, realized suddenly that she was still wearing her United Species T-shirt. Breathing in the thick odor of spices, she watched as he carried back two eggs in a china dish, a cup of milk, balancing them deftly on top of a yogurt container which he said was full of potato soup. *I'm so hungry I could eat a horse. Well, no, not a horse.* She thanked him profusely, longing for ordinariness, for days when she had automatically trusted the smooth white shells of eggs, days when she had simply pulled on her knapsack, grabbed her bike and, without looking over her shoulder, gone shopping. Her bike was still locked outside the City Hall, but if she went out the door now, she'd probably be followed. There was no going back. Her twin lives had converged—she'd made them converge.

In the dark, moonlit kitchen, she opened the fridge. At the back of the freezer, a few old ice cubes still lay in the ice tray. She broke one into the palm of her hand and slipped it into her mouth, sucking the liquid out, then crunched it slowly. She chucked another couple of ice cubes into a glass. Chemicals whose names she didn't even know leaked and traveled through her body. She imagined Foster and Elena hurrying up a street, talking furiously about her, or, alternatively, not talking about her at all. Even that afternoon she had known what the risks were, although retrospectively they seemed clearer than ever: Foster and Elena would never want to have anything to do with her again. Everyone, including Paul, would insist on seeing what she'd done in terms of its effect on her mother. And yet she remembered what it had felt like to be standing in the pool: the headiness, her own solidity, the sweaty press of bodies. She tried to cup this feeling inside her, like a small white pebble that held the heat of the day.

She tried Foster's number again: still no answer. "Hello," she said, and her voice barely sounded like her own. "It's Helen. Please call me." *I'm here.* She wanted to wave her arms down the phone line. *I haven't disappeared. It's still me.* Maybe she should have leaped out of the taxi as it slowed at a red light, raced back to the police station, tried to find him then.

She dialed the space station, digging her toes under the sofa cushions, as if this would ground her, at least keep her steady. She did not turn on the television. "Hello," her mother said in a taut, official voice. "Barbara Urie."

"Hello," Helen said, "it's me." Somewhere a toilet flushed and a man began singing along to a radio. Up her voice traveled, reduced to particles, thin as air, quickly reassembling, up and up. Her heart was speeding.

"Are you going to tell me what's going on?"

"There was a chemical spill in the lake."

"I know. Helen, that's not what I mean. I *was* worried about the spill but I'd heard everything was under control."

"I'm drinking old ice cubes right now. There's water from the tap and they say it's all right, but the spill was right near the

271

water intake pipes so I *am* kind of nervous about drinking it."

"All right," Barbara said. "There was a spill. But for the last few hours people have been calling up and asking what I think about what you've been doing. Of course all the calls have gone to mission control, I haven't spoken to anyone directly, and I don't have to make any comment. But I would like to know, Helen, what *have* you been doing? You were with some activist group. You were arrested in some protest. Is that right?"

"We were at City Hall. We had a rally at City Hall and then five of us chained ourselves to the arches over the pool."

"Five of you," Barbara said emphatically. "So it wasn't as if this happened in the heat of the moment. It sounds as if this was quite planned."

"It was quite planned."

"United Species. Is that the name of this group?"

"Yes," Helen said. "I thought up the name." She curled her toes tightly, then uncurled them. She wanted to open her mouth wider and wider, for everything to come pouring out at once. "We've actually been working together for a few months now. It started off with just a few of us. I mean, I didn't start it, but I got involved, and things are gradually getting bigger. I've been going out with one of them, someone named Foster, but it happened afterward and that's not *why* I did any of it. But I was the one who came up with the name."

"You never—"

"There's more," she said. "I'm sorry. But work like this doesn't pay. So I've been working as a waitress in this natural foods café, a waitress and food recycler—it's really a two-part job these days."

"Helen, how can you sound so matter-of-fact? How can you possibly talk like this? You told me you were working on a research project this summer."

"Well, I know." Her voice dropped to a whisper. "I know, but I'm not, and I actually haven't been at university since just after the launch, only I didn't want to tell you. I didn't want to upset you."

"Since the launch."

"I know that's a long time."

"Helen, I'm trying to make sense of this, of your reasons. Do you think I'm not upset now?"

"I've been meaning to tell you."

"I'm five hundred kilometers away," Barbara said. "In a way it's a huge distance, and in a way it's not so far at all. And I've been trying as hard as I can to stay in contact with you. You do realize that, don't you?"

"Yes." Helen leaned forward, her hand hovering over the remote control device without turning the TV on. "But I didn't know *how* to tell you. And I know you want to stay in contact, I know that, but even if you were down here, I don't think you necessarily need to know exactly what I'm doing all the time. Say you were in Australia, you wouldn't necessarily know. And I *was* frightened that you would be upset. I thought you'd be horrified, actually. But I don't know if you have any right to be upset about what I'm doing or what happened this afternoon."

"Any right?"

"If you're not upset about everything else that's going wrong down here. Everything that's getting destroyed and contaminated. I don't see how you can be worried about anything I'm doing."

"Helen, why didn't you ask me? Why didn't you talk to me?"

"I thought you ought to be able to see for yourself what was going wrong. But you're not here, you're in space."

"I'm in orbit—not on Mars. Helen, I look down all the time."

"But you've left everything down here behind. You escaped."

"An escape," Barbara said, and her voice slipped, or perhaps her grip on the handhold slipped, "is that what I'm doing looks like to you? Just an escape?"

"Not all, maybe not all." She switched on the TV and Barbara stared blindly, intently in front of her. "But, yes, it looks like an escape. It looks like you really wish you were on Mars. You want to prove that people can live in space. It's looked like that for years. I mean, it's true, what David said, that there's a difference between people who just want to go up in space and say they've experienced it, and people like you, who think that the important thing is to find a way to stay out there, that this is our future somehow. You said it was in our genes, you really did. And maybe you never said to us directly that you wanted to get away from us, but we're not stupid, that's still the flip side of it. These are still the facts. What else are we supposed to think?"

"Helen, the facts? Is that the main thing you grew up with? The thing more than anything else that you took away?"

"You wanted us to look after ourselves. We always had to be prepared to look after ourselves because you dreamed about space and you wanted to be an astronaut. We always had to live with the expectation of people leaving, and you left. You both did."

"Going away doesn't always have to mean abandonment," Barbara said. "I've said that before. And it's not as though I'm gone forever. I will come back."

"No, I know, I know. But I didn't always see it like that. And I'm trying to tell you, you asked me to tell you what it felt like. And I can tell myself you both had good reasons for what you did, but, still, where does that leave us?"

"I've always tried to take you into account. I really have. I've

274

always asked your opinion about things. You really can't say I ignored you. If at any point things were intolerable to you, you should have told me they were intolerable. And I've never, never tried to pretend that any of these decisions were easy ones."

"But we had to agree with you. It would only have been worse if we hadn't agreed with you."

"Helen, that's not true." Her mother's voice was rising.

"I know you've wanted to stay in contact. I know how much you value communication, but what good does it do if the farther away you are from people, the closer you want to be to them? You say you miss things but you've never said you wanted to come back. I mean, what kind of model is that for us? How are we ever supposed to figure out how to get on with other people?"

"Helen, we—"

"I'm glad you're both doing important things, but sometimes I really don't understand why you decided to have children."

"Helen, don't. Don't say that. We wanted to. We believe in you. What else in the end can we say to justify ourselves?" There were tears in her mother's eyes: She could see them.

"So you both left. And then it was OK, you know, it really was. We got used to it. But why did you refuse to say you were separated? How were we ever supposed to know what was going on when you wouldn't talk about it? How can it possibly be a marriage when you don't even speak to each other for years?"

"Maybe we needed some time apart from each other. Maybe we genuinely did. Listen—maybe, even then, the need to be apart didn't seem reason enough to give up entirely, to conform ourselves to what other people expected us to do. I didn't want to be the one to cut myself off. I wanted there to be a possibility—I'd always said that my wanting to do this didn't have to undermine everything else between us, between any of us. I still believe it. I wanted to prove things with David were possible, just as I've wanted to prove it was possible to be close to you, even from here."

"What if it's not possible?" Helen whispered.

"What?"

"What if that's not possible?"

"Well, then maybe I'm crazy. Maybe all my optimism is just a delusion—but I refuse to believe that, I really do."

"What if I don't see things the way you see them? What if I don't see the future the way you do?"

"In what sense?"

"What if I don't see our future leading into space, toward Mars, wherever, but human beings going into space? Not coming back. I think about the future. I've been trying to have some sense of the future—I *do* have some sense of the future—but what if I see it being here, right here?"

"Why does it always have to be one thing or the other?" Barbara's eyes were shining. "I'm trying to offer people—I'm trying to offer you—a possibility, what I think is an important possibility. That doesn't mean I want to rule out, eliminate everything else."

"But we have to change things here, the whole way we think about things here. I don't think it's good to act as if everything might get better by being someplace else. I don't have any choice about escaping or ignoring things. I have to deal with things here. And even if everyone's acting like the only reason I was arrested at that rally was to get your attention or prove something to you, it isn't true. Maybe I don't know exactly what I want to *be,* but I know right now what I want to do. And if it means I get arrested or whatever, well, fine. You have to be prepared to take certain risks. Didn't you teach us that? So these are the risks I'm prepared to take."

"Perhaps you didn't expect there'd be this much attention," Barbara said dryly.

"Oh, no, I did. I knew it would be like this because of you. I didn't want it to be but I knew that was another one of the risks."

"Helen, are you OK?"

"Right now, sure, I'm OK."

"I wish I'd known," Barbara said. "If there's ever been a point where I've felt trapped up here, it's now. It's horrible, actually. I want to see you—really *see* you. I wish you'd told me. Helen, I love you. I would give you a whole new world if I could."

"I don't want a whole new world," Helen shouted. "Don't you see? I want this one. I want a future here. I think about you, too. I think about you a lot. And I worry about what's going to happen to you. I mean, I love you. I worry about all the terrible things that could happen to you."

"We have to trust we'll all be all right," Barbara said quietly.

"I have to go. Maybe we will be all right, but maybe we won't be." Helen's voice began shaking. "I'm sorry, I have to go."

She pressed her hand over her eyes, listened to her heart beating, to the silence ringing through the room. She took out a handkerchief, wiped her eyes, and blew her nose. Slowly the room crept back into focus. The blue light on the floor had shifted. Through the window, the moon itself was visible now, nearly round and rising above the houses and the trees. Even when she went to the window and stared out, all she could see was that one huge satellite, not even any stars. The picture on the feed kept shifting relentlessly; she could not see if Barbara

277

was still gripping the handrest by the phone, or was pressed against a window or floating fiercely back and forth between the space station walls.

She did not actually wish her mother was in the same room as her. That was the strange and contradictory thing. If Barbara had not been in space, if they had not been stretched apart, tugged to the limit, the whole ionosphere pulled tight between them, maybe they would never have said what they'd just said. Wasn't this what Barbara herself had dreamed would happen when she left the planet? They'd discover a new intimacy, say things to each other that they had never said before. Maybe she'd learned Barbara's distance lessons too well. Contradictions were everywhere. Maybe she could barely see the ways in which she was actually like her mother. Everything swam into sudden relativity: They were two people on moving objects, both floating in space, trying to shout across the void between them.

Breathe in; breathe out. The room swam back into focus. On a braided rug in a room not unlike this one lay a young woman, only a few years old than Helen was now, while a small girl crouched beside her, pounding the woman's back, horrified at her own strength. She was staring across the room at her mother, the day of the shuttle crash, pressing a Kleenex over her mouth, shocked by the recognition that she could hurt her mother—simply by saying something. She wasn't, as she'd thought until then, hurling herself endlessly, furiously against Barbara like a weight or a target, or running around the edges of a swimming pool while her mother skimmed through it. Everything came down to cause and effect: She could have an effect on her mother. In a way, her mother became permeable.

The room itself seemed magnified, luminous and still. Helen could feel her own body quietly expanding into the space around her, into the silence, drawing its own sharp, shimmering outline in the air. She had asked some of the questions. And yet she still wanted the intimacy, love, whatever it was, to be seen, for Barbara to see her as she really was. Was this a contradiction?

At least, she told herself firmly, pacing back and forth, *I'm trying to make myself clear.*

At seven in the morning, thunder rolled on the horizon. Helen woke up listening to the voice of a Japanese journalist who spoke into the machine in halting but precise English, asking if he could get an exclusive interview with her. It would die down, though. In a day or so, everything would die down. She lay on her side, trying to recall a dream in which she'd been talking volubly to someone—but who? At eight, when she got up, the rain began, slow and heavy, whirring faster and faster. Each time the phone rang, she waited, poised and hovering over the machine like a wary animal, to see if it would be Foster. Maybe Barbara would call back. *I'll leave you some questions,* said one voice, *and then you can call me with the answers. Number one, do you really think that by chaining yourself in a pool of water you can save the world? Number two, where is your father?*

Helen shoved up the windows as high as possible, drops of rain speckling her arms, breathing in vigorously, savoring the clean, damp smell of ozone. "All I need is a sub," she said out loud. "I don't need a clone or a double, but please let there be a sub who can work for me tonight because I don't think I can deal with serving people their tofu burgers and curried salad and sorting through their leftovers right now."

Water safety levels, said a voice on the radio, *continue to improve. In London, England, thousands of people attended an outdoor memorial service after the death of one of the world's last tigers. The Europeans delay the launch of a new communications satellite.* On the local TV news, she found a shot of her own apartment building, a shot of the sign she'd taped to the inside doors. *Astronaut Barbara Urie has not yet commented on the recent arrest of her daughter in a Toronto environmental protest.*

Words from her conversation with Barbara kept coming back to her. Unexpected words like *trust* and *love*. She wondered again about her parents' mysterious, frustrating loyalty to each other and about their early days, how much the pull between them was polar, magnetic, born out of their differences, how deep their passion and their memory of that passion really went. *Maybe all my optimism is just a delusion.* Helen stood very still in the middle of the floor. What if she was deluding herself? What if she had done everything these last few months, or gone public at the rally anyway, simply as a way to get Barbara's attention, wanting nothing more than to be seen? She was terrified that she had not done *the right thing.* There was, as always, no way back. Would the young woman who had played her at the launch be appalled if she'd heard, the young woman who only knew how to be a good daughter? The monkey named Trouble had pulled his arm free in a Soviet spacecraft while space scientists on Earth tried desperately to duplicate every possible thing he might do—but how could you predict what anyone else was going to do when you couldn't even figure out your own actions? What if she had sacrificed everything she shared with Foster and Elena to this need for attention or was following some perverse instinct for self-sabotage?

"Helen," said another, urgent voice, "it's your father. Please pick up if you're there. I'm down at the corner."

In a way she wasn't even surprised. It made perfect sense that at a time like this he would come back, that her whole split-apart family would suddenly start hurtling through the thinning air toward each other. She lifted the receiver. "Hi," she said, "how are you?"

"I decided I'd give you a little warning this time, instead of just arriving on your doorstep," David said. "Not a lot, because that might have been too much of a shock, but a little. And then there are these young men out here with this thing called a Live Eye. They make it a little harder to slip on in, and I figured if you were trying to avoid them, you might think I was them and decide not to let me in anyway."

"Can you do me a favor first? Please?"

"What's that?"

"I don't have any food. I'd really like to have some breakfast. I'd really like to offer you some breakfast, but I can't get out very easily. There's a place down the block where I usually shop. I'll pay you back when you get here. If you can pick up a few things." It felt peculiar and wonderful to ask him to do something for her.

David set the paper bag of groceries on the kitchen table, lowered his flight bag carefully to the floor, and kissed her cheek. Droplets of rain floated like tiny bubbles in his hair. He looked just the same, only this time he was wearing his windbreaker instead of carrying it over one arm. When he took off his glasses, his eyes seemed to shrink and widen at the same time. Pulling a handkerchief out of his pocket, he sat down easily, as if at home in Helen's kitchen, and began to wipe the lenses clean. "I shouldered my way past those people using the groceries as a shield," he said cheerfully, "but they filmed me anyway. I managed to pull the front door closed before they could follow me through, and then I dashed up the stairs, and here I am. So how are you?"

"I'm sorry about all the fuss."

"Well, I guess you knew—"

"Yes," she said, "but I'm fine. Really." Seeing her father without his glasses on always made him seem oddly naked, a sensation that she remembered from childhood. The contours of his face changed, became almost unrecognizable, as he stared back at her curiously. Then he slipped his glasses on again. It was hard to believe it was just days since she had last seen him; so much had happened in the meantime. And yet already something like habit was binding itself between them, dissolving the time that separated them into almost nothing. "How did you find out?" she asked.

"About what? I heard about the tanker and the spill on the news. On the radio. Which had me worried. And I was thinking about coming back even then, but then I heard about the rally and that you got arrested. Well, I saw that actually, on the news on TV. And then Barbara called me."

"When?"

"Last night."

"After she talked to me?" He nodded. "So I told her," Helen said slowly. "Finally I told her what I'd been doing. And she was angry, well, more upset, I guess, that I hadn't told her before this but it ended up all right."

"You probably can't blame her for being a little upset," David said.

"All right, I know."

"Have they set a court date for you?" He sounded astoundingly matter-of-fact.

"Not yet."

"I was frightened I might find you locked away in jail. Or you'd be totally distraught. Or they'd set your bail so high we'd never get you back." Was he just joking or was he being serious? "What about the water?" he went on. "Are you managing? It's such a terrible thing. Here, I brought something for you." He pulled over his flight bag, wedged it between his feet and unzipped it; then he lifted out one plastic jug of water, and another. "Spring water. I've imported these for you, because I heard it was pretty much impossible to get anything here right now. I know it's not much. I couldn't carry any more. And I know there's no guarantee that bottled water is any better than tap water, but here you go, if it's a risk you want to take."

"Thanks." She kissed him and hefted the bottles onto the counter.

He gave a small shrug. "It seemed the least I could do."

"Are you through in Ohio?"

"Not necessarily. It depends. They're still trying to determine the extent of ground toxicity. Some of those people could be permanently homeless."

"I'm just curious." Opening one of the bottles of water, she poured them each a glass, then carried both glasses back to the table. His gaze followed her, which made her feel smaller somehow, a thread of uneasiness. "About what you said. About what reasons you gave for having to come back here so soon."

"Well, I said you were in some kind of trouble. And I mentioned the spill, of course."

"So you want to save me."

"Well, no, not exactly." He gave her a puzzled smile.

"Yes," Helen said, "like all the other people stuck in the middle of disasters. Rescue me and keep me out of trouble."

"Helen, I wanted to see if there was anything I could do to help you. That's true. I wanted to support you. What's wrong with that?"

"But you came back *now.*" She stood and paced back and forth across the kitchen. "It just feels weird to me because you come back when things are getting terrible. You reappear when we don't have any water, when things are reaching extremes. But what about before this—because there were times when we needed you before this, during all the years when you weren't around."

"Helen, I can't go back." The starkness of his voice threw her: She'd meant to catch him off guard, and now he was the one pitching her off-balance, as if she'd probed the deepest wound she could. "I'm sorry," he said after a moment, rubbing his fingers back and forth across the edge of the table. "I won't pretend things were any different than they were. I thought I was doing the right thing. If I regret it too much, then everything starts to collapse, doesn't it? I did what I thought I needed to do to stay alive. I was in terrible pain. And now I can only be a realist and say I wasn't there when I could have been, when probably you did need me. And I missed you terribly. But does that mean I shouldn't come back now? We are, after all, still a family."

"What does that mean?"

"What does it *mean*?"

"I mean, we all live in totally different places and live totally different lives." She covered her face with her hands. "I just don't want to feel like a child. I don't want you to come back and make me feel like a child. I want to see you, but I can manage, you know, I really can. I didn't get arrested in this protest as a way of making you come back. Of course we all need to help change things but if I get myself into trouble, I'll have to find my own way out of it. And I *have* needed support, but you learn to look elsewhere. I mean, I have, because I had to. You can't just come back now and expect we'll want the same things you want or the same kind of family you want."

"I'm not trying to fit us into some kind of mold," David said. "I think there's great value in elasticity. Helen, I'm not trying to interfere. My motives are a mixture of idealism and selfishness, I'll admit that, but whose aren't? You're still my child. I want you to be all right. I wish there were more I could do for you. I look around at the way the world is going and I want—perhaps I *am* moved by extremes, perhaps that's true, but can you understand how much I don't like to feel useless?"

"When you think of home," Helen asked suddenly, "where do you think of?"

"The house," David said, but it sounded like a question. "I don't know. Perhaps I'm someone right now who does not have a home."

"Sometimes I think of us all in space," she whispered. "I can't help it. I imagine us as these tiny balls in orbit—no, more like these lines moving through the air above the planet, like this very thin web. Transmissions. I don't know, but when I think about a family, that's what I see. Not people. Just lines or particles, like trajectories. Sometimes that's all I see."

David reached out his hand, clasped hers, and held it tightly, with all the heat and density of skin meeting skin, as if to prove that they were not just transmissions, not merely dependent on satellite communication. Helen squeezed back tightly, then let go.

"I don't think you should stay here," she said, sitting down at the table again.

"You don't."

"I mean, I think you should stay for breakfast, I want you to stay for breakfast but what I really think is that you should go and see Paul."

"Oh, I was going to, absolutely, but I didn't think I necessarily had to leave today."

"But what if he finds out that you're here? He wants to see you. He knows you came back here before. I went to Montreal last week to tell him I'd seen you. And I know I probably look like the one who needs more attention because of the things I do but it isn't true. It isn't fair to either of us."

"I was hoping maybe the three of us could meet up in Montreal."

"Not right now," Helen said quickly. "I can't. I'm really busy. And I have to work. If I give away any more shifts, I may even lose my job." She imagined Foster's lips, his eyes, the dark hollows around his eyes, imagined him nervously watching his telephone, didn't know whether it was better to summon him up or block him out. "You could catch a flight out, or you could take the train. Why don't you take the train? And maybe call him once you get there, just to let him know."

"He's all right?"

"Yes, he's fine." She'd leave Paul to tell David about Carla, let him make his own revelations. She didn't feel she had any right to do it for him.

"There is no single return," David said thoughtfully. "I don't know what I expected." He ran his hands back through his thin hair and smiled. "Only I do hope that one day in the not-too-distant future we can all manage to meet up in the same place at the same time—the three of us at least. I can't tell you how much that would mean to me."

"Yes," Helen said. She clenched her fists. The problem was she could barely even imagine it.

Faint rain falling. A halo around the streetlights. With her hands in the pockets of her jacket, Helen walked toward the strip of Korean neon blinking ahead of her. She was supposed to meet Foster in a bar, somewhere she'd never been, west from where he lived. *Somewhere neutral,* he'd said, and added, *somewhere you're not likely to be recognized.* She had let that pass. Cool air streamed through the streets. Past the window of a Korean bakery where two tiny wedding mannequins stood frozen on top of a huge white cake. There were still food scents on her skin and under her fingernails from her dinner shift at The Million. People *had* begun to recognize her there; one way or another, word had gotten out, and she was thinking of quitting, only then, of course, she would have to find some other job.

Ten days after she'd called her mother, Barbara had called her back and begun speaking as if no time at all had passed since they'd last spoken. *I get so worried when I hear you talking the way you've been talking, that you're losing your sense of wonder. Because if there's one thing I ever wanted to pass onto you, it's a sense of joy, of finding wonder in the world. There are so many marvelous things—I don't want you to forget. You don't even have to talk to me right now, it's all right, but I wanted you at least to think about this.* Then she'd hung up.

The day before, David had called to say that he was staying on for another week in Montreal, that he was taking Paul and Carla into the mountains for the weekend. Helen missed him, but this time in a way that seemed completely manageable, almost ordinary. *At first it was strange to see him,* Paul had said when he came on the line. *He is thin. But he and Carla get on well. Actually, it's been kind of cool to have him staying in our apartment—to be able to offer him a home.* She told herself there was no reason to feel jealous.

What did you say to Mum about Carla? she asked instead.

I told her I had a girlfriend, Paul said. *I said I'd known her for a few months and she was moving in with me. I didn't say she already had. But I told Mum she couldn't complain about it happening so fast when that was how she and Dad did it.*

Sometime in the past week, people had gone back to drinking the water, and Helen had decided to do it, too, an act of faith. *Wonder:* She tested the notion, holding the word in her mouth, eyeing the street around her.

A woman stepped out of a doorway, opening a Chinese waxed-paper umbrella, a young woman in a black cotton coat with a thin, patterned scarf around her neck, her face half-hidden. Elena? Helen wasn't close enough to be sure. Had the woman just stepped out of the bar? One sharp glance down the street, and then, with swift, economical grace, she disappeared around a corner.

Foster was sitting near the back of the bar at a table by himself, reading in the terrible light, two empty bottles of beer in front of him, which either meant that someone had been with him or he had been there for a while, fortifying himself. His face looked pinched, his dark hair pulled back tightly. "Hello," he said carefully as Helen sat down opposite him. "How was work?" Three men at the counter were watching football on television, and there was one other couple at the back, dressed in serious black leather. Two rings of water pooled in the middle of the dark green Formica table.

"I'm fine," Helen said. If Elena had been there, what had they been talking about? Foster's canvas bag sat on the chair beside him, papers sticking out of it. He was reading his well-thumbed copy of *Animal Liberation*. Ridiculously, she wanted to duck under the table and make sure that now, three weeks since she'd last seen him, he was wearing the same red hightop sneakers as always. Maybe that was just perverse nostalgia. She wondered if he was considering going back to relatively simpler actions like the anti-meat stickers and slaughterhouse attacks. Two weeks after she had called Foster, just when she'd almost given up hope, he had called her back.

"How's your mother?"

"She's fine. Foster, listen."

"Two hundred and forty-two days in space, and counting."

"I know. Foster."

"It was a real shock. I'm not sure if you can begin to imagine what kind of shock it was. I mean, there we all were, chained in a row, and all of a sudden you say, 'I'm Helen Urie,' and everything goes crazy. Maybe you thought it would be a great way to get us into the news, and you're right, of course, I can accept that. But no warning, Helen. Nothing to me. Nothing to Elena. Nothing for *months*. I mean, what am I supposed to think?"

"It wasn't a joke." She could see the edges of his running shoes now, bright red, brand new ones. He looked ready to bolt. "Nothing I've done was a joke."

"Helen, I've been involved with you and you never even told me your real name."

"That's not true," she said fiercely. "Stockton's still my name. It's my middle name. I just dropped the Urie. Stockton is even my mother's name. I'd been using it before I met you, when I started working at the restaurant, because there had been so much fuss, and all I wanted was some privacy."

"All right," Foster said. "I understand that. At least I understand that at the beginning, but then what? Helen, you know that's not all of it. You've been lying to me like crazy. Your mother does not work for the World Health Organization in Australia. Your father does not work in radio in Yellowknife. I actually went to the library and read a few articles about Barbara Urie and her family. You didn't just hide a few facts, you made all these things up. Your brother isn't some whiz-kid financial analyst, and as far as I can make out, you didn't grow up in L.A. and London and Montreal and Toronto, which is what you told me. You grew up in Toronto, didn't you? Helen, why have you been doing this?"

She tried to pour a bottle of beer into a glass without foam spewing over the edges. She'd thought somehow that her longing to see him would make things simpler than they'd been with Barbara, but now they didn't feel simpler at all. "I didn't really think it mattered who my family was." Her hand kept shaking. "I didn't think it really had anything to do with the work we've been doing or what's gone on between us."

"Did you just think you could go on and on like this?"

"No." She watched Foster's long fingers rip the corner off his beer label and roll the paper into a tiny ball. "Maybe I thought you would guess. In a way it seemed so incredible that you didn't ever guess. I've been on the news before. Sometimes there have been pictures. I was at my mother's six-month celebration, the night the lights went out, the night you were protesting. I was up on stage, I was even on TV, but you didn't see. I felt as if you didn't want or didn't need to see."

He paused for a moment. "Didn't you want to tell me?"

"Partly," she said slowly, "and partly not."

"Helen, what does that mean? You're not a spore. You're not something that floats about and generates itself out of thin air. At some point, at least at some point between us, don't you think it's going to matter who your family is? I mean, are you trying to tell me that the Helen I've known and the Helen who gets up on stage at her mother's celebration are not the same person?"

"Yes," she said. Or did she mean no? She forced herself to look at him. "I'm the same person. But Foster, that's not all of it. It's more complicated. I mean, I've always been defined by my family before anything else. Do you have any idea what that's like? And this was a chance for once, for the first time, not to do that. To make myself into someone else. To have some kind of independent life. And that was important. It's been wonderful, actually. That's real. That was a real need, too."

"How am I supposed to know this wasn't some game, a way of slumming, I don't know, some kind of escape?"

"It wasn't an escape. Foster. Even if I've made things up. All right, I've made things up about my family, but it's not an escape. I haven't lied about what I feel or what I believe or what I've been doing. I'm still the same person who was on top of the chicken bucket with you or on top of your roof with you, and I was there at the protest, wasn't I? How was I supposed to explain to you that all these things were true? I didn't know what to do about the contradictions. And maybe I fucked things up but I'm not running away."

"This time I'm supposed to believe you."

"I thought about telling you, but I was—look, what would you have said if I'd told you who my mother was? If I'd said, guess what, my mother's trying to set a record for the length of time a human being has lived in space?"

"Isn't it a little late to ask me this now?"

"But what would you have said?"

"Did you ever look at it this way, that you could have helped things by telling us?" His fingers kept moving, ripping the beer label, twisting the paper into tiny balls, jittery, tearing her, still beautiful.

"Helped how?"

"Well, you could have talked about the issues, maybe in interviews, or helped with fundraising, or whatever, and partly because of your name, because you're Barbara Urie's daughter, people would listen to you."

"Foster, listen to yourself." She took a fast swallow of beer. "If you want to know why I didn't say anything, that's why. You make me feel as if I'm being held hostage to a name, as if all you want is my name, or my mother's name. It's like some kind of product endorsement. Nothing else I've done, none of the work, not even thinking up a name for you, none of that counts. What I feel doesn't count. That's what I was frightened of more than anything, I really was. That you wouldn't see me at all. Just my name."

He was stacking the paper balls into a small pyramid on the tabletop. "You don't have to look at it quite as cynically as that," he said. "I don't look at it quite like that."

"How else am I supposed to look at it?"

"If you really believe in what you're doing, you think you'd want to let people know. What's wrong with going public? Isn't that what you did at the protest?"

"Foster, the TV guy knew." She squeezed her hands together and released them. "I didn't want to have it happen like that. I didn't want you to find out like that. But I couldn't figure out the right way to tell you and then he recognized me, he was going to say something."

"Maybe what we do embarrasses you."

"It doesn't embarrass me. I just don't want to be manipulated!"

"Don't shout." He was staring at the tiny pyramid in front of him as if for the first time. Then he looked up at her, his eyes very lucid and dark. "No one wants to be manipulated."

"Do you think I should call Elena?"

"Probably." He swept the balls of paper into the ashtray.

"Do you think I hurt Elena?"

"Probably."

"I'm sorry."

"You're sorry you hurt Elena."

"No," she said. "I mean yes, but not just Elena. Foster, what about us? We haven't been talking about what's going to happen to us."

"Elena was here," he said, "before you came. We were talking for a while. I was trying to decide if I ever wanted to see you again. It's hard, you know, because I can't really, logically say don't work with us. I guess I could, but it also seems kind of hypocritical."

"It isn't just about work."

"Helen, the problem is I still feel fucked around with." The muscles in his face were working furiously.

"I'm sorry," she whispered, leaning toward him. "I couldn't see a way that things weren't going to be messy." She pressed her fists against her head. "Whose motives are always clean, anyway? Foster, if I'd told you—I hadn't told my mother either. I hadn't told her about you or about what I'd been doing."

"Have you?"

"Well, she found out, of course. And then I told her."

"What did she say?"

"Why does it matter to you what she said?"

"Just curious."

"She still believes the things she's always believed in. Foster, she's an astronaut. And she's hard to argue with because she wants to make everything seem possible at once. Foster, what about us? I want to keep working with you but I don't want to give up on us either. I've been happy, you know. I don't want everything to seem like a waste. Maybe everything's changed but I still want to try to work things out."

"Did you just assume everything would be possible, that you'd tell me all the things you hadn't told me and then everything would keep going the way it had been?"

"No," Helen said. She bit her lip. "I didn't assume anything." She had no rules for this, nothing to go on. In the distracted angle of his gaze, his parted lips, the white triangle of skin that shone above the collar of his T-shirt, she saw keenly how much she'd hurt him. "But I didn't mean to tell you and disappear either. I didn't want things to end here. I don't think they have to end here. Only of course it makes a difference what you want." There was still a thin layer, like a screen, like an extra skin that separated them.

"Can we walk for a while?" Foster stood up abruptly, pale and strained. "All I really want to do right now is walk."

17

COUNTDOWN

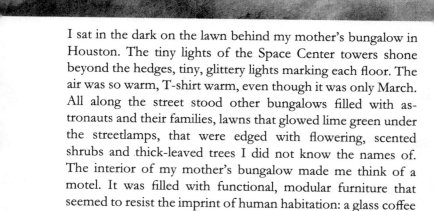

I sat in the dark on the lawn behind my mother's bungalow in Houston. The tiny lights of the Space Center towers shone beyond the hedges, tiny, glittery lights marking each floor. The air was so warm, T-shirt warm, even though it was only March. All along the street stood other bungalows filled with astronauts and their families, lawns that glowed lime green under the streetlamps, that were edged with flowering, scented shrubs and thick-leaved trees I did not know the names of. The interior of my mother's bungalow made me think of a motel. It was filled with functional, modular furniture that seemed to resist the imprint of human habitation: a glass coffee table and dining table, bookshelves that housed a huge TV set, a beige fold-up couch.

We had been at a party. But first I had watched my mother practicing for a space walk in one of the Space Center pools. I had thought at first that it would be like a swimming pool, like our old swimming pool in Toronto, but it wasn't: For a start, it was much deeper, with ladders descending its walls, and near the bottom, projecting from one wall, was a life-size model of the long white remote manipulator arm. They had simulations for everything here: a launch simulator; an exact model of the space station. They used the pool to simulate weightlessness. She was supposed to fix the manipulator arm.

And I had watched her climb into her huge, oversized astronaut suit as well, the kind they used for EVAs—extravehicular activities. The suit ballooned around her arms and legs, and was so heavy that the top half had to be wheeled in on a separate stand. Her head was lost inside her helmet. All I could see was the shiny bulb of her helmet as she lumbered, with excruciating slowness, taking great mastodonlike steps, toward the pool. She had to fix the arm, she'd said. Not try to fix it, had to. It was an emergency. She did not say a simulated emergency. Peter Carter was in a room just off the pool, beneath water level, separated from her by a window, operating the remote manipulator arm. All around me, space agency officials hooked up to wires and headphones were taking notes. And there was a real time limit: the length of time her oxygen supply would last.

I hadn't known until after she had pulled her heavy astronaut body up the ladder, stripped to shorts and a T-shirt, after she had talked to the officials and walked exhaustedly toward me, if she'd managed to do it. *It's semifunctional,* she said. *I managed to rig it, not perfectly, but I did.* Her face was reddened, her hair soaked and flattened with sweat. All sense of effortlessness was lost.

At the party, we had stood eating nachos and chips in a room full of other astronauts, among people who had already gone into space and back, among astronaut children who were all much younger than I was, children who lived here and had grown up surrounded by other astronauts and space engineers. To them, none of this would seem unusual. People came up to me with the graciousness you bestow upon a visitor.

"Have you had any thoughts about becoming an astronaut yourself?" one of the female astronauts asked me.

"No." I'd worked out my answer to this question carefully. "I think one in the family's enough."

"You're right." She gave a low, delighted laugh. "I'm *sure* one in the family's enough."

What had struck me above all was the astronauts' ordinariness. I wasn't sure exactly what I had expected from them in person: to be stranger, more alien, more obviously convinced of their own invincibility, perhaps in some way I could hardly describe to myself, more American. And yet it was this very quality that caught me off guard, that elided all the differences between us.

Behind me, a moving square of yellow light: The screen door to her bungalow slammed. My mother walked through the darkness across the lawn toward me, changed back into casual clothes. "I'm going to give you a massage," she said, as she sat down on a lawn chair, enclosing me between her legs, and then she slipped her hands inside the collar of my T-shirt. Her fingers were cool and silky. She squeezed my shoulders, probing the muscles under my skin.

"It's funny," she said, her calm, hollow voice issuing from somewhere just above me, "the kind of adjustments I had to make when I came down here. Not the kinds of things you'd necessarily think. Like squash. Everyone here plays recreationally but almost religiously. And I'd hardly ever played so I had to teach myself how. I'm not bad. I've even started to beat people occasionally."

Her fingers moved up the back of my neck, as if counting each vertebra, as if her very deftness and precision could secure some new intimacy between us, while I tried to relax, to concentrate simply on the motion of her fingers, that exquisite blurring of pleasure and pain. "Something happened the other day," she said.

"What?" Something in the simulator, I guessed.

"David called."

"He what?"

"Helen, it's OK, just relax." Her voice was low with private excitement, although her hands kept moving methodically. "It was one of those chance things. He managed to catch me while I was here, and I'm not often here. But the phone rang and I picked it up and there was his voice. Well, we were both shocked. We've been in touch, of course, but it's been over a year since we've spoken to each other directly. It was hard to know what to say at first, although he did tell me he'd called because he thought it was time we stopped canceling each other out—time we found a way to enlarge our vision. That was how he put it, anyway."

"Had he been meaning to call?" (Because even though I had been talking to him, not frequently but still, he hadn't said anything about it to me.)

"He didn't really say."

"What will happen now?"

"What do you mean?"

"Well, is anything going to happen? Do you think you'll try to see each other?" I could not begin to figure out what, if anything, they wanted from each other, what they believed was going on between them. They baffled me, infuriated me. Her fingers worked their way around the base of my skull as if gently probing new terrain, as if trying to smooth away scars.

"I don't think he would come here," she said quietly. "I don't think David wants to come here. And there's no way I can get away right now. Helen, we honestly didn't even get that far. But I think we'll talk by phone again. In fact, I know we'll talk again before too long."

Before my eyes, just above the tree line, a meteorite exploded silently, one wish, a shooting star. "Did you see?"

"Yes, I saw." The whir of her private excitement again. "Helen, sometimes the air's so dry here that you can see everything with such crystalline sharpness, so deeply into the sky that it gives you this utterly intense sense of the scale of things. I love it." The indigo sky above our heads grew thicker with stars, wild and fervid and plunged with deep holes of the unknown. What did she wish for?

Sometimes, at night, walking down a street in Toronto, I'd stop and look up at the few stars I could see and wonder why my restlessness and passion didn't translate into something like my mother's. Now I closed my eyes, breathed in, and felt a stirring all at once, like a chrysalid, pale green, the small, fierce flutter of wings inside me. Could she feel it? Softly, I prowled the tiled floors of the simulation room, looking for a key, a doorway.

18

Tele-vision = 1. Vision at a distance. 2. Vision with a purpose.

"At least part of the point," Elena said, "is that I want the astronauts to see us." She looked at Helen as if testing her response. The small windows, high in the white, thick walls of Elena's basement apartment, shone like tiny cubes.

"You can never depend on the weather," Helen said, "but if it's a clear night and they actually look down at where you are, then they should be able to see something." With her feet hooked around the rungs of her stool, she kept folding flyers, trying to match her rhythm to Elena's, waiting to see if Elena actually asked her if she could tell her mother about the rally they were planning. At this, she drew an interior line: She did not want to become some kind of go-between.

"You said she could see fires."

"Yes, I know," Helen said carefully. "In the desert, or forest fires. I did." It was so hard to begin talking about these things, not to want to retreat, to resist the first impulse to hide or lie—not to feel thrown sometimes by Elena's bluntness, which had always been there, and suspect it was still residual anger. The house hummed with late-night quiet. Rapti, the white cat, lay sprawled across the turquoise kitchen floor, twitching with dreams. A plate of fruit dumplings, made by Elena's grandmother and dipped enticingly in icing sugar, sat on the counter in front of them. From the back room came the chatter of Elena's new TV, which she'd bought a few weeks before she quit her daytime job. Foster was taking a break, but then he'd been up proofreading, he said, for two nights running. He was probably sprawled across the futon sofa, legs up, fast asleep.

"Candles," Elena said intently. "We'll have a whole crowd of people holding up candles and marching down University Avenue. We'll start at the top of Queen's Park, right by the planetarium, which seems appropriate, and head south from there. We need a big crowd and I'm going to be optimistic and say we can get a big crowd, not just traditional animal-rights people but people who have a broader range of concerns, because we're the ones right now who are addressing those concerns. I dream of filling all University Avenue with people, and if there are enough of us, they'll be able to look down and see us, in spite of all the other lights, because we won't look like cars and we'll be moving." She was wearing a soft, gray flannel shirt, a shirt that was too large for her and that Helen had a funny feeling she'd once seen Julie wearing. Elena's face was flushed with an almost childlike excitement as she leaned down and rubbed the white cat gently behind the ears. "Of course we'll have to have an alternative date and make sure everyone knows why we need a clear night to do this."

"Helen," Foster said tersely from the edge of the room, a darker outline, as if he'd suddenly materialized there. "Hurry. There's something I think you should see."

The look on his face, the quick, uneasy smile that crossed it and vanished, threw her completely.

In the back room, she found him standing in front of the TV. On the screen, in its real and artificial darkness, a space shuttle rested on a launchpad, lit by the beams of floodlights that swayed back and forth across it. The shuttle and the rockets attached to it remained absolutely still. *The rescue mission is scheduled to lift off at eight fifty-five EST,* said a man's head.

"Cable news channel," Foster said. "This report just came on."

This is Muhammed Johnson, said the man, *at the Space Center.*

There was a mission going up this week, a routine mission, Helen knew, knew they'd already started the countdown, but she was also pretty certain there was still another day before the lift-off.

"He said something happened to the other guy, the American. They're sending up a rescue mission and they may be bringing both of them down."

Rescue, she thought, *not routine but rescue.* Someone had simply switched two words on her, words that made all the difference in the world. She reached out and touched the screen haltingly, in disbelief.

"Helen, he didn't say anything had happened to your mother." She could feel Foster watching her, his gaze grazing her. A moment ago she and Elena had been folding up flyers for a strategy session and even Elena had assumed that her mother would be up there for a while, was in a sense depending on it.

You're tuned in to our special rescue mission report, said the man named Muhammed, *on the channel where news never sleeps. At two hundred and seventy-six days, what was supposed to be the longest-running space mission ever may be over.*

Over. Her father was in Montreal. He'd come back from Ohio a second time and gone straight to stay with Paul. For hours they or the family liaison man in Houston had probably been trying to get hold of her, but she hadn't been expecting any messages, hadn't bothered to call her machine. *The mission may be over.* The astronauts were coming down. She sat on the edge of Elena's sofa with her hands over her ears and raged against the mere possibility of it. *No.* She wasn't ready. It didn't matter whether or not she was ready. In the moment of trying to imagine it, her mother's return became the most inconceivable thing of all. The line between the possible and impossible kept shifting, and her whole realm of expectation had to shift as well, her entire vision of the future. Was it that she didn't know how or didn't want to imagine Barbara coming down?

And yet another part of her brain kept running lucidly, efficiently, just as it had done that day nine months ago when they'd watched Barbara's launch—and even afterward, when she and Paul had seen that other family on TV and raced out of the Florida diner. You could not simply change the time of a launch at the last minute. Even if this was an emergency, the American space agency for one must have known something was wrong in time to reorganize the mission, reprogram the computers. That took more than half a day. Even if someone had been trying to call her, even if Paul and David were trying desperately to get through to her right now, they were the ones finding out at the last minute.

Four days, no—she counted back—five days since she'd last talked to Barbara, but that wasn't so unusual; she'd automatically assumed that time was passing for her mother as it was for her, with ordinary speed, in routine busyness. Maybe something had happened to Peter days ago, time slowing around the two of them in their space capsule, stretching, space expanding on all sides of them, a true vacuum. Had it been an accident or was it some virus or debilitating condition that could infect them both? Maybe he had floated away, spiraling downward in a fiery blaze. Maybe he was already dead. *No.* Why hadn't Barbara called? Couldn't she at least have managed a quick, warning call? What if she was up there alone?

"You can use the phone," Elena said from the doorway,

MINUS TIME

where she stood with her arms crossed, velvet, sequined slippers glittering on her feet. "Call wherever you have to."

They were both watching her carefully, from either side of the room, an old allegiance reasserting itself, in which they shared the comfort of familiarity and Helen was the stranger, growing stranger. It didn't matter that she and Foster had shared a hurried and slightly testy dinner in a Chinese restaurant before riding the streetcar here or that they had started sleeping together again with a new mixture of passion and wariness.

When she tried Paul's number in Montreal, it was busy. The space station number was busy, too. She kept almost forgetting the numbers, her mind sliding. She even tried the public access space station number, usually filled with the jargon-laden voices of mission control, but an automated voice told her it was temporarily out of service. All umbilical lines were severed. They'd been told that contact was always possible, but of course it was not always possible. She'd been freed suddenly, perversely: on her own. Even her own phone line was busy, not because anyone was there, but, she supposed, simply because people were trying to reach her. She longed for the space station feed with a violence she'd never felt before, for its semblance of closeness, its calm, interior sweep from room to room, even if there was no guarantee that she would see what she wanted to see, her mother's face, her lips moving in reassurance, and Peter Carter's body, so familiar after all these months, chest heaving gently.

"You can't go home," Foster said, pulling his hair back into a tighter ponytail, which made his face look more taut and extreme than usual.

"No, I know," Helen said. "I know I can't." She could picture the scene by now: reporters not just at the door to the building but knocking on her own apartment door, waking people up and down the hallway. She slapped one hand over her mouth. "The goldfish." They floated belly-upward, starved to death.

"They'll be all right for a day," Foster said, "and then, if you lend me your keys, I'll go over and feed them. I'll climb in the window if I have to."

"Shh," Elena said with preemptory harshness, flicking off the light switch. "Foster, the TV." In the darkness, the picture exploded in a burst of light, its afterimage glowing like radium. Out on the street, a van door opened and closed, voices and footsteps on concrete blurred in a soft shuffle. A beam of white light flashed through the windows at the front of the apartment, ricocheting off the dark walls of the tiny hall. "If it's what I think," Elena's voice said, "then they must have got hold of my name and address through the United Species arrests, which means they probably have all our names and will try and track you down through each of us. Helen, stay here. Maybe I look suspicious because I'm up and dressed at three in the morning, but it's none of their bloody business what I'm doing up. I'll take care of it." Her footsteps hurried purposefully away.

But how could she possibly stay? What if there were more after these? What if the ones at the door pushed in anyway? How did she even know what Elena was going to say? There had to be a window—the windows right at the back of the basement. Foster was in the room with her, but she could breathe silently, move as stealthily as he could, hidden by the sound of Elena's footsteps in the kitchen and the insistent knock on the side door. Easing herself away from the couch, Helen slipped into the hall, toward the blacker stretch of curtain hanging over the doorway to the furnace room, into its clean, acidic-smelling darkness. She wasn't abandoning them but there was no reason why they needed to be pulled into the circus surrounding her family for the next few days: She was just trying to be considerate.

Through two windows at the back, beyond the bulge of the hot water tank and the furnace, a little light shone like phosphorescence. The TV burst on again suddenly, an eruption of sound, louder than before. (Was Foster simply going to hoist his feet up on the couch, shove a pillow under his head, and keep on watching it?) The curtain gusted behind her as Elena opened the door.

At least the furnace room wasn't piled high with junk; it was easy, after a moment, to make her way across the cement floor, through the darkness, without bumping into anything. She headed for the window behind the water heater. A block of wood had been wedged against the top of it, to keep it locked, although the whole paint-sealed surface looked unbudgeable.

She sensed him without hearing anything, an animal sense, every hair on her body prickling and standing on end, every particle of skin probing the place where he changed the shape of the air. "Are you ready?" Foster whispered, as if they had choreographed their movements perfectly. Helen did not jump. If she looked out of the corner of her eye, she could almost see him; a trace of light rippled across his face. Could love be tied up with utter relief? *He was here.* There was a roll of masking tape around one of his wrists. He wore his own denim jacket and another jacket tied by the arms around his waist. "Can you climb on my shoulders?" She nodded.

He handed her the masking tape, and she realized suddenly what she had to do, from reading books if nothing else: She stretched two pieces over the glass in the shape of an X. Foster passed her a small hammer. (Where had he found these things? Unless he knew exactly where they were stored in the darkness of Elena's basement, part of some kit that he and Elena had once used in raids on university labs.) "Don't hit it too hard."

On her second try, the glass cracked and collapsed soundlessly against the tape. "Shit," Foster whispered, "no gloves. Put the pieces on the windowsill. I'm going to drop you for a sec."

A wave of cool air blew in across Helen's face. She wished madly that she could hear what Elena was saying. Foster boosted her by the feet this time, pushed her toward the window until she had her hands, then her knees on the sill, and was squeezing past the shards of glass onto the outer sill of concrete, into the damp, black edges of Elena's vegetable garden. She gulped eagerly for breath. Was Foster coming with her, was he staying?

When she turned, his hands were already on the sill, his boots scrabbling against the wall. Wedging her feet against the ground, she grabbed him by the shoulders as he jumped, pulling his weight forward. She lurched out of his way, as if they were simply performing some terrible comedy routine, trying to stay clear of vegetable stakes, watched him wriggle and swear and tug himself free, sucking the side of one hand. The air around them smelled of dying leaves, dying tomato plants, the bitter decay of geraniums. She was ahead of him, making for the gate at the back of the garden that led into an alley lined with aging, wooden garages. When she glanced back once, a white halo of light rose behind them, from the side of Elena's house. "Walk, don't run," she whispered. "Don't look as if you're fleeing anything." Her own inclination was to run like crazy.

"I'll get Elena a new window," Foster whispered. "Tomorrow, whenever." He held out a blue jacket that must have been Elena's. "Here. I couldn't find yours. I guess you left it in the kitchen." No money, Helen thought suddenly, no ID. Nothing. "She'll be fine. She probably told them that if they woke up her grandmother there'd be hell to pay. Magda's a great believer in freedom of speech, but she's an even greater believer in being able to sleep through the night in your own house. That's what she once actually said to me."

"Where are we going?" Helen demanded. "We can't go back to your place either." They were heading south, shoulders bent forward, elbows bumping, toward Gerrard. Months ago, she had followed Foster through the dark, elastic with adrenaline then as now, all her senses focused acutely, eyeing him, matching her pace to his across the distance that separated them, trying to guess his destination.

"I think I know where we can go," Foster said. "We can even walk there. It'll take a while, but we can stay pretty much out of the way."

"As long as there are telephones. I need to stay close to a telephone."

"Helen, there are telephones everywhere," he whispered, swinging one arm around her. "Even the ravines are wired, these days, as a precaution, whatever, just in case anyone needs to make a call."

From a phone booth outside a closed doughnut shop on Gerrard, Helen tried dialing Paul, the space station, mission control: all lines still busy. It was as if a huge silence had descended, ringing in her ears, spreading through the empty streets and over the brown and opaque sky, as if even the beep, beep, beep of missed connection had become a kind of silence.

"This way," Foster whispered, "we'll go west." They headed across the footbridge over the wide Don Valley, over the parkway lit by its rows of orange sodium lights, a lone taxi arcing down one lane, over the dark and sluggish river, the viaduct rising in ghostly arches north of them. On the far side, Foster turned, as if to follow the road that curved toward the floor of the valley, only he bolted down the hill next to it instead, hugging the shadows of the cement overpass. On the road that stretched ahead of them, running south between the backs of warehouses and a weedy, abandoned railway track beside the river, there were no cars in sight.

In hours, or if not hours then days, her mother could be coming down, but right now Helen felt instead as if Barbara had disappeared. The whole sky bulged with her absence. She had lost all sense of her mother's gaze bearing down from above, whether powerful or benign.

"I used to walk down here," Foster said conversationally, "on the path by the river. After my episode in the ravines. I'd keep walking, I guess, to see how far I could go."

"And?"

"Well, I never went out for longer than a day, and then I went home."

They were like comets, Helen thought dizzily. She was moving through this landscape not as if it were a place but itself a kind of moving scrim, wavering a little in the air beyond her, streaming away from her at its own speed. If she had a home at all, it would have to be something she could carry with her, inside her, an invisible packed bag, an endless movie, an eye always open in the darkness, an insistent voice telling its own story. They both trailed their pasts behind them like comet tails, vaporous and filled with detritus. In the present, receding into the future, she still multiplied and divided, seeing through several eyes, longing for too many things at once, but in the past she was singular; her past made her singular, it was hers and no one else's, and whatever else happened, she still carried it with her, like a portable home.

Beside them the river shone, quiet and viscous, running between its cement banks, seeping toward the lake, toward the thick, tall pillars that held up the Gardiner Expressway as it ran beside the lake. They dashed across the road beneath the highway, under the leached stains and the rusted pipes protruding from the pillars, this crumbling stretch of concrete sky. Even the lights on the CN Tower were turned off for the night, although its intermittent warning lights kept flashing.

Ahead of them stood a telephone booth, leaning slightly beside a desolate stretch of railway tracks. Helen stepped inside the canted doorway. *Please hang up,* an automated voice told her, no matter what number she dialed, *and try again.* Kicking the phone booth made no difference. She imagined the computer screens on the space station blinking vacantly, bursting with small photon explosions. No connection, no connection. "Hey," Foster said softly, his face gaunt and smooth and close to hers, "there'll be another one."

Where she'd walked once with her mother, tugging the string of a paper-bag kite that gusted, intermittently airborne, they walked now along a skinny stretch of silver beach so quietly that even the sleeping, headless Canada geese barely stirred as they passed. Helen could no longer tell whether she was walking away from or toward something. Each step reverberated in its own infinite present, binding the two of them lightly together. A car passed like a memory, a long sigh.

When they walked into the motel lobby, the woman behind the front desk nearly jumped, shocked at the sight of them.

"I didn't hear your car," she said. She had the creased and baffled look of someone who had just been woken up.

"We don't have one," Foster said. Helen stayed by the door, turned toward the parking lot and the view they'd left behind them, the curve of the lake streaming away into the darkness, the sky graying in the east, the whole skyline of the city contained within the curve like a tiny movie set. "Cash," she heard Foster say. "Actually, since we probably want to stick around during the day, I'd better pay for tomorrow night, too." It was nearly morning, already morning, a little after five o'clock, and it was easy to guess what the woman behind the desk was thinking. At least they came cloaked in ordinary furtiveness: just another couple desperate for a room key, a DO NOT DISTURB sign, an anonymous bed anywhere along the Etobicoke motel strip.

The red indoor-outdoor carpeting, even the potted artificial plants looked worn out by transience. Behind a door, presumably the door to the cramped motel office, two TV experts were battling over whether or not her mother should come back to Earth. *On the one hand, Urie has always managed to stay on very good terms with American mission control.* She longed to talk to Barbara before it was too late: There were still things she wanted to tell her, things she needed to say. "You ready?" Foster whispered, cupping the key in his palm and winking at her, with a quick and nearly salacious grin.

She dreamed that she was flying with her mother in a small plane. Just once—out of the blue one day—Barbara had asked if she wanted to come with her, and Helen had thrown her resistance and hesitation to the wind and said yes. They were climbing. Each nudge of the controls registered in their own bodies as well as in the air, each swoop of the wings moving through them. They'd tilted toward a bank of rolling cumulus clouds, at a steep, precise angle, the earth plunging sharply beneath them. The engine's throbbing was deafening: nothing around them but that thin metal skin, which seemed so frail, so animal tenuous.

It could not be morning, but the sky beyond the chiffon curtains was slowly brightening. It did not feel like the beginning, just the desperate middle of something. Helen sat up. How could it be so quiet? Somewhere buildings were tilting, lives crumbling, the space station keeling dangerously out of orbit. She tried calling Paul once more, no luck, and imagined him yelling into the void of his own phone line, *Why isn't she there? Why does she always disappear when things get difficult?* He meant her, of course, not Barbara.

In the bathroom, water splattered against the bathtub: Foster was taking a shower. She was floating in a capsule, tiny globules of sweat forming around her hairline and above her upper lip. What if the TV reporters were lying and there *was* something horribly wrong with her mother? For that matter, what proof did she have that her mother was even up in space? The more she thought about it, the more convincing this seemed: Barbara could be anywhere, or nowhere, in a desert in Australia, a cave in New Mexico, a Los Angeles TV studio, even a studio blocks away in Toronto. Her own faith, as much as anyone's, had kept her mother in the air, and without it of course she began falling.

Foster opened the door to the bathroom, a skimpy white motel towel wrapped around his waist, steam breathing through the doorway all around him.

"Everything's fake," Helen whispered.

"Why don't you take off your boots?" Foster said. "You'll get mud all over the bed." He lay down easily beside her with his hands folded behind his head.

"Foster, listen to me." She propped herself up on her elbows. "What if everything has been faked?"

"Wait a sec," he said. "What? What everything?"

"I keep thinking, for a start, what if they're not really in space?"

"Didn't you see the launch? Didn't you see them climb into the shuttle?"

"No," she said. "It doesn't happen quite like that. Maybe that's what people think because that's what you see on TV, but you're too far away. I mean, you can watch them climb inside on these video screens at the official launch site, but that's all. And that's no proof. Only I wasn't at the launch site. Paul and I drove down and stood by our car at the side of a highway. No one stopped us. We saw a rocket go into the air—and it was great, it was amazing to see it without any interference—but that's no proof that anyone went with it."

"Wait a sec," Foster said. "You were where? Helen, I've seen pictures of you at the launch."

"It's no proof," she whispered. "It wasn't me. These other people took our place. And no one seemed to notice, which sounds crazy, but I'm telling you what happened to me."

Foster stared at her, shaking his head from side to side. "Helen, people would notice. I'd notice."

"No." She watched him carefully. "You didn't. No one did. I don't care that you couldn't tell, but I want you to believe me."

She felt as if each quiver of thought were visible in his face, in each twitch of muscle, each blink of his eyelids, flinch of his eyes. His skin turned paler blue as the light through the curtains strengthened, a resonant, tender gray. She explained about the other family. "It's pretty wild," he said, "but then again, it's not really so incredible, is it? You'd say no. In a perverse way it makes a lot of sense." He rolled toward her, growing more serious, tucking his wet hair behind his ears, his long fingers smoothing planes in the sheet between them as he talked. "There's no reason I would have noticed anything funny at the time, because I didn't even know you, and when I looked at the pictures recently, when I was in my phase of doing a little research on you, I was trying to convince myself that the person I knew *was* Helen Urie, even if I didn't want to believe it. Helen, this is terrible. I love it. It's awful and wild and think of the possibilities."

"Foster, think about what it *feels* like. Don't you see why it's been so hard for me to trust anything?"

"I believe you," he said. "The launch. The whole thing. I believe your mother is really up in space." He pulled her on top of him and rolled them both across the bed, pressing his face against her, biting her neck with infinite gentleness.

"Wait," Helen said breathlessly, maneuvering herself from underneath him; she sat up and took off her boots and socks. Even from a slight distance, Foster's body emanated a thick, interior warmth. Turning, she pressed both hands against his chest, his ribs, the heat of him. Start with a body: Start by believing in her own body, building herself a body limb by limb, and then by believing in another body, and not any body but this particular one, the sharp curve of Foster's pelvic bone, the line of dark hairs below his navel.

She was doing what she'd once almost accused Paul of doing, turning her back on the television, even though its drama intimately concerned her—not losing herself but concentrating hard on what was right in front of her. She pulled off her turtleneck and bra. There were voices in the background, but she did not hear them. She licked her fingers and touched the slight concave dip at Foster's temples in amazement, the ridge of bone that ran along his nose: the pure wonder of it. As his hands moved across her body, her skin grew as springy as moss, as if touch itself could redefine the two of them, hurl them into the present, clear some space and time for them. Gravity held them within the room. The mere weight of Foster's body on hers made her nearly delirious. She was filled with an immense, an endless sense of discovery. "I left my bag at Elena's," Foster whispered. "It's got everything in it. You don't have anything on you, do you?"

"Doesn't matter," she whispered back. "There are plenty of other things we can do."

His tongue left a liquid trail across her stomach; then she felt his fingers on her body, very softly. She opened her legs and at the same time touched him, listening to his breath rise. With his free hand he reached out suddenly, a strange, urgent gesture that lurched through her heart; she grabbed his hand, listening to their breath, the speed of it. Her whole body felt so thick and clear and dense, stretching past the point where she could feel his touch as separate from her skin, rocked by him, by each tight shock through her pelvis, his. She did not float away. She filled her body absolutely.

She woke again in minus time, those terrible, anticipatory moments just before the launch. The screen crackled with flames. With slow, monstrous propulsion, the shuttle nosed above the launchpad. "Foster, wake up." Helen shook him by the shoulder until he groaned. "You said you wanted to see it." She squeezed her hands together, nervous in spite of herself. The camera eye suddenly seemed to pull back miles, lenses swiveling, the shuttle rising now beyond a glittering marsh, against the rodlike silhouette of rushes, the dark, flapping wings of a crane.

"Nature," Foster said groggily, "my God." He scrubbed his hands over his eyes and shook out his hair, as if emerging from a swimming pool. The rocket boosters toppled away in a pinwheel of flame while the shuttle climbed higher, burning through the blue.

Without warning, he leaped out of bed in his manic, instantly reinvigorated way, and crouched by the television. "I want to see if there's any difference between what the American channels and the Canadian channels are showing."

"I keep thinking maybe the Americans want to bring her

down and the Canadian space agency doesn't." Helen hugged her arms around her knees. Sense by sense the world returned to her. Voices, the occasional opening and shutting of doors drifted in from the hall; habit made her cautious, she kept her voice down even though she didn't really think anyone could hear them.

Nora Carter, Peter Carter's wife, appeared, courtesy of a Buffalo channel, standing on a bright green lawn in Houston, wide-rimmed sunglasses hiding her eyes, a breeze gusting her streaked hair. *Whatever happens,* she said, *he's still a hero.* Her mouth was trembling.

"Do you know her?" Foster asked.

"I've met her." The sight of Nora Carter brought her near tears, despite all their differences and the fact that Nora had always seemed to disapprove of Barbara's family. The sliver of identification ran deeper. And yet, on the American channels, there was barely any mention of Barbara at all. The spaceship continued to climb unstoppably, undisastrously, like a tiny, gold-flecked needle.

Then they were on the streets of Toronto, where an earnest reporter was asking people whether they thought Barbara Urie should stay up. *Of course she should stay up,* a man in a baseball cap said adamantly. Helen gasped; Foster tipped onto his heels. Elena stood at the door of her pale green house, in daylight now, dressed in a light trenchcoat that made it seem as if she were on her way somewhere, impossible for either of them to know by what sequence of events she had gone from fending off journalists in the middle of night to standing there. *I think she should come down,* Elena said calmly. *I don't think any of them should be up there.* ELENA SKOPEK, read the identifying tag in the corner of the screen, ACTIVIST. *Spending billions of dollars to rescue one man who's sick in space is the kind of thing that should only happen in a movie. Except it isn't a movie I'd pay to see.*

"She's good," Foster said after a second. "The weird thing is, she's really good." The conviction that Elena always conveyed in person somehow translated itself into a bright stillness, an electric fixity in her gaze that made it impossible not to stare right back at her.

Especially in times like these, the woman reporter said, *I think we all need heroes.*

"Please." Helen put her hands over her ears. "Can you turn it off for a sec?"

"Do you think she wants to be a hero?" she heard Foster ask.

"It isn't that simple," she said passionately. "She never used to like the word 'hero' at all, but how do I know what she's feeling now? Maybe she's changed. A week ago she was telling me how all these people have called up mission control, the number where you can leave messages for the astronauts, to say they're naming their daughters after her. There'll be all these little girls running around named after my mother, and I don't know how that makes her feel." She tightened her arms around her knees. "I get so tired of the way everyone wants to reduce things to black and white, when they're not. I don't even have to go to my apartment to know exactly what the media crews hanging out there would say to me. I'm her radical-environmentalist-animal-rights-activist daughter. And so I have to say yes, I want her to come down, not because I'm a good daughter, and I want her back, or I miss her, which I do, but because I think it's morally reprehensible, and everyone will somehow see that as shocking, whereas wanting her to stay up is somehow more *loyal.* No one will even quote me if I say what I really feel, which is that I feel ambivalent, in the truest sense, Foster, I feel two things at once. No one wants to hear me say that or hear me talk about the contradictions because it gets too complicated. I *want* to talk about the contradictions and yet that's taboo. Elena makes it look so easy."

"Elena's a different kind of pragmatist than you are," Foster said calmly. "She believes you have to take a clear position in order to take action."

"Oh my God," Helen said, throwing up her hands, "what am I doing? I have to call my brother."

Miraculously the phone rang on the first try. When Paul's machine picked up, she shouted her name into the void after the recorded message.

"Helen," David said almost immediately. "Hello. I don't need to tell you that we've been worried sick about you."

"I'm sorry," she said. "I've been trying and trying to get through to you but it's been busy—and I can't help it that I wasn't home when all this happened, and you know how crazy it would have been if I'd tried to go home."

"Where are you now?"

"In a motel. With Foster. I've told you about Foster."

"It's just there have been these reports." David's voice trailed away oddly, ending with what might have been a cough. "Sightings of you in various places around Toronto. Even televised shots of you. It's been highly disconcerting. Obviously they can't all be you."

"Did Paul tell you what happened at Mum's launch?"

"Yes," David said, "another surprise after all this time. Yes, he did."

"So either there are people impersonating me, or it's some kind of weird, collective hallucination. I don't know. Dad, how are you?"

"I'm tired." His voice went suddenly ragged at the edges. "Sometimes I feel like my whole life has been reduced to dealing with emergencies, and I know this is neither the time nor the place to say this, but I'm outrageously tired. I long to see Barbara. I long to see her walk into a room and smile or put down a coffee mug—something completely matter-of-fact. Can you understand that? But I know that right now, whatever happens, any kind of ordinariness is out of the question, and yes, more than anything else, I simply want her to be all right."

"Have you managed to get through to her?"

"No," Paul said, which startled Helen only until she realized that sometime since her last visit he must have hooked up an extension phone in the kitchen or his bedroom. She stared at the speckled carpet, glad that neither of them could see or would picture her sitting crosslegged and naked on the disheveled, squeaky motel bed. "And they've temporarily blacked out the feed," he went on. "We've talked to the family liaison guy. They keep saying she's fine, everything's under control. They say Peter's suffering some kind of heart problem, but who knows? That doesn't explain why she should have to come down. The American space agency wants us to fly to Houston and the Canadian agency wants to move us into a hotel suite here in Montreal, and they couldn't believe we didn't know where you were." Was he terrified at the prospect of seeing their mother thwarted, her fury, her despair at being forced to come down?

"We are encouraged to talk to their return trauma psychologist," David said dryly. "Just in case."

"Return trauma?"

"Well, they say that based on past experience, the return to Earth is just as difficult, and sometimes more difficult, than going into space—and not just for the astronaut but for the family. The assumption is, of course, that the longer they're up there, the worse it's going to be for all of us. We'll be the guinea pigs."

"So she's coming down."

"We don't know that," Paul said.

"What will you do if she doesn't come down?"

"If she doesn't?" David paused, the air between all three of them growing suddenly fragile, separating and binding them. In a Montreal apartment, he hunched his worn shoulders forward. Maybe she shouldn't have asked. Maybe she already knew the answer: A path stretched out ahead of him and resolutely he kept walking. "We'll see what happens first."

"But do we have any idea whether she wants to stay up or come down? Do we even know if she has a choice?"

"No, we don't," Paul said soberly. "We all wish we did but we don't."

Foster's cool fingers closed around Helen's arm. He'd turned the TV back on. "I'll give you the number here," she said, "so you'll know how to reach me." Lit by floodlights, glimpsed through the windows of a new, radical vegetarian restaurant called Chaos where she'd actually been thinking of looking for a job, stood a young woman in black jeans, a black waiter's apron around her waist, whose purposeful, malleable face looked remarkably like hers. The young woman gave the invisible camera the finger.

"Wonderful," Foster said gleefully. "Maybe Elena said she'd seen you there."

Astronaut Urie's activist daughter appears intent on ignoring the current space station crisis.

"It doesn't explain—" Crouched low over the handlebars of a mountain bike, a sand-colored braid hanging loose beneath her bike helmet, another figure in black turtleneck and biking tights zoomed through traffic on Bloor Street.

"At least this time people can *see* what's going on," Helen said, gesturing toward the screen. "How can they be taken in? There are too many of me. The contradictions are evident."

"Helen, listen," Foster said. "I'm being very serious. Are you sure this isn't something you've managed to do yourself?"

There was a door in the sky, the outline of a door stretched like a drum across the pale sky, only Helen could not see what lay on the far side or who might step through it. A woman in a red sweater burst through a door into a dark hall. A woman stepped through the doorway of a homemade lunar landing module and waved. A woman stumbled out of a landed space-craft, nearly toppling to the ground, arms grasped by two space agency officials, men who maneuvered her forward through the heavy, uncompromising air while behind them, another figure, a man on a stretcher, had to be carried from the runway. Whatever happened, there would never be actual pictures like these, every effort would be made to keep a moment like this shrouded in secrecy: Sick astronauts were invisible ones. She strove to imagine what she could not see.

Beside her, Foster's body lay sprawled across the motel bed with careless, unconscious abandon. Leaning against the head-board, still wrapped in a sheet, Helen listened to the quiet teeming of blood through her veins and did not try to wake him, knowing he wasn't asleep out of any disregard for what was going on but from utter exhaustion. *Is he right about the other Helens, is it something I have done myself?*

Neither the Canadian nor American channels had made any further statements about Peter Carter's health, or even de-clared whether he was alive or dead. Everyone was too busy talking about heroes and national dreams with a kind of mounting hysteria, as if somehow this had become the news story everyone had been waiting for. *They'd better let her stay up,* she'd heard a man in a business suit say, *or if not, I hope she has the guts to say no and put up a fight.* It would be hours yet before anything actually happened; the rescue mission hadn't even docked yet. The voices of its astronauts crackled from orbit. Time pressed through the room relentlessly, without any way to gratify people's expectations for instantaneous action. Each second pulsed like distant thunder.

She stared into the distance and saw a woman who peered into a mirror, lifting one lock of her short hair and then another, hair that had turned suddenly, miraculously white from the shock of her return to Earth, her fall from space. A woman's hair turned slowly white during the tortuous months of physical and psychological tests that awaited her on her return. Her face betrayed her anguish.

If it was hard wrestling with the fact of Barbara's reappearance, it was harder still to imagine what Barbara would do afterward, what further transformations lay ahead. Would she fly back to Toronto, move back into the house on Glenforest Street, go back to work in the lab? Would she let herself be identified perpetually as Barbara Urie, former astronaut, travel the world on lecture tours, talk on endless TV shows, write her autobiography? A woman stood in front of a window in a darkened room at night, paralyzed by her impossible longing to be back in space. *The light,* she whispered to herself, *the light.* More galvanized than ever, she strode into other people's offices, prepared to fight tenaciously, in spite of all opposition, for the continuation of the Mars project, its goals of international solidarity and a safe haven for the future. Was there a man reading beneath a tiny halogen lamp in the next room? Was her father the man in the next room? One day the phone would ring and it would be her mother, asking in a cheerful, matter-of-fact way if Helen wanted to meet her downtown for a quick meal at a Chinese restaurant and a movie.

There remained something chimerical and wavering about these scenes. For months, the memory of her mother's skin, her smell, her touch, had begun to seem abstract, a sensory field grown worn, that she could nearly see through. Was this what the space agency psychologist meant by the trauma of return? Only it wasn't exactly a return: The woman who left did not come back. Those she'd left behind were not the people who came to greet her. The idea of a mother as someone who could enter the room in which she waited seemed nearly alien. And what about the small, scandalous voice that whispered incorrigibly, in spite of everything Helen had said to Barbara about abandonment and escape, how much it liked having the planet to itself?

Foster shifted in his sleep, eyelids twitching, and called out. With quick, protective passion, she watched his chest rise and fall and wondered if Peter had had time to warn Barbara that he was in pain. Perhaps Barbara had found him slumped over the treadmill or discovered his body bumping unconsciously against the walls of their sleeping quarters. A woman held a man's face gently between her hands and lowered her lips to his, breathing in and out, as once she had taught her daughter to do on the warm tiles of a patio beside a swimming pool. In and out. The woman's heart closed like a fist around her fear. Real fear. In and out. Until this became the crux of everything, their months in space, their lives. *I'm the child on the tiled patio, waiting for the warm touch of my mother's lips. I'm the woman who leans over, exhaling softly.* As carefully as she could, the woman steered the man's weightless body into the health-monitoring area, tethering his arms and legs to a wall to keep him still while she hooked him to the thin tubes of oxygen. And then: Did his heart keep beating?

She floated through the rooms and corridors of the space station, listening to the shocked thumping of her own heart, the only human sound against the constant machine hum. A small needle of joy shivered through her, as she peered through the window, pressing closer and closer, past the liminal point where the frame dissolved. The scale shifted absolutely. *I'm here. There's no one else. I'm facing the huge reach of the universe alone.*

But wait. She was still making one crucial assumption, still taking the space agencies' and the TV reporters' word that Barbara was well, that only Peter Carter had been felled in space by something as bizarre and ordinary as a heart attack. *What if my mother is dying?* Helen's body began to shake and would not stop. What if the astronauts had simply proved that long-term habitation in space, at least under the conditions of the space station, was *not* possible? *Even if it takes everything,* Barbara whispered, pressing her ear to Peter's chest, *it's worth it.*

Keep breathing. In and out. Breathe deeply.

On the TV screen, at the far end of the bed, the sealed entrance between the docked shuttle and the space station sprang open. The four rescue mission astronauts, three men and one woman, floated into vacuumland, moving a little jerkily, like nervous fish or cowboys, their faces wobbling as they tried to hide their delight at weightlessness: They had to stay serious, concentrate on the drama assigned to them, convince their audience that there was a crisis—a real crisis, fake crisis, did it matter which as long as they kept people's eyes on them, their TV audience increasing minute by minute, in the millions now, possibly into the billions if they played it right? The real drama, how to take one breath, the next, wait through the still point between each breath, went on imperceptibly all around them.

When Helen dialed Elena's number, Elena's machine told her, *You can leave messages here for Elena Skopek or United Species. If you are calling about the rally, meet us at the north end of Queen's Park at eight tomorrow night.*

"It's Helen," was all she said.

"Who are you calling?" Foster asked clearly.

"Elena," Helen said. His eyes were wide open, making their instant transition to alertness. "Either she's moving up the rally or else she's planning a different one, but she's organizing something for tomorrow night."

He stretched his arms out wide above his head. "Will you go?"

"There's something I need to do." She spoke calmly, sliding down in the bed until she faced him, her head beside his head. The idea had risen in her suddenly, like a bubble, perfectly round and unassailable. "I want to go and see my mother."

"See her land?"

"No. See her in the sky. And I know there won't be much I can see, only this little yellow light if I'm lucky, but in all these months I haven't ever done it, I haven't even tried, and I want to before it's too late."

"Where?" Foster asked. "You can't do it from here."

"Somewhere up north. I'll take the train. Is there a train that goes to Sudbury? My mother always used to say she would take us to Sudbury, back when she built us the lunar landing module in our garden, because the land up there looked like the moon. I know it doesn't look as bad as that any more. Maybe I won't go that far, or maybe farther, as long as it's somewhere where there aren't a lot of people and it's dark."

"What if someone recognizes you?"

"I'll be careful," she said firmly. "They won't. If they do, I'll just jump off the train somewhere when it slows, but, honestly, who's going to be looking for me on a train bound for Sudbury?"

"It doesn't leave until this evening."

"How do you know?"

"It's just one of those things I know," Foster said with a

sigh. "There's only one train now and it leaves this evening."

She touched his dark hair with her fingertips. "I need to do this," she whispered. "I really do, and I need to do it by myself, and then I'll come back."

"You think she's on her way down?"

"I don't know. Foster, listen to me. Part of me would love to stay right here in this room with you, in spite of everything that's going on, and not even get out of bed. I can barely pull myself away, but there's another problem. I'm starving. All right, not starving but I'm so hungry I'm starting to get a headache. Aren't you? We haven't eaten since last night."

"Takeout." He rolled onto his back and stared at the stuccoed ceiling with a small frown. "Or we can go back sort of the way we came and there's this Vietnamese restaurant, no one ever seems to go there but the food's not bad. I have to find Elena. I told her if we needed candles, I'd be the one to get hold of them. Because I will be there tomorrow night. I *want* them to see us—and it isn't because I want anything terrible to happen to the astronauts. Is that inconsistent? I don't think of that or even being here with you as inconsistent."

"I didn't necessarily think you did," Helen said. Her stomach growled.

"I'll miss you." Foster grabbed her arm. "Everything that's wonderful and difficult about you. I'll miss you so much I'll walk around feeling rubbed raw from missing you."

"I love you," she said. She kissed his lips, the corded, salty taste of his neck, the milky lobes of his ears. "I have to go, but then I'll come back."

His eyes shone, inches from hers, bloodshot at the edges, bright as a dare. "I never said don't go. The proof comes afterward, doesn't it? Just come back."

A train sped on silver tracks through the darkness. A car followed the beam of its headlights over the curve of a hill.

Darkness: above Helen's head, the density of deep space that still looked like darkness even if it was really a mixture of cold dark matter or hot dark matter and flying light. Clouds swept across it. The darkness of a road outside a city, no cars for miles it seemed, only a thickening expanse of trees, hacked at the edges. At the verge of the road gravel crunched under her feet. In one hand she held a flashlight, which she'd bought in a hardware store in Toronto before she'd caught the train. For the first while she had kept it on, a thin beam ahead of her; then she had switched it off again.

She was walking through a wilderness of satellite beams and radio waves, somewhere beyond Sudbury, through a world that seemed to her like a map of voices in the darkness, lost voices, place names she remembered from all the province-wide weather reports she had listened to in childhood: Temagami, Kapuskasing, White River, Atawapiskat. Places linked not by roads but by the speed of light. Time itself seemed vaporous, lapping in small waves around her. She had stepped off the train after hours of travel and followed a road into the darkness, her eyes still dizzy with sleep, with the image of the large, bearded man sitting across from her who cradled a tiny TV set like a child in his lap, who kept whispering bits of news to her, telling her about the three people who had appeared in the Houston airport claiming to be Barbara Urie's family, while satellite dishes swelled and vanished like ghosts across the dark field of her window.

Soon it would be morning. She was tired, tired of walking through the cold air, wishing she had more than Elena's blue jacket and Foster's denim one to keep her warm, tired of the interior vigilance of pressing down fear and jumping off the verge whenever a car tore by, imagining a solitary, dangerous man inside. The distant sound of water drew her like a lure: She wanted the trees to fall away suddenly at the edge of a lake, for the sky to open gloriously, cloudlessly wide above it. *Remember there's still the uncontrollable weather,* she heard David's voice say gently.

A light rose beyond the horizon of the road, a stationary light, not a car approaching but a sign blinking, a plastic sign lit up from within. The Glenn Gould Motel, she read as she approached. One tractor trailer cabin, without its load, stood pulled up in the parking lot, looking top-heavy and off-balance, as if it really ought to tip over. The gassy, nighttime smell of a parking lot in North Carolina months before filled her nostrils, the last time she had been in a place anything like this. Although the door to the office was locked, there was a button beside it, which she pressed, and a bell rang. A tiny, silvery band of music spun out of an unseen window.

"Are you open?" Helen asked the man who answered the door. He wore a dressing gown over his regular clothes. The compressed sounds of a faraway orchestra rose and fell behind him. She told him that her boyfriend had dumped her out of his car and driven off.

"Is he coming back?"

"No." She hoped her voice sounded firm and convincing enough. "There won't be anything violent or messy. I'm just going to call a friend of mine to pick me up. I mean, I want a room. With a TV and a telephone." There would never be a way to stop lying altogether.

The man gave her a short, peculiar look, as if she'd landed from another world. "All the rooms have TVs," he said. "And telephones."

A black, upright piano stood in the dusty shadows against

the wall behind him, and Helen wondered if Glenn Gould had ever stayed in the motel, or if this man, with his ribbed, slicked-back gray hair, who tuned to orchestras as his beam through the night, was simply an aficionado, or some kind of musician himself.

There was, as the man had promised, a television with old-fashioned, wood-grained sides, although at first all Helen could pick up were Detroit channels, bouncing off satellites and streaming down through the atmosphere toward her. A car had exploded on State Street. The president was trying to telephone Peter Carter. She wedged the black phone against her shoulder, poised on the edge of the bed, and called out her own name again and again, waiting for Paul or David to disengage the answering machine and respond, only what she heard instead was a woman's throaty, sleepy voice.

"Helen?" Carla said. "They tried to call you but you weren't at that hotel. They left."

"They left?" They were in a plane, they were flying south to meet—.

"David had this plan. They made a dash for it in the middle of the night." Carla's voice grew stronger, sure and strangely intimate. "They took his rented car and headed off to find somewhere they could see the space station."

"Where did they go?"

"Well, they would've told you, Helen, but they couldn't."

"Are you going to talk to them?"

"They said they'd call. They hoped you would call. I told them it was OK, if they wanted to go, then they should do it, and I'd stay here. Someone had to stay and be command central."

"So you *can* get a message to them?"

"I hope so."

"Because they could meet me. The amazing thing is, that's what I decided to do, I'm up here already." She could barely keep from laughing. "I took a train. Somehow we've all decided to do the same thing. I'm at this motel—a different motel. They could be heading in some totally opposite direction but I have to believe they're not. If they called, you could tell them where I am—I'll give you the number. I don't even think I could give directions on how to get here but the guy who runs this place would know. There's a lake. We could see her from there." *Serendipity.* The word spilled out of her. The world had never felt so serendipitous as it did at that moment.

"Helen," Carla said softly, "this is totally weird."

"No," Helen said, "not really. They will call. Oh God, they'd better. Has my mother called?"

"She hasn't. Sorry."

"If she calls—just in case—will you give her this number?" She needed Carla, they all did: All at once Carla had become the essential link between them, and she was fervently grateful for Carla's aura of dependability.

"Let me grab a pen," Carla said. "I don't know if you've heard or seen, but there's this crowd gathering at the base of the CN Tower in Toronto to support her. They say they're going to show her how many people want her to stay up. At first it was just a few people but it keeps growing, gaining momentum. Some people were out there all night."

"No," Helen said, "I didn't know."

We need a dream, a voice said. *She's giving us a way to dream.*

It was as if a web of connection stretched through her, out toward Carla and beyond, toward Foster and Elena, too. Helen's hands were tingling. She unzipped the canvas knapsack she'd bought at the same hardware store as the flashlight, checked the three boxes of candles, a box of matches, two bottles of apple juice, three cheese sandwiches, two chocolate bars. Survival gear. There could, of course, be a gas station and a package store around the next curve of the road or, alternatively, nothing for kilometers. In the front pocket of her jeans lay a thin wedge of folded bills, the money Foster had lent her. Subtle and tensile, the web stretched farther, around the world and back again, binding them all, stretching tighter and tighter without breaking. She imagined a rope of film, all the miles, the hundreds, no thousands, of kilometers of film containing images of her mother, all the videotape transcripts that had accumulated in the last number of months, tapes from the years before that. She imagined them uncoiling, reeling outward, twisting into a ladder that climbed into the sky.

She was holding the telephone. It was a moment of absolute discontinuity. How did she come to be holding it? Someone said, *Hello? hello?* The bedspread had been pulled off the bed, was folded, nestlike, in the armchair. When had she done this? With a shock, Helen realized what had happened: Fast asleep, with the ease of utterly unconscious habit, she had walked across the room and answered the phone. *Helen, hello?*

"I'm awake," she said out loud, pinching herself, pinched harder, as the voice on the far end of the line said, "Can you imagine if I'd dialed a wrong number?"

"You're all right?" It was the most inadequate question in the world. She meant it exultantly and desperately to encompass a thousand questions.

"I'm all right," Barbara said. "I've spent the last eight hours secluded in the health-monitoring room undergoing the most exhaustive series of tests I've ever—"

"Is Peter all right?" Helen touched the bureau, the phone, as if their density could prove she was awake.

"Not as all right."

330

"Is he dead?"

"Helen," Barbara exclaimed. "Are people saying that?"

"They're saying all kinds of things. Maybe not that. I was frightened."

"The cumulative effects of strain. He should be all right. Listen, Helen, I don't have that long but I wanted to speak to you. I said if I was going to make a decision I had to speak to my family first."

"Paul and David are in a car," Helen whispered. "Did Carla explain you may not be able to reach them?"

"The horrible part is that I may not be able to wait, and I have to make a choice. That's why I'm calling, because that's what it comes down to. I know about all the hoopla going on down there and I've heard about some of the things people are saying but the point is, I've passed the tests. I'm all right. I'm holding up—physically, psychologically. I have been commended on, of all things, my elasticity. And the final test, by the way, is that I have a choice, to stay up or come down. Of course there are and have been negotiations, endless negotiations between the space agencies, but still, in what privacy remains of my life up here at the moment, I have a choice."

Helen's heart beat so loudly it threatened to drown out Barbara's voice. "There are crowds," she said, "crowds and crowds of people who want you to stay up."

"Yes, I know."

There were no clues outside herself that could help her now: The horror of responsibility filled her, too. "You haven't decided yet."

"Not yet," Barbara said.

"I can't tell you what—"

"I'm not asking you to tell me what to do, only I wanted to hear what you think, what you want. Helen, after everything you've said."

"Maybe what we want right now can't be totally separated from what you want." She closed her eyes and began again slowly. "It has to be your choice. Maybe that's all I want." She pressed her fingertips against the bureau, as if she could push thoughts out through them. "But if you do decide to stay up, please don't say you're doing it for us. Perhaps that's the most important thing. It sounds so cruel, but what I mean is, why can't you say, even to us, that you're doing it because it's what you want to do? Mum, it's your dream. I know, if you stay up, it will only be for a few more months, but our lives will keep on going down here. They have their own speed and momentum. We'll think about you, we always do, but we'll keep moving, we can't just be here waiting. And anyway, I don't really think you'd want us to. But if you decide to come down, then we'll come to meet you. Even if everyone says the return is as hard as going up, I'm not frightened. We'll go through that. But you have to want to come down. You can't turn it into something we made you do."

"Helen," Barbara said quietly, "there are so many kinds of simultaneous desire, you do realize that? If you want to know the truth, I feel more torn than ever, which isn't what I hoped at all. And probably I shouldn't say things like this, but I feel as if it wouldn't take much for me to divide completely in two, as if another part of me is out there walking somewhere. I wish someone could give me proof that everything I've done has been worth it, but on the other hand I don't know what the proof would be."

"What's Peter going to do?"

"He has to go down. Two of the other astronauts are staying on, two men. Look, are you anywhere that people will pressure you to release this information?"

"No," Helen said, "I'm not. I'm in a motel, on an empty highway, beyond this tiny, tiny town called Crow. I came up

332

here because I wanted to see you in the sky. None of us ever has, did you realize? And the completely amazing thing is that we all must have realized it at almost exactly the same time, because David and Paul set out without knowing I was going, too. And all you have to do is look down. They're going to meet me. We'll be by this lake called Titanium Lake. Is it on any of your maps? Can you find it? Maybe you won't be able to see us but at least you'll know we're all here together, looking at you. If it's cloudy, we'll try tomorrow night. It *won't* be cloudy. And if you hear any other reports about us—"

"What kind of reports?"

"Well, that we're in Houston or Toronto or Montreal, we're not. If anyone tries to convince you we are, don't believe them."

"Helen, why would anyone—"

"We've always tried to do what seemed like the right thing or at least the right thing to us," Helen said calmly. "And I know this isn't the easiest time to tell you something like this, but at your launch—well, Paul and I went to Florida and watched the launch but not from the official site. We wanted to be on our own, just stand there and watch it, in privacy. There was some risk, and we took it. But no one ever guessed we weren't in the stands because another family appeared in our place." She heard the catch in her mother's voice. "Wait," she said. "Please. I know no one told you. We didn't tell you because we decided not to tell anyone, that we would only be making things worse for ourselves if we did. Mum, I live in a world where this doesn't seem fantastic and whether we like it or not, it's happening again. We're not hiding. I'm trying to figure out how to be true to myself in a world like this. I'm trying to figure out how to see."

"A world like this," Barbara said. "Helen, my God, I have just over an hour to make this choice. Do you think telling me this helps? I think I understand why you did it, I think so, but I can't help wondering what else don't I know? Do things like this happen all the time? I want an impossible thing. That's probably no surprise to you. I want to see through time, see what the world will be like depending what I choose. I'll drive myself crazy thinking that each breath drawn in, each dispersal of cloud makes a difference, becomes a kind of demarcation of choice, the infinitesimal division of worlds. I long just for one millisecond to surrender responsibility, to have someone else tell me—I can't, I won't. This is my promise. Whatever happens, I'll look down tonight. Your night. We'll synchronize our watches. And look up at me, please. I want to know you're doing that while I keep my eyes open and look for you."

My mother wants impossible things. It was, all at once, a statement of fact, a description rather than a recognition blurred by anger or despair. *She wants to confound contradictions.* David and Paul were coming, they had called excitedly to say they'd been heading north anyway, they were on their way, and David had joked that he couldn't quite believe the three of them were actually going to be in the same place at the same time, or at least he'd believe it when he saw it. *Call the space station,* Helen said urgently. *Keep trying. Identify yourselves. Try mission control. There's a chance you'll be able to get through to her.* It was as if they were all still walking through their own version of minus time, toward the moment of cumulative choice.

She pulled on her jacket and her knapsack. In daylight she had found the lake. A sign just beyond the motel, which she had missed in the darkness of her arrival, led her down a short dirt road. Beyond a row of pines spread a long stretch of pebbly beach, then water extending toward a thin rim of trees on the horizon. All around her, the leaves of deciduous trees

334

were yellowing, an occasional burn of red, the bare branches at the top scrabbling like fingers toward the expanse of sky. A small plane buzzed through the few, fair-weather cumulus clouds, its tiny shadow darting like a minnow across them. A sign nailed to a tree read FISH AT YOUR OWN RISK. Underneath it, someone had nailed another, handprinted sign: THERE ARE NO FISH. A duck dove and vanished beneath the water surface. The tall pines sighed and shivered like a tribe. Among the trees on the southern horizon rose something that could have been a smoke stack or a tower, or perhaps it was simply a branch, a tree trunk that had grown in the shape of a tower.

The crowds were growing, Helen knew, not just at the foot of the CN Tower but elsewhere, in other cities and towns across the province and the country, in front of the Canadian space agency headquarters in Montreal. Other crowds, American crowds, were gathering in Houston and Florida, shouting Peter's name and Barbara's name as well, waving signs. There was even a crowd outside the gates of the space program's desert landing base, waiting to see which astronauts came down. The news blackout had not been lifted and yet, or perhaps because of this, there was for the moment no other news—although a second story was developing: *the mysterious case of Barbara Urie's family.*

There were the three people who had played them at the launch: Nine months later and they seemed barely to have changed. *If they don't show up,* the other Helen said adamantly, surrounded by flashbulbs, *we are prepared to be her family. We have nothing to be ashamed of. We'll be here whenever she needs us.*

Does Barbara Urie's family really exist? a voice asked. *If they do, why don't they show themselves?*

As darkness begins to fall once more, people ready themselves, waiting for some outcome. When these crowds raised their faces to the sky, what did they see? The old shots of Barbara that kept appearing on the screen seemed out-of-date, almost distorted, as fragile as memory.

The light curled away softly outside Helen's motel window. She and Paul and David were waiting, too, which was agonizing, but they were also moving forward, pressing through the space they had created for themselves, borne, as Helen had told Barbara, by their own momentum, their own volition. There was, as always, little time to lose. In the twilight, Foster and Elena would be setting up their sound system, working breathlessly, stacking their crates of candles in the park, against the trunks of trees. People hurried through the streets toward them.

Stand up and be counted, a voice whispered.

No, Helen thought. *Stand up and be.* When she turned off the TV set, the silence was haunting. She checked her watch. Closing the door of the motel room behind her, she wedged a note between the door and frame telling Paul and David where to find her, trusted it would not blow away. Then she set off down the road. Voices and tiny images zipped through the wild air around her. *Choose,* the trees whispered, *choose.* At least what was at stake no longer felt like a matter of who was orbiting whom.

The water clucked and murmured against the pebbles at the shore. No lights glimmered around the edges of the lake. A small breeze rose like a wish and dropped away. And the sky: It took a while for Helen's eyes to shift perspective, into the distance, and then, the longer she looked, the more stars it seemed she could see. Hours passed, or minutes. Her heart quickened: no clouds, just those clear points of burning gas, endlessly multiplying. Under her feet the Earth turned slowly. Land scrubbed bare by glaciers stretched on all sides, sensed if not seen. Crouching, she unslung her knapsack and opened it purposefully, pulling out the boxes of candles and matches; then she halted. In that instant the darkness did not seem dangerous or frightening. She did not feel lonely. Wonder stretched beneath her skin like a network of capillaries. *Everything seems magnified,* she told Foster silently. Gathering up the boxes of candles, she walked a little, then crouched, rooting the candles one by one among the pebbles, in the shape of a star. She had just enough candles to set a second row beside the first.

A burst of light rose above the southern horizon, freezing her in horror, turning the distant trees a ghostly pink. The northern lights—no, don't be crazy. A lower, flickering explosion, a boom that rolled toward her, more reverberation than sound, and past her, ricocheting through the trees. An orange star fell upward and cracked into a million tiny stars that soared glitteringly back toward the Earth. Before Helen's eyes, the horizon grew alive with fireworks, which meant—

Keep breathing. There was no doubt about what it meant. If she listened hard, she could hear people shouting, distance collapsing, the whole sky humming, city after town lit simultaneously by cascades of artificial fire. Barbara had made her choice. If she concentrated even harder, Helen could see the CN Tower rising before her, lit by a fury of laser lights, fireworks bursting over the lake behind it, while the huge crowd below roared and cried in jubilation, calling her mother's name over and over, as if the power of their excitement had sent this dream of themselves rising into the sky.

And another crowd: She focused as hard as she could. A sea of tiny, flickering yellow lights moved slowly south toward the Tower, toward the lake, between an avenue of soaring buildings, accompanied by police squad cars, their warning eyes revolving. The candles quivered but did not blow out. She was there among them. A black-haired woman at the front of the crowd shouted through a megaphone, *You cannot ignore us. This is our home. We will not give up.* A glimpse of Foster's pale, illuminated face. The sea of candles stretched and stretched, for a block, another block, and Helen nearly gasped in amazement because still she could not see the end of it.

She opened her arms. Something lifted away from her. Her mother was up in space, and she stood here. Untraversable distance reasserted itself. The ache inside her grew and settled, grew and settled. Her skin closed freely around it. And it was true that to let go did not mean that her mother disappeared or that she had abandoned her; it did not eliminate the things that separated them or those that bound them, their own horizons. A forest curved around a lake inside her, as well as outside. The CN Tower soared like a needle beneath her ribs.

She lit a match so that it flared in the darkness with a sulphur sting. There was no time to lose. She held a lit candle to the wick of one candle after another, cupping her hand around the tiny flames.

A star of candlelight burned all around her. A tiny globe of light trembled on the horizon, just above the trees. She stared at it keenly. The dark lake and dark sky shone before her like a doorway, shimmering in time. There was so much to be done. *A small step.* Barbara, more than anyone, would appreciate these words. *A small step into tomorrow.* Shoes crunched on the pebbles behind her. Two voices called out her name.

I'm here.

She held out her hands to them, and stepped through the doorway.

The author would like to thank the Fine Arts Work Center in Provincetown, the MacDowell Colony, the Explorations Program of the Canada Council, the Canada Council, the Ontario Arts Council, and the Toronto Arts Council for their essential support during the writing of this book.

Thanks to all those who offered their generous encouragement, including Malaga Baldi, Ann Close, Aaron Jay Kernis, Jean Hanff Korelitz, Mary Ann Naples, and all my family. Thanks to Nigel Hunt (for love and slogans) and to the wild boys, Menno and Gibreel, who were with me through all of it.

Sources consulted during research for this book include:

Ark II; *Animal Liberation* by Peter Singer, Avon Books, New York, 1977; *In Defense of Animals,* edited by Peter Singer, Basil Blackwell, Oxford, 1985; *Canada in Space* by Lydia Dotto, Irwin Publishing, Toronto, 1987; *Entering Space* by Joseph P. Allen with Russell Martin, Stewart, Tabori & Chang, New York, 1985; and *Space* by Christopher Trump, Fitzhenry & Whiteside, Toronto, 1987.

A child of the Apollo era, Catherine Bush was born in Toronto in 1961. She graduated from Yale University with a B.A. in comparative literature. She has been active as an arts journalist and dance critic in Toronto and New York City. Her work has appeared in a variety of publications in the U.S. and Canada, including the literary journals *Canadian Fiction Magazine, Descant, Epoch* and *The American Voice.* She lives in Toronto, around the corner from the U.F.O. snack bar.